CONFESSION

For Martha,

Love

to Greet
you in

the big,

Apple!

Cey

CONFESSION

CAREY BALDWIN

WITNESS
IMPULSE
An Imprint of HarperCollins Publishers

This is a work of fiction. Names, characters, places, and incidents are products of the author's imagination or are used fictitiously and are not to be construed as real. Any resemblance to actual events, locales, organizations, or persons, living or dead, is entirely coincidental.

EPub Edition MARCH 2014 ISBN: 9780062314109

Print Edition ISBN: 9780062314116

10 9 8 7 6 5 4 3 2 1

For Shannon.
First little light of my life.

CONFESSION.

CONFESSION

PROLOGUE

Saint Catherine's School for Boys
Near Santa Fe, New Mexico
Ten years ago—Friday, August 15, 11:00 P.M.

I'm not afraid of going to hell. Not one damn bit.

We're deep in the woods, miles from the boys' dormitory, and my thighs are burning because I walked all this way with Sister Bernadette on my back. Now I've got her laid out on the soggy ground underneath a hulking ponderosa pine. A bright rim of moonlight encircles her face. Black robes flow around her, engulfing her small body and blending with the night. Her face, floating on top of all that darkness, reminds me of a ghost head in a haunted house—but she's not dead.

Not yet.

My cheek stings where Sister scratched me. I wipe the spot with my sleeve and sniff the air soaked with rotting moss, sickly-sweet pinesap, and fresh piss. I pissed myself when I clubbed her on the head with that croquet mallet. Ironic, since my pissing problem is why I picked Sister Bernadette in the first place. She ought to have left that alone.

I hear a gurgling noise.

Good.

Sister Bernadette is starting to come around.

This is what I've been waiting for.

With her rosary wound tightly around my forearm, the grooves of the carved sandalwood beads cutting deep into the flesh of my wrist, I squat on rubber legs, shove my hands under her armpits, and drag her into a sitting position against the fat tree trunk. Her head slumps forward, but I yank her by the hair until her face tilts up, and her cloudy eyes open to meet mine. Her lips are moving. Syllables form within the bubbles coming out of her mouth. I press my stinging cheek against her cold, sticky one.

Like a lover, she whispers in my ear, "God is merciful."

The nuns have got one fucked-up idea of mercy.

"Repent." She's gasping. "Heaven . . ."

"I'm too far gone for heaven."

The God I know is just and fierce and is never going to let a creep like me through the pearly gates because I say a few Hail Marys. "God metes out justice, and that's how I know *I* will not be going to heaven."

To prove my point, I draw back, pull out my pocketknife, and press the silver blade against her throat. Tonight, I am more than a shadow. A shadow can't feel the weight of the knife in his palm. A shadow can't shiver in anticipation. A shadow is not to be feared, but I am not a shadow. Not in this moment.

She moves her lips some more, but this time, no sound comes out. I can see in her eyes what she wants to say to me. *Don't do it. You'll go to hell.*

I twist the knife so that the tip bites into the sweet hollow of her throat. "I'm not afraid of going to hell."

It's the idea of *purgatory* that makes my teeth hurt and my stomach cramp and my shit go to water. I mean, what if my heart isn't black enough to guarantee me a passage straight to hell? What if God slams down his gavel, and says, *Son, you're a sinner, but I have to take your family situation into account. That's a mitigating circumstance.*

A single drop of blood drips off my blade like a tear. "What if God sends me to purgatory?" My words taste like puke on my tongue. "I'd rather dangle over a fiery pit for eternity than spend a single day of the afterlife in a place like this one."

I watch a spider crawl across her face.

My thoughts crawl around my brain like that spider. You could make a pretty good case, I think, that St. Catherine's School for Boys is earth's version of purgatory. I mean, it's a place where you don't exist. A place where no one curses you, but no one loves you, either. Sure, back home, your father hits you and calls you a bastard, but you *are* a bastard, so it's okay he calls you one. Behind me, I hear the sound of rustling leaves and cast a glance over my shoulder.

Do it! You want to get into hell, don't you?

I turn back to Sister and flick the spider off her cheek.

The spider disappears, but I'm still here.

At St. Catherine's, no one notices you enough to knock you around. Every day is the same as the one that came before it, and the one that's coming after. At St. Catherine's, you wait and wait for your turn to leave, only guess what, you dumb-ass bastard, your turn is *never* going to come, because you, my friend, are in purgatory, and you can't get out until you repent.

Sister Bernadette lets out another gurgle.

I spit right in her face.

I won't repent, and I can't bear to spend eternity in purgatory, which is I why I came up with a plan. A plan that'll rocket me straight past purgatory, directly to hell.

Sister Bernadette is the first page of my blueprint. I have the book to guide me the rest of the way. For her sake, not mine, I make the sign of the cross.

She's not moving, but her eyes are open, and I hear her breathing. I want her to know she is going to die. "You are going to help me get into hell. In return, I will help you get into heaven."

I shake my arm and loosen the rosary. The strand slithers down my wrist. One bead after another drops into my open palm, electrifying my skin at the point of contact. My blood zings through me, like a high-voltage current. I am not a shadow.

A branch snaps, making my hands shake with the need to hurry.

What are you waiting for, my friend?

Is Sister Bernadette afraid?

She has to be. Hungry for her fear, I squeeze my thighs together, then I push my face close and look deep in her eyes.

"The blood of the lamb will wash away your sins." She gasps, and her eyes roll back. "Repent."

My heart slams shut.

I begin the prayers.

ONE

Santa Fe, New Mexico
Present Day—Saturday, July 20, 1:00 P.M.

Man, *she's something.*

Luke Jericho halted midstride, and the sophisticated chatter around him dimmed to an indistinct buzz. Customers jamming the art gallery had turned the air hot, and the aromas of perfume and perspiration clashed. His gaze sketched the cut muscles of the woman's shoulders before swerving to the tantalizing V of her low-back dress. There, slick fabric met soft skin just in time to hide the thong she must be wearing. His fingers found the cold silk knot of his tie and worked it loose. He let his glance dot down the line of her spine, then swoop over the arc of her ass. It was the shimmer of Mediterranean blue satin, illuminated beneath art lights, that had first drawn his eye, her seductive shape that had pulled him up short, but it was her stance—her pose—that had his blood expanding like hot mercury under glass.

Head tilted, front foot cocked back on its stiletto, the woman studied one of Luke's favorite pieces—his brother Dante's mixed-media. A piece Luke had hand-selected and quietly inserted into this show of local artists in the hopes a positive response might bolster his brother's beleaguered self-esteem.

The woman couldn't take her eyes off the piece, and he couldn't take his eyes off the woman. Her right arm floated, as if she were battling the urge to reach out and touch the multitextured painting. Though her back was to him, he could picture her face, pensive, enraptured. Her lips would be parted and sensual. He savored the swell of her bottom beneath the blue dress. Given the way the fabric clung to her curves, he'd obviously guessed right about the thong. She smoothed the satin with her hand, and he rubbed the back of his neck with his palm. *Ha*. Any minute now, she'd turn and ruin his fantasy with what was sure to turn out to be the most ordinary mug in the room.

And then she did turn, and damned if her mug wasn't ordinary at all, but she didn't appear enraptured. Inquisitive eyes, with a distinct undercurrent of melancholy, searched the room and found him. Then, delicate brows raised high, her mouth firmed into a hard line—even thinned, her bloodred lips were temptation itself—she jerked to a rigid posture and marched, yeah, marched, straight at him.

Hot ass. Great mouth. Damn lot of nerve.

"I could feel your stare," she said.

"Kind of full of yourself, honey."

A flush of scarlet flared across her chest, leading his attention to her lovely, natural breasts, mostly, but not entirely, concealed by a classic neckline. With effort, he raised his eyes to meet hers. Green. Skin, porcelain. Hair, fiery—like her cheeks—and flowing. She looked like a mermaid. Not the soft kind, the kind with teeth.

"I don't like to be ogled." Apparently, she intended to stand her ground.

He decided to stand his as well. That low-back number she had on might be considered relatively tame in a room with more breasts on display than a Picasso exhibit, but there was something about *the way she wore it.* "Then you shouldn't have worn that dress, darlin'."

Her brow arched higher in challenge. "Which is it? Honey or darlin'?"

"Let's go with honey. You look sweet." Not at the moment she didn't, but he'd sure like to try to draw the sugar out of her. This woman was easily as interesting and no less beautiful than his best gallery piece, and she didn't seem to be reacting to him per the usual script. He noticed his hand floating up, reaching out, just as her hand had reached for the painting. Like his mesmerizing customer, he knew better than to touch the display, but it was hard to resist the urge.

Her body drew back, and her shoulders hunched. "You're aware there's a serial killer on the loose?"

Luke, you incredible ass.

No wonder she didn't appreciate his lingering looks. Every woman he knew was on full alert. The Jericho charm might or might not be able to get him out of this one, but he figured she was worth a shot. "Here, in this gallery? In broad daylight?" He searched the room with his gaze and made his tone light. "Or are you saying you don't like being sized up for the kill?" He patted his suit pockets, made a big show of it, then stroked his chin thoughtfully. "I seem to have misplaced my rosary somewhere; I don't suppose you've seen it?"

Her shoulders eased back to a natural position.

"Seriously, do I look like someone who'd be called the Saint?"

If the glove doesn't fit. . .

Her lips threatened to curve up at the corners. "No. I don't suppose you do." Another beat, then her smile bloomed in earnest. "Looking a little is one thing, maybe it's even flattering . . . but you seem to have exceeded your credit line."

He turned his palms up. "Then I'd like to apply for an increase."

At that, her pretty head tipped back, and she laughed, a big genuine laugh. It was the kind of laugh that was a touch too hearty for a polished society girl, which perhaps she wasn't after all. It was also the kind of laugh he'd like to hear again. Of its own accord, his hand found his heart. "Listen, I'm honest-to-God sorry if I spooked you. That wasn't my intention."

Her expression was all softness now.

"Do you like the painting?" he asked, realizing that he cared more than he should about the answer.

"It's quite . . . dark." Her bottom lip shivered with the last word, and he could sense she found Dante's painting disturbing.

Always on the defensive where his brother was concerned, his back stiffened. He tugged at his already loosened tie. "Artists are like that. I don't judge them."

"Of course. I-I wasn't judging the artist. I was merely making an observation about the painting. It's expressive, beautiful."

Relaxing his stance, he pushed a hand through his hair.

She pushed a hand through her hair, then her glance found her fancy-toed shoes. "Maybe I overreacted, maybe you weren't even staring."

Giving in to the urge to touch, he reached out and tilted her chin up until their eyes met. "I'm Luke Jericho, and you had it right the first time. I *was* staring. I was staring at—" He barely had time to register a startled flash of her green eyes before she turned on her heel and disappeared into the throng of gallery patrons.

He shrugged and said to the space where her scent still sweetened the air, "I was staring at your fascination. Your fascination fascinates me."

Saturday, July 20, 1:30 P.M.

Faith Clancy strode across her nearly naked office and tossed her favorite firelight macaron clutch onto her desk. After rushing out of the gallery, she'd come to her office to regroup, mainly because it was nearby.

She could hear Ma's voice now, see her wagging finger. *"Luke Jericho? Sure'an you've gone and put your wee Irish foot in the stewpot now, Faith."*

Well, it was only a tiny misstep—what harm could possibly come of it? She braced her palms against the windowsill. Teeth clenched, she heaved with all her might until wood screeched against wood, and the window lurched open.

A full inch.

Swell.

Summers in Santa Fe were supposed to be temperate, and she hadn't invested in an air conditioner for her new office. She sucked in a deep breath, but the currentless summer air brought little relief from the heat. Lifting her hair off the back of her damp neck with one hand, she reached over and dialed on the big standing fan next to the desk with the other. The dinosaur whirred to life without a hiccup.

That made *one* thing gone right today.

The relaxing Saturday afternoon she'd been looking forward to all week had been derailed, thanks to Luke Jericho. Okay, that wasn't even half-fair. In reality, the wheels of her day had never touched down on the track to begin with. She'd awakened this morning with a knot in her stomach and an ache in her heart—missing Danny and Katie.

Walk it off, she'd thought. Dress up. Take in the sights. Act like you're part of the Santa Fe scene, and soon enough you will be. Determined to forget the homesick rumbling in her chest, Faith had plucked a confidence-boosting little number from her closet, slipped on a pair of heels, and headed out to mingle with polite society. Even if she didn't feel like she fit in, at least she would look the part. But the first gallery she'd entered, she'd dunked her foot in the stewpot—crossing swords with, and then, even worse, *flirting* with the brother of a patient.

Rather bad luck considering she had just one patient.

Her toe started to tap.

Her gaze swept the office and landed on the only adornment of the freshly painted walls—her diplomas and certificates, arranged in an impressive display with her psychiatric board certification center stage. A Yale-educated doctor. Ma and Da would've been proud even if they might've clucked their tongues at the psychiatrist part. She blinked until her vision cleared. It wasn't only Danny and Katie she was missing today.

She kicked off her blasted shoes and shook off her homesick blues . . . only to find her mind returning to the gallery and her encounter with a man who was strictly off-limits.

There was no point chastising herself for walking

into the art gallery in the first place, or for refusing to pretend she didn't notice the man who was eyeing her like she was high tea in a whorehouse and he a starving sailor.

Care for a macaron, sir?

Had she realized her admirer was Luke Jericho, she would've walked away without confronting him, but how was she to know him by sight? It wasn't as if she spent her spare time flipping through photos of town royalty in the society pages.

She'd recognized his name instantly, however, and not only because she was treating his half brother, Dante. The Jericho family had a sprawling ranch outside town and an interest in a number of local businesses. But most of their wealth, she'd heard, came from oil. The Jerichos, at least the legitimate ones, had money. Barrels and barrels of it.

Luke's name was on the lips of every unattached female in town—from the clerk at the local Shop and Save to the debutant docent at the Georgia O'Keeffe museum:

Single.

Handsome.

Criminally rich.

Luke Jericho, they whispered.

When she'd turned to find him watching her, his heated gaze had caused her very bones to sizzle. Luke had stood formidably tall, dressed in an Armani suit that couldn't hide his rancher's physique. The gallery lights seemed to spin his straw-colored hair into gold and ignite blue fire in his eyes. She could still feel his gaze raking over her in that casual way, as if he didn't wish to conceal his appetites. It was easy to see how *some* women might come undone in his presence. She eased closer to the fan.

"Dr. Clancy."

That low male voice gave her a fizzy, sick feeling in the pit of her stomach, like she'd just downed an Alka-Seltzer on top of the flu. When you're all alone in a room, and someone else speaks, it's just plain creepy.

Icy tendrils of fear wrapped themselves around her chest, squeezing until it hurt her heart to go on beating. The cold certainty that things were not as they should be made the backs of her knees quiver. Then recognition kicked in, and her breath released in a *whoosh*. It had only taken a millisecond to recognize the voice, but at a time when someone dubbed *the Santa Fe Saint* was on a killing spree, that was one millisecond too long.

It's only Dante.

She pasted on a neutral expression and turned to face him. How'd he gotten in? The entrance was locked; she was certain of it.

"Did I frighten you?"

She inclined her head toward the front door to her office, which was indeed locked, and said, "Next time, Dante, I'd prefer you use the main entrance . . . and knock."

"I came in the back."

That much was obvious now that she'd regained

her wits. "That's my private entrance. It's not intended for use by patients." Stupid of her to leave it unlocked, but it was midday, and she hadn't expected an ambush.

To buy another moment to compose herself, she went to her bookcase and inspected its contents. Toward the middle, Freud's *Introductory Lectures on Psychoanalysis* leaned haphazardly in the direction of its opponent, Skinner's *Behavior Therapy*. A paperback version of *A Systems Approach to Family Therapy* had fallen flat, not quite bridging the gap between the warring classics.

Dante crossed the distance between them, finishing directly in front of her, invading her personal space. "Quite right. I didn't mean to startle you."

She caught a blast of breath, pungent and wrong—a Listerine candle floating in a jar of whiskey. In self-defense, she took a step back before looking up at her patient's face. Dante possessed his brother's intimidating height, but unlike Luke, his hair was jet-black, and his coal-colored eyes were so dark it was hard to distinguish the pupil from the iris. Despite Dante's dark complexion and the roughness of his features—he had a previously broken nose and a shiny pink scar that gashed across his cheekbone into his upper lip—there was a distinct family resemblance between the Jericho brothers. Luke was the fair-haired son to Dante's black sheep, and even their respective phenotypes fit the cliché.

Dante took a step forward.

She took another deep step back, bumping her rear

end against wood. With one hand, she reached behind her and felt for the smooth rim of her desktop. With the other hand, she put up a stop sign. "Stay right where you are."

He halted, and she edged her way behind her desk, using it as a barrier between herself and Dante. Maybe she should advise him to enroll in a social-skills class since he didn't seem to realize how uncomfortable he was making her. Though she knew full well Dante wasn't on her schedule today—no one was on her schedule today—she powered on her computer. "Hang on a second while I check my calendar."

"All right." At least he had the courtesy to play along.

When he rested his hand on her desk, she noticed he was carrying a folded newspaper. She'd already seen today's headline, and it had given her the shivers. "Any minute now." She signaled to Dante with an upheld index finger.

He nodded, and, in what seemed an eternity of time, her computer finished booting. She navigated from the welcome screen to her schedule, then, in a firm, matter-of-fact voice, she told him, "I'm afraid you've made a mistake. Your appointment isn't until Monday at 4:00 P.M."

As he took another step closer, a muscle twitched in his jaw. He didn't seem to care when his appointment was. Gesturing toward the leather armchair on the patient side of her desk, she fended him off. "Have a seat right there." If she could get him to sit down, maybe she could gain control of the situation; she really ought to hear him out long enough to make sure this wasn't some sort of emergency.

Dante didn't sit. Instead, from across the desk, his body inclined forward. Her throat went dry, and her speeding pulse signaled a warning. If this were an emergency, he most likely would have tried to contact her through her answering service; besides which, he'd had plenty of time already to mention anything urgent. He must've known he didn't have an appointment today, so what the hell was he doing here on a Saturday?

Dante had no reason at all to expect her to be here. In fact, the more she thought about it, the less sense his presence made. Pulling her shoulders back, she said, "I am sorry, but you need to leave. You'll have to come back on Monday at four."

The scar tissue above his mouth tugged his features into a menacing snarl. "I saw you talking to my brother."

He'd followed her from the art gallery.

Even though Dante's primary diagnosis was schizotypal personality disorder, there was a paranoid component present, exacerbated by a sense of guilt and a need to compensate for feelings of inferiority. His slip-and-slide grip on reality occasionally propelled him into a near-delusional state. She could see him careening into a dark well of anxiety now, and she realized she needed to reassure him she wasn't colluding with his half brother against him. "I wasn't talking to your brother about *you.* In fact, I didn't have any idea I had wandered into your brother's art gallery until he . . . introduced himself."

"I don't believe you."

As fast as her heart was galloping, she managed a controlled reply. "That hardly bodes well for our relationship as doctor and patient, does it? But the truth is, we were discussing a painting."

"Discussing my painting, discussing me, same difference."

His painting?

That bit of information did nothing to diminish her growing sense of apprehension. That painting had had a darkness in it like nothing she'd ever seen before. A darkness that had captivated her attention, daring her to unravel the secrets it belied.

Dante dropped into the kind of predatory crouch that would've made a kitten roll over and play dead.

But she wasn't a kitten.

Defiantly, she exhaled slow and easy. If she didn't know better, she'd think Dante was intentionally trying to frighten her. "I'm happy to see you during your regular hour, and we can schedule more frequent sessions if need be, but for now, I'm afraid it's time for you to go."

He returned to a stand. "You're here all alone today."

A shudder swept across her shoulders. He was right. No one else was in the building. She shared a secretary with an aesthetician down the hall, and today,

Stacy hadn't been at her post. The aesthetician usually worked Saturday mornings, but she must've finished for the day and gone home. Home was where Faith wanted to go right now. She wished she'd kept her clutch in hand. *Her phone was in that clutch.* "We'll work on that trust issue . . . on Monday."

With Dante's gaze tracking hers, her eyes fell on her lovely macaron bag, lying on the desktop near his fingertips. He lifted the clutch as if to offer it to her, but then drew his hand back and stroked the satin shell against his face.

The room suddenly seemed too small. "I don't mean to be unkind. We've been working hard these past few weeks and making good progress up to this point, and I'd hate to have to refer you to another psychiatrist, but I will if I have to." She paused for breath.

"You're barefoot." Slowly, he licked his lower lip.

Feeling as vulnerable as if she were standing before him bare naked instead of barefooted, she slipped back into her shoes. Jerking a glance around the room, she cursed herself for furnishing the place so sparsely, as if she didn't plan on staying in Santa Fe long. It wasn't like she had anywhere else to call home anymore, and now here she stood without so much as a paperweight to conk someone on the head with. Under these circumstances, she'd have little chance against a potential attacker. Her Krav Maga instructor wouldn't approve of her lack of preparedness. The window was open; at least she could scream for help if necessary. "We're done here."

"I'm not leaving, Dr. Clancy." He opened her purse, removed her cell and slid it into his pants pocket, then dropped her purse on the floor.

Her stomach got fizzy again, and she gripped the edge of her desk. Screaming didn't seem like the most effective plan. It might destabilize him and cause him to do something they'd both regret. For now, at least, a better plan was to stay calm and listen. If she could figure out what was going on inside his head, maybe she could stay a step ahead of him and defuse the situation before it erupted into a full-scale nightmare. "Give me back my phone, then we can talk."

Here came that involuntary snarl of his. "No phone. And I'm not leaving until I've done what I came here to do." Carefully unfolding the newspaper he'd brought with him, he showed her the headline:

SANTA FE SAINT CLAIMS FOURTH VICTIM.

TWO

Faith's vision stuttered across the bold block letters of the headline. Her knuckles throbbed from gripping the edge of her desk, and the nerves that ran from her wrists to her elbows buzzed like bees.

Fourth Victim.

Was she destined to become the fifth?

A chill swept over her, and a fleeting wish that someone wonderful would appear and throw warm, protective arms around her, made her breath catch. *Ridiculous.* Jerking her chin up, she pushed away the useless thought and focused on the dark, contorted face of the man standing on the opposite side of her desk.

Dante Jericho.

His black hair stuck up wildly from the way he'd been yanking it here and twirling it there. As his gaze flitted rapidly about her office, a distended vein pulsed frantically in his forehead. His pumped arms finished in balled-up, ready-to-smash fists, and his nostrils flared like those of a bull that had been offered the matador's cape. If the look he was going for was enraged serial killer . . . then, well done indeed.

Her throat contracted in a painful spasm. Part of her wanted to scream. *Most* of her wanted to scream. But then, the professional corner of her brain kicked in. Suppose her gut, which was telling her she was in real danger here, was right. She certainly needed a better strategy than shouting out a window or knocking her *patient* over the head with a nonexistent paperweight . . . and she needed that better strategy now. Turning over the facts, she sifted them through a rational filter, one constructed from education and training, if not from experience. She was a psychiatrist, facing the unexpected from a disturbed, and *perhaps*, a dangerous man.

Yet, fear of her patient in no way relieved her of her duty toward him.

As her professional persona wrestled her anxiety into submission, her heart rate slowed, and her thoughts sharpened. What was really going on here?

Dante clearly *wanted* her to believe he was dangerous—reminding her they were alone in the building, confiscating her phone, showing her that horrible headline. And yet, he'd done nothing to hurt her—so far—despite the fact that he'd had ample opportunity. He hadn't brandished a weapon, but, of course, that didn't mean he wasn't in possession of one. Her legs wobbled beneath her, and she pressed her knees together to steady herself. Then she softly smacked her fist into her palm. She'd decided on her course of action.

She would wrench control back from Dante, then treat this like any run-of-the-mill therapy session . . . as long as he kept his distance and made no overt threat.

After taking a moment to summon her nerve, she tiptoed to gain height, then leaned forward across the desk until her forehead nearly touched his. Infusing her voice with authority, and then some, she said, "Sit. Down."

For a two-second lifetime, Dante stood his ground, their faces so close she could feel the heat coming off him, smell his camouflaged whiskey breath. Then he stepped back and dropped into the leather armchair across from her desk.

Aborting a relieved sigh before it could go on long enough to give her away, she sat down. Dante lowered his eyes, and when he looked up again, the fierce expression in them had dissipated by half. So far so good.

He dug in his pocket and pulled out her cell, studied it, then put it back in his pocket. His way of intimidating her. She ignored the gesture, and a taut silence stretched between them like a high wire—whoever lost his balance first would shift control to the other side.

Only a moment or two passed before Dante fell. "You want your phone back. Who exactly are you planning to call, Dr. Clancy?"

He wasn't going to return her phone, and begging

him for it would only weaken her position. Leaning back in her chair, she crossed her arms over her chest and said nothing.

"Nine-one-one? The men in white coats?" A warble crept into his voice, then he hid his face with his hands.

That's when she knew for sure . . . Dante was scared.

Well, that made two of them.

His hands dropped to his lap. "Surely, you're not thinking of calling your brother-in-law—the detective. What's his name? Oh, yes, Benson."

Her body jerked in response to his words. What did he know about her family? He couldn't possibly know the mere mention of her brother-in-law left her feeling as though her heart had been carved out of her chest and the remaining cavity packed with sawdust.

"Judging by the look on your face, I'd say I hit a nerve . . . but, wait, Benson's not actually your brother-in-law anymore, is he? Not now that your sister, Grace, is dead, and he's remarried."

She shot him a perky smile and kept her shaky hands hidden. Dante knew nothing important. He couldn't possibly know she'd spent years traipsing after her dead sister's husband like a substitute wife, all the while knowing she could never measure up to the original. Not even *Danny* knew that. As far as Danny and the rest of the world were concerned, she was just good-old-reliable Aunt Faith. Always there when he needed a home-cooked meal or a sitter for Katie and just as ready to disappear into the background when he didn't.

Dante might have gone digging and uncovered a few facts about her past, but he *understood* nothing. This was little more than a shot in the dark on his part. But why had he bothered to go digging into her past at all? She suppressed a shudder and remained silent.

Dante tilted his head, making him appear almost sympathetic. "I mean once your sister died, that severed any true family connection with Benson, and your parents, they were killed in a car accident when you were, what? Eleven years old? Poor Grace was eighteen. Do I have that right?"

She flashed back twenty years to Grace, waiting for Faith outside her classroom, arms reaching out, eyes swollen with tears. Touching her necklace, the one her sister had given her, she willed her breathing to steady, then glanced indifferently at her watch and said, "Time's almost up. You've got five more minutes."

"Speaking of Grace, she raised you after your parents died, but when you were just seventeen, she swallowed an entire bottle of happy pills, leaving you with let's see . . ." He tapped his chin with his forefinger. "Leaving you with *no real family whatsoever*. And, of course, you're new in town and can't have made many friends, so let's face it, you don't need your phone after all because you, my dear doctor, have no one in the wide world to call." Studying her reaction and seeming pleased with it, he patted his pocket. "I think I'll just hang on to your cell until I've said my piece."

Her heart thudded heavily in her chest, and she looked toward the door. It might as well have been miles away instead of just across the room. She certainly couldn't reach it without going through Dante. As much as she wanted to run far away from him, she straightened her back and leaned toward him. He had no words that could make her feel more alone in life than she already did, and she would not allow him to frighten her into behaving foolishly. Determined to keep her wits about her, she did her best to smooth her face into an expressionless mask.

"Don't look so alarmed."

Poker was never her game.

With a wave of his hand, he sat back. "I can't trust just anyone with my deepest darkest secrets, now can I? I've done my homework, that's all. *You've* nothing to fear from me because I *like* you. You're smart and hardworking. Well educated. But most importantly, I know I can trust you."

Oddly, his tone had turned sincere.

"You *can* trust me." She meant what she said. Dante was her patient, and she felt her responsibility toward him as keenly as she felt the room closing in on her like the walls of a coffin. If there was any way she could keep them *both* safe, she would.

"I trust you because we're alike. We're both of us all alone in the world. I know you understand how desperate that feels, and I know you'll try to help me." He arched one brow high and enunciated each word sharply, "No matter what I've done."

No matter what I've done.

Her body started to rock, and she stiffened, stilling

herself. With all her heart, she wished the man in front of her had done nothing terrible at all. He had a massive guilt complex—that much she knew from the few therapy sessions they'd already had. Most of it to do with his mother, Sylvia, and his brother, Luke.

"You're not alone, Dante." His parents might be dead, but unlike Faith, Dante still had a living sibling. "You have your brother."

His brow lowered, and the corners of his mouth drooped until he seemed more sad clown than raging bull. "You think a man like Luke Jericho cares about me—his useless bastard half brother?"

The self-loathing reflected in that comment only reinforced her suspicion that Dante was carrying far too much guilt around—guilt that belonged elsewhere—like on his father's shoulders, for example. And from what Dante had told her, Luke did care about him. Lowering her voice to a soothing tone, she reminded him of his own words. "Didn't you say that even though your father left his entire estate to your brother—"

"You mean my *half* brother. Remember, I'm a *bastard*. My mother was my father's housekeeper."

She steepled her fingers and rested her chin atop them. "Didn't you say Luke has set his lawyers working to divide the estate equitably between the two of you? Didn't you say Luke's invited you to move back to the family ranch?"

"He's trying to buy me off."

She shook her head. "I don't see why he'd need to do that. I won't pretend to know what's in Luke's mind and heart, but judging by his actions, I'd say he's trying to build a relationship with you. I'd say he's trying to be a good brother."

When Dante raised one hand to press his fingers against his eyes, she noted a faint tremor. As a rule, though she knew of certain exceptions, serial killers weren't prone to nervous tremors—not with all that ice running through their veins.

Her head was clearing, and the facts were shifting into a new, if confusing configuration. She couldn't be sure, of course, but she was beginning to suspect Dante's antics were more a cry for help than a true threat to her safety. In this moment, he seemed calm enough that she dared a confrontation.

"Dante, what's this all about?" Then in a firm tone, she added, "I'm willing to hear you out, but I don't like playing games."

He reached for the newspaper, rolled it up, and began slapping it into his open hand.

Thwack. Thwack. Thwack. Thwack. Thwack.

She couldn't see the headline, but with each slap, the words she'd read earlier echoed in her mind.

Serial. Killer. Claims. Fourth. Victim.

Her own hands still trembled, so she kept them hidden beneath the desk. Her body didn't seem to be getting the message her brain was sending:

He's doing his damnedest to scare you. Don't react.

The sound of the fan's whirring and the slapping of the newspaper set her teeth on edge. Deliberately, she relaxed her jaw and waited while Dante struggled with his demons. At last, he dropped the paper and met her gaze. Tears had formed in his eyes, and his lips twitched into an apologetic smile. Whatever game they were playing, she was about to learn the rules.

Her heart picked up speed.

"I'm him."

Her cheeks went numb. "You're who?"

He passed one hand over his face. "*Him.* I'm the Santa Fe Saint. *I* killed those people."

The whirring of the fan in the quiet room grew so loud she had to stop herself from covering her ears. The numbness in her cheeks spread to her mouth and tongue, and she couldn't swallow or speak. Her skin felt waxy, and she pinched her arm like a child trying to wake herself from a bad dream.

Then Dante started to cry in earnest, to sob really. He sobbed and shuddered until blood, just a trickle, leaked from his nose onto his face. She frowned. A psychopath wouldn't feel remorse. He simply wouldn't. Was Dante's display of emotion real, or just another show put on for her benefit?

If Dante was feigning his distress to trick her, he was not only the embodiment of a textbook, conscienceless killer, but a consummate actor to boot.

But if his emotion was real . . . then he most likely was *not* a killer at all. And if Dante wasn't the Santa Fe Saint, why would he confess?

As desperately as she tried to make the pieces of this puzzle fit, they weren't falling into any known psychiatric algorithm.

"I-I'm not certain . . ." Her voice trailed off. She didn't want to accuse him of lying and risk angering him. If he was indeed the Saint, he could turn on her in a heartbeat, and she'd have no defense other than screaming out that window and hoping she wasn't dead by the time help arrived.

And yet she didn't believe he *was* the Saint. Not completely anyway.

Dante spread the newspaper, almost reverently, on her desk and laid out his case for her. "See right here." He jabbed the headline with his index finger. "It says the police are closing in on the killer. They're about to make an arrest." He looked up at her with pleading eyes. "You have to make it stop. I can't sleep, knowing they're coming for me."

A fresh trickle of blood joined the drying stain under his nose, and he wiped it off with the back of his sleeve. "I can't go on hiding in the shadows, looking over my shoulder, waiting for the moment the cops handcuff me and haul me down to the station. Last night, I locked myself in the closet, in case they came for me. I mean, they might say I tried to escape and shoot me. It happens, you know."

Filling her lungs with a deep breath, she looked past him and tried to focus on what he was telling her. His words seemed paranoid, delusional. As if he was convinced the authorities were out to get him, and he wanted *her* to hand him over, here and now, in a place where he felt safe. That meant he hadn't come to harm her. He'd come because he needed her help. Her pulse still thumped in her ears, but it was growing slower and softer. "You believe the police are closing in on *you*."

"Yes." He huffed out a breath, as if relieved she was finally getting it. "It says so right here in the *Gazette*."

She pulled her bottom lip between her teeth. She needed to choose her next words carefully. "Not exactly. The paper doesn't say the police are closing in on Dante Jericho."

"Yes. It says so." He jabbed his finger harder.

"Dante, the headline says the police are closing in on the Santa Fe Saint. It doesn't say they're closing in on *you*. Have you been interviewed by the police regarding these murders?"

"No." He wrung his hands.

"Have you been interviewed by the police regarding anything at all?"

"Yes. Yes." He nodded emphatically. "They called my home on the pretense of wanting donations for the policemen's ball. But I can see through their tricks. I know that phone call was merely a ruse to get me to incriminate myself."

"Dante, do you remember how we talked about the fact that some of what you believe may be a distortion of truth, a trick of your mind?"

"The police are the tricky ones."

His thinking was circular and distorted, containing loose associations—like the thinking of a man with a very tenuous hold on reality. At last, here was a clinical diagnosis she recognized. Dante was displaying clear signs of a thought disorder, of impending psychosis.

She tried to remember what she'd read about false confessions, but most of what she knew applied to co-erced confessions, not voluntary admissions of guilt. This was uncharted territory for her. "You've admitted to me already that you feel guilty for many things that we know are not your fault. Such as the fact that your mother died in a car accident."

"But it *is* my fault. Her life was ruined when she got pregnant with me."

These deep-seated beliefs could not be expunged with a simple reassurance, but her heart was heavy with the need to offer one anyway. "Your mother's death is *not* your fault." As she reached out her hand, palm up, she pushed away the memory of her own sis-ter's suicide.

He dug out her cell phone and placed it in her open hand. Her breath released in a relieved rush, but she took no pleasure in what she knew was coming next. "Do you actually remember committing these crimes?"

"I just said so. Do you want me to tell you all the details?"

She put up one hand to stop him. "No. You need a lawyer before you talk to . . . the police."

"Then you will call them? You *have* to call them—before I kill again." And then he smiled . . . and she knew he knew he'd won. "You don't want another dead body on your conscience now, do you?"

Her shoulders sagged under the weight of Dante's confession. Even if she might consider betting her own life that the man before her was *not* the Santa Fe Saint, and she wasn't at all sure she'd make that particular wager, she could never bet someone else's.

The matter was out of her hands.

The moment Dante said he would kill again, whether she believed him or not, she was morally and legally bound to report him to the police. The statutes were clear on this matter. If a patient presented a danger to others, doctor-patient confidentiality no longer applied. She had a duty to warn.

Her hands were steady, but the sinking feeling in the pit of her stomach left her fighting off a dry heave. Dante slumped in the chair across from her, his cheeks and chin streaked with dried tears and blood.

He'd grown up unloved, unwanted. He believed he was nothing. He believed he'd killed his mother merely by being born.

Her heart squeezed painfully, and her knees rattled against the bottom of her desk.

Either she was currently cloistered in her office with a demented serial killer, or she was about to send an innocent man—*an innocent man with whose welfare she'd been charged*—to prison.

She powered on her cell and hit 911.

THREE

Sunday, July 21, 7:00 A.M.

Once again, his brother, Dante, had broken his promise to breakfast with the family. Luke crumpled a napkin in his fist and turned his attention to his mother, who slouched across from him, clanking her spoon around in a cup of hot chocolate. He tapped his fingers together, then ran them over the cool surface of the mosaic table that'd been in his family for generations. There, a river of blue and violet tiles raged across a white background while light from the east window bounced off the vibrant mosaic chips. His jaw tightened. If these shattered bits of broken glass could lose their sharp edges and come together to form a functional pattern, surely his fractured family could do the same.

His brother's absence, while disappointing, was

hardly a surprise. Luke didn't know whether Dante had simply overslept, or if he hadn't come home at all last night, but Luke didn't intend to let anything spoil the morning. His gaze flicked to the panorama outside the breakfast room's east window—his favorite view of Gran Cielo. To him, a good day started off sipping a man-up cup of Aileen's blackest coffee while perusing the morning paper and watching the high grasses undulate across his family's ranch. The way the soft hills of his land battled and finally surrendered to the hard peaks of the distant mountains pleased him, and he liked nothing better than watching the sun come up, and as its first order of business, turn the snowcapped summits of the Sangre de Cristo Range bloodred to match their name.

He loved Gran Cielo for its beauty, but even more for its toughness. He loved the way the hard ground fought back at planting time because that made a man strong. He loved the way the summer heat cooked a man's bones because that called him up before dawn and drove him home in time for dinner with his loved ones—not that Luke's father had ever made it home by dinner . . . or breakfast much, either. Thanks to his father, life on Gran Cielo had been harder than most.

But life's not supposed to be easy.

Not unless you're keen to turn out soft.

Besides, not counting the bachelor penthouse he'd occupied in his college days, Gran Cielo was the only home he'd ever known. He'd been born right here on the ranch. That little alcove off to the right was where he'd rushed into the world and thrown an entire set of monkey wrenches into his mother's elaborate birth plan. A million times she'd sat at this very table and scolded him:

I was supposed to give birth in the new hospital downtown. I was supposed to be attended by the finest physicians. Here, she usually paused to whither him with a particularly disappointed look. *I was supposed to get an epidural. You've always been so willful, Luke. What kind of a Jericho has the common manners to be born at home?*

And then she'd wrap her arms around him and give him a loud smacking kiss on the cheek, and he'd know his mother was secretly proud of managing to bring him into this world all on her own. Just as his mother would always be his mother, Gran Cielo would always be his home, and everything about the place felt right to him. Everything, that is, except that damn casita— the tiny house Dante and his mother, Sylvia, had occupied.

He'd burn the thing to the ground if only Dante weren't so attached to it.

But there was no need to ruin this day or any day dredging up the past. Banishing the thought of the casita and all it represented, he shaded his eyes. By now the sun was shining bright and lucky as a dime on a sidewalk, flooding the room with warmth and filling Luke's heart with hope for the future. Hope for his family. "Beautiful day for riding, Mother."

She slurped her chocolate and gave her cup one last round of her spoon. Then she let out a lingering sigh, just like she used to do when he was a kid.

"I'll take that as a no to the ride."

Back in the day, his mother's pity-me sigh meant she'd just finished with her latest romance novel and would have to wait *an eternity* for the next installment in her favorite series. This morning, the sigh meant she'd just finished with her latest husband and had no intention of waiting long for another.

"Mom?"

Finally, she seemed to notice he'd spoken and turned her fabled blue eyes on him. The local press liked to describe Rose Jericho's eyes as the color of robin's eggs—and she liked to blush and point out how hackneyed the phrase was to anyone who'd listen— her hairdresser, the bank teller, even the parish priest: *My eyes, a bright blue reminder of spring? Have you ever heard such drivel?*

He never let on that he knew she loved the flattery. Hard to argue with a spot-on comparison and even harder to argue with a happy mother, especially since happiness had been so hard for her to come by.

"I think the gallery would be the best venue for the benefit, don't you?" Her brassy tone smacked of feigned cheerfulness. She set down her spoon and stared dismally into her empty cup.

"I'll leave the venue to you. I don't have time for minor details. I lasso the donors. You plan the party.

That was our deal, remember?" He shoveled a spoonful of corned beef hash into his mouth.

"No thank you, Aileen." His mother held up a well-manicured hand to indicate she didn't want a second helping of waffles, and the cook promptly forked the extra onto Luke's plate, then left the room.

"Choosing a venue is hardly a minor detail, sweetie. Don't pretend this event isn't important to you because I know better."

It was true he'd been planning the Big Brothers and Big Sisters benefit for the better part of a year, and he'd put a lot of energy into securing a guest list that contained both the wealthiest and the most generous members of Santa Fe society—these being two distinct groups. It was also true his secretary was more than capable of handling anything and everything related to the benefit, but no one could throw a party like his mother, and more importantly, having just left her fourth husband, Rose Jericho needed a distraction. Otherwise, Luke was liable to wind up with yet another stepfather in short order. His mother was a serial monogamist, and her cooling-off period was growing shorter between victims.

She picked up a set of bifocals she was breaking in and promptly set them down again, pulled her long blond hair back, and snapped it absentmindedly into a ponytail. In the right light, his mother looked thirty, and she knew it. She pushed the bifocals as far away as her arm would reach. "I'm onto you, you know."

"No idea what you mean."

"I mean you're handing me something to do so that I won't moon and mope about Bernie."

He hadn't expected her not to see through his ruse, but he had expected her to play along. This was their dance, and she knew the tune well. She was supposed to follow his lead, pretend she didn't know he was trying to cheer her up. It irked him she wouldn't just go with the flow.

He let loose his best imitation of her pity-me sigh. "I truly need your help, Mother. Because you're right, this benefit is important to me. And I am sorry about Bernie." He slathered syrup on his waffles and spoke with his mouth full. "I don't understand why you don't just date these men. Why do you have to marry them? It's costing you a small fortune."

"You're one to talk about throwing away your fortune. And don't speak with your mouth full. I raised you better than that."

"I'm not judging you." He wasn't. "I'm merely curious as to why you keep . . ."

"Making the same mistake over and over again? Because I believe in love, and I believe in marriage."

"So you keep getting divorced? Bernie's a nice guy. Maybe you should've stuck it out a while longer."

She slid lower in her chair. That wasn't fair of him. He knew how hard she was trying. And she'd stayed with her first husband, his unfaithful father, more than eighteen years, until Luke was in college. That hadn't been easy on her. He knew because it hadn't been easy on him, either. Now, at the age of fifty-four, his mother had decided to go on a no-holds-barred search for her soul mate, her one true love, and he didn't want to stand in her way. It was just that seeing her sad every time things went south made Aileen's best cooking taste more like unsalted mush than gourmet cuisine.

Crossing her arms on her chest, his mother looked at him slyly. "Speaking of love, are you bringing that Heaven woman to the benefit?"

He gulped his coffee too fast and singed the roof of his mouth. So *this* was the game his mother was looking to play. "No, Mother, I won't be bringing *Celeste*. I'm sure it'll devastate you to know I haven't been out with her in months." And it'd been far longer than that since he'd grown tired of her.

As lovely as Celeste was, she was a virtual clone of every other beautiful woman who ran in his crowd. Her hair, her dress, even her taste in art conformed to what was expected. Suddenly struck by the memory of a less predictable woman, he rubbed the back of his neck.

Faith Clancy.

Yesterday, at the gallery, his dulled appetites had roared back to life at the sight of her. And he'd been certain the attraction was mutual—right up until the moment she'd abruptly cut him off. After she left, he'd asked around, but no one seemed to know her. Finally, his assistant remembered the woman had signed the guest book, and only then did he learn her identity. Instantly, he'd recognized the name. Faith Clancy was his brother's psychiatrist. His people had run a background check on her, but he hadn't seen a photo, so he hadn't recognized her at the time.

"Luke?"

His eyes drifted to his mother, and he thought she might've called his name more than once.

"What were you thinking of just now?"

"Not Celeste." He waved a hand in reassurance lest his mother think he was pining after the girl.

"Your father?" Her voice softened with sadness.

He shook his head, and his spine stiffened as his thoughts returned to his family. His father's death had not only drilled a hole in his heart, it'd left him with every regret in the book. But Roy Jericho's passing had brought one good thing with it: a chance for the living members of the family to come together. His father had long ago banished Dante from Gran Cielo, and while his father lived, his mother had banished herself.

Now, Luke had it in mind to bring about a family reconciliation. It was time to put the past where it belonged and to right the wrongs that had been inflicted on his brother by his father. All of them—his mother, Dante, and yes, even Luke himself—needed to reconcile the accounts in order to heal and get on with their lives.

His mother must've read his mind because she looked up from the origami bird she'd begun crafting from her napkin, and said, "Do you really think it's a good idea for your brother to move back to Gran Cielo?"

To her credit, she never referred to Dante as his half sibling. Unlike his father, his mother never wanted Dante to feel like a second-class Jericho.

"I do." He answered curtly, hoping a decisive response would put the question to rest. He hated the idea of Dante's going back to live in the casita, but he wanted him home, and his brother had adamantly refused to move into the main house.

"I think you should proceed with caution as far as your brother is concerned. I'm not saying you shouldn't attempt to repair your relationship with Dante, only that he seems, well, a bit unstable." His mother's voice rose a bit at the end.

Luke had to admit that six months ago, when he'd first contacted Dante to notify him of their father's funeral, he'd noticed a dramatic change in him. It'd been almost twenty years since he'd seen his brother, and the confident, aggressive demeanor Dante had possessed as a youth had vanished entirely. It was as if the years had hammered him down into a lifeless piece of sheet metal: flat, dull, and brittle enough to crack at any moment. Dante kept his head down, his voice low. He startled at the smallest noise. At times, his speech wandered.

"I don't disagree," Luke said. "Which means he needs his family more than ever. And you and I both know that if Dad hadn't sent him away that night—"

"Dante has a psychiatric disorder. Not that I claim to know exactly what kind, but I recognize a loose screw when I see one. Your father wasn't perfect, Luke.

He made a lot of mistakes, but you can't pin Dante's mental health, or lack thereof, on him."

"Oh, but I can. And I wish you wouldn't defend Dad after the way he treated you. I wish for once you'd look me in the eye and say: *Your father was a selfish prick, and I wish I'd never married him.*"

The way her eyes darkened made him wish he could take back his words. His mother had suffered through a miserable marriage, with his father keeping a lover and an illegitimate child on the grounds of Gran Cielo. The casita might have been out of sight of the main house, but it was never out of anyone's mind.

Her back straightened, and her eyes misted over. She blinked hard, too proud to let the tears fall. "Your father was a flawed man who made a terrible mistake. But I don't regret marrying him because if it weren't for your father, I wouldn't have you. And whether you choose to believe it or not, he loved you more than life itself."

"My father loved no one but himself."

"You're wrong, Luke. He loved *you.*"

He turned away from his mother's insistent gaze. "Even if he did, that's still not good enough. A man doesn't have the right to choose only one of his sons to love."

"Maybe it wasn't a choice. Maybe circumstances forced his hand." A tremor crept into her voice. "Oh, Luke. You don't think your father sent Dante away for *my* benefit, do you?"

He should put a stop to this right now. This subject was too painful for his mother, and she was far too vulnerable at the moment. But the harsh words kept coming, despite the hurt welling in his mother's eyes. Dante had suffered too much, and not even for his mother's sake would he gloss over it. "I will not honor my father's legacy of injustice. I want Dante here at Gran Cielo, back with this family, where he belongs. I'm sorry if that hurts you, Mother. Please believe me when I tell you that's not my intent."

She shook her head. "Don't worry about me, Luke. I never blamed the poor child . . . I never blamed Dante, for your father's infidelity. I wish your brother only the best. But I do worry about his odd behavior, and I don't think it's wise to force things. Dante's made it clear he doesn't want to live in the main house, which says to me, he's not as ready as you are to become one big happy family."

"He wants his privacy is all." Luke didn't mention he'd found Dante with a prostitute shortly after he'd moved back to the casita. The incident had made both brothers uncomfortable, and Dante had since taken his amorous adventures off the ranch. He'd often disappear for a couple of days at a time, and Luke speculated he was with prostitutes, but he didn't pry.

"This business of splitting your inheritance with Dante doesn't seem wise. Your father wanted to make sure his entire estate went to you, or else he wouldn't have put all those clauses in his will to try to stop you from sharing with your brother. What if Dante ruins the family businesses?"

His hands tensed into tight balls, and he struggled to keep the frustration out of his tone. How like his father to try to control everyone else, even from the grave. How unlike his mother to take his father's side. "The day-to-day operations are mostly overseen by others—"

"Not the ranch. Not the gallery."

Her words echoed all his private doubts—doubts he'd shoved aside as if they were bullies who wanted to do more harm to his troubled brother. "They're as much Dante's to ruin as mine. According to my lawyers, those nasty clauses Dad put in his will are unenforceable. The estate belongs to me, and I can do whatever the hell I want with it." His fist came down on the table hard enough to bounce a fork onto the floor.

His mother covered her mouth with her hand, but not before a sharp cry escaped her lips.

He could be a real a jackass sometimes. "I'm sorry, Mother."

"No. It's just I didn't hear him come in." She pointed over his shoulder, and Luke turned to find a uniformed policeman standing in the room, hands out in front, palms up like he was offering them an olive branch.

Luke scraped his chair back and rose with deliberate calm.

His mother's face drained of color. The last time he remembered a uniformed cop at Gran Cielo was twenty years ago, and then to deliver very bad news. "How can I help you, Officer?"

The man planted his hands on his hips. "The chief asked me to come out here as a courtesy to the family. Your brother, Dante Jericho, was taken into custody yesterday afternoon."

Luke drew a deep breath, bracing himself. "That's impossible. He would've called me."

"Believe me, we encouraged him to do so. But your brother insisted he had no one to call. And . . . he's waived his right to counsel."

"What the hell do you mean he waived his right to counsel? He can't do that." Luke clenched his fists at his side. No one was going to railroad his brother. Not without a fight from him.

"Again, we encouraged Mr. Jericho, your brother I mean, either to retain an attorney or allow the court to appoint one for him. And not just out of respect for your father. The chief and the DA want everything by the book on this one. Nobody downtown wants your brother to walk because we didn't do our job. Maybe you can convince him he needs representation."

Luke already had his cell out of his pocket, poised to make the call to his corporate lawyers. Whatever Dante had done, if Luke's attorneys couldn't help him, they'd be able to recommend someone who could. "What are you holding him for? Be specific please."

"Like I said, the chief wanted you to know before the news hits the papers. Your brother's psychiatrist turned him in to the police."

"His psychiatrist? Faith Clancy?" He gripped his phone tighter. "What's Dante done?"

"First, he told his shrink, then he signed a confession down at the station." His eyes came level with Luke's. "Your brother's the Santa Fe Saint."

FOUR

Sunday, July 21, 2:00 P.M.

SANTA FE SAINT CLAIMS FOURTH VICTIM.

Scourge Teodori prowled his studio apartment, digging his fingers into his wavy black hair, pulling it until his scalp burned. Afternoon light swept in through the big kitchen window, and a shadow dogged his steps across a polished maple floor that smelled faintly of lemon oil. While he lapped the room, he ruminated on the article in the day-old *Gazette*.

With his Fourth victim, The Saint has grown careless. A source close to the Santa Fe District Attorney's Office revealed new clues found at the scene may soon lead to an arrest.

That was yesterday. But today, there'd been no further mention of the Saint. *New clues? Grown care-*

less? Scourge prowled and perseverated. His sneakers squish-squished. The refrigerator rumbled. In one corner of his apartment stood a single bed, covers pulled coin-bounce tight, a white sheet folded down to cuff a navy blue spread. A thin pillow in a freshly ironed case lay flat above the sheet cuff. The white of the pillowcase was beginning to dim, and he added a bottle of bleach to his mental grocery list. He considered sitting on the bed, but the thought of mussing the covers made his throat itch. Carefully, he lifted the pillow and removed the book that lay beneath his head while he slept. He kept the book under his pillow night after night, wishing he could absorb its lessons by dream osmosis.

Carrying the book beneath one arm, he made his way to the kitchen, where he pulled a shake out of the freezer and set it on the counter to thaw for an afternoon snack. The shake was his own special blend: egg yolk, barley, whey, a garlic clove, two teaspoons of soy sauce, and a block of tofu. As always, he recited the ingredients to keep the recipe safe in his memory. Like crossword puzzles, memorization was good exercise for the brain. He liked to avoid writing things down whenever possible. He wasn't lazy, and he admired that quality in himself . . . and in others. For example, suppose a waiter took his order without writing it down—he would give that waiter an extra tip because he respected servers who were not hebetudinous. *Hebetudinous,* meaning: *slacker,* was on his list of vocabulary words for the day.

Hebetudinous, perseveration, imperious—all good words to have in your hip pocket.

Before taking a seat at the table, he went to his calendar, marked a black X over today's date, and counted the days until the fifteenth of August.

In exactly twenty-four days, he would fulfill his destiny.

Once seated, he placed the book on the table next to the newspaper and squared the corners of both. His gaze ricocheted back and forth between the book and the newspaper. Both called to him with an intensity that made his eyes water and his stomach churn. First, he traced the raised gold letters of the book title with his index finger, then dragged that same finger over the smooth, cool newsprint.

. . . *New clues found at the scene may soon lead to an arrest.*

His pulse thudded relentlessly in his ears like footsteps following him down a dark alley. The air in the kitchen grew thin and unsatisfying. He inhaled a sharp, lemon-scented breath. Of course, the article might be a bluff, one of those planted stories used to draw out a criminal and trick him into making a mistake. It was a well-known fact the cops often used the media as part of their strategy to catch a killer, or even as a temporary means of mollifying the public in high-profile cases—like this one. He heaved out a breath, loosening his constricted chest, but on the inhale, his lungs clamped down again.

With only twenty-four days remaining until The

Big Kill, he made the sign of the cross and vowed not to let anything or anyone stop him. But . . . suppose the story wasn't a trick. Suppose the cops really did have evidence that would lead them to his door.

Why leave those damn beads?

The voice was scratching at him again, and the footsteps were thudding in his ear.

Those beads are going to get us caught.

"Shut up." A spasmodic cough followed his words, and he pounded his chest with his fist. He'd heard all the arguments, and they were not without merit, but he would not get caught. He needed the rosaries. He had to help his victims get into heaven, the way they were helping him get into hell. He wasn't so cruel as to chance leaving the poor souls in limbo.

By the book. He tapped the book, his blueprint to hell, with his forefinger.

That's how this must be done. His targets were a means to an end, part of a carefully-thought-out plan, only . . . he didn't intend to wind up hanged. The book was to be admired and emulated but not copied without thought. Certain necessary corrections, adjustments to the course outlined therein were in order. Unlike Perry, Scourge would get it right. Perry had tried to commit the perfect crime.

Scourge would actually do it.

He'd rewrite the book's ending, live to a ripe old age, and make the most of enjoying life as a free man on earth—because there would be no reward for him in heaven. There would be no heaven, period.

Not for someone like him.

He pulled his hair until his scalp burned to life again.

I am not a shadow.

His friend, the voice in his head, was wrong about the rosaries. Scourge would not be caught. He'd studied the book long and hard, and he knew all the mistakes that had been made in the past. He wouldn't repeat those mistakes. He wouldn't take on The Big Kill until he'd mastered the art of the *small kill*. He'd already succeeded with four practice victims, one for each Donovan, and he wasn't done perfecting his technique. He'd not be caught unprepared.

He'd not be *caught*, period.

He'd found another one to practice on now. She didn't fit the profile, but so much the better for throwing the police off course. Not that the authorities had a clue how he selected his victims. They had no idea that what tied his victims together was the book. The cops were too focused on the rosaries to figure things out. His chest puffed up.

No bullshit police-planted headline was going to alter his course.

No voice was going to tell him how to handle his business.

Twenty-four more days.

His breathing grew easy. Rising from the kitchen table, he placed the book under his arm and carried it to the bed, slipped it back under the pillow. Then he pulled open the nightstand drawer, where a pamphlet lay beside a black velvet bag. At the first touch of velvet against his fingertips, his pulse began to pound in his ears again. Turning his palm up, he stared at the blue veins snaking beneath his white skin. He could see the black blood whooshing inside them. His head went light, and he flexed his hand open and shut until his head cleared. He grabbed the pamphlet and unfolded it. Inside was a headshot of a young woman with sad green eyes and long, flaming hair. She wore clear gloss over tempting red lips.

Open to new patients. Accepting most insurance plans. Call for a free initial consultation. Faith Clancy, MD. Psychiatrist.

His breath hissed out through his teeth. He didn't need a shrink, and he considered it an insult that his doctor had given him the pamphlet and suggested he call one instead of testing his blood for toxins as he'd requested. He only kept the pamphlet because he liked imagining the reasons for the sadness in the woman's eyes and because he liked looking at her picture. Last night, he'd dreamt about her red mouth. He swallowed with difficulty and passed his hot palm over his hardening dick.

He might not need a shrink, but he did need more practice.

Practice makes perfect.

Just this once, he would indulge his urges and practice on someone who could give him pleasure. He dropped the brochure, then lifted the velvet bag and pulled its drawstring open, allowing the contents to fall into his hand.

Pop, pop, pop.

Electricity shot through his palm and up his arm as he curled his hand around the beads.

Good.

He had plenty of rosaries.

FIVE

CONTERSON S

pulled its drawstring open, allowing the contents to
. . . . . . into his hand.

". . . . . . ?"

Electricity shot through his palm and up his arm as
he . . . . . . his hand around the beach . . . .

. . . .

He had plenty of roubles.

Monday, July 22, 6:00 P.M.

As she steered her Toyota Corolla onto Calle De La
Cereza, Faith's shoulders lowered, and her hands loosened on the steering wheel. It'd been a tough couple
of days, what with having to turn Dante over to the
police, and she couldn't wait to soak in a hot bath and
sip a crisp Zinfandel. Her head felt heavy. Her arms felt
heavy. Her skin weighed her down like a suit of armor.
She smiled to herself at the thought. This was just how
she liked to end her day—dog-tired.

Somewhere around the time of Grace's death,
Faith had discovered that if during the day she worked
her muscles to the point of exhaustion, her troubles
wouldn't keep her awake at night, and ever since
making this blessed discovery, she'd stuck to a routine. Most mornings she rose at five for a six-mile run.

One night a week, she attended a Krav Maga class—this at her brother-in-law's insistence that she learn to defend herself. Other evenings, she hit the gym for a round of heavy weightlifting, then followed that up with a warrior-level spin class. Half measures were not enough to overcome her insomnia, and that suited her fine, because in her heart she'd always been an all-or-nothing kind of girl—just like Grace.

By the time Faith's head hit the pillow at night, no matter how much she longed to review and recycle her list of problems, her physical need for sleep was too great. She'd trained her body to outsmart her brain, and it'd been years since she'd needed the sleeping pills that had threatened to become an addiction after Grace died. There were other benefits to Faith's exacting regimen as well. She never felt lonely—or rather she did, but was simply too tired to care. She'd grown accustomed to her isolated ways, the comfortable if unexciting rhythm of her routine. Solitude had become an old and trusted friend, one to be welcomed with open arms rather than shoved away.

Admittedly, she still thought wistfully of her old life in Flagstaff. But two years ago, Danny had remarried, and she knew it was time to let go. He wasn't her brother-in-law anymore, not really, and the last thing he needed was his dead wife's baby sister intruding on his newly wedded bliss.

But Santa Fe was growing on her, and this in large part because of her lovely adobe bungalow on her lovely tree-lined street. Despite its name, Calle De La

Cereza was lined not with cherry trees but with radiant crabapple. The stunning pink flowers of spring had recently given way to clusters of bright red miniature apples the neighborhood children simply could not resist. Never mind that the flavor turned their happy little faces into sour pusses every time. With exhaustion rolling off her body in waves, she let up on the accelerator, scouring the landscape for said neighborhood children, who always seemed to be looming around every curve in the road.

Home at last, she pulled into her carport and killed the engine, stepped out of her car, and lifted her hand in customary greeting to the little boy hunkered down on the sidewalk a few yards away. The boy, however, didn't return her wave or her smile. A frisson of disappointment rippled through her. Little Tommy Bledsoe was part of her quiet routine. Every evening when she returned home, she waved and smiled to him, and he waved and smiled back. She and Tommy were friends. Not the kind of friends who hung out together, but the kind of friends who had an unspoken agreement they could count on each other for a cheery wave and an I've-got-your-back smile. At least that's how Faith viewed it.

Tommy and his mother, a hardworking woman who looked to be about thirty going on fifty, lived in the two-bedroom bungalow next door to Faith. She'd learned from her single visit to the Bledsoe home that the floor plan was identical to hers, only reversed. Both homes had identical adobe exteriors painted a brilliant terra-cotta red that screamed: *Welcome to New Mexico, Land of Enchantment.*

Viga tails extended beneath the flat roofs, and square windows were framed with heavy wood and shuttered in bright blue. High arches loomed over the front doors, making the tiny homes appear midsize. The only differences a casual observer might note between the two houses were the ten-speed bicycle leaning against the side of the Bledsoe residence and the small garden filled with cutting flowers in Faith's front yard.

Flowers were her weakness, and she loved to fill the house with the most fragrant kinds cut fresh from the yard. She had another overflowing garden in the fenced-in backyard and a water bill that would've gotten her booted out of the Sierra Club if her membership hadn't already been canceled for nonpayment.

Faith was just about to head inside for that bath when the image of her young friend's slumped posture and downcast eyes came back to her. She turned and headed over to say hello. Tommy was ten, possibly eleven, and he was *that* kid. Every neighborhood has one, a child who never seems to be included in the after-school games of Frisbee or street hockey and rarely gets invited to birthday parties. This particular block was filled with school-age kids, and the parents liked to put out Child-at-Play signs—yellow plastic figures sporting jaunty red caps and waving warning flags that said SLOW.

Tommy's mother had little to worry about since

Tommy usually hung on the sidelines, only wishing he could be in the street mixing it up with the other children. So finding him sitting alone on the sidewalk was nothing new. But today, Faith could sense something wasn't right. Although he was rarely called to join in the fun, he typically wore a hopeful, prepared expression that signaled he was ready to step in at any moment, just in case someone more popular got called inside for dinner or homework.

Today, however, Tommy's chin was tucked to his chest, his expression dejected. He hardly seemed to notice the lively game of tag taking place in the yard across the street. As she approached, he didn't bother to look up. And there was something else. Crouching beside Tommy, its nose nudging the boy's armpit, was a spotted dog that resembled a bag of bones covered in dusty fur.

Her body tensed as she assessed the situation, but quickly relaxed when she noted the dog's docile nuzzling of Tommy's axilla, neck, and face, not to mention the mewling noises more akin to a kitten's than an adult canine's. By now she was close enough to see tears dripping down Tommy's nose, hear his sniffles. The animal's nuzzling accelerated in an urgent attempt to comfort the boy.

"Hey-a." Faith tried her wave and cheery smile again, but Tommy still didn't look up.

The dog, however, gave her a doleful look and whimpered at her, perhaps looking to her to help buck up Tommy.

"Where'd ya find this fellow?" Faith knelt on the grass and scratched behind the dog's ears. More whimpering, then a vigorous tail wag.

"Chica's a *she*."

Faith gave Chica the once-over and soon decided Tommy was right. Despite the bony rib cage and lack of subcutaneous fat, the dog's belly bulged. Could be bloating secondary to the obvious malnutrition, but when Faith examined the dog's swollen belly, she could clearly feel the cause. Chica was pregnant. And starving. Probably also flea- and tick-infested. Poor Chica. Her hand swooped over the short polka-dotted fur and found denuded areas. "You're right. Chica is most definitely a she. Where'd ya find her?"

"She followed me home from school today. She wants to be my dog." Chica wagged her tail and licked a fat tear off Tommy's cheek.

"I can see that."

A screen door slammed. Faith turned her head and watched Tommy's mother scurry down the front steps and out to meet them. Mrs. Bledsoe slowed her pace once she saw it was only Faith chatting up Tommy and Chica.

"Still not here?" Tommy's mom stuck her hands on her hips and made a raspberry noise with her mouth.

"No, ma'am," Tommy whispered.

"I called animal control nearly an hour ago." Mrs. Bledsoe filled Faith in. "Guess I better call them again."

At that, Tommy jumped to his feet and threw his arms around his mother's waist, burying his face in her apron. "Please, Mom. Please don't let them take Chica away."

With a firm but gentle hand, Mrs. Bledsoe untangled her son from around her middle. "She's sick, Tommy. Lord knows what diseases she's carrying. For all we know, she could have rabies."

Chica wagged her tail, and this time her butt got in on the action.

"She doesn't have rabies, Mom. Anyone can see that. Rabid dogs don't make friends with you. They growl at you and foam at the mouth. Don't you remember Old Yeller?"

"Well, maybe she doesn't have rabies then. But she's got the mange for sure." Mrs. Bledsoe's voice dropped. "I'm sorry, Tommy. I know how much you want to keep her, but we can't afford a sick dog. I'm sure some nice family will adopt her."

Chica was scrawny, mangy, covered in nicks and cuts, *and* pregnant. Despite her winning personality, adoption didn't seem the most likely outcome after animal control transported her to the shelter. Faith did a quick mental calculation of what she had left in her bank account. With no money coming into the practice as of yet, she'd been living off the start-up loan the bank had given her. She had just enough funds remaining to pay office rent and live frugally for six months.

If she was careful.

If she didn't take on any unnecessary expenses.

No doubt she could scrape up the money for pet food and a doggie bed, but judging from Chica's debilitated yet expectant condition, the vet bill alone could run thousands of dollars, and that was definitely more than Faith could afford.

Biting her lower lip, she rose and looked down at Chica. Chica gazed up at her with a hopeful, please-choose-me face—the doggie version of the look Tommy usually wore—it was the kind of heart-melting expression that went to work faster than a hot match on a tick's rump.

If push came to shove, she supposed, she could always look for a second job. She'd moonlighted in the ER to pay bills during med school, and she knew hospitals always needed someone to work the graveyard shift. If her loan ran out before her practice took off, so be it. She could manage perfectly well.

Mrs. Bledsoe, on the other hand, was a single parent with too much on her plate already. She couldn't be expected to take on another hungry mouth to feed. Especially when that hungry mouth had puppies on the way.

Tommy'd gone back to crying in his hands. His whole body shook with muted sobs.

"I'll take Chica," Faith said, and immediately felt right and warm inside.

Mrs. Bledsoe's eyebrows shot up. Her jaw dropped ever so slightly. "Why on earth would you do a thing like that?"

Faith shrugged, then winked at Tommy. "I could use a good watchdog, and besides, sometimes I get lonely all on my own." That last bit sort of slipped out, and she realized there was more truth to it than she'd like to admit. "It'd honestly be swell having someone to come home to at night."

The expression on Mrs. Bledsoe's face went from disbelief to confusion, as though she couldn't quite figure Faith out. "But, I don't think *this* dog—"

Faith tapped her chin with her index finger and addressed Tommy. "Of course, I'd need someone to help me with Chica. Someone who could maybe walk her for me while I'm at work. Someone who could keep an eye on the puppies when they're born and help me find them good homes."

"Puppies!" Tommy yelped. "I knew there were puppies. I just knew it. I can walk Chica. I can help with the puppies." Tommy bounced on his toes, then flew around the yard in a circle, arms out, airplane style, before coming in for a landing back on the sidewalk and hugging Chica's neck.

"We'll have to get her healthy first, of course. Until the vet gives me the okay that she's safe and disease-free, I'll handle everything. But, if your mother says it's okay, Chica will still be your dog. You found her. You named her, and its only right you help make decisions about her toys and her diet. She'll live over at my house, but you can visit anytime you want. As long as it's okay with your mom. We can't forget your mom's the boss."

"I-I suppose that would be all right." Mrs. Bledsoe eyed her sideways but raised no objection, and even helped Faith load Chica into the backseat of her Toyota.

She'd have to hurry if she was going to make it to the vet before they closed for the night. "I'll let you know what the doctor says, Tommy."

As Faith pulled into the street, she smiled, knowing Tommy was back to sitting on the sidewalk watching the game of tag across the way, his hopeful, prepared expression in place. Out of her peripheral vision, she saw Mrs. Bledsoe put her hand on her son's shoulder, then lift the corner of her apron and swipe her cheek.

In the backseat, Chica started to pace. The weak kitten noises she'd been proffering changed first to low growls, then to full barks. "I didn't know you had it in you, girl. But don't worry, you'll see Tommy again soon."

Faith eased her foot on the brake until the car came to a gentle stop. A quick glance in the rearview mirror verified no cars were coming, so she turned fully around to check on her new friend. Chica's tail stood at attention. She pawed the side window, her claws clattering against the glass. Faith's body tensed as she looked past Chica toward her house. A man with black hair appeared in her kitchen window, then ducked out of sight. Her foot came off the brake, and the car lurched. Heart racing in her chest, she stomped the brake and reached for her phone.

SIX

Monday, July 22, 7:30 P.M.

Scourge bolted into his house and slammed the front
door behind him. Unable to catch his breath, he doubled over and waited for his chest to stop heaving, his
racing thoughts to slow. A full minute passed before he
could breathe and think normally again. He straightened, went back outside, and craned his neck, looking
in every direction to ensure no one was there. His ears
pricked, but he heard no sirens. He was sure Dr. Faith
Clancy had spotted him inside her kitchen—he'd certainly seen *her*, phone in hand, no doubt calling 911.
Then he'd raced out the back and scrambled over the
fence before the police could arrive.

He told himself to calm down. After all, he'd made
it home safely. His breath still hitching occasionally, he
retrieved the evening paper from the porch and went

back inside, shutting the door behind him again. This time he engaged the dead bolt and chain.

How could he have been so careless? He knew Dr. Clancy's schedule, and yet he'd timed his scouting expedition to her house poorly. True, she usually returned home a good forty-five minutes later, but he'd cut things far too close. Not everyone stuck to a routine as faithfully as he did.

Once more, accusing words replayed in his head.

It's not like you to get detoured by a pretty face. You should just throw that brochure away. Faith Clancy was never part of the plan, and you don't need more practice.

But he did! He wasn't ready for the Donovans. Not yet.

And he had twenty-three days left, so where was the harm?

Admit the real reason you chose her. You're letting your dick lead you around. You're no different than any other man.

In truth, his dick was hardening now, just thinking of the beautiful psychiatrist with the sad eyes. Well what of it? After the Donovans, he'd be headed for Mexico to live out Perry's dream of sun and sand and freedom. Before he retired, he deserved, *just once,* to kill for his own pleasure. He'd earned that right.

Perspiration beaded on Scourge's upper lip, tickling his skin in a most unpleasant way. He pulled out his linen handkerchief and dabbed his upper lip dry. Holding the scrap of linen by the corner, he hurried to deposit it in the dirty-clothes hamper, then thoroughly washed his hands. After returning to the living room, he seated himself in a hard-back chair and unfolded the evening paper. He read the headline, and a fine tremor started up in his hands, intensifying until his entire body shook—so hard the chair seemed to vibrate beneath his thighs. He tried to swallow, but his throat was too dry. A strangled cry escaped his lips.

SANTA FE SAINT IN CUSTODY. LOCAL MAN CONFESSES.

Tuesday, July 23, 7:00 A.M.

Scourge woke up with damp hair clinging to the back of his neck and cold sweat dripping down his forehead. One of his arms was flung off the side of the bed. The other was smashed between his stomach and the mattress. From above, a lightbulb buzzed loud enough to make his teeth vibrate. But that wasn't the worst of the noise.

Click.

Clack.

Click.

His mind still clouded with sleep, he didn't immediately recognize the source of the metallic noise coming from above his head. His heart hesitated, then began to race. *Make it stop.*

Click.

Clack.

Click.

The beats jolted down his spine one vertebra at a

time, and his body jerked like a man in the electric chair.

Please make it stop.

His hand crept up, fished beneath his pillow, and caressed the book. *Still there.* The book hadn't abandoned him like his friends had. He banished all thoughts of abandonment from his mind, and his heartbeat slowed. He flipped onto his back, forced his eyes open.

Click.

Clack.

Click.

Fucking ceiling fan. For as long as he'd lived in these rooms, the fan above his bed had been making that noise—why, he didn't know. Maybe the blades were loose. Maybe the fan wasn't seated properly in its mounting. He'd requested the fan be fixed, of course. In writing. Many times. He believed in going through proper channels, in following protocol. He'd never been the type to make undue trouble. And whenever he sent a note, his landlord responded promptly, promising to take care of the matter right away. But no one ever came to fix the fan.

This had been going on so long, Scourge was beginning to worry his landlord had nefarious motives. Last night, Scourge had been lying peacefully in his bed, about to doze off, when he suddenly envisioned the fan crashing down from the ceiling. Next he imagined a blade flying off, decapitating him, and a geyser of blood spraying his perfect white sheets. His throat had closed so tightly, he couldn't swallow his saliva.

Drool had slipped from the corner of his mouth, like it was doing now. He wiped away the spittle.

It was time to write another note. Either fix the fan or find a new tenant.

An empty threat.

This place was set up perfectly for him. The apartment was well located, just around the corner from the lab where he worked, so he didn't have to take the bus. He truly did not like public transportation. Too many people, too many smells, not to mention the surfaces he'd have to touch—handrails and doors, teeming with bacteria.

Also within walking distance—Scourge's favorite diner, The Blue Moon Café. At The Blue Moon, everyone knew him by name. He was a big tipper, and Suzie had eventually learned just how he liked his place set: nice and neat, the silverware perfectly parallel. Suzie never took offense when he removed his antibacterial wipes and used them to clean the forks and knives. Sometimes she took one of the wipes and helped him. That was Suzie for you. Always ready with a friendly smile and clean silverware.

Of course, he had a truck, but that was only for Special Duty. He kept it parked inside a storage locker, registered to Bernadette Smith. He thought that was a nice homage to Sister. Anyway, he couldn't afford to be seen driving around town in that truck.

That was the kind of mistake that led to death row.

He wasn't a student of the craft for nothing. If Ted Bundy hadn't driven around every day in the same

Volkswagen Beetle he used for Special Duty, he might never have been caught and executed. If Israel Keyes, who'd been almost as meticulous in his long-term planning as Scourge, hadn't parked his rental car in front of an ATM camera, he'd be alive today. So no, he wasn't driving his truck on routine errands, and he wasn't discarding his cozy apartment, which was within walking distance of all his regular haunts, just because of a malfunctioning ceiling fan.

Click.

Clack.

Click.

Then again, until today, that sound had never made his hands shake. A drop of perspiration dripped from his forehead down the tip of his nose. He sniffed and turned his face to the side, toward the pungent odor seeping up from the sheets. The ammonia-like smell gagged him, and he struggled to move air in and out of his lungs, breathing through his open mouth like a landed fish. As he writhed, the sheets stuck to his skin.

That's when he knew. The tacky moisture against his buttocks, his thighs, wasn't sweat at all.

It was urine.

He hadn't wet the bed since Sister died.

A tear slid down his cheek, then he started to sob.

I'm sorry. It was an accident.

Lazy. You lazy dirty boy. God doesn't want us to lie in our own urine. Maybe you defecated, too.

No! No. I didn't defecate. And I'm not lazy. I was asleep. I can't help what happens when I'm asleep.

He could feel the explosion of pain from Sister's flashlight slamming down on his back, then across his bare bottom.

Lazy. Thwack. *Dirty.* Thwack. *Boy.* Thwack. *Sinner.* Thwack. *Scourge!* And then that echoing laugh. *That's what you are, a scourge among us, and from now on that's what you'll be called. Scourge.* Thwack. Thwack. Thwack.

Click.

Clack.

Click.

He was on his knees beside the bed, desperately ripping off the sheets, trying to hide the evidence of his sin—from his own eyes. But it was no use. The filthy urine stained his sheets like his shame stained his soul. Sister Bernadette was right to punish him. He longed to be punished.

He buried his face in the sheets and made himself inhale his sin, the way Sister would have him do if she were here. On trembling limbs, he rose and stumbled into the alcove that housed his stacked washer-dryer unit. He stuffed the sheets into the wash, poured bleach into the dispenser until it overflowed into the bin, then added laundry detergent and fabric softener. He slammed the lid and dialed in *bulky load, extraheavy soil, extra rinse.* The machine shimmied to life, and his chest loosened, his shoulders lowered. He headed for the bathroom. He could fix this. All he had to do was get clean.

He could make this right.

He stripped. Turned the shower dial all the way to

the left, and stood just shy of the jet, replacing the sheen of urine with sweat. His lungs opened fully. He could breathe normally at last. He dialed the water temperature back just enough that he could force himself to stand in the stream of scalding water. He'd forgotten the scrubber. The new one with the wooden handle he'd bought for cleaning the floors. He retrieved it from beneath the sink and jumped back in the shower.

A moment later, he'd soaped up the bristles and begun scraping the brush between his thighs. He was a dirty, filthy boy. But he could make himself clean. He stayed in the shower a long time. Eventually, the hot water ran out, but he didn't care. He stood in the spray and scrubbed until his skin was raw and bleeding. The cold water soothed his burning skin. Then he slapped his forehead with the back of his hand. The blood pooling in the drain had reminded him of work. He was going to be late.

"Have you ever had your blood drawn before?" Scourge asked.

According to Mrs. Wilhelmina Stovall's face sheet, she was seventy-three years old. The caustic look she gave him served as her answer and indicated to him she was an impatient woman who didn't understand he was only doing his job. First of all, it was entirely possible that somewhere there was indeed a seventy-three-year-old woman who had never had her blood drawn. Second of all, phlebotomy was important business, and he took his job seriously and always followed protocol.

Really, he took everything seriously.

Many people were afraid of needles and blood. According to the phlebotomist manual, he was supposed to ask every patient the same question. A good phlebotomist informed and reassured his patient. The question was standard. He never skipped it. Not even for seventy-three-year-olds.

Managing to maintain a professional manner despite the nervous knot that had been forming in his gut since he'd woken up today, he said, "Make a fist please."

"Oww!" she hollered, as he tightened the blue rubber tourniquet above her elbow, a fine mist of her saliva spraying him in the face. "You're not doing it right."

"Sorry." Again, best to be professional, but he cringed at the thought of the germs now saturating the air he breathed. When he thumped the veins in Wilhelmina's antecubital area, she squirmed, making his job more difficult. Her veins ran beneath her skin like thick ropes, rolling away from his touch, and he knew she was the sort who would complain if he didn't hit pay dirt on the first try. So he took his time, which should have made her grateful, but had the opposite effect instead. By now, she was practically snarling at him.

Perhaps a little small talk would help her relax, put her in a more friendly frame of mind. "Is Wilhelmina a family name?"

"Keep your flirtatious remarks to yourself, young

man. I'm here to get my blood drawn, not start a relationship."

His face flushed. She was making fun of him. "I was only trying to be polite."

"I don't mind a little conversation, in fact I enjoy it, but let's stick to the news or weather. I don't like personal questions."

Leaning forward, he thrust his tongue out between his lips, carefully studying her veins, somehow keeping his composure in the face of her imperious attitude. Finally, he thought he'd found a less roly-poly target. He lifted the venipuncture needle, already encased in its hub, with the purple-top tube in go position. He looked up and smiled at her, signaling the impending poke.

"D'ya hear they arrested that monster—the Saint?" Her tone let him know she found the whole story titillating. *This* was the type of conversation she enjoyed.

He blinked hard, imagining her lips moving in reverse, and her words being sucked back inside her mouth. If no one said them aloud, maybe they weren't true. Maybe the police hadn't arrested anyone at all. Returning his focus to her veins, he said nothing.

"I'm telling you they caught the Saint," she repeated just as he pushed the long flat needle into a vein.

His hands started to shake. "No. They didn't."

"Oh, but they did."

His fingers fumbled. Sweat stung his eyes. His vision blurred, and he couldn't pop the needle into the vacutainer.

"Turns out it's that illegitimate Jericho brother—Dante, and he *confessed*. Do you believe it?"

"No!" His hand seized, plunging the needle deeper. He jerked his arm back, and the needle ripped her skin before flying across the room. The empty purple-top vacutainer rolled onto the floor between his feet.

"You miserable little fool! Look what you did!"

Big fat drops of watery purple blood oozed down her forearm and dripped onto his gloved hands. Dripped onto his trousers—soiling them over the fly. "I'm sorry. It was an accident," he whispered hoarsely.

"You stupid, stupid boy."

Lazy, dirty boy. You're a scourge.

Expecting her fists to rain down on him, he protected his head.

Her mouth dropped open, and her eyes went so wide he could see white all the way around her irises.

"I can clean up my mess." He grabbed some gauze and swiped at the blood on her arm, but she knocked his hand away.

"I'm going to have to report you."

Dirty boy! Wait until I tell the other Sisters what you did.

"No, please don't tell anyone . . . I'll lose my job." His voice sounded weak, plaintive. He was good with the needle. He knew exactly where and how hard to poke it in. It was all her fault for not holding still. He got his needle in the vein, but she wouldn't be still, she wouldn't shut up. She'd unmanned him with her nasty remarks. His eyes flicked to his pants, wet with blood and ruined. He crossed his hands over the wet spot. "I'll clean up my mess. I promise, Sister."

"Are you a retard?"

He looked up through his tears, expecting to see Sister Bernadette, bounding to her feet, shaking her fist at him. But it wasn't her.

Bernadette was dead—he'd killed her years ago.

For the second time that morning, he fell to his knees, and the oddest thing happened. As he wiped the blood drops off the floor, they burned right through his glove. Right through his skin, sizzling like spilled acid. He saw blisters rising on his arms, the blood boiling inside his veins. If he didn't get the blood off him, his whole body would catch fire. "No! No! No!" Tearing off the bloody gloves, he crawled across the floor, as far and as fast as he could go.

Wilhelmina screamed for help.

He covered his ears.

Curled into a tight ball.

Began to cry.

SEVEN

Tuesday, July 23, 9:00 A.M.

Faith winced at the clock in the police interrogation room. Nine in the morning. She'd been here since seven, and the detective who'd insisted she arrive promptly had just now swaggered into the room. Last night, despite her weariness, she'd tossed and turned for the better part of the night, unable to forget about either Dante's confession or the black-haired man in her kitchen. New locks and the authorities' assurance that the man would not likely return had been some comfort, but not enough to result in a restful night. And now, thanks to the tardy detective, she hadn't gotten her morning run in, which meant she wouldn't be sleeping tonight either. It was far too easy for her to regress to her old insomniac ways. Ways that harkened back to the time of her parents' accident.

Closing her eyes, she pictured Grace, sitting at the foot of her bed offering a cup of warm milk, after Ma and Da died. *Do you want me to sing you a lullaby?* Grace had asked. But Faith had declared she only wanted Ma to sing to her and turned her sister away.

She swallowed past the lump in her throat and set down her water bottle, glaring around the stark room. Detective Howard Johnson referred to this oversized closet as an interview room, but she knew it was the same place the police interrogated murderers and thieves. Wire cages that covered not only the windows but the ceiling tiles as well were strategically placed to prevent suspects from escaping through the vents. The whole ambience was designed to wrest control from the interviewee and give the interviewer a decided psychological advantage. Which was all well and good for prisoners and suspects, but she was neither. She was a trained professional, and she was cooperating fully. Narrowing her eyes at the big two-way mirror on the far wall, she barely managed to resist the urge to shoot the bird at whoever was behind it.

Sleep deprivation made her cranky.

"Nobody there. They're all across the hall watching us on computer screens. These two-way mirrors are practically obsolete, but it's not worth tearing them down." Detective Johnson balanced his beefy body, made even bulkier by the Kevlar vest buttoned under his shirt, atop a flimsy laminate table, and swung his feet off her side. Rather than sitting across from her in the opposite chair, he loomed over her, invading her personal space. A controlling and completely unnecessary move.

When one giant, swinging shoe narrowly missed her kneecap, she flinched. "Is there some particular reason you're treating me like a hostile witness, Detective?"

"You've got the wrong idea there, little lady." He winked at her and followed that up with a loud belch, making her wonder if he'd just had a long leisurely steak-and-egg breakfast while she sat waiting obediently in an interrogation room that stank of body odor and sour milk.

Her teeth clenched, and she deliberately relaxed her jaw, smiled sweetly. "Do I really have it all wrong, *Howie*?"

His face flushed. "I'm just trying to get to the bottom of this very serious matter. You wanna Coke or something?" He snapped his fingers and addressed the camera. "Somebody bring Dr. Clancy a Coke. She thinks we don't treat her right."

"No, thanks."

"Coffee? I can't really recommend the brew here, but we'll scare some up if you like."

"No, thanks. You said you wanted to talk to me about Dante Jericho?"

"If you're sure, then." He trailed a hand through his close-cropped wheat blond hair. "Heard you had a possible break-in at your home last night."

"Not a *possible* break-in. I saw a man in my kitchen."

"But there was no sign of forced entry. Nothing missing."

"Not that I can tell so far, no. But I saw a man in my kitchen window. It wasn't my imagination."

He gave her the once-over. "If he wasn't after money, maybe he was after you. If I were a pretty lady living all alone, I'd keep my doors locked."

"The doors were locked. But thanks for the tip." The sarcasm in her tone matched the condescension in his. Bring it on. She'd rather be mad than scared any day, and the macho detective was providing a nice, fat, diversionary target.

"You look beat, Doc. You sleeping okay?"

"No," she snapped. "Look, Detective, I came down here voluntarily, and I'm prepared to give you all the help I can. But I don't know what you want from me. I've already told you everything I know."

"Doctors got a funny way of thinking their responsibility is to their patients. But a cop's responsibility is to the public. See, *my* job is to look out for Jericho's victims."

"Allegedly, Jericho's victims."

"He confessed. But okay, *allegedly*. And you just proved my point with that remark . . . *little lady*." Johnson leaned as close as he could get without touching her.

She could smell that coffee he couldn't recommend on his breath.

"So maybe you can understand how I might want

to be sure I'm getting the whole story from you. That you're not holding anything back."

Her hands twisted in her lap. Johnson's argument wasn't without merit. She had a duty to warn the public about a potentially dangerous criminal, both legally and ethically, and she'd fulfilled that duty. But Dante Jericho was technically still her patient. She had real moral and legal obligations toward him, too, and she felt the weight of those rather heavily at the moment. What the Saint had done to his victims froze her bones and cracked her heart into little pieces, but what if Dante Jericho wasn't the Saint?

Dante's grasp on reality ebbed and flowed with the phases of the moon. Surely, the police should confirm the facts, gather some evidence, before accepting his confession and closing the case.

"We've subpoenaed your records on Dante Jericho," Johnson said.

"And they've been provided to you." Faith used an EHR, an electronic health-record-keeping system, and that meant no waiting for transcriptions or photocopies like the old days. The police had been given full access to everything in her files the same hour she received the subpoena.

"They weren't much use." Johnson shrugged and slid a consent for release of information, signed by Dante, into her line of vision. The release wasn't necessary. Unlike the communication between a lawyer and a client, doctor-patient confidentiality didn't extend to criminal matters. Plus there was the subpoena. The fact that Johnson obtained a consent that was entirely superfluous confirmed her belief he didn't trust her. He was trying to preempt any possible protest on her part.

She tried again to set him straight on her intentions. "Detective, I'm not going to pretend I enjoy being interrogated."

"Interviewed."

"Whatever. But I won't withhold information. I want the truth to come out as badly as you. So maybe we can just get down to it."

"Got places to go?"

Her only patient was in jail. She hadn't a single friend in town, and Johnson likely knew both of those facts.

"I've got an important conference later today, and I need time to prepare for it." Not a complete lie. She *hoped* she had an important conference. On Saturday, she'd e-mailed Dr. Caitlin Cassidy, requesting a consultation.

Dr. Cassidy was the foremost expert in the country on false confessions, and she had recently been involved in the release of a man on death row—a man who'd been clearly exonerated by DNA evidence after new witnesses came forward. It was absolutely possible Dr. Cassidy would respond to her today.

"An important conference." He made a harrumphing sound. "Well then, down we'll get." Johnson slapped a photograph of a young woman in front of her.

Faith immediately recognized Nancy Aberdeen.

In this photograph, which had been plastered all over the news, Nancy posed with a cherry pie, a big blue ribbon, and a hometown-sweetheart smile. Nancy wore a gingham dress and had her hair pulled back in a neat ponytail. Her skin shimmered with a rich, inviting sheen, like a bowl of cream waiting for a cat. Her wide eyes sparkled with happiness, perhaps because of that big blue ribbon she'd won, or perhaps because happiness was simply in her nature. Nancy Aberdeen was both a breath of fresh air and a blast from the past. The perfect picture of more innocent times. An unexpected teenager. Why had the Saint chosen this particular girl?

"That picture was taken at the state fair." Johnson's face contorted, covering whatever emotion the photograph called up in him. Not good for his tough-cop image to show he cared.

"And this." He slapped a second photo down beside the first. "This is Nancy Aberdeen after the Saint got done with her."

All Faith had in her stomach was water, and she had to fight to keep that down. Tears welled behind her eyes, and she blinked those back, too. She forced herself to keep her gaze on the picture. The girl had been hog-tied, her skull blown apart by a shotgun blast. What was left of her face was shrouded in blood, unrecognizable. In her hand, she clasped a rosary. "You're a real jerk, Howie, you know that, right?"

"I could give a rat's asshole if I am."

"What the hell do you want from me?" She refused to allow her voice to quiver.

"I wanna know every single goddamn thing you know about Dante Jericho, the bastard who killed this sweet sixteen-year-old girl." She could practically hear his teeth grinding.

"I'm afraid you're going to have to narrow that down a bit. *Tell me everything you know* covers a lot of ground. What's your question?"

"You call this cooperating?"

"You call this an interview?" She leapt to her feet.

Raising one hand, Johnson's expression turned coaxing. "Sit down . . . please."

He pulled out her chair, politely.

She sat back down—her legs were shaking anyway.

"I wanted you to see his evil with your own eyes. I apologize for not preparing you first. I may have been out of line."

Swallowing hard, she met his eyes. "Apology accepted."

His shoulders relaxed, and a bit of the fight seemed to go out of him, as if he'd finally realized she might not be the enemy after all—or maybe that was her remembering he was one of the good guys.

"Did Jericho ever mention the name Nancy Aberdeen or the names of any of the other victims to you before last Saturday?" he asked.

She shook her head.

"For the record, please."

"No, he never mentioned the names of any of the Saint's victims." Turning toward the camera, she enunciated clearly. "Not that I recall. But I've only been treating him a couple of weeks."

"Is there anything you might've omitted from your notes that could help us?"

"Anything that seemed important to me at the time, I put in the notes. Of course, I wasn't looking for clues to catch a serial killer."

"But looking back, is there anything at all that would've suggested Jericho might be the Saint."

"He never said anything to me that would specifically connect him to these crimes."

"Other than his confession."

Ah. The condescending Johnson she knew and loved.

"Right."

"If you think of something, you'll let me know." He handed her his card. Twisting his mouth like he was spitting out a bite of sour apple, he said, "Sorry if I shocked you with the photo."

She nodded. A not-so-random thought came to her mind. "Detective, I've been wondering. Were any of the victims sexually assaulted?"

His brows shot up in surprise. "I can't disclose that information."

"They weren't. I can see by the look on your face. Seems unusual. So many serial murders are sexually motivated. And based on what I've read in the papers, I don't see a common thread among the victims. Finding that thread and pulling it would be the key to unraveling the mystery—wouldn't it?"

He opened the door to the interrogation room, seeming suddenly anxious to see her out. "Make you a deal, Doc. You stick to head shrinking, and I'll stick to crime solving."

Before leaving the police station, Faith ducked into a bathroom to splash cold water on her face, then hightailed it out of the building, racing down the front steps two at a time, occasionally reaching for the handrail to keep from falling. Her car was parked in a lot to the left. She turned right. She needed fresh air. Needed to walk it off. Being forced to look at a picture of Nancy Aberdeen's mangled corpse had scalded her skin like acid injected beneath the epidermis. Only someone who'd lost all connection to his fellow man could've committed such a crime.

Outside, the sun shone as brightly as before, going about its business oblivious to the evil in the world. She halted and closed her eyes, wishing she could be that strong. The street was quiet at this hour. With most people manning their desks on a weekday morning, there was very little foot traffic, giving her room both to open up her stride and to stop and breathe whenever she liked. As the clean air filled her lungs, she felt the toxins washing out of her system.

She scoured the area, searching for a good thing—any good thing. A waft of sweetness drifted by when a flower vendor carrying armfuls of Castilian roses passed. Faith spotted a street performer and crossed the street to listen to him wail on a tenor saxophone. Three tunes later, she tossed a twenty into his instrument case.

"God bless you, ma'am."

"God bless you, sir." She smiled, then turned around, headed back to her car. With every step, her shoulders felt lighter. A pang of hunger reminded her that she hadn't had breakfast, and she quickened her pace, imagining a nice plate of waffles at Denny's.

Pulling up short to avoid a toddler barreling down the street in front of his mother, her hand came up to shade her eyes against the sun's blinding light. When the child's laughter faded away, she took off again, but this time, she heard footfalls padding close behind her.

She slowed.

The padding slowed.

She sped up.

The footfalls sped up.

As the fine hairs on the back of her neck made their presence known, her mind began to race. What had she learned in class?

Do not wait to be attacked.

That's what her Krav Maga instructor always said.

Trust your gut. Don't be the gazelle. Be the lion.

She stopped, crouched, readied herself to spin and face her stalker with raised fists.

Get back! she'd yell. *She'd be the lion, not the gazelle.*

Her hands came up as she pivoted and found her-

self facing a wall of well-dressed, muscled chest.
Brute strength and a starched collar. Wild possibilities
flashed across her mind, but none made sense. A mob
enforcer? Secret Service? In the nanosecond that passed
before she could jerk her chin up and look him in the
face, the man deflected her fists and spun her around.
When he grabbed her by the waist, her breath rushed
out. She dug her nails into his arms and stomped on his
instep, but he lifted her off the pavement, leaving her
feet kicking helplessly in the air.

Help!

She screamed. But as in a dream, no sound came
out of her mouth. Her heart roared in her chest like the
lion she wanted to be, but her vocal cords had frozen.
The man took several giant strides forward. With
blood rushing to her head and storefronts passing by,
her stomach lilted in protest. The sun, reflecting off a
long, black car, hit her in the eyes, all but blinding her.
The man opened the car door. Dumped her inside.

"Help!" At last her voice returned.

Snap.

She heard the sound of doors locking.

EIGHT

It'd been a crime of opportunity . . . and a monumentally bad idea. Luke had never anticipated bumping into Dr. Faith Clancy on his way to meet Detective Johnson at the police station. If he had, maybe he would've run through the scenario in his head a few times and thought of a different way to handle matters—a way that didn't have the potential to land him behind bars. But he hadn't anticipated, he hadn't planned, and when he saw the woman who'd turned his brother in to the police, sauntering down the street, smiling at the flower girl, and chatting up the sax guy, enjoying life without a care in the world, his core temperature had started to rise.

Injustice was a repeating theme in Dante's life, and Luke had had enough of standing by and doing nothing while his brother suffered. So he'd followed her, and when she turned, fists up, ready to pummel him, he'd lost it. No other way to describe how reason had fled and animal instinct had taken over. His skin had grown clammy. His pulse had bounded in his neck, and his body had charged off on its own ill-considered mission without a care as to consequence.

He never decided to scoop her up and carry her to his limo; he'd simply acted on impulse. He'd grabbed her in broad daylight on a public thoroughfare, and now here she was bucking in his arms in the backseat of his limo, screaming at the top of her lungs like . . . like a woman who'd been abducted off the street.

Nice going, Luke.

He should find a way to calm her down—fast. His arms released her. Maybe an apology to start. "I—"

She drew back. A hard slap across his jaw shut that idea down, and he didn't have a Plan B, but at least she'd stopped screaming. Apparently, she couldn't slap and scream for help at the same time. Or maybe she'd finally gotten a good look at him and realized he wasn't the bogeyman. He thought he'd seen a flash of recognition in her eyes just before she'd slapped him, and her terror seemed to have been replaced by fury.

Her hand came up for another whack. His blood still simmering, he clasped her by the wrists, yanked her against his chest. The tremor in her arms sent vibrations through his own, and her heart beat wildly against his. He took a gulping breath. Her skin smelled like flowers. Her breasts rubbed against him as she struggled. Arousal, as unreasoned as the act of swooping her up in the first place, shot through him. He looked down at her, and her breath caught. Her eyes widened. He knew she could feel his erection growing against her belly.

"Oh, man." He dropped her hands like he'd been zapped with a cattle prod. Maybe he should start by calming *himself* down before calming her.

Breathe. Try not to throttle her, and whatever the hell else you do, do not kiss her.

"Let me out of this car immediately."

"It's not a car, it's a limo. And no one's stopping you." Could he be charged with kidnapping if the vehicle never moved? After all, they were parked on a public street, a mere stone's throw from the police station.

She reared back, as if preparing to head-butt him, then seemed to change her mind. Holding up her wrists to display the red marks his grip had left, she said, "The doors are locked."

"My bad. That's an automatic safety feature. Autolocks when a passenger gets in the back. Cuts down on carjacking, kidnapping . . ." His voice trailed off lamely. His hand went to his heart of its own accord. "I'm honest-to-God sorry if I scared you."

Her eyes flashed. "You're always honest-to-God sorry for scaring me, and I honest-to-God don't give a damn about your apologies."

Seemed she remembered the first time they'd met all too well.

So did he.

"Fair enough. But I just want to talk you. I have no intention of holding you against your will." He turned his palms up. Maybe a silent *sorry* would get around her defenses. He pressed a button and the privacy glass whirred down. "Unlock, please."

The privacy window whirred back up, and the locks snapped open.

Faith grabbed her door handle, and he shook his head. "Just hold on one second. You don't need to go jumping out into traffic. I'll get out first, then you can slide out this side. The sidewalk's safer."

"The sidewalk *used* to be safer." Her voice seethed, but she let go of her door handle, the tremor in her hands dissipating with each passing moment.

"Or, if you like, I'll have my driver take you wherever you're headed. I won't be going along for the ride, so you don't have to worry. I've got an appointment with a police detective."

There was a moment of cold silence. She continued to eye him warily. "I'm free to go?"

"You always were."

"Except when I wasn't."

"I explained about the locks." But she had a valid point. "I never should have grabbed you like that. But I've seen my brother hurt so many times, and you're his psychiatrist. You're supposed to help him, not call the cops on him. Surely you can see how I could get wound up enough to forget my manners."

"Forget your manners?" she intoned through gritted teeth. "Technically speaking, you assaulted me, maybe even kidnapped me. I could press charges against you if I wanted."

"Technically speaking, I scooped you up off the sidewalk about a half second before you put that fancy toe of yours in doggie doo. Then I placed you in a luxury vehicle and offered to have my chauffeur drive you home. And don't forget, you had your fists up in a very threatening manner. I feared for my safety. I honest-to-God did." If he laughed at himself, maybe she'd laugh with him.

The corners of her mouth curved ever so slightly. He caught the briefest flash of pretty white teeth. "You feared for your safety?"

"You looked positively ferocious." If she hadn't forgiven him yet, it was only a matter of time. He was on a roll. "It would've been a shame to ruin those great shoes."

Her foot wagged, her heel slipping in and out of her stiletto. He could swear those were the same shoes she'd been wearing at the gallery, and he was up for saying anything to distract her from his bad behavior. This might be as good a topic as any. "Those your only pair of stilettos?"

"Yes, if you must know." Her tone was granite, and her shoulders were steel.

Maybe he'd overestimated his charm, or maybe he'd inadvertently insulted her. He chose to believe the latter. Most of the women he knew had closets full of Jimmy Choos, Ferragamos, and Louboutins. He knew because he was usually the one who paid the bill. Women he dated never wore the same pair twice. "These are lovely." He pointed at her foot.

It jittered faster. "You can't possibly be interested in my shoes." By now, the pink had returned to her cheeks, and she seemed to have successfully gathered her composure—or maybe that was just what she wanted him to think.

"What can I say? I noticed your shoes because I like your legs. I mean generally speaking, I'm a leg man." How much worse could this conversation get? He wasn't distracting her. He was pissing her off. He hadn't been this off-balance with a woman since high school. "Look, I'm not asking for a medal here although I did save your one pair of fancy shoes, but maybe you could cut me enough slack to hear me out."

"Mr. Jericho, I can assure you that these Rambo tactics . . ."

Rambo. Not a compliment. He retrieved white wine from the limo's bar, poured a glass, and pressed it into her hands. So what if it was before noon?

Her jaw dropped, and she stared at the goblet. As she sat beside him in the limo, back ramrod straight, eyes gleaming with both a hard determination that made him believe in her will and an underlying vulnerability that softened his heart, it struck him: Faith Clancy could be a powerful ally.

Besides, his brother trusted her, and that meant

Luke needed her help. "I've got red if you'd rather." He was back in Luke-mode. If anyone knew how to win a woman over, it was him.

She slid farther away from him. "Mr. Jericho, I can assure you that you needn't resort to either force or seduction to have a conversation with me. If you want to talk to me about your brother, all you have to do is call my office. I've got Dante's signed consent to speak with you on file."

"And I can assure you I don't need to resort to seduction. I don't seduce women. Women seduce me." He sat back, enjoying the way his words made the color deepen in her cheeks. "I only gave you wine to settle your nerves."

"I'm not nervous." She steadied the hand that held her wine and took a slug. "And I happen to agree with you."

"Great," he said before he'd fully processed her remark. Then, "You agree that women seduce me, not the other way around?"

She tossed back another sip of wine. "I agree with you that it's my job to help your brother. *First do no harm* is the doctor's credo after all."

"And yet you turned him in to the police."

"He confessed to horrible crimes."

"He's fragile. He can't always distinguish what's real from what's not. You must know his confession can't be taken at face value."

"I get what you're saying. I truly do. But I can't

afford to risk someone else's life on my working diagnosis. I'll do what I can—"

Suddenly, a loud *pop* sounded, followed by the crackling of breaking glass.

He saw Faith flinch as her window's safety glass fractured but didn't dump into the backseat. A lurch of the limo jolted them both, spilling Faith's wine and knocking her head against the window.

Goddamnit.

Reaching across her, Luke locked Faith's seat belt in place. His breath was coming in short angry bursts. He lowered the privacy window, and growled, "Drive like hell."

Faith's eyelids fluttered open and the room—scratch that—the interior of the limo came back into focus. Through the fog in her head, she heard the driver's voice. "Sorry, Mr. Jericho, I had my eye on a pretty girl across the street when I saw a man dart into the road with a rock in his hand. I didn't have time to pull away before—"

"You sure it was just a rock?" Luke asked.

Faith noticed Luke's arm around her shoulders, supporting her, and shoved it away, then straightened out of her slump.

"Yes, sir. I'm sure of it. May I slow down, sir?"

Luke pressed his face in front of hers. "Let's get Dr. Clancy to the nearest hospital."

In his eyes, she saw genuine regret, and her body relaxed. She proffered a weak smile. "No. Just take me home, please. I'm perfectly fine, and I don't want to spend my day in an emergency room."

A deep wrinkle formed between Luke's brows.

"Please. I'd like to go home."

He gave a reluctant nod, and she gave the driver her address.

"By the time the limousine pulled into Faith's driveway, the lump on her head had started to throb in earnest. The driver came around, opened the door for her, and she climbed out, still clasping the small blue ice pack Luke had given her against her skull. Turned out the limo contained not only a well-stocked mini-fridge, but a well-stocked first-aid kit, too.

"Thanks for the lift . . . I think." She gave Luke an *adios-amigo* smile, but as she'd anticipated, he was already shoving out of the limo and waving off his driver. "No. Really, I'm perfectly fine. There's no need to trouble yourself any further on my account," she added hastily.

He took a step toward her, and the look on his face made her take a step back lest he scoop her off her feet for the second time that day.

"I'd like to see you inside, make sure you're okay if you don't mind."

"Not necessary." Her vision grayed, and she bent her knees slightly to steady herself.

"But it's not offensive? Just for my own peace of mind. You look like you might faint."

"Fine." She kept her tone matter-of-fact. Her head might be light and her legs soupy, but she had no intention of fainting. Still, it wouldn't hurt to let him walk her inside. Yesterday, she'd nearly interrupted a thief in her house.

A thief who took nothing.

Because he'd seen her spot him and hightailed it out of there before the police arrived.

She had little of value, certainly not anything that would entice a criminal to risk a return visit. But slice it any way you like—Luke's presence made her feel safe.

Which was the last thing she should feel around a man like him.

Her breath released, and she tossed the ice pack back to Luke's driver, who caught it with ease. "Don't go anywhere. Mr. Jericho'll be right back." Luke placed his hand on her elbow, but she shook him off. "I can walk."

But her next step was unsteady, and her knees threatened to buckle.

"Either I help you inside, or I carry you inside. You make the call, because you're not whacking your head again on my watch."

She gave him the eye roll, but let him steer her slowly up the steps and into her home, where she promptly sank backward onto the couch, splaying her limbs like one of those chalk outlines on *CSI*.

"I still think we should get you checked out at the hospital. You might have a concussion."

"Nothing to do for a concussion but watch and wait.

What's known in the biz as COMI, catlike observation and masterful inactivity."

"Then I'll observe you." He looked at his watch and frowned. "Damn it to hell. I missed my appointment with Detective Johnson."

"Just go."

"It's too late anyway. He mentioned he had to leave by noon. I'll have to reschedule."

Luke continued to fuss with her between making phone calls, during which he presumably rearranged his day's appointments and rebooked with Johnson. She closed her eyes, reviewing the day in her head. First, she'd sat in that hot, smelly interrogation room over two hours, then she'd been forced to view that awful picture of poor Nancy Aberdeen. Next, she'd been dumped in a limo against her will and banged her forehead on the window when said limo blasted off to escape what might've been bullets but turned out to be a hurled rock instead. Now she had a goose egg the size of a Chihuahua forming on her parietal bone, and an impossible-to-ignore man in her living room. A man who would not stop bossing her around: *Put this pillow under your head like so. Prop your feet up here. Don't take that bag of frozen peas off your noggin for another fifteen minutes.*

All in all, it'd been a truly terrible day.

Oddest thing though—she drifted right off to sleep—with more ease than she had in a long, long time.

By the time she opened her eyes again, sunset coated the living room in soft pink light. The lace cloth on her dining-room table looked like a ballerina's tutu—what was up with that? She blinked until it looked like a tablecloth again. Her eyes focused on Luke, sitting cross-legged on the floor, reading a *Psychology Today* magazine while Chica sprawled in his lap.

"Hey there, sleepyhead," he said when she sat up and yawned.

"Hey there back." A warm feeling spread across her chest, but it was quickly followed by a pulsatile ache in her head. For a moment, she couldn't get her bearings. What was Luke Jericho doing in her living room petting her dog . . . and when did she get a dog? She touched the throbbing spot on her forehead.

Oh yeah.

Chica.

The limo.

The rock.

"Who do you think threw that rock at the limousine?" Too many things were going on at the same time. Hard to sort out what was important and what was coincidence. A man breaking into her house, a rock thrown at a limo while she was inside. She didn't know if it was just bad luck or something more.

"I'm sure the rock wasn't intended for you if that's what you're worried about. Dante's confession is all over the news, and the limo has a personalized plate:

JERICHO ONE. People are scared, and they're looking for a scapegoat. Right, now, my family's that goat."

"JERICHO ONE. How many limos do you have?" she asked, hoping it wouldn't turn out to be more than the number of pairs of shoes in her closet.

"Three."

She had four pairs of shoes. "Well, that's a relief."

He threw back his head and laughed. First time she'd seen him do that. He looked . . . very attractive when he laughed. He also looked very attractive when he didn't.

"I like this dog." He scratched Chica under the chin. "She wandered out of that bedroom, right after you fell asleep. Nosed around a little, then once she found you, she wouldn't leave your side, so here we both are." Pulling Chica's face up, he studied her eyes. She mewled and wagged her tail in response. "What happened to her?"

"Don't know, really. The vet says she's most likely been on the streets for a very long time. Prior to that, suffered some abuse. She's malnourished, pregnant. She followed the little boy next door home from school, but she's too much for Tommy's family to manage, so I'm sort of her foster mom."

"Lucky dog."

"Lucky me." She patted her knees, and Chica came bounding over to her. "If I hadn't needed to take Chica to the vet, I would've walked in on a burglar, and who knows what would've happened." She shuddered just thinking how close a call she'd had.

She never saw a man get to his feet so fast. "You had a burglar. When was this?"

His alarm alarmed her. No one else had seemed impressed by a black-haired man appearing in her kitchen window. Not the uniformed officer who'd taken the report, certainly not Detective Johnson. But Luke stalked across the room, flexing and unflexing his hands, his brows drawn down into a tight V between his eyes.

"Last night, but nothing was taken, so I guess all's well that ends well."

"How did he get in? I didn't see broken windows anywhere in the house."

"You didn't see any broken windows *anywhere in the house* when?"

"When I was checking out the place."

"Oh." Her hand went to her throat. It was only natural he would've looked around. But most people wouldn't own up to it. Luke Jericho was turning out to be a very forthright man, and she couldn't make up her mind whether that was a good thing or a bad thing. "I don't know how the burglar got in. The police say there's no sign of forced entry, but I'm absolutely certain I locked my doors and windows." She stared at her fingernails. "I do have a hide-a-key, but it hadn't been moved."

Luke had his phone in his hand again. He and that phone seemed tight. Very tight.

"I need a locksmith. I'm at . . ." He looked over at her. "What's the address?"

"What're you doing?"

"We need to get the locks changed."

"What do you mean *we* need to get the locks changed?"

"I'm somewhere on Calle De La Cereza, just tell the guy to look for the limo in the driveway."

Her chagrin doubled. This was simply too much. Luke's profile was making her heartbeat launch into outer space, but she no longer cared. "You made your chauffeur wait outside for you this entire time?"

"Good to know you think I'm a complete ass, but no, another driver picked him up. Left me the limo." He laid his phone on the coffee table and sat down next to her, touched her hair in a way that had that rocket-ship effect on her heart again. "You had a break-in. No sign of forced entry means you either didn't lock your doors and windows like you say you did, or the intruder had a way in. Most likely he used your hide-a-key. Plus you're renting, right? No telling who has keys to this place." Without giving her time to respond, he continued, "We're changing the locks tonight."

Her jaw clamped down, and she had to take a few deep breaths before she could open her mouth and respond. "Whether I change my locks is my decision, not yours. You don't get to just barge in here and take charge of my life."

"What life?"

"Excuse me?"

"Don't think I didn't have my guys check you out

the moment I found out you were my brother's psychiatrist."

"You had no right."

"I have every right to protect my brother."

"Well you don't have a right to protect me. No wonder Dante has a problem with you. You're an interfering control freak."

"And you're a stubborn, infuriating woman who doesn't know how to say thank you when someone offers her help."

"Oh, did you *offer* me help? Because I must've missed that part. So call your guy off. I don't need your locksmith."

He handed her the phone. "Then call your own. Do it now."

"I've *already* had the locks changed," she ground out. "And you can't tell me what to do, Luke Jericho." Even to her, the words sounded silly. "We hardly even know each other."

"That's about to change."

She arched a single eyebrow—high enough he ought to get the message.

"Look, I owe my brother, and, you said so yourself, you owe my brother, too. That puts us both on the same team, so yeah, we're going to get to know each other real well, real fast." He picked up her hand, traced his thumb along her palm, trailing fire everywhere he touched. "And one of the first things you're going to learn about me is that I don't mess around. I don't cajole. I don't persuade. I don't seduce. Subterfuge isn't in my nature." First his breath was in her hair, fogging up her brain. Then he was whispering close in her ear, melting her like warmed sugar. "When I see something I want, Faith, I don't apologize. I just go get it."

NINE

Friday, July 26, 7:00 A.M.

Without finding anything he could choke down for breakfast, Scourge slammed the refrigerator door and sidled along the kitchen wall, one arm covering his eyes. Unable to bear looking at the calendar while its red dates pulsed at him, taunting him like the very blood that surged through his veins, he'd been forced to begin chronicling time in a spiral notebook.

Twenty days.

That's all the time he had left until he was supposed to fulfill his destiny with the Donovans.

Just last Sunday he'd been itching with anticipation, but now—he pressed his palms to his eyes—after all his practice, all his dedication everything was falling apart. Thanks to that incident at the lab, he'd hardly slept in days. The sight of the red vessels fanning across the whites of his eyes sent shivers racing down his back and thick waves of nausea rolling through his gut.

With determination, he hobbled to the bedroom and pulled the book from beneath his pillow. As he traced its title with his fingers, electric volts shot up his arms and jolted his heart into a terrifying, galloping rhythm. He jerked his hand from the book and fell to his knees.

Pressure welled behind his eyes. How could he fulfill his destiny now?

Of all the obstacles he'd prepared for, all the possible complications and hindrances he'd imagined that might keep him from executing his plan, this particular problem had never occurred to him. And so he hadn't been ready. Not for this.

Still disbelieving, he tried one last time. Clawing his arm, he gouged his nails deeper and deeper until red droplets began to ooze from his skin. An agonizing scream tore from his throat as a wave of terror swamped him. It couldn't be true.

But it was.

Tears streamed from his eyes.

He was afraid of blood.

Faith Clancy had just become an *official* part of Scourge's master plan.

Pleased with himself for coming up with the perfect solution to his problem, Scourge settled himself in the big leather chair on the patient side of Dr. Clancy's desk and smiled. If he'd had any qualms about choosing a target—about choosing *Dr. Clancy*—off book and for his own pleasure, those points were all moot now.

This was destiny, plain and simple. No wonder he'd been drawn to her so deeply, so inexplicably, from the first moment he'd seen her face in that brochure. And here she was, the very one who'd turned Dante Jericho over to the police. Dr. Clancy's fate was sealed. She was meant to be his.

Though he despised a man who couldn't regulate his appetites, waiting for this temptress would be the ultimate exercise in self-control. His release would come, but only at the appointed time. Although this hemophobia he'd developed posed an unexpected problem, he was quite certain he could overcome it in short order and keep to his schedule.

A great vocabulary word: *Hemophobia*.

And Dr. Clancy was just the person to cure him of it.

Irony.

Also a good word. He made a mental note to use both words in a sentence at least once today and nestled deeper into the comfy leather armchair. The buttersoft animal hide felt like living skin as he dragged his fingers over it and imagined stroking the soft hollow of Dr. Clancy's throat. A space so creamy, so pure—so exciting. Then he thought about her stroking him, and his dick hardened. His heart beat fast and loud. Too loud. If she heard it, she'd know he was a dirty boy.

Dirty boy. What's that in your pants?

Thwack.

He could feel the hot sting of Sister's ruler slapping his dick. She'd seen his erection and taught him a lesson.

It's for your own good. You don't want to go to hell, do you?

But that was just it. He *did* want to go to hell. More than anything he wanted to find a place where he belonged. At least in hell, he'd fit in with all the other dirty boys. He looked down at his crotch and saw that his dick had deflated, and his chin dropped to his chest in relief. He'd regained his self-control.

"What brings you here today, Mr. Teodori? How can I help you?" Dr. Clancy asked.

Behind a smile that was all innocence and light, she hid her own dirty heart. Dr. Clancy didn't see through him, but he could see through her.

"Scourge. Please call me Scourge."

The corners of her mouth pulled down, and then a neutral expression quickly replaced the look of someone who'd just had an unpleasant surprise. "All right, Mr. Teodori . . . Scourge. Is that your given name, or a nickname?"

"It's my *name*. A friend helped me change it. Would it be on my insurance card if it weren't my legal name?"

"Oh, certainly, right. I see."

But she didn't see. He could tell by her frozen face she didn't think *Scourge* was a proper name for a man. Probably thought a name like that'd make a person feel bad or worthless or cause some deep psychosocial injury. But she was wrong. Sister Bernadette had fixed

him with that name because it was true to his character. To be a scourge upon the earth was a fine destiny,
and he had the ambition and the will to live up to his
name. He was glad to have a purpose. He was glad to
own his name. His back straightened, and he met her
eyes—those sad eyes that made him want to fuck her
and then slide a knife across her throat.

Dr. Clancy didn't look away.

She wanted him, too.

Patience.

"Scourge . . ."

Yes. She definitely wanted him—he could hear it in
the throaty dip of her sensual voice when she called
out his name.

"I understand your family physician referred you to
me last month. Perhaps you can tell me what brings
you here *today*. What finally made you decide to follow
through and seek therapy?"

"Hemophobia." A grin tightened his cheeks. Hadn't
been hard to fit that word into the conversation.

"I see."

Was she going to keep saying that all day? He
scratched the arms of the chair with his nails, and the
leather made an anguished sound. Would Dr. Clancy
make that sound when he fucked her?

"I think I might be able to help you with your fear
of blood. How long have you had this problem?"

"A few days." *Might* be able to help? He needed her
to cure him immediately. "I-I can't go on like this. You
don't know what I'm going through." His voice trem-

bled like a fool's, and he had to cross his arms over his chest to keep his hands from shaking. "I've already lost my job."

Now the sadness in her eyes looked more like compassion, as if she was thinking only of him and had forgotten about her own problems. The idea of someone like her worrying about someone like him made his chest constrict, then explode—like he'd been underwater holding his breath and finally managed to kick his way to the surface for air.

But breathing in all that oxygen was painful, and it made him want to dive back down into the depths where he belonged.

"You lost your job?"

How was Dr. Clancy going to help him if all she ever did was repeat his words back to him? "Is there an echo in here?"

"It's called reflective listening. Quite an astute observation, Scourge. Now then, about losing your job, you were saying?"

He squeezed his eyes shut. *Patience.* He must exercise patience with her. Reveal enough so she could do *her* job . . . but not enough for her to discover who he really was. "I'm a phlebotomist. Isn't it ironic?"

"It's practically an Alanis Morissette lyric." She gave him the innocent eyes again.

"Ha." He forced a laugh. She was trying to relax him with humor. He didn't find the joke particularly funny but wanted her to know he was sophisticated enough to get it. "You a fan?"

"Oh, well not really, but it's a fun song. Anyway, yes, I do find it ironic that your job involves the very object you fear."

He wanted to tell her more. He wanted her to understand. He couldn't fulfill his destiny as long as he feared blood. But sadly, it was his fate to be misunderstood. "Can you cure me?"

"I can't make promises, but I'm very optimistic. You see, you've only had the problem a little while. Technically, your fear of blood doesn't qualify as a phobia because it hasn't been present six months, but . . ."

The urge to choke her was almost too much to resist. Strangulation would be bloodless . . . but not at all satisfying. No. He'd come too far to give up on his plans now. He would wait for his cure. "I haven't slept in three days. I couldn't eat my breakfast this morning because I can't pour ketchup on my eggs, and that's the only way I like them. Yesterday, I saw a man with a barbecue stain on his shirt, and I passed out, right there on the street." He gritted his teeth. "I qualify. I promise you, I qualify."

She steepled her fingers and rested her chin atop them. "I agree with you, Scourge. We can't always go strictly by the book. What I was about to say is that when the problem is severe enough to interfere with your ability to carry out your work—"

He came up on his haunches. "I need to do my work. We can't always go by the book. Sometimes we have to change the book to get the job done right."

She nodded. "Agreed. If your symptoms interfere

with daily living, I'd say you've got a true phobia. The good news is phobias are highly responsive to treatment. Often, a month or so of simple behavior therapy is all it takes."

He dropped back into his chair. He only had *twenty days* left. "I can't wait that long."

"I can see you're terribly eager to get back to work, and that's a good thing. Your desire to get better may move therapy along more quickly. I can't promise a fast cure, but like I said before, I'm optimistic." She leaned back. "I think we should start with systematic desensitization. It's a simple but effective technique involving relaxation therapy, and I think you could benefit from learning to relax no matter what. You seem a little . . . on edge."

A muscle in his jaw was twitching. He wished she hadn't noticed. He didn't want her to think he was a weakling. "Relax me now. Hurry, please."

She hid a flash of a smile with her cupped hand. "Hurry up and relax? Slow down a minute and think of what you're saying. Take a deep breath, Scourge."

He gulped air as fast as he could.

"Okay. Good start. Now take a *long,* deep breath, let it fill your lungs, then slowly, *slowly* exhale."

He released his breath in a long exhale just like she said. Oddest thing. His heart slowed in his chest, his clenched hands opened and fell to his side. The muscle in his face stopped twitching. "I actually feel better. Am I cured?"

She pushed her chair back from the desk. "Hardly.

But I'm glad you feel better than when you arrived. Try practicing slow, deep breaths before you go to bed tonight. Put your hand on your stomach and make it rise with each inhale. It'll help you sleep." She leaned back, stretched her legs, placed her hand on her belly, and closed her eyes. She started to breathe, rhythmically, hypnotically.

As he watched her body rise and fall, his dick grew hard again. He stroked the leather chair while she breathed in, then out, demonstrating the technique. Yes. Dr. Faith Clancy was the perfect person to cure him. He could feel it in his bones. He'd be back at work in no time, and she would make a very pleasurable first order of business.

TEN

Monday, July 29, 2:00 P.M.

No wonder Faith's secretary had sounded excited. When Stacy had buzzed Faith to announce a man was here to see her, her voice had jumped with energy— like she was about to give Faith the down and dirty after a hot date. As Faith rose to greet the visitor, she ran a hand beneath the length of her hair, fluffing it a little. And she wasn't the type to fluff for a pretty face.

The pretty face in question crossed her office, reached over her desk and offered her his substantial hand. "Please don't get up."

"Too late. I'm already up." She snapped her mouth shut. His grip, not surprisingly, was strong, his voice low and deep, the kind of voice that rumbled and reso- nated and commanded attention. As she quickly as- sessed his face, the hard angles and strong chin, she noticed him doing the same. They were sizing each other up in the time it took to shake hands. And that quickly, she decided she liked this man.

He smiled, a warm, broad smile that made the skin bunch up around keen brown eyes—eyes that took in the room in one fell swoop. "I'm special agent Atticus Spenser. FBI."

Her brows lifted, but she hurriedly smoothed her expression.

"Mom was a Harper Lee fan. Let's move on."

Apparently she hadn't smoothed her expression quickly enough. But who could blame her? After all, it wasn't every day a man who looked like a taller, handsomer, cockier version of a young Greg Peck strode into her office and announced he'd been named after Atticus Finch, the hero of *To Kill a Mockingbird*—only her favorite book of all time.

"Me too—I mean I'm a Harper Lee fan. So as you were saying . . ." She cleared her throat and narrowed her eyes to signal she was all business and completely unaffected by either his looks or his name. "Let's move on."

He motioned for her to sit, as if he were the host and she the guest. This was *her* office. She remained standing and gestured for him to take a seat on the other side of the desk. He shrugged, dropped into the chair, and bent his long legs neatly, squaring his knees over his massive feet. Okay, good. Now he knew who was in charge. Smiling politely, she sat down opposite him.

"You're Dr. Faith Clancy. May I call you Faith?"

"Of course. May I call you Atticus?"

"No." He stretched out his legs and relaxed back into the chair. "Everyone calls me, Spense."

"I bet your mother calls you Atticus."

"You got me there. But *only* my mother."

"Well, Spense, I presume you're here about Dante Jericho. I didn't realize the FBI was involved."

"Officially, we're not. But serial killers make people nervous. Detective Johnson, for example, has gone downright squirrelly over this one. Anyway, the Santa Fe Police Department requested unofficial input from the Feds. I was in Phoenix working another case, but Johnson and I go way back, so I volunteered to come out for a curbside consult."

She tilted her head. "I doubt that Detective Johnson would appreciate the squirrelly remark."

With a wide grin, he said, "I call 'em like I see 'em."

"So do I."

"And you don't like Johnson."

This guy was nervy, and she didn't want to talk about his buddy, Johnson. "For the record, I don't think that's relevant. You have questions for me regarding Dante Jericho?"

"I like your office."

Given how sparsely furnished her office was and how little thought she'd given to the décor, his remark took her by surprise. "You do?"

"I really do." Leaning forward in his chair, he ran

his palm over her desktop. "Your desk is different. An antique?"

"Yes, it came out of an old mining office in Jerome, Arizona."

"Arizona's your home state. You chose an unusual desk like this because it reminds you of home. Home and family are important to you."

"You're pulling this out of thin air, drawing conclusions with few if any substantiating facts."

"Which is precisely what Uncle Sam pays me to do." He sat back and put his hands behind his head.

"Are you a profiler?"

"I like to think of myself as a puzzle solver. I'm a whiz at puzzles." His eyes took another turn around the room. "You're sentimental, but you'd rather not show that side of yourself to others. Thus no family pictures in the office. People are more important to you than things, which is why you don't have the typical office knickknacks on display."

"Maybe I just haven't had time to decorate."

He shook his head. "You had time to hang your diplomas, shelve your books, the things that matter to you. You don't care about knickknacks. You care about people." He came out of his chair, leaned across her desk, and sniffed her hair.

The only reasonable response to such outlandish behavior would be to call him out, ask him to leave immediately. But part of her found Special Agent Atticus Spenser far too fascinating to dismiss. She didn't know what it was with men sniffing her hair lately, but she was dying to find out what this one would say or do next.

"You love fresh flowers, but you don't keep them in your office—because you're concerned they might trigger a patient's allergies."

"How did you know?" He should take this show of his on the road. He was that good.

"Your hair carries the faintest scent of gardenias, which means you keep an abundance of them around you in your home. But your patients are more important to you than your flowers. As I said before, I like your office." He smiled and sat back down. "And I like you, Faith. I know it was difficult for you to turn Dante Jericho over to the police, but I hope you know you did the right thing."

"Did I?"

"Absolutely. Which brings me to why I'm here."

Spense retrieved a set of photographs from the briefcase he'd brought with him. On top was the photo of Nancy Aberdeen's bloodied corpse. The same picture Detective Johnson had blindsided her with a few days ago. She felt just as queasy now as then, but this time she didn't flinch, didn't change posture or expression.

Their eyes met, and Spense quickly chested the set of photographs, rearranging them so the picture of Nancy's corpse was on the bottom. "Mind if I show you some photographs of the Saint's victims?"

Unlike Detective Johnson, Spense didn't seem interested in intimidating her. His tone was respectful.

Nor did he strike her as the type of man to get into a power struggle—too much confidence for that. No doubt Agent Spenser had his reasons for asking her to view those awful photos again, but she didn't see what those reasons could be. "Like I told Detective Johnson, I'll do anything I can to help, but I don't see how looking at these gory crime-scene shots will make a difference. I'm not a detective."

"But you are a trained observer of human behavior . . . as am I. And I don't intend to show you crime-scene photos. I should've made sure the photos were sorted properly before I took them out. I want you to look at pictures of the victims taken when they were still alive. You told Johnson that during your therapy sessions, Dante never mentioned anything that would connect him to the victims."

"That's right, because he didn't."

"But you can't say for sure unless you really know who these people were. Maybe if you knew more about them, something might click." Gently, he placed one of the photos on her desk, oriented it toward her. "This is William Herbert Carmichael, the Saint's latest victim. Forty-seven years old, a deacon in the Methodist church. Made a fortune with some miracle-grow crop fertilizer he invented."

"And you want to know if I think this Carmichael might represent Dante's father."

His silence indicated that was exactly what he wanted to know.

She shook her head. "I don't see it. Dante's father

passed away this year at sixty-three, so the age doesn't fit. The victim was a wealthy farmer, and Dante's dad was a wealthy rancher, but I still don't see Carmichael as a likely stand-in for Roy Jericho. Roy Jericho had a reputation as a drinker and a womanizer. People say the man was handsome as sin, had women trailing behind him like breadcrumbs." With her index finger hovering over the photo, she traced Carmichael's chubby-cheeked grin. "This guy, probably not so much."

"What about the brother, Luke? He inherited all the money and all the perks of being a legitimate Jericho as well. Dante has to resent him." Spense added a second victim to the lineup. "This is Kenneth Stoddard. Fifteen years old. Average student. Involved with his church group."

"Methodist?" She peered hard at the photo.

"Yeah. So far that's all we've got to tie the victims together. All Methodists."

"So the Saint's murdering Methodists and leaving rosaries in their hands. Maybe he's trying to save their souls."

"Possibly. Your boy Dante's Catholic, I believe."

She tensed at his use of *your boy*, but let the remark pass. "No. According to Dante, his family attended mass on Christmas and Easter, and he considers them hypocrites for it. He not only refuses to participate in organized religion, he's an avowed atheist. I can't imagine Dante Jericho trying to save someone's soul." Closing her eyes, she tried to set all bias aside and wrack her brain for a true connection between Dante and the victims. *Nada*. She looked at the photo of Kenneth Stoddard again. "Even assuming Dante hates his brother, and I don't think I can stipulate to that, this boy is not a good stand-in for Luke Jericho. The age doesn't fit, but mostly he's just too average to represent Luke. Tell me about the women."

Spense laid down a third, then a fourth photo. "Linda Peabody. Forty-four years old, a soft-spoken housewife and stay-at-home mother of four. And finally, here's Nancy Aberdeen. Sixteen. Straight-A student. Popular girl. Never in any trouble."

"I understand Nancy won this ribbon at the state fair."

"For her cherry pie." Grimacing, he looked away.

They were all so different, and yet . . . "These people take living average lives to the extreme. I think that's what sets them apart from the crowd. How many sixteen-year-old girls enter baking contests and wear gingham dresses these days? That has to mean something, Spense."

"Agreed." He closed one eye and raised the opposite eyebrow. "Suppose we put these photos together like so."

"A visual puzzle?" she asked, as he arranged the photos in a square, with the man and woman on the top row and the boy and girl below, like four pictures in a single frame.

"This reminds me of something. You see it too, right?"

Her chest tightened. "I see a family." Her eyes

moved from one photograph to the next. "But it's definitely not *Dante's* family."

"That's how I see it, too. Separately, there's no logical pattern. A mixed bag of age, gender, and geography. But put them all together, and you have the perfect all-American family. A throwback to the past." He let loose a rough sigh. "We mean to nail the bastard who did this. Tell me you're on board with that, Faith."

"With nailing the bastard who murdered four innocent people? Absolutely. But just so we're clear, I believe a man is innocent until proven guilty. I don't intend to rush to judgment or let myself be blinded by hate because of the heinous nature of the crimes."

"Dante Jericho confessed."

She put her forearms on the desk and stared hard into his eyes. "I'm the one who called the police. I don't need you to remind me that he confessed."

A woman's voice, soft and cold like frozen silk, cut into their conversation. "And Spense here doesn't need me to remind him that a confession doesn't seal the deal. A confession isn't proof a man's guilty. Right, Spense?"

Faith's shoulders jumped. She'd been concentrating so hard on the photographs, been so intent on finding that common thread among the Saint's victims, she'd failed to hear the door open. For the second time that morning, she had to snap her mouth shut to avoid appearing rude. The woman standing in the doorway, sidelit by afternoon sun shining in from the window, was none other than Dr. Caitlin Cassidy. At least in this light, her hair had the sheen of melted chocolate. With a complexion just short of olive, and jet-black lashes, her vivid blue eyes came as a surprise. Not so surprising, they looked every bit as keen as Spense's.

When Faith had e-mailed Caitlin Cassidy for advice, she'd hoped to speak with her by phone or possibly set up an online conference. She never expected a face-to-face meeting, at least not so soon.

Spense bounded to his feet, and Faith followed suit, quickly making her way around the desk to greet her surprise guest.

"Well, well," he said. "If this isn't an unexpected displeasure, I don't know what is. How the hell are you, Caity?"

"I'm well, Spense, and believe me, the displeasure is all mine."

Apparently, Dr. Caitlin Cassidy and Special Agent Atticus Spenser had met.

"You gunslinging for the Jericho family now?" Spense swaggered over to Dr. Cassidy and pulled his jacket aside, revealing his service weapon.

Faith stopped dead in her tracks, her breath catching, her hands clenching at her sides. Spense pretended to draw his gun, and as he blew fake smoke off his finger, she released a long breath.

Dr. Cassidy fake fired back at Spense, then blew imagined smoke from her own finger. "I'm nobody's hired gun, and if you don't know that by now, you're not as bright as everyone thinks you are. I'm just a concerned citizen who believes in justice for all."

"You get paid by defense attorneys. In my book, that makes you a hired gun."

"I'm pretty sure you get a nice paycheck from Uncle Sam, so according to that definition, you're a gunslinger, too."

"But I'm not paid to set murderous clients free."

She didn't let a beat go by. "Nor am I. I'm a psychiatric consultant hired to render an *honest,* expert opinion."

"Yet you specialize in getting killers off death row. Come to think of it, there's no death penalty in New Mexico, so what the hell are you doing here?"

"I asked Dr. Cassidy for help." Faith finally got a word in. "Dr. Cassidy, thank you so much for coming. I wasn't expecting you to show up in person, but I'm terribly grateful you did."

"I would've been here sooner, but I was in Phoenix working another case."

Spense lurched toward her. "Goddamnit, Caity. Judd Kramer is guilty. Just take my word for it and go home, why don't you."

Dr. Cassidy's lips pursed, and her smile was all innocence. "You're on Kramer, too? What airline you flying? Maybe we can sit next to each other on the plane back to Phoenix."

"Maybe you can kiss my ass."

She addressed Faith, "I apologize for Agent Spenser. His manners get worse every time I see him."

A low growl came out of Spense's mouth. Dr. Cassidy got on her tiptoes and up in his face. "I specialize in discovering the truth. Not getting killers off. And as you know, I'm especially interested in cases where a confession factors heavily into a guilty verdict. The number of false confessions in this country, and the number of innocent men and women who're convicted based on those false confessions is unconscionable."

Spenser smacked his fist into his open palm. "And the bulk of those false confessions are based on sloppy police work and coercion. No one's arguing that, Caity. But let's stick to *this case* for a moment. Even you have to admit that Jericho's confession wasn't coerced. It was a spontaneous, voluntary, good confession. And as such, is highly credible."

"The fact that Dante volunteered his confession doesn't make it credible. Maybe he's looking for his fifteen minutes of fame. Maybe he's lost touch with reality. Police fielded more than two hundred confessions after the Lindbergh baby was kidnapped. None of those confessions was coerced, and every one of them proved false. But you know that already, Spense."

Faith could see a vein pulsing in Spense's forehead, his posture tightening. "Let's not do this in front of the kid, Caity. You and I got time for a pissing match later. If you're flying Delta, I'll change my seat on the plane, and we can see how long it takes for the flight attendants to separate us."

He turned to Faith, took her by the hand, and uncurled her fingers, which had drawn down into a closed fist, then he pressed a card into her palm. "Despite your first impression of him, Detective Johnson's a good man. You should trust him. But just in case you don't, and you get in a jam, you can call me. I've got connections, Faith, and I can make things happen, even from Phoenix."

Back at Faith's desk, Spense reverently lifted each photograph and held them up to the light for inspection before replacing them in his briefcase. "Remember these victims, Faith. Linda Peabody. William Carmichael. Nancy Aberdeen. Ken Stoddard. You think about *them*."

Spense brushed past Caitlin Cassidy, scalding her with his gaze on his way out the door. Then he looked back over his shoulder at Faith. "One more piece of advice, kid. If you're going to treat confessed serial killers in this office, you should consider keeping a weapon here for self-defense. You're afraid of guns, so figure something else out."

Faith didn't bother asking herself how Spense knew that. After all, the man was a whiz at puzzles.

"Again, I apologize for Spense . . . and for me, too. There's something about that man that gets me every time. But that's no excuse for that little scene you just witnessed." Dr. Caitlin Cassidy stuck out her hand. "Dr. Faith Clancy, I presume."

Faith let out a long breath. "No worries. And please, call me Faith. I can't believe you're here. Thanks again, Dr. Cassidy."

"Call me Caitlin. I guess my timing wasn't the greatest."

"Your timing was perfect. Please . . ." Faith gestured toward the seat recently vacated by Spense.

Caitlin plopped down and stretched her arms, then settled them behind her head as Spense had done. To Faith's eye, the two apparent enemies seemed to share a lot of personality traits.

"Tell me what happened with you and guns," Caitlin said.

Yep. Another puzzle solver. "Maybe you and Agent Spenser could form your own special team."

"Not a chance in hell Atticus Spenser and I will ever be on the same team, and you can take that one to the bank. Now then, about your fear of firearms." When Caitlin's voice thawed, it warmed the whole room, instantly putting Faith at ease.

Something in her eyes made Faith want to trust Caitlin, made her want to let her guard down. "Sure. I'll tell you all about it. But first you tell me how you knew."

"A few minutes ago, when Spense pulled back his jacket and flashed his service weapon, your face went white. No. Not just your face, your lips, too. I swear, your lips and your skin were the exact same color. I was sure you were going to faint."

"I've found if squeeze my fists, it raises my blood pressure and keeps me on my feet." Faith walked to the window and looked out onto the street below, then turned back to Caitlin, twisting the turquoise ring she'd bought on the street last week.

Caitlin looked at her expectantly.

"I was six. My best friend Gina and I were playing cops and robbers at her house. Her dad was a cop, so we played that game a lot. Anyway, Gina's mom had a pocket Beretta. It was so small, we thought it was a toy. Gina picked it up." Faith pumped her fists, went to her desk and sat down hard in her chair. Just remembering that moment raised the hairs on her neck and sent her heart racing. "One minute, I was playing with my best friend, the next, I was watching her die."

"I'm sorry."

She looked away, folded her hands on top of her desk. "Yeah. Me, too."

Caitlin reached out and touched Faith's hand. If another person had done that, Faith would've pulled away. But Caitlin had a way about her.

A moment later, Caitlin sat back and crossed her arms. "Have you ever thought about trying to overcome your fear? Maybe take a gun class so you could learn to handle a weapon safely."

"I've never had a reason . . . before now. But we digress."

"Shrinks like us do tend to digress don't we?" Caitlin shrugged one shoulder. "And we have important matters before us. I read about Dante Jericho's confession in the papers even before I got your e-mail. I could tell you I was planning a trip to the darling city of Santa Fe and just happened to drop in, but that would be a lie, and you'd see right through me."

"I'm not sure I can see right through anyone at the moment."

"I believe you can. Don't underestimate your instincts, Faith. You've got the training and the heart for this business. That's apparent by the way you've handled yourself so far. All you need now is experience."

"This isn't the kind of experience I planned on getting when I went into psychiatry. I'm not a forensic specialist, like you."

"Believe me, nobody wants something like this to fall in her lap, but in life, you get what you get. This is a highly unusual case. Try to look at it as a rare opportunity."

"A *very* rare opportunity, I hope."

"Listen, I brought up all those false confessions in the Lindbergh kidnapping mainly to get Spense's goat."

"Mission accomplished." Faith refrained from raising her hand for a high five.

"But Spense makes a good point. A false confession that did not result from external influence is more akin to a zebra than a horse. They don't show up at the watering trough that often. Confessions are my thing, but I've never seen an *unsolicited* false confession in my career. I'm only thirty-three, but still."

So that was why Caitlin Cassidy had flown all the way from Phoenix to Santa Fe. She was hunting zebras.

"Now that it's just us girls, how about you fill me in on Dante Jericho?"

"Does this mean you're be available to assist in his

case? If I could come up with the funds I mean. I'm sure Luke Jericho would be willing to pay you whatever you ask."

She waved her palm in the air. "No can do. When I said I wasn't in this for the money, I meant it. I'm involved in a big pro bono case right now."

"Judd Kramer?"

"Uh-huh. I'm here for one day only, so we have to make the most of our time."

Faith's body sagged with disappointment.

"I'll get you started, and I'll stay available for you by phone or e-mail. I wish I could take this one for you, but I can't."

"Then where should I begin?"

"Let's start with your working diagnosis for Dante Jericho."

"His diagnosis." Faith drummed her fingers on the desktop. "Truthfully, I'm not sure anymore. In the beginning, his presentation was classic. A schizoid personality disorder in the throes of a major depressive episode—some paranoid features. He met criteria under DSM-5."

"Don't you hate the new manual?"

"With a passion. But hey, at least they got rid of those irritating roman numerals."

Bonded together by a mutual dislike of the new Diagnostic and Statistical Manual for classifying mental disorders, they shared a high five after all.

"So Dante didn't fit the diagnosis of psychopath." Caitlin frowned.

"No. Schizoid. Depressed. Possible delusions, but he exhibited no psychopathic features at all. At least not until the day he confessed."

"Interesting."

"That day, his behavior was entirely inconsistent with his past behavior—and my working diagnosis. He followed me from his brother's art gallery, snuck into my office the back way, and more or less ambushed me. He grabbed my cell, made all sorts of menacing gestures and remarks. I'm certain he was deliberately trying to frighten me. And he seemed to be getting off on it . . . like a psychopath would."

"Scary."

"Very. I had to force myself not to show fear." Her hands closed into fists. "I decided to behave as if we were in regular session. And that's when Dante suddenly turned back into his old, docile—and depressed—self."

"What do you make of that? *Two incompatible diagnoses*. Is the guy schizoid and depressed, unable to carry out a simple plan, or is he a ruthless psychopath?"

"If I knew the answer to that, I suppose I could tell you for certain whether Dante is capable of having committed such highly organized crimes."

"What's your gut telling you?"

"My gut goes first one way, then the other. Like you said, I don't have a lot of experience to guide me. But *logic* tells me his menacing behavior in my office was all an act. He never planned to hurt me. He wanted to scare me good and proper though because he wanted to be sure I'd phone the police."

"Then my advice is to keep digging. Don't stop until you find the truth, Faith, because I'm telling you from my heart, if you ever stop searching, you'll never be able to live with the consequences."

ELEVEN

Wednesday, July 31, 11:00 A.M.

One more piece of advice, kid. If you're going to treat confessed serial killers in this office, you should consider keeping
a weapon here for self-defense. You're afraid of guns, so figure
something else out.

Special Agent Atticus Spenser's words to Faith had
missed the mark. She wasn't *afraid* of guns, she was
flat-out *terrified*. She figured Caitlin Cassidy was right:
It was time to face her fear. So the next morning, after
filling her tank with a hearty breakfast and three cups
of coffee—the sole purpose of which was to raise her
blood pressure sufficiently to prevent fainting—she
headed downtown and marched intrepidly through
the doors of Todd's Gun World.

And if it hadn't been for its puke pink grip, she
might've walked back out as the proud owner of a

Ruger LCP. Faith had gotten through the nerves that nearly stopped her from entering the gun shop in the first place. She'd sucked down the queasy feeling that came over her when she saw the rifles, thick as locusts, covering the walls. But when Todd, the earnest owner of Todd's Gun World, gently placed a lightweight compact pistol with a pink handle in her palm, she'd almost lost her breakfast.

Focusing on the gun's silly-looking grip seemed like a good way to ward off an outright case of the jitters. "Why's the handle this color?" she asked though she already knew the answer. Todd had taken one look at Faith and decided the gun she needed was lightweight, lethal . . . and pink.

"Err . . . because you're a lady? Goes good with your shoes?" His puzzled smile had finished his sentence off for him with an unspoken *why'd ya think?*

She knew she shouldn't have worn her Jimmy Choos. A gun was not an accessory. Nor was it a toy, and she hated the way the pink grip made her feel like she could be playing Barbies with her girlfriends. Her throat clogged, and she got that watery feeling in her legs. This was exactly the type of weapon a child might choose to stuff in her ear, like her friend Gina had done. Two deep inhales later, she'd regained her land legs. "What? You don't have bedazzled?"

Giving her hand a paternal pat, Todd had said, "Far as I can tell, nobody dragged you in here, Missy. You asked me to assist you in finding a weapon for self-defense. This model is compact, so it's safe and easier for you to fire. It's easy to load, and you can handle the recoil. But that don't mean it's for sissies. This here compact pistol packs a punch. It's a favored BUG for our boys in blue."

"What do you mean BUG?" Oh, Lord. Did she really want to know the lingo?

"Backup gun. Now, the question is, do you want a gun for protection, or don't you? If the answer is yes, I got plenty without the pink for you women's liber types."

"I haven't burned a bra in years." Some people giggle when they get nervous—Faith got mouthy. Still, she bit her lower lip. Todd had hit the nail on the head . . . and then hammered it home.

Do you want a gun or don't you?

She'd let the question roll around in her head. If she hadn't understood the need for personal defense before, she understood it now. Being holed up in her office with Dante, with her wits as her only line of self-defense had been a wake-up call. No, he hadn't harmed her. Yes, she now believed his confession to be a lie, but she could never go back to that false sense of security she'd had before. She'd turned the gun over once or twice, testing the grip. The weight of her decision was as palpable as the cool pistol in her hand. She blew out a hard breath.

She didn't think she could take a human life—even in self-defense. "Thanks anyway, but I guess I don't want a gun after all."

"No worries." He'd grinned widely and thumped

her on the back. "I see what your deal is, and I got all kinds of nonlethals. Uncle Todd's gonna fix you up right."

Now, Faith stood smack in the middle of her unprotected office with no gun and the full knowledge she simply didn't have it in her to use lethal force. But that was okay. She hadn't given up on the idea of personal safety. She'd re-upped for her Krav Maga class, and added an additional night per week. Plus, Todd had made good on his promise, and she'd left his shop with enough bells and whistles to befuddle an attacker into believing *she* was the badass.

She also had a few tricks of her own up her sleeve. She closed the door to her office, flipped the dead bolt in place, and started to unpack her personal-defense arsenal. First came the letter opener, brass-plated and pointy. Not sharp enough to kill someone, but it could put an eye out in a pinch. She slipped the letter opener in her top desk drawer and moved on to the next item.

It took both hands to lift the glass orb from her shopping bag. None of the paperweights at the office-supply store had been treacherous enough to suit her, so she'd gone to a Christmas specialty shop and picked up this little beauty—a giant snow globe of the Sangre de Cristo Mountains, mounted on a wooden base. An absolute steal at ten dollars and guaranteed to knock an intruder out cold. She marched the heavy globe over to the bookshelf. When one end of the shelf lifted like a teeter-totter, she rearranged, then rubbed her hands together in satisfaction.

Two down; two to go.

She snapped her pepper-spray ultra system, which included an earsplitting alarm and blinding strobe, onto her belt. To prove she was a good sport, she'd selected the spray with the pink holster. Remembering Todd's *attagirl*, her chest puffed. Then her foot began to tap. She still had one final item to place. Circling her office, she kept her eyes peeled for the perfect spot. The desk seemed an obvious choice, but that zone had already been secured by the letter opener. She circled the room again, but nothing came to mind—this place really could use more furniture. But the third circle was the charm—her gaze fixed on the plantless plant stand near the doorway. If she turned the boxy mahogany stand against the wall just so, its sliding door would be hidden from view and, voilà, became a secret panel.

When she pulled her Taser from its case, her hands stayed steady—a very good sign. Constructed from black plastic, the stun gun felt light and comfortable in her grip. With a simple click, she activated the laser sights. Sweeping the red dot about the room, she straight-armed the Taser.

"Clear," she whispered.

No. That wasn't right.

"Clear," she said, in soft but audible voice. Yes, that was a bit better. She turned off the red light and resolved to practice handling both her Taser and her pepper-spray ultra system again tomorrow. Lightning doesn't often strike twice, so it seemed unlikely she'd ever actually use her assembled arsenal, but one thing was damn sure, on the off chance lightning did strike again, she wouldn't be caught unprepared.

TWELVE

Wednesday, July 31, 12:00 P.M.

Fifteen more days.

Scourge flexed his aching fingers. He wished he'd popped some aspirin, but he'd been too wound-up to think of it. Now, as he palmed his homemade bump key, the ache in his joints brought a sense of pride for a job well done. The first time he'd been in Faith's home, he'd used her hide-a-key to get inside, but unfortunately, his timing had been off. Faith had arrived home earlier than he'd anticipated and spotted him inside the house, forcing him to scramble over the back fence before the police arrived.

And now, just as he'd figured, she'd changed her locks and ditched the hide-a-key.

Smart girl.

But not as smart as him.

He ran his fingers over the cold edge of the key he'd sanded down earlier today, closed and opened his palm around it, then smiled at the way his flesh blanched and retained the triangular pattern of the key's shaft. The faintest of quivers beset his hands. What if the key didn't work? What if he hadn't sanded and smoothed it properly? With no one there to guide him, his confidence was low, but he'd followed the Internet instructions to the letter, and he'd made several practice keys first. He'd been diligent and careful and polished every speck of dirt off the shaft.

The key will work.

On a long inhale, he slipped the bump key in the back-door lock. The shaft sank in easily.

So far so good.

He pulled the key back just a bit, remembering what he'd read—this was the art of the bump. Next, he removed a small screwdriver from his pocket and used the handle to tap the key, just so.

The bump.

The bump, the click, the snap of the lock resonated down his arm.

Yes!

The key turned. The door opened, and once again he'd successfully penetrated Dr. Faith Clancy's private sanctuary.

The house itself was not much, but the master bedroom was magnificently located on the east side of home. A large, eight-paned window banked with heavy wood allowed morning light to come flooding in, igniting the mustard-colored walls. He stuck his arms out and lifted them over his head, like a circus master inside a ring of fire, posturing for the crowd.

The screens had been removed, and the windows were kept crystalline clean, no doubt to enhance the coveted view of the Sangre de Cristo mountain range.

Sangre de Cristo.

The blood of Christ.

His skin grew hot, as if the walls of fire were closing in on him. He turned his back on the window, grabbed his knees, and took deep breaths until his nausea passed. He stood back up and wiped his forehead with his sleeve. No cause for alarm. True, at the moment, he couldn't even think of blood without panicking, but Dr. Clancy would have him cured in no time, which is why he was here in her home, on a little scouting expedition. He was a planner. He liked his ducks in a row before he carried out a kill, and with Dr. Clancy, it was more important than ever to get things right.

Pacing her bedroom, he caught sight of something that interested him on the nightstand—a rather striking picture of Dr. Clancy cradling a newborn babe. He halted, lifted the picture, and tilted his head. Upon closer inspection he realized his mistake. The woman with the baby wasn't Dr. Clancy. Her eyes were a paler shade of jade—by a fraction—her expression every bit as lost as the one Dr. Clancy wore when she thought no one was looking. A freckle dotted the corner of the woman's lips, which were full and luscious like Dr. Clancy's. Oh, yes. Of course.

This must be Grace.

His hand trembled as he replaced the photograph on the nightstand. How terrible for Dr. Clancy. Like Scourge, she had no one left. He pressed his index finger to his lips. Yes. She'd be happier, better off joining her sister and her parents in the great beyond. He'd take the utmost care to ensure her path to heaven was straight and easy. Scraping his fingernail across his teeth, he thought of a special touch. He'd leave Dr. Clancy with his very best rosary—the one Sister Cecily had given him in school. Many times he'd thought of leaving it at a kill, but he'd never felt the occasion was right. Now he knew why. That rosary was meant for Dr. Clancy, his healer, his savior.

All he had to do was get well so he could give it to her.

That decided, he moved on to the living room. There, a kiva fireplace extended to the viga-beamed ceiling. A creamy leather sectional decorated with an assortment of brightly colored throw pillows, a distressed wood coffee table, and a Navajo rug finished off the casual Southwestern look nicely. He approved of her taste and was especially glad to note she'd stuck to one theme for the house. Her office décor, what there was of it, was decidedly eclectic, and that threw him off-balance.

He liked things to match.

Speaking of disorder, a number of books were spread haphazardly on the coffee table, and a copy of

Arizona Highways lay folded open. Several hiking trails had been marked with a sharpie. Oh, that was too bad. She was planning a trip. Sorry to know she wouldn't be able to make that journey, he shook his head.

But what could he do? The clock was ticking.

He made a few quick entries into his notepad regarding the placement of doors and windows, the floor plan of the home, and especially noted any potential weapons Dr. Clancy might have at her disposal—best to stay out of the kitchen, where a cast-iron skillet and a block of butcher knives might ruin his whole day.

Just a final look around the backyard for brush that could provide cover and the best place to scale the fence in the event of another emergency, and he'd have all the information he needed. Last time, he'd suffered more than a few scratches getting over that fence. A spot near a bench or tree would be ideal. He pushed out the back door, and the smell of gardenias hit him in the face.

Followed by an earsplitting high-pitched bark.

"Heel, Chica! Heel. There's no one back there," called a small, boyish voice trying its best to sound stern.

More barking.

"I said heel!"

His eyes darted around the yard. The brush was scant around the house, and he didn't see a ready hiding place.

"She's not home, girl. I'll show you."

Footsteps on gravel.

The gate squeaked open. No time to scale the fence and disappear like last time.

His blood cooled in his veins.

A very good sign. He didn't feel even the slightest flutter of a palpitation. That meant he was getting better already.

Smiling, he dropped into one of the lounges on the back porch, flipped open the *Arizona Highways* magazine he'd pilfered from inside, crossed his feet at the ankles, and whistled "Dixie"—literally.

"Hello? Is someone there?" That Vienna Boy's Choir voice again.

Then there they were, a boy and his dog—a pair straight out of a Disney movie—except for the fact the dog was more bone than bark. Certainly wasn't the type of dog to cause him any trouble. She looked like she barely had the strength to stand. "I like your dog," he offered casually, peering over his magazine.

"Her name's Chica. Who're you?"

"I know. I heard you calling her. Chica's a nice name."

Chica tugged forward on her leash, growling.

"I'm Tommy. Who're you?"

Scourge said nothing, merely waited. The boy frowned, began backing toward the gate. Oh dear. This kid had seen his face. As much as he didn't need the extra trouble, he couldn't let this slide. This boy and his dog were exactly the type of thing that might come back and bite him in the ass. A loose end.

That meant collateral damage could not be avoided.

The boy kicked the gate open with his heel and was just edging out of sight when Scourge answered, "Who do you think I am?" He put down the magazine and stared directly into the boy's eyes. What did it matter now if the kid got a good look at him? The damage was done.

"Are you Faith's brother?" Tommy asked.

Why not? "I am. You're a very good guesser."

"Is Faith here?" Tommy asked, as Chica strained forward on her leash again, still making those aggressive noises in her throat.

"No. She's at work." He got to his feet, went to the boy, and offered his hand.

The boy's palm was sweating when he shook with Scourge, pumping his arm up and down a bit less than enthusiastically.

"And the thing is, my sister doesn't know I'm in town. It's a surprise. So you're not to tell. You wouldn't want to spoil the surprise."

"N-no. But my mom says I'm not allowed to keep secrets."

"Oh, sure. That's right. Never keep a secret. But you know, Tommy, a surprise and a secret are not the same thing. I missed my sister today, and it might be a while before I get back over here. You like Dr. Clancy, right?"

"Oh, yes."

"Then don't ruin this for her."

Tommy reeled Chica in close to his body. Patted her head. "It's okay, girl. Hush." Then he nodded. "Okay. I promise I won't tell."

"Attaboy. Where do you live, son?"

Tommy pointed to the house next door, but then suddenly dropped his hand, as if he knew he'd made a mistake. "I gotta go. I'm not supposed to talk to strangers."

"Maybe I should take you home to your mother. Is your mother home, Tommy?"

The boy shook his head violently. "Please, don't do that. I'll get in trouble if my mom finds out I was talking to you."

He scratched his chin. "I guess if you won't tell, I won't tell. Your mom's right. You shouldn't talk to strangers or keep secrets either. Good thing I'm not a stranger, just a brother with a big surprise for Dr. Clancy. I won't take you home, Tommy. I won't get you in trouble. I'd rather be friends."

"Me, too." Tommy's hunched shoulders relaxed.

"Shall we shake on it, buddy?"

They pumped hands again, then Scourge gave Tommy a high five.

Tommy turned to go and then looked back over his shoulder. "Will I see you again?"

Scourge threw his arms wide and chuckled. "You better believe you will, buddy. You can count on it."

THIRTEEN

Thursday, August 1, 10:00 A.M.

Where was Torpedo?

It wasn't often anyone kept Luke waiting, and he didn't care for the experience. Especially not in his own office. Especially not when he'd invited Faith to join him. His corporate attorneys had insisted Teddy *Torpedo* Haynes was not just a showboating media darling. He was the best criminal-defense attorney money could buy—never lost a capital case and played exceptionally well with Southwest juries. Luke pushed a hand through his hair. This asshole better be good because he was wasting Faith's time as well as Luke's.

The door to the conference room in his downtown business suite swung open.

Swallowing his irritation, he got to his feet and offered his hand to Teddy *Torpedo* Haynes. "I'm Luke Jericho. Call me Luke." He inclined his head toward Faith, who'd also risen. "That's Faith Clancy, my brother's psychiatrist. Call her Doctor if you don't mind."

"Oh, I don't mind a bit. I'm Teddy Haynes but y'all can call me Torpedo." The squat, well-fed attorney pulled his black Stetson off in a backward sweep, revealing a strawberry blond comb-over. The combination of hair spray, Stetson, and male-pattern baldness left some patches of hair glued flat to his scalp while others stuck straight back behind his ears like Winged Mercury.

"Any relation to Richard Racehorse Haynes?" Faith walked over and shook the Torpedo's hand.

"Not far as I know. But winning in the courtroom is in my DNA just the same as it is in his, so never you mind the technicalities." Torpedo hooked his black Stetson on a coat pole in the corner of the conference room and took a seat at the head of a table that seated twenty.

That was Luke's seat. Once again, he swallowed his gall. The only thing that mattered was Dante. "Shouldn't you be wearing a white hat? For the jury's sake?"

"I don't see a jury in here, son. So no, I'll let my true colors show."

Out of the corner of his eye, Luke caught a definite rise in Faith's eyebrows.

"And this pretty little filly"—Torpedo winked at Faith—"knows a jury would pick up on a cheap trick like that anyway. I got a better one up my sleeve." He proceeded to swing his arm wide, knocking Luke's cup off the table and dousing himself in cold, black coffee. "Now that little stunt will buy the jury's sympathy for sure." He ripped off his Gucci jacket and tossed it on the floor. *"Poor Torpedo, he's a walking disaster. I hope his client's innocent. Hate to see him have to lose the case on top of being a boob."*

Haynes was known for his theatrics both inside and outside the courtroom, and apparently Luke and Faith were going to get the full dog and pony. Which was no problem just as long as Torpedo made good on his promise to bring Dante back home where he belonged and wipe the Jericho name clean. If the Torpedo could do that, Luke didn't give a flying fuck about the man's hat size.

Torpedo rubbed his hands together. "Shall we get down to business then?" He motioned a stay-put to Faith and Luke, who'd both gotten up to clean up his mess. "You got people for that, son." He thumped a microphone on. "Testing, testing."

Faith reseated herself and openly rolled her eyes. "We can hear you perfectly well without the mic."

Torpedo shrugged and clicked off the microphone, plopped his bared elbows on the table. "First thing you should know is my courtroom skills are every bit as good advertised." He pounded his chest with one fist and made a sound reminiscent of hocking a loogie. "Trust me, the jury loves a common man. They're pudding in my hands."

"You mean putty?"

"Whatever. The point I'll make is this." His tone changed here, and he pulled his shoulders back, looking shrewdly at Luke, his beady black eyes suddenly gleaming with intelligence. "You don't want me to prove myself in the courtroom. If I'm really earning my keep, this case won't get that far."

Up until this very minute, Luke had been seriously doubting his choice of counsel. But if this guy was good enough to trick him into believing he was a poor Country Joe, no telling what he could do with a jury. He wasn't sure he liked the Torpedo, but he decided right then and there he was going to have to trust him. "Okay. How do we accomplish that?"

"First, it would help an awful lot if we could establish an airtight alibi for your brother for at least one of the murders. If we can eliminate him as a suspect in even one case, it casts grave doubt on the validity of each and every one of his confessions."

"That shouldn't be hard; I mean, assuming he's innocent, he should be able to account for his whereabouts in at least one of the four cases," Faith said.

Torpedo pulled a toothpick from his pocket and stuck it between his teeth. As he spoke the toothpick pumped up and down. "That might be true in most cases, but I'm afraid in this situation there are some complicating factors. For one thing, the guy's a loner—that means he spends a lot of time alone." Chortling at his own joke, Haynes almost choked on the toothpick.

"My brother's innocent. And he's not always alone." Luke's mind went to the prostitute he'd caught Dante with at the casita. There were bound to be others. Maybe one of the women could vouch for his brother. Luke dragged a hand across his face and forced himself to smile. He knew what language Torpedo spoke, because he spoke it too—money. "If you need funds for a PI to help locate . . . and motivate . . . witnesses, it's no problem."

"If money were a problem, I wouldn't be here. It's a given you'll provide whatever I need."

Luke wheeled his chair back from the table, crossed his arms over his chest. "Whatever you need."

"Good." Torpedo spit his toothpick at the trash and missed. "Now then, the complicating factor I was referring to is time, not money, and I don't mean ordinary time. I mean *time of death*. You see, there isn't one. Not really. No one can say exactly when any of the victims went missing, and the bodies were found at least several days postmortem. So the medical examiner had no physical indicators to establish a tight time of death."

"You mean like liver temperature and rigor mortis." Faith frowned, her eyes darkening with concern for Luke's brother. He touched his heart to signal his appreciation for that concern, but she kept her attention focused on the attorney.

"Yep." Haynes nodded.

"What about social media?" Faith started taking notes on the tablet she'd brought with her.

"You're on the ball there, darlin'. You sure you haven't done this kind of thing before?"

Luke didn't follow, but before he could ask, Faith turned to him, and explained, "Two of the victims were teenagers."

"Which makes this whole situation even more horrifying, but I don't see what that has to do with establishing time of death." He rubbed his eyes, his head beginning to ache, his impatience with the showboating Haynes growing greater by the minute.

Torpedo took back the reins. "These days, our best markers for time of death are social-media-related. Too true. Too true. When was the last tweet or Facebook post? Last text message sent? Teens today text almost continually while they're awake, even while they're in a classroom or at the movies. So Dr. Clancy is onto something. The tightest timeline we'll get will likely come from Ken and Nancy. But there's still going to be a large window of opportunity to cover. Unless your brother can account for his whereabouts for the entire window, we're shit out of luck."

Luke snapped a pencil. He was no longer willing to let Teddy Torpedo Haynes run the show. "My brother is an innocent man. He wouldn't harm a fly, much less brutally murder four people. He's simply not capable of such an act."

"I'm not saying we're not going to try. I'm just saying—"

"Shut up, Teddy. I'm not done talking."

Teddy's head jerked a nod.

"Now then, as I was saying. My brother is innocent, and I'm not paying you to sit there and spit toothpicks and tell me all the reasons you can't prove his case. I'm paying you to figure a way. So do your damn job or get the fuck out of my office."

Torpedo's mouth flattened. "I hear you, and believe me, I intend to deliver on my promise. I've never had a client convicted of murder, and I don't plan on breaking my streak now. I'm not saying I won't work the angles. I'm just saying that even *if* your brother is innocent, it won't be easy to bulletproof his alibi. So we need *more* angles. You can never have too many angles going at once."

"Keep talking." Luke got to his feet and went to stand about an inch in front of Haynes.

"I'll get my team working the alibi, but in the meantime, the best thing for your brother would be to convince him to recant his confession." Haynes flicked his gaze to Faith, eyes all over her in a way that made Luke want to grab him by the collar and kick him back to Texas, where he came from. "And that's where, you, Dr. Clancy, come in. Long as you're on our side, that is," Haynes said.

Her face reddened, and Luke's fingers flexed. Maybe he'd take Torpedo by the collar after all.

"Are you suggesting I won't do everything I can to get to the truth—to help my patient?" Faith sat straighter in her chair.

"No offense, Dr. Clancy, but getting to the truth and helping your patient may not turn out to be one and the same. You and I are not in the same position. An attorney advocates for his client. That means my job here is to do anything and everything I can, short of breaking the law"—his face screwed up as if it pained him to admit to any scruples whatsoever—"to get my client, Dante Jericho, off the hook. His guilt or innocence is not my concern. You, however, most likely would not wish to do anything to help a guilty man go free." He waved his hand in the air. "Which is fine. In fact, it makes you a damn good consultant. You'll have all kinds of credibility with the jury. But before I send you in to talk to Dante as my agent, I need to know which side of the fence you're on."

"I'm on the truth side." Her eyes rose to meet Luke's even though she spoke to Haynes. "I don't believe Dante's confession is factual. I don't think he killed those people."

"That's good," Haynes said. "Then you'll likely work harder to get him to see reason and recant. And now more than ever we need him to take back that goddamn confession."

"How can he be in any more trouble than he's in now?" Faith asked.

Luke braced his hand on the edge of the conference table, dreading the answer he knew was coming.

"Last year, there were 345 executions in my home state of Texas."

"But New Mexico doesn't have the death penalty." Faith came halfway out of her seat.

Luke kicked his chair and sent it spinning across the room. It hit the opposite wall with a loud thud. "One of the victims, Kenneth Stoddard, disappeared from Amarillo. The body turned up a week later in Lubbock."

For the first time, Haynes dropped his eyes like he gave a damn. "If you can get Dante to recant his confession, Dr. Clancy, it'd be a big help. Texas wants their piece of the Santa Fe Saint. They're already making noises about extradition. Dante respects you. He trusts you. So you gotta let him know it's his life on the line. All or nothing. We're not talking life in prison. Get him to take it all back, and you just might save an innocent man's life."

FOURTEEN

Friday, August 2, 6:00 P.M.

Luke wasn't sure why he'd come. A phone call would've
been more efficient, and he had no doubt Faith would
do her best to persuade his brother to recant that
damning confession without more prompting. Yet
here he was, lounging on Faith's sectional, waiting for
her to return from the kitchen with his beer. He tore
his gaze away from the kitchen door, but his thoughts
remained on Faith.

He pictured her smiling, leaning over to hand him
a cold bottle. Her sleek red hair would fall loosely over
her shoulders, and her collar would gape open . . . just
enough for him to glimpse the tops of her lush breasts.
He might even get a peek at a nipple. Their hands
would brush. She'd look at him a moment too long
before casting a glance around the room, then he'd

touch her cheek, turn her face back to him, and drag her into his lap.

And that would spook her for damn sure.

He remembered their first meeting at the gallery. Faith had been standoffish. He'd worked hard and finally managed to put her at ease. Her smile had opened. Her posture had softened. The space between them had grown smaller and smaller until they were separated only by a vanishing layer of highly charged air. Then he'd reached out his hand to touch her, and just like that, she'd disappeared. So no. As much as he'd like to take her in his arms the moment she walked in the room, as much as he'd like to show her how good they could be together, he couldn't chance it.

He needed Faith to convince Dante to recant. Until then, he'd keep his hands off. But once she succeeded in that—and she *had* to succeed or else there'd be no hope for his brother—he intended to make good on his word.

When I see something I want, Faith, I don't apologize. I just go get it.

So who was he kidding? He knew exactly what he was doing sitting on Faith's couch. He dusted his hands together, got to his feet, and went to wait for her by the window. If she leaned over him, he'd wind up doing something he'd regret. Sensing her approach, he turned to face her.

"I only had a light. I hope that's okay." Faith touched his shoulder, then handed off the beer.

She'd poured it for him into a frozen mug, and the

frosted glass nearly froze his palm. Good. He could do with a little cooling off. From this distance, he could smell that fresh-flower scent on her skin, and he willed her to back up a little.

Instead, she came closer.

"Light's perfect." He licked ice off the rim of the mug, then took a slug. The beer burned his chest on the way down, and he sputtered out a cough.

Smooth, Luke. Real smooth.

He didn't care for small talk, so he jumped right in. "I know I've been a jerk up to now, Faith, but I promise I'll do better in the future."

Her eyes opened a bit wider. "No worries. I turned your brother in to the police. It's only natural you'd be angry."

"You did what you had to do." He should've told her that from the get-go. Instead, he'd blamed her, made her feel worse than she already did. "When I heard my brother had been arrested and accused of murder, I couldn't think straight. But like I said, I get it now, and I came to thank you for agreeing to talk with Dante. If anyone can make him see reason, get him to recant, it's you." He took another sip of beer, slowly this time. "You seem to be the only person he actually trusts."

"You're a good brother, Luke."

He didn't deserve the admiring look she was giving him, but he definitely liked it. "I'm not perfect. Hard to believe, I know."

"Oh, it's not hard at all." Her tone was teasing. "I wasn't laboring under the impression you were anywhere close to perfect. But what you've done for your brother is admirable. Even for brothers raised together, it'd be difficult for one to give away half his inheritance to the other. But that's exactly what you're doing for a man you haven't seen in almost twenty years—a man you barely know. Right now, the whole world is against Dante, but you're standing by him, and you won't let him turn you away no matter how hard he tries."

"Dante doesn't know what's good for him. I barely trust him to choose his own breakfast, so no, I can't let him face a murder charge alone."

"A lesser man would breathe a sigh of relief and wash his hands of the whole matter the moment his brother refused his help."

He shook his head, uncertain if he should disillusion her. What if she heard him out and decided he was more toad than prince? On the flip side, if he won her heart—and it seemed her heart might be the very thing he was after—based on a lie, that would be worth nothing to him. He needed her to see the man he truly was, not the man she wanted him to be. "When I was a kid, I begged my father to send both Dante and his mother, Sylvia, away."

Faith's body stiffened, and she quickly smoothed away a fleeting frown.

"I don't feel good about it, but it's true. When I was five, our housekeeper, Sylvia gave birth to Dante. Once it came to light that he was my father's son, the tension between my parents became unbearable. For nearly a decade after, if my father entered a room, my mother would walk out. I don't know how many times I caught her crying in secret. Then one day I had enough of seeing my mother cry, and I begged Dad to get rid of them. Sylvia and Dante lived in small guesthouse we called the casita. I thought if they left the ranch, things would go back to normal."

"So your father sent them away?" Faith asked softly.

"Not that day, no. But later, a month or so maybe, my father came and told me Dante was leaving for good."

"Only Dante? Not his mother, too?"

Saying this out loud was harder than he'd anticipated. "It was early morning." He tried, but he couldn't keep his voice from cracking. "A policeman came to our house. He stood in the kitchen and talked with my father a long time. That afternoon, Dad explained what had happened—Sylvia had died in an accident. She'd been drinking, and her car went over a railing on a mountain pass."

Faith's eyes flickered up as if she were trying to remember something. "Dante told me his mother died in a car accident, but he never said anything about your father's sending him away that same day." She shook her head slightly. "You'd think he'd have told his therapist something like that."

"Maybe it's too hard for him to talk about. You hadn't been treating him very long."

"Long enough for him to confess murder."

"Long enough for him to give you a *false* confession to murder. The things he confessed to you are in his head, whereas this really happened. So it's not the same at all. Anyway, the point is I wanted Dante and Sylvia out of my life. Out of my *family*. And suddenly they were gone. My father sent Dante away that very same night. He wasn't even allowed to attend Sylvia's funeral."

"I can hardly believe your father sent Dante away the same night his mother was killed."

"Heartless bastard." He jerked his hand, and beer sloshed over the side of the mug. "Even I knew that wasn't right, and I was just a selfish kid."

Her sigh was heavy, and he wondered again if telling her the truth had been the right the thing to do. But he'd kept his family's secrets far too long. Besides, the more Faith knew about the family, the more likely it was she could help his brother. "So you see, I got my wish. I never wanted Sylvia to get hurt, but the result of her death was that I got everything I asked for. Suddenly, I was an only child, the center of my parents' world. My mom and dad stayed together. Without Sylvia and Dante around as a constant reminder of my father's infidelity, they were able to tolerate each other until I left for college. I got everything, and Dante got nothing. It was almost as if my father erased them. Like Dante and Sylvia never existed."

"The fact that you resented Dante when you were a child, and for very understandable reasons, doesn't diminish what you're doing for him now." Her expression hadn't altered during the entire conversation. She still thought better of him than she should.

"I'm only doing what's right, so don't give me too much credit. Nothing I do will ever make up for what my father did to Dante, or for my own selfish part in it. But I have to try because I'm all he has left."

Like he'd imagined earlier, Faith held his gaze a moment too long, then cast a glance around the room.

His hands itched to touch her. He headed back to the couch and made a production of choosing a coaster for his beer. She sat down beside him—too close. He gripped his fingers together tightly and changed the subject. "I've decided we should have a security system installed in your house—on my dime. After all, you're helping with the case, and a woman shouldn't—"

Now her expression altered. He found what he read as her *miffed face*, adorable—and he wasn't the type of guy who found things adorable. "I don't need you to pay for a security system. I'm already shopping for the best deal, and I can handle this myself." She fiddled with the hem of her blouse. "I don't think you came here to thank me at all. I think that was just an excuse to check up on me."

He had indeed wanted to check up on her. "Busted." He grinned. "I'm checking up on someone all right, but not you. I wanted to see how my good friend, Chica, is doing."

In immediate response, a howl came from the other room. Then, Chica herself, looking a good five pounds heavier already, trotted into the room and plopped at his feet. "Good girl." He leaned down and scratched behind her ears.

Faith's smile returned. "The vet says she's a genuine miracle dog. She's not only getting fat and happy, but she should be able to carry her pups just fine." Her enthusiasm showed in both her voice and her hand gestures. "And I can tell you I didn't want to have to break the news to Tommy if there weren't going to be any puppies. He's already picking out names."

"Tommy's the kid next door, right?"

"Right." Faith's phone-messaging alert sounded. She pulled her phone from her pocket, and said, "Speak of the devil, look at this cute pic I just got of Tommy making the rounds with Chica." Her brow drew down. "Says contact unknown. Maybe Tommy's mother got a new phone."

She passed him her cell, and sure enough, there was a small boy with a big grin on his face and a tail-wagging Chica by his side.

The message alert sounded again, and Faith took her phone back. "Tommy's so—" Her voice broke off midsentence. Her hand opened, and the phone slid to the floor. She grew so still, he couldn't tell if she was breathing or not.

With one arm, he pulled her against him, and with the other hand he picked up her cell. "It's going be okay, babe."

"No. It's not going to be okay," she said in a strangled voice.

He tightened his hold on her, glanced down at the cell, and found himself unable to look away, unable even to blink. There were now two images, both from the same unknown contact. The first was the picture of Tommy and Chica. The second photo showed a bloodied boy with his hands and feet bound. Luke's heart stopped, then started again when he recognized the photo of Kenneth Stoddard.

The Saint's first victim.

Keeping his hand steady, he eased his own cell out of his pocket and hit speed dial. An operator picked up. He took a long, controlled breath. "Luke Jericho for Detective Johnson. Tell him it's urgent."

FIFTEEN

Thursday, August 8, 2:00 P.M.

Faith sat down at her desk, with Scourge across from her for their two o'clock session. She was slowly getting back to her routine, a run in the mornings, work in the afternoon, which meant either seeing her lone patient or visiting primary-care docs to introduce herself and leave her brochures. In the evenings—a Krav Maga class, or a good hard workout at the gym. But she was still having trouble sleeping, and that horrible photo sent to her cell had only made matters worse.

Her brow tightened. Detective Johnson had taken the report but hadn't seemed impressed. After verifying that Tommy was okay, and that he didn't recall anyone's bothering him or taking his photo, Johnson had promised to interview the rest of the neighbors but had not yet gotten around to it. At least the police had stepped up the patrol in Faith's neighborhood. But not only did Johnson say he didn't think there was any danger, he'd actually implied she might've somehow sent those photos to herself . . . for attention! She let out a long breath and mentally shook herself. This wasn't the time to dwell on her own problems, this was the time to focus on her patient.

Bouncing a pen between her fingers, she studied Scourge. He'd been on time for therapy as usual, dressed in a crisp white linen shirt and tan slacks as usual, greeted her politely as usual, and his eyes flitted around her office in a frenzy—also as usual. His outer perfection seemed an attempt to contain an inner chaos she discerned only by his eyes. If he lost a cuff link, or heaven forbid a shoelace came untied, she suspected it would send him hurtling over the edge. Scourge wasn't just tightly wound. He was a bomb with feet, just one tick shy of exploding.

This was their third session, and things were going nowhere fast. Despite the fact that Scourge had easily mastered the deep-muscle relaxation technique Faith had taught him, he was completely unable to remain composed when presented with the most innocuous stimulus. Last session, she'd helped him achieve a state of profound relaxation. Then she'd presented him with what she believed to be a remote and safe representation of blood: a paper scribbled in red crayon.

He'd practically levitated off the seat in a full-blown panic attack.

Bottom line: Systematic desensitization therapy wasn't working.

Her pen bounced faster. The dark circles under his eyes, the pallor of his skin, the pitiful way he picked at his nails signaled a man in genuine distress. Of note, too, was the long-sleeved shirt Scourge always wore and kept buttoned up to the collar. It was hot outside. No air-conditioning in her office, just that whirring fan, so he didn't need extra layers in here.

He's hiding something under those long sleeves.

A myriad of possibilities came to mind. At the top of the list: pickers sores. Scourge's obsessive-compulsive personality traits predisposed him to picking not only his nails but his skin as well. Or perhaps he was hiding track marks. Quickly, she discarded that hypothesis—he hadn't exhibited any signs of substance abuse, and an addict would never be able to maintain such a highly organized lifestyle. Self-inflicted scars from past suicide attempts? *Maybe.*

Her body tensed. "How's your mood?"

His eyes rolled back in his head. He twisted a hair around his finger and yanked it out. "My mood would be perfectly fine if I didn't have all this blood running through my veins. How much longer is this cure going to take?"

She had no idea. "Been sleeping?"

Bleary-eyed, he merely shook his head. This man needed relief, and he needed it now. She wasn't a fan of anxiolytics—antianxiety agents—for phobias, because while the drugs provided temporary relief, they did nothing to correct the underlying problem and often led to dependence. In this situation however, maybe tranquilizers could buy her the time she needed to cure Scourge's hemophobia, which was proving to be quite resistant to behavior therapy.

She scribbled out a prescription for oxazepam and handed it across the desk. Deliberately, she gave him a week's supply only, just in case he decided to swallow them all at once. "This'll help you sleep."

"Thanks." Relief flashed across his face, lasting mere moments before his eyes began roving the room once more.

"Scourge . . ." She truly hated to call another human being by that moniker, but for whatever reason, he seemed to be highly attached to a name that had not been provided by his parents. A few times, she'd questioned him about the origin of the nickname, but he hadn't been forthcoming. "Scourge, you've done a great job with the deep-muscle relaxation, and I think that will be a good tool for you to have in your arsenal. But—"

"It's not working," he said dryly.

"We need to try something different." She closed one eye, considering. Participant modeling would be just as slow and somewhat more cumbersome than systematic desensitization. So scratch that.

"I saw someone on *Dr. Phil* who got cured by flooding. How exactly does that work?"

Thanks a bunch, Dr. Phil. "Flooding exposes you to your feared object all at once, in a big way. At first, it's terrifying, but eventually your adrenaline response burns out. Flooding doesn't always work, but when it does, it works quickly." She shook her head. Flooding was a popular, well-established technique, but . . . "I don't think it's right for you."

His expression brightened. "I think it is. Where would we get the blood? Maybe I could cut myself."

"No." She kept her voice even, despite the troubling nature of his response. "Fake blood, like the kind in the movies, is what's generally used, but as I said, flooding isn't right for you."

"I don't want fake blood. I prefer the real thing." His eyes stopped flitting around the room and fixed on her in a way that made the hairs rise on the back of her neck.

She clenched her pen hard and dropped it onto the desk. "Scourge, has there ever been a time in your life when you felt . . ." Her voice trailed off, and she gulped a breath. "Have you ever felt attracted to blood?"

His body canted forward. His mouth curved into a half smile. A sheen of sweat formed on his brow. He pressed his index finger to his lips like a child guarding a secret. "Why certainly *not*, Dr. Clancy."

The way he said her name, drawing out each syllable, that little high-pitched lilt at the end, gave her a creepy, sick feeling in the pit of her stomach. She mentally shook herself back into therapy mode. This man needed relief, and it was her job to help him. "You have to admit some affinity for blood, though. I mean, you were working as a phlebotomist."

"I'm not sure what you mean."

"I mean that can't be a coincidence. First you're drawn to blood, and then you're repelled by it. There's more going on here than a simple phobia. I'm sure of it. Suppose there's some factor that draws you to blood, but that same factor is responsible for your fear of blood. Like a switch that flips on and off."

"What kind of factor?"

"A past trauma. Maybe a childhood memory."

"I'm telling you, I've never been drawn to blood." He smiled a half smile again, and she knew he was lying.

There had to be some way to get around his defenses. "Have you every heard of personal constructs?"

"No." He yanked another strand of hair.

"According to personal construct theory we all have unique constructs that organize our world in meaningful ways. For example, in my world, love and hate may be opposites, but to another person, indifference might be the emotion that operates in opposition to love. In any case, when we're challenged by a stressful event, change often comes in the form of what's called a slot change. We simply slide to the opposing pole of our personal construct."

"Sounds like psychobabble to me."

"But it's not, and you're smart enough to understand what I'm saying. Think about the radical atheist who suddenly finds religion. He doesn't become a believer in moderation, he becomes a fanatic about his new belief system, just as he was previously fanatic about his *disbelief*."

"Because he's fanatic by nature. I do see your point. There's only one problem."

She leaned forward, waiting.

"I'm not a blood fanatic. I've never been attracted to blood."

"I see. Mmm hmm." She stalled, gathering her thoughts. Scourge had an unnatural attachment to blood, an obsession perhaps. Only he didn't want to admit it. Perhaps if she could uncover the traumatic event that led to his obsession, she could alleviate the shame surrounding it and effect a cure. "We're done with behavior therapy—and that includes flooding. We need to dig deeper to get to the root of your problem."

"If I agree to the movie blood, then could we try flooding?"

Scourge was too unstable for an extreme technique like flooding. If she doused him with fake blood in his current, fragile state, it might even precipitate a psychotic break.

Too dangerous.

She firmed her voice. "We need a deeper therapy."

"Like dream analysis."

"Exactly, along with some other methods. The root of your fears is buried deep within your psyche, and we have to dig it up to get you well."

"That's going to take a long time." His knuckles whitened as he gripped the arms of his chair.

"Perhaps, but the tranquilizers I've prescribed will help you, and the sooner we get started, the sooner you'll get permanent relief. I'd like to start by giving you some tests."

"Ink blots. I've seen those in the movies. They seem unscientific to me, and I don't think I'd like that."

In his own way, Scourge was quite psychologically sophisticated, and yet that only seemed to make her job more difficult. "The inkblot test is called a Rorschach, and yes, that's one of the tests I'd consider, but we could start with something else if you prefer."

"I don't see how taking a psychological test will do any good. You said flooding works fast. All I need is to be exposed to blood, lots of blood, and then I'll be cured. I don't want to waste my time with inkblots and dreams. I want the fast way."

"No you don't. You want the fastest way that will help you *without making things worse*. I won't put you in jeopardy like that, so let's move on." She went around to the front of her desk and stood beside him, placed a hand on his shoulder, a gesture that should've come naturally to her. Yet somehow, with Scourge, she felt uneasy, as if she were reaching for a fanged creature who might turn and strike her down without warning. Forcing herself to maintain contact long enough to offer him some comfort, she felt his body begin to tremble beneath her palm. "I need to find out how your mind works. That's my job. You've asked for my help, and I need you to trust me in order to do that job."

"Just ask me whatever you need to know straight out. I'm not a liar." His voice rose an octave. "Veracity. You can trust in my veracity."

Scourge had the oddest way of dropping ten-dollar words into conversation. "Look. I'm not doubting your veracity."

"Then cut the bullshit."

And then at other times his phraseology strayed to the common side. "It's not bullshit. I believe you're being as truthful as you're able to be. After all, *you* came to *me*. You want to get better. You're motivated to be truthful."

"Exactly."

"But . . ." She bent down and tried to look him in the eyes. He averted his gaze. "Everyone has psychological defenses. Unconscious barriers we build up to protect ourselves from sad or frightening or shameful things. These tests are simply a way to get around those barriers."

"Kind of like psychological truth serum." He looked up, and his eyes pierced through her. "Let's just hope the truth turns out to be something you can handle, Dr. Clancy."

SIXTEEN

Faith went to her office bookcase and retrieved her set of TAT cards before returning to her usual seat behind her desk. Since Scourge was apparently skittish where psychological tests were concerned, she took it nice and easy and slowly placed the closed blue box on the desk for him to examine.

Scourge reached out and, with shaky fingers, traced the embossed gold lettering. *"Thematic Apperception Test* for adults." He crossed and uncrossed his legs. "If this TAT test circumvents my defenses like it's supposed to, you'll see all those shameful secrets you think I'm hiding."

"Not to worry. I'm only a psychiatrist, buddy, not Kreskin—and this test is only a tool." She propped her elbows on her desk. "A tool that may give me insight into your personality, into the way your mind works."

"You have secrets, too, Dr. Clancy. Shameful ones. I can see them in your eyes."

Scourge was merely displaying a classic defense mechanism: projection. He was projecting his own guilt onto her. She knew this, and yet her mind immediately turned to Grace. Her face heated. "We all have secrets. We've all done things we feel guilty about. *All of us.* Not just you. Mistakes are part of being human, nothing to be embarrassed about."

She knew these words by heart because she'd recited them to herself more than once. Hopefully, they wouldn't ring as hollow in Scourge's ears as they did in her own. "We're all human." Her fingers toyed with the necklace Grace had given her—one-half of a heart. The other half had been buried with Grace.

Scourge's gaze bounced to her throat, and she suddenly felt like the mouse to his toying cat.

"You show me your secrets, and I'll show you mine," he said, his voice a coaxing purr.

Keeping her tone all business, she said, "I'm not the patient, and this is not show-and-tell. Either you're in or you're out, but I can't help you if you're not willing to trust me."

His fingers drummed the box. He shifted in his chair, bent, and looked around on the floor as if he'd dropped something, which he certainly had not as far as she could tell. Finally, he straightened and stilled. "What do I have to do?"

"Inside this box is a set of cards." She held up her hand to block his protest. "Not inkblots. There are pictures on the cards, mostly of people. I show you a picture, and you make up a story about it. Simple and painless and we can stop anytime if anything makes you uncomfortable."

"But I don't know what story to make up."

He needed more reassurance. "Any story you want. Anything at all."

He jerked a nod. "Fine by me, then."

Infusing her tone with encouragement, she said, "Try to remember, my job is to help you. I'm on your side."

His lips trembled, and he wiped his mouth.

"Why don't you go grab a water, take a pit stop if you need one?" Faith needed time to select the cards she wanted to use with Scourge, and he shouldn't see them beforehand.

"You're trying to get rid of me."

"I certainly am." She smiled at him. "I have to set the test up privately, or the results will be spoiled. Just give me five or ten minutes, if you don't mind."

He hesitated but then complied with her wishes. While he was out of the room, Faith selected ten cards from the assortment in the box, focusing on the subject matter she thought most likely to bring Scourge's problems to the forefront, all in the safe guise of a make-believe story. She'd just completed her selection when he returned with two styrofoam cups of water.

"Thanks. How thoughtful of you." She accepted the water he held out and waited for him to take a seat, make himself comfortable. Which was going to take a while, judging from all the repositioning of legs and folding and unfolding of arms.

Finally, he seemed settled in.

"Ready. Here we go." She handed him a card, and just having something to hold in his hands helped him relax. He breathed in and out slowly. "That's great. You're using your relaxation techniques without being prompted." He actually seemed to be learning to cope with his anxiety in a productive way, and that was a very good sign.

"I'm recording." She turned on a handheld recorder. Later, she'd use the playback to score and analyze the results.

He turned the card upside down, sideways, looked at the back side, flipped it over again. "This is a very strange-looking picture."

No argument there. The images on card 13MF were indeed strange—the kind that stirred the imagination . . . and the psychosexual urges. In residency, they not so jokingly called it the sex card. It depicted a woman lying in bed, nude from the chest up. Beside her, a man stood hanging his head, hiding his eyes with his forearm.

Scourge continued to look at the card, but when he didn't volunteer any more information she prompted him. "I'd like you to make up a story about what you see. It can be any story you like, but it should have a beginning, a middle, and an end. Try to make it as dramatic as you can. Oh, and I'll want to know what the characters in the story are thinking and feeling."

"Sure. But what's going on with the woman in bed. Is she asleep, or is she dead?"

"Up to you. I'm afraid I can't answer any questions about the cards. There's no right or wrong story, only what you choose."

He was quiet a good five minutes. Faith relaxed into her chair and stretched her legs; rushing him would be counterproductive.

At last, he said, "She's dead."

Keeping her voice and face neutral, she reminded him, "I need you to tell me a beginning, a middle, and an end. I want to know what the characters are thinking and feeling."

"Right. Well, that's her son, and he killed her. He's upset, that's why he's hiding his eyes. He's glad she's dead, but he's also sad because now he doesn't have anyone to take care of him. Only he's stupid because his mother never took care of him in the first place. He's already forgotten that's the reason he killed her. Drunks shouldn't have kids."

"And?"

"And he runs away and makes a new life for himself and lives happily ever after. The end."

Faith took mental notes only—she had the recorder to review later. Scourge's response to the first card lacked the typical elements. Most patients saw the man and woman as being near the same age, and while some described the woman lying in the bed as dead, most said she was sleeping. Typical stories contained either overt or subtle sexual elements. Scourge's story held none. The fact that his story was so different meant it was very personal and very significant.

Mother issues.

After presenting Scourge with several more cards, he seemed to relax into the task and get the hang of things. She no longer needed to remind him to tell her what the characters were thinking and feeling or tell a complete story. In response to each story, she offered no judgment or evaluation.

But her heart squeezed a little at Scourge's reactions. While she kept her expressions as neutral as possible, he beamed like a boy who'd just brought home a straight-A report card to his parents. For Scourge, the mere absence of criticism seemed equal to the highest of praise. If only she could touch his sleeve, tell him *well done,* but that would've contaminated the process.

Each story grew more elaborate than the next, and Scourge was on a quite a roll. But it'd been over an hour, and she still had one more card to show him. Card 2 depicted a family—a teenage girl holding books in her arms, a man plowing a field in the background, and a pregnant woman standing to the side. Faith leaned forward, eager to learn his reaction to the family card.

"Oh," he said in a loud voice. He set the card on her desk and jabbed it repeatedly with his index finger. "This is going to be my favorite story."

Okay. People didn't usually get quite that jazzed about the farm family, so maybe she'd been right to select the card. Suppressing a smile, she made no comment.

"So, this girl looks to be around sixteen. Let's call her Nancy."

First character he'd named. She twisted in her chair.

He looked up, eyes glittering with excitement. "See these books? Nancy's a good student. She's on the honor roll, student council, the whole nine yards. But today she has to hurry with her homework because she's getting ready for a meeting of the 4-H club."

It wasn't easy for to hide her surprise. The animated way Scourge recounted his story, the rich details—giving the characters names and ages—was highly unusual. She bit her lower lip and focused her eyes on the bookcase. "Mmm hmm."

"The father's a rich man, he's done very very well for himself with that farm of his, but he's strict and a tough disciplinarian. Nancy's a good girl, though, so he doesn't need to worry about her. She's helpful and kind. Everyone loves her. She's the type of girl who'll go straight to heaven when she dies."

"Mmm hmm." Lots of people dying today.

Jumping up, he nearly spilled his water on the card but caught it at the last moment. "The mother, let's call her Bonnie, doesn't look happy. She's got four kids, and her husband doesn't pay attention to her anymore. He's too busy with church and running the farm to take notice of his wife. Some days, Bonnie doesn't even bother getting dressed."

He'd named both the mother and the daughter. Highly unusual. Maybe he'd had an aunt named Bonnie, or a cousin named Nancy. You'd never know he was constructing a family from thin air. He talked as if he knew them well. Perhaps he'd imagined himself in a different, happier family than his own. Perhaps this wasn't the first time he'd thought about Bonnie and Nancy. She checked her watch.

"You want an end?"

She nodded.

"Because they're good people, they have nothing to worry about. The end."

Scourge handed her the card, his face flushed and glowing. This being the final card, there was little risk of her contaminating the process any longer. She decided to venture a question. "What do you mean, *because they're good people, they have nothing to worry about?*"

A wide smile on his face, he said, "I enjoyed this, Dr. Clancy. I really did."

She tried again. "Why doesn't this family need to worry?"

"Because they're going to heaven—all of them."

SEVENTEEN

Friday, August 9, 5:00 P.M.

Faith had come to the jail to convince Dante to recant—if he was in fact innocent—and she wasn't leaving until she'd accomplished her mission.

"This place robs them of their dignity," Sergeant Sheila Nesbitt remarked as she gave Faith a thorough pat down. "Try not to let it get to you." Her low voice had the kind of soothing tone that could quiet a spooked animal. "Losing your dignity is worse than losing your freedom, so I never show my prisoners I notice. Act cool. That's the best way if you can manage it."

Faith felt a little of her own dignity drain away as the sergeant checked her for contraband. Teddy Torpedo Haynes had appointed Faith as his agent and managed to get her a private visit with Dante at the jail. The pat down was necessary for everyone's safety, and it was no big deal compared to the searches the inmates endured.

"I'll be right outside this door." Nesbitt, a stately African-American woman with soft eyes and a hard body, gave Faith a look full of meaning.

"Thanks." Faith wasn't worried. After all, she'd been alone with Dante on many occasions with no security, and from what she could see, there was simply no way Dante could do her harm under these circumstances. Her gratitude to Sergeant Nesbitt was not so much for the protection she offered as for the kindness toward the prisoners reflected in her words. Prior to this, Faith's image of jailers had been constructed mostly from television shows and B movies. Sergeant Sheila Nesbitt had dramatically altered Faith's image for the better in the less than five minutes they'd spent together.

A loud *clank* sounded as the door latched shut behind Nesbitt. Faith placed a hand on her stomach and took a slow breath. A shiver ran down her spine as she surveyed the visitation room, where a sense of hopelessness gusted out the air-conditioning vents along with the too-cold air. The room was all concrete, painted the dirty gray of slush on a highway. Concrete walls. Concrete floors. Even the furniture was poured concrete. Nobody was going to pick up a table or chair and use it as a weapon in this place.

The *click* of her heels echoed through the room as she approached the picnic-style table in the back. No way Dante didn't hear her coming, but he kept his head down, avoiding the moment when he'd have to meet her eyes. That gave her a chance to compose herself and blank her expression. Or as Nesbitt would put it, to regain her cool. She allowed herself one and only one glance at the chain that wrapped Dante's midsection and looped through a metal ring bolted into the floor. As she sat down at the table across from him, she kept her head up, her back straight.

Dante was dressed in a gray jumpsuit that matched the color of the walls, floor, and furniture. His shackled hands rested on the tabletop, and they, too, were chained to a ring, this one bolted into the concrete bench.

"Thanks for agreeing to see me," Faith said in as casual a tone as she could summon while her heart was withering in her chest. This place did indeed rob a person of his dignity.

"You're wasting your time, Dr. Clancy." Dante whipped his head up, raised his hands, and literally rattled his chains.

"I've got plenty of time, and I don't consider you a waste."

His eyes had grown dimmer, or maybe it was just all the gray that made them look so flat. Dark bags puffed out the area under his lids, and his skin drooped off his carved cheekbones. He must be refusing food altogether to lose noticeable weight in such a short time. Her chest grew heavy, and a lump formed in her throat. Beneath the table, her feet twisted. But she hadn't come here to pity him. She'd come to empower him, to make him understand he could change his circumstance by telling the truth.

Keeping her tone all business, she asked, "Do you mind if I record our conversation?" Torpedo needed to know everything Dante said, verbatim.

"Suit yourself." Dante's forehead wrinkled. "I don't mind talking to you. But don't think you can convince me to withdraw my confession. I'm guilty as charged."

Ah, so he knew exactly why she'd come. If this were a therapy session, she'd have time to help him reach a good decision on his own, slowly. But this wasn't a therapy session, and there was simply no time to coddle him. It was entirely possible this was the only private interview she'd be allowed. "Then why did you agree to let Mr. Haynes enter a not-guilty plea for you at the arraignment?"

"Mr. Haynes?"

The startled look that passed over Dante's face reminded Faith of a child awakening from a bad dream.

"Your attorney, Teddy Haynes."

He jerked his hands, and his chains clanked together. "He's not my attorney. I never agreed to anything."

"Yes, Dante, you did. You told your brother you wanted a lawyer, and Luke hired Teddy Haynes." Hopefully, the facts would pull him back to reality.

His eyes rolled back in his head. "Right. Teddy

Haynes. Luke got me a lawyer." He pushed his body as close to her as he was able. "You want to help me, don't you, Dr. Clancy?"

Automatically, she reached out her hand to touch his arm, and when she did the cold metal of his shackles brushed her fingers, jolting her. "Yes. That's why I'm here. I want to help."

"Then tell my brother to back off." His lips pulled at the corners, and he bared his teeth at her. He was putting on a show to scare her again.

She pulled her hand away. This time she wouldn't be manipulated. "I'm afraid I can't do that, and even if I tried, Luke would never walk away from you, Dante. He cares about you too much."

"It's all an act. He doesn't give a damn about me. He just doesn't want the Jericho name dragged through the dirt."

"I don't believe that, and besides, he's all the family you've got." She gave him a pointed look. "You should give him a chance."

"Like you gave your family a chance?" Again with the manipulation.

She forced herself not to drop her eyes, but inwardly she cringed. Dante knew things about her—about her family. He'd told her so on the day he confessed. Her fingers went to her throat, but the necklace Grace had given her wasn't there. No jewelry allowed. "I didn't come here to talk about me. Maybe this is a waste of my time after all." She came to her feet—time to get tough, for both their sakes.

"Wait. Don't be mad." A muscle beneath his eye started to twitch.

"Why shouldn't I be mad?" She might be using her anger strategically, but she wasn't faking it. It pissed her off that he'd invaded her privacy—and more importantly that he'd invaded the privacy of people she loved.

"I don't want you to go." His eyes turned glossy. He wasn't faking either.

She hesitated, pretending to debate whether to stay or go. She turned her head from side to side before looking back at Dante. "Then answer this question. If you're guilty as charged, why did you enter a not-guilty plea?"

His feet tip-tapped on the concrete floor. "I had to. If I had pleaded guilty, there wouldn't have been a reason to try me. I want to go to trial. I want my day in court."

"I don't understand."

"I want a jury to convict me, and I want a judge to confirm my guilt." The way his voice cracked was heartbreakingly earnest.

Her hands formed tight balls. Oh God. She could actually see some sort of sick logic at work here. "Just to be clear. You want a judge and jury to publicly declare you a guilty man. Have I got that right?"

"Exactly." He breathed a sigh, and his shoulders lowered.

"But Mr. Haynes says that there's nothing in your confession beyond the information that was made public through newspaper accounts. Mr. Haynes thinks you might not have killed those people at all."

"If I did kill them, I deserve to be locked up for the rest of my life."

"*If* you killed them?"

"I killed them. I know I did. I told you, the police were closing in on me. They wouldn't be after me if I hadn't done something very, very bad."

Classic paranoia. And this particular delusion of guilt was going to buy him a lethal injection if she didn't find a way to get through to him. "Dante, do you or don't you actually remember committing any of the murders to which you've confessed?"

"No."

No!

"In your statement, you said you blew Nancy Aberdeen's head off with a shotgun and then put a rosary in her hand. Did you do those things?" She firmed her voice, letting him know she'd be angry if he lied to her. It was clear he valued her approval, and if the only way to save his life was to withdraw that approval, she wouldn't hesitate.

"No."

"What about William Carmichael, and Linda Peabody and Ken Stoddard. Did you have anything to do with any of their deaths?"

"No."

"Then why, Dante, why would you say you did?"

"Because I'm a guilty man. I killed my mother."

She slapped her palm on the table, and the concrete bit back. "Your mother died in a car accident nearly twenty years ago."

"Because of me!"

"Stop being childish. You weren't even in the car." She turned up the heat. Let him hear how ludicrous his assertion was. "You were eight years old, whad'ya do, cut the brakes?"

"She had too much to drink. She argued with my father . . . about me. She wished I was never born. That's what she said."

He was sobbing now.

Steeling her heart against his cries, she turned her back and took a step toward the door.

"Don't go. Please don't go," he gasped.

"I'm done here." Her throat closed, the cruel words nearly choking her, but she had no choice—not if she wanted to save an innocent man from going to prison . . . or worse.

"What do you want from me? Please don't go. Just tell me what you want."

Whirling to face him, she said, "I want you to agree to meet with Teddy Haynes, and I want you to tell him the truth."

He shook his head. "I can't. I need to be punished. And I have nowhere to go. No one to care if I live out the rest of my days in prison."

"Dante. Listen to me very carefully. I'm done playing games with you. You think you're being honorable, but you're not. Your brother cares about you, and you're hurting him by lying to the police. You're hurting a lot of other people, too." She had his attention so she kept going. "The minute you confessed, the police stopped looking for the Saint. So if the real Saint kills again while the police are wasting their time with you, you really will be guilty of murder." She took a backward step toward the door.

"I'll talk to my attorney. I swear. Just promise you'll come to see me again."

"After you keep your end of the bargain."

His head bobbed excitedly. "Yes. Yes. I promise."

She sought his gaze and held it. "And there's one other thing, Dante. Texas wants to extradite you for the Saint's crime there. And unlike New Mexico, Texas has a death penalty. So when Teddy Haynes comes by to see you, you better listen to what he says. You better start telling the truth—on the record—because if you don't, I promise you, you won't see me again."

EIGHTEEN

Saturday, August 10, 11:00 A.M.

Five more days.

The light changed to green, and Scourge eased his foot on the gas, careful to maintain a speed well below the limit. The last thing he needed was to make another mistake. He pulled his lower lip between his teeth and sucked hard. He shouldn't have sent those photos to Dr. Clancy, but he hadn't been able to resist the urge to let her know that the Saint was still on the loose. He hadn't been able to resist the urge to let her know he was watching her . . . and her friends. Despite the sweltering heat, his teeth chattered loudly as he considered what would happen if the boy told the police about the black-haired man he'd seen at Dr. Clancy's house. This damn phobia had thrown his whole system off. He'd never have made a mistake like that in the past.

Concentrate on the task at hand.

Only five more days.

He needed his cure sooner than later. Right now, that was the only thing he should be thinking about. Scourge fixed his eyes on the road ahead. This was one of those rare occasions he'd decided to take his truck on a nonduty run. Generally, he preferred to walk, and when that wasn't possible, he'd bite the bullet—the metaphor made him chuckle, easing the tension in his chest—and rake up cab fare. But with his cure just around the corner . . . literally . . . it was time to gas her up, air the tires, and take her for a spin to make sure she was in good working condition.

The cab of his Special Duty truck was cramped, unlike the large, open-roofed bed in the back, flanked only by wooden slats. The vehicle had previously been owned by a landscaper who used it to haul debris. There was room to breathe in the back, for the living, that is, and more than once, Scourge wished he could ride in that big open bed with the cargo instead of up here in this hot, closed space.

This was one of those times.

He'd rolled down the windows, but that offered little relief. Sweat leaked from his scalp into his eyes, and as soon as he blinked the sting away, more followed. In order to keep as much distance as possible between the roof of the truck and the top of his head, he kept his chin tucked to his chest. Reaching around, he rubbed the cramp out of the back of his neck and scratched the area where his collar rubbed against his skin.

Too much starch perhaps.

No.

No such thing as too much starch in a collar. His cotton shirt clung to his back, and he knew his perspiration had ruined its pristine appearance. Thank goodness Three Little Pigs was around the next turn.

He swerved around the corner. The act of driving didn't faze him—quite the contrary. The feel of all that power roaring to life when he fired up his truck's ignition, the ability to control that heavy mass of steel with a spin of the wheel gave him a charge. Too bad a convertible wasn't in his budget. It was only this damn claustrophobic cab that made his head ache.

But he would manage. Understanding why closed spaces gave him the willies helped him to cope during the times when driving his truck was warranted. At school, he'd dreamt of white plastic walls, over him, under him, around him. He'd dreamt of peering through metal bars, his eyes wet, his throat hoarse from crying, and he'd wake up with his heart racing in his chest and the certainty he was going to die.

For a time, a young novitiate at Saint Catherine's had taken him under her wing. Cecily snuck him sweets and books and once she even hugged him after a particularly vivid nightmare. On that night, he'd recited his dream to her in detail, then next morning, she'd taken him aside and explained that his dream wasn't a dream at all.

It was a memory.

According to his case file, his mother used to keep

him in a puppy crate whenever she drank, which was every night. She claimed this was for his own safety because she was prone to passing out and couldn't properly supervise him. The kindhearted novitiate told him that misguided though it might have been, the crating was an act of love, and anyway, God expects us to forgive those who've wronged us, and he should pray to God to give him the strength to forgive his mother. But Scourge didn't really think there was anything to forgive. Putting a child in a crate seemed logical enough to him.

True, it'd left him with a slight touch of claustrophobia, but nothing he couldn't handle. When absolutely necessary, he could grit his teeth, climb in his truck, and get where he needed to go. And here he was now—at Three Little Pigs.

The real challenge was not the journey here but rather how to cope with the hematogenous sights and smells of the butcher shop.

Hematogenous: involving or arising from blood.

He removed a surgical mask from his glove compartment and placed it over his mouth and nose, then looped it around his ears. Typically, he used the mask on public transportation, while grocery shopping, and the like, to protect himself from the germs of the masses, but today it would serve to filter out the smell of blood. A scent he'd relished in the past. Once, that scent had made his dick hard and his confidence soar. Now, a mere whiff could bring him whimpering to his knees.

Not for long.

Hoping to mediate the red color of the meats, he donned a pair of dark glasses and exited his car. With his shoulder, he pressed open a glass door painted with a mural of Porky Pig, then eased himself into the butcher shop one body part at a time.

He snorted. If he were the owner, he'd make sure the mural depicted the correct swine, but Hugo apparently didn't see the need for consistency. He seemed perfectly content to allow Porky to welcome customers to Three Little Pigs. Hugo wasn't the sharpest knife in the butcher's block, but he was a jolly good fellow, and Scourge trusted him.

With one hand stuck out behind him, he backed up to the counter and cleared his throat to get Hugo's attention. Just in case backing into the shop wearing a mask hadn't done the trick. Anyway, he had no intention of turning around so that he could face off with a long counter of meaty steaks and fatty rolls of fleshy sausages, all leaking juicy red blood onto the white butcher paper below.

"That you, Scourge?" Hugo boomed in a louder than normal voice, perhaps assuming Scourge's mask signaled some sort of hearing impairment.

That would be very Hugo.

Scourge was one of Hugo's best customers, and in the days before he'd developed his hemophobia, he'd loved lingering in the shop, discussing the butchering process and hearing details from Hugo's glory days at the slaughterhouse. Hugo still had slaughterhouse connections, and this enabled him to get extraordinary deals and pass on the savings to his customers.

It hadn't been unusual for Scourge to spend the better part of a Saturday chewing the fat (again, he chuckled under his breath) with Hugo. Once, Hugo had even given Scourge a tour of the meat locker, allowing him to make the acquaintance of the carcasses as they patiently awaited their turn to be carved into the finest fresh meats in Santa Fe. It'd thrilled him, and his mouth watered in anticipation of being able to enjoy such a treat in the future—the very near future.

"It's me," Scourge said.

"Do you maybe wanna turn around and tell me why you're wearing that mask? You sick or something?"

"Not sick exactly, but no, I can't turn around. Come out from behind the counter, and I'll explain everything." Scourge sidled up to a round Formica table with a steel base and sat facing the window, his back to the dangerous meat counter. Even filtered through his mask, the smell of fresh blood made his palms sweat and his knees knock. He blew out a few panting breaths. *Hee hee hee*—like expectant ladies do in Lamaze class, but it only made him dizzy.

Hugo pulled up a stool facing him. "What'cha need, buddy. You sure you're not sick?"

"I already said I'm not. I've got a job for you. A very important one."

Hugo eyed him sideways. "This job you got for me. Is it legal?"

"Pays real good."

"I'm up for most anything if the pay is right. Mrs. Simpson—that saucy gal works down at the lab with you—said you had some kind of a crackdown and lost your job. You sure you can pay me?"

"Breakdown, Hugo, not crackdown, and yes, I promise to make it worth your while." His hot breath, trapped beneath his mask, blew back against his face as he spoke. "You still got a buddy down at the slaughterhouse?"

NINETEEN

Saturday, August 10, 7:00 P.M.

Faith had begun the celebration early. One more sip
of champagne couldn't hurt, she thought, and swilled
what remained of her third glass. Yesterday, Dante had
met with Torpedo and officially recanted his confession. Tonight, Luke was treating her to a nice dinner as
a thank-you, which seemed a perfectly civil, perfectly
reasonable thing, given her role in persuading Dante
to recant. But as she'd prepared herself for an evening
out with Luke, she'd felt anything *but* reasonable.

This morning, she'd awakened even earlier than
usual and gone for a run, followed by a hard workout
at the gym, but upon returning home, she'd found
herself still full of restless energy. After cleaning her
kitchen twice, she'd picked up the latest Sandra Brown
but couldn't concentrate. She'd then decided to treat

herself to a rare mani-pedi. At the salon, the manicurist had commented on her trembling hands. She dripped more champagne into her glass. She hadn't been this keyed up since senior prom—the night she gave it up to Ricky Charleston.

And Luke wasn't helping matters any by being ridiculously thoughtful. Not that Luke had been thoughtless to this point, far from it, but she hadn't expected all the extra little touches he'd added to make tonight special. This wasn't a date. They'd both agreed on that much, but for a thank-you dinner, he seemed to be going a bit overboard.

Earlier today, he'd messengered over a case of white-chocolate-covered dog bones for Chica—an impossible-to-resist gesture—and three menus. One each from El Meson, Geronimo, and Café Pasqual and asked her to choose her poison. She'd wound up selecting Geronimo because she wanted to try the *mignardises*, a treat described as pâté de fruit, toffee, fudge, truffles, and housemade marshmallows. House-made marshmallows—just think of it. Later, the messenger had returned for her reply and delivered a large bouquet of flowers, all white, all fragrant: lilies, roses, carnations, and her favorite—gardenias. A stunning combination that not only filled her entire home with sweetness and light, it showed Luke had been paying attention. He already knew her tastes. That was the kind of chivalry a man couldn't fake. He hadn't sent the most expensive flowers; he'd sent the flowers she loved most.

When the doorbell rang, she knocked over her champagne flute—fortunately it was both plastic and empty—and stepped outside. Golden porchlight sifted across Luke's profile, striking his face just so, darkening shadows and highlighting his strong jaw, polishing the hard blue of his eyes into shining lapis. His appearance was so striking, she had to hold back a little gasp of appreciation.

He offered her his arm.

She took it, and he stole her breath when he bent and placed a tender kiss on the top of her head.

"You're stunning, Faith." The low timbre of his voice sent shivers racing down her spine. Her knees went weak. She was a cliché walking—no, make that stumbling. Next thing you know, she'd have butterflies in her tummy. He smiled and shook his head. "Absolutely stunning."

Yep. A whole swarm of winged creatures took flight right on cue.

"Thanks," she said, and drew a shuddering breath. "But this is all too much and oh, my goodness, you *really* didn't need to pick me up in the limo."

"Oh, but I *really* did." His eyes probed hers, as if searching for approval. "You and I got off on the wrong foot right from the start. First at my gallery, then later, when I scooped you up—"

She flapped a forgiving hand as she wobbled down the drive. "To stop me from putting a heel in doggie doo."

He grinned. "Sure. Let's go with that, and then I

locked you—inadvertently locked you—in my limousine." He opened the door for her, and she slid inside. He climbed in after her. "I know how frightening my imitation of a caveman must have been. I was completely out of line, and I'm hoping you'll forgive me. I brought the limo tonight because I want to wipe the slate clean. I want a do-over . . . if you will."

"I will," she whispered. "But believe me, Luke, this whole pampering and seduction scenario is truly unnecessary. I'm thrilled that your brother recanted his confession, and I'm very glad that I was able to help convince him. But I don't need expensive dinners and my favorite flowers. I consider Dante my responsibility."

"And you think that's what this is about. I'm plying you with flowers and champagne in order to secure your ongoing help with my brother?" He reached for a bottle of bubbly.

No more alcohol. She covered a hiccup and waved a no-thanks. "Aren't you?" Apparently, she was as susceptible to the Jericho charm as any other woman because even though she knew Luke had ulterior motives, her tummy had gone fizzy as a flute of Dom Pérignon.

"No." His voice came out gruff, and he looked away so quickly she couldn't see the reaction in his eyes. If she didn't know better, she'd swear, his feelings were hurt.

On impulse, she reached out and turned his face back to hers. Heaven help her, his eyes had deepened to a blue-black that reminded her of the sky just before midnight. She dropped her hand quickly to her lap. "Then why go to all this trouble?"

"I've already told you. I want a do-over. Is it really so difficult for you to believe I like you?" He leaned in, and she detected a highly male scent rising off his heated skin.

She wished she could just close her eyes and inhale, enjoy the moment like any other woman.

"Dante's recanted his confession. I promised myself I wouldn't make my move until then. But now I don't see any reason not to pursue what I want."

She drew back, fanned herself with her hand. "And . . . are you saying . . . me? You want me?" Her voice squeaked out in the most juvenile way.

Their eyes met. There wasn't a hint of falseness in his expression. In fact, he looked almost vulnerable. Her gaze fell on his massive shoulders, his powerful arms. Maybe *vulnerable* wasn't exactly right. *Sincere.* Yes, that was more like it.

What was the big deal anyway? Luke was right. She was no longer treating Dante. She'd succeeded in persuading him to listen to his attorneys. She planned to refer him to another psychiatrist as soon as he was released from jail, and anyway, *Luke* wasn't her patient. She would never be foolish enough to allow herself to fall for a man like Luke Jericho, or any other man for that matter, but there was no harm in one night of . . . celebration. "I'm thirsty," she said, and closed her eyes, inhaled, enjoyed.

"I'll pop a cork." He reached for the bottle of champagne, and she reached out, touching his forearm. The softness of his skin and the brush of fine hairs on her palm made her head feel lighter than champagne ever could.

"I'm not thirsty for champagne." She walked her fingers down his arm all the way to his hand and turned his palm up, traced circles with her thumb, like he'd done to her that day in her living room. The dusky look that came over his face, the way his eyes took on a hooded appearance encouraged her. "What was it you said before?"

He sat perfectly still and silent, his mouth tipped into the slightest smile.

She leaned toward him, tilted her face near his, and closed her eyes. "I believe you said something like, *I don't seduce women, they seduce me.*" Heart fluttering in her chest, she found and kissed the tip of his nose. "Well, Mr. Jericho, prepare to be seduced."

She waited a beat and let her hand fall to his lap, exploring. She opened her eyes, leaned in closer, then she heard a hoarse moan.

"No way, Clancy. If anyone's in charge of the seduction tonight, it's me." His hand clasped the back of her head and pulled her in for a kiss. A rough, hard unapologetic meeting of the lips . . . and of the minds. He kissed her until she couldn't breathe, and when she pulled back for air, he slipped his hand around her back and unzipped her dress.

Another moan. This time from her. Anticipation pulsed through her, softening her, making her ready.

Beneath her palm, he was already hard, his erection straining against his slacks. She rubbed her hand over the fine linen, delighting in the heat seeping through the cloth. She traced his long shape with her fingers, and then it was her turn to unzip.

"Faith." He closed his hand over hers. "I know how to control my body, but even I have my limits, and we're reaching them fast. So if you think this is something you might regret—"

Her eyes squared with his. "I want this. I want you."

"Right here? Right now?" His Adam's apple worked in a hard swallow.

The briefest moment of doubt flashed across her mind. The tenderness in his voice, the hunger in his eyes reached someplace deep inside her heart, and like a hand snatched away her defenses. She might indeed regret this later, but for now . . . She slipped her dress down to her waist and unsnapped her front-closure bra. Her head fell back, and her eyes closed once more.

Luke pressed the intercom—she assumed. Because she heard him bite out an order to the chauffeur. "Drive around. I'll let you know when to take us to the restaurant. Until then, I don't want to be disturbed."

"Yes, sir," the driver responded without intonation.

"Open your eyes, Faith. This is your last warning."

His commanding voice both excited and terrified her.

Luke wasn't the safe, controllable type of man Faith usually allowed herself to be with. He was warning her, and she knew she should heed his message. She opened her eyes to find his gaze scorching her bare breasts. She touched her nipples, pinching them between her fingers. "No, Luke. This is *your* last warning."

A sound very much like a growl came out of his throat, and he reached under her dress, pulled her thong to her ankles and urged her onto her back in one swift motion. The leather seat squeaked as her skin slid over it. Luke slipped off her shoes and thong, then pushed her dress to her waist so that now both her top and bottom were exposed. Her body was tightening and aching and demanding his touch.

He plucked her hands from her breasts, then leaned back and took a long look. "You're even more beautiful than I imagined." Cradling her breasts with both hands, he said, "Your nipples are so pink." His head bent between them. "You always smell like flowers." He murmured something else against her skin and pulled one nipple into his mouth, setting off ripples of pleasure.

Her back arched, and he tugged and nipped at her until she was writhing beneath him. Fumbling with his slacks, she finally managed to push them down and dip her hands inside his silk boxers. The waistband pressed against the back of her hand and his cock leapt beneath her palm. Scents of musk and leather mingled heavily around them as she sank deeper into the billowed cushions.

Luke kicked off his shoes and boxers and lifted her leg in the air, caressing her ankle. Her other leg bent at the knee and fell back against the seat, opening her to his devouring gaze. "I've thought of you like this, you know."

His words stole her breath with their intensity. His open desire set her body ablaze. She was helpless against the whispering in her heart. *Yes. More please.*

Watching her eyes, he spread her folds with his fingers, then his gaze traveled to her most intimate places. "I've imagined stroking you." He reached between her legs and pressed two fingers inside, working them higher, deeper.

Luke.

"I've imagined tasting you," He kissed his way up her thigh and pressed his tongue between her legs, his fingers and mouth playing in unison until she cried out with need. Her heart fluttered dangerously with every caress, but it was too late to stop this now.

"Please." She tugged at his shoulders, and he surged over her. His weight crushed her chest, but she didn't care. She wanted him closer, on top of her, inside her.

"Faith." He kissed the corner of her mouth, and she opened her lips. He slipped his tongue inside her mouth and ground his pelvis against hers. She was ready, so ready, arching into his touch, her hand stroking him, and guiding his hard length to where she needed it. "Please," she begged, and brought him against her opening.

"Not yet."

He slid higher so that his shaft rubbed over her. "I love the way you feel, Faith. So wet, so sweet." He slipped his fingers inside again. "So tight. I want to feel that tight energy around my cock."

He swirled his fingers inside her and circled his tongue over her nipple, and she felt herself climbing up, up, up toward that tight, aching peak.

"Now." He moaned in her ear, slid his fingers out, then pressed into her. And when he'd sunk himself to the hilt, he began to thrust, slowly at first then faster and harder. The limo hit a dip in the road and drove him even deeper, adding to her pleasure . . . and her torture. There was no holding back now. As her muscles clamped around him, he whispered in her ear, "That's it Faith, come for me. Since the first moment I saw you, this was what I wanted, to feel you shatter in my arms."

Unable to stop herself from doing just what he'd asked, she cried out. He drove into her over and over, still whispering in her ear, urging her forward until at the very moment she soared to her peak, he jerked his head back and let out a low moan.

After, when they'd put themselves back together and reassembled their clothing as respectably as possible, she rested her head on his shoulder.

He pressed a soft kiss to her lips, and the realization of what she'd done started to sink in. She'd held nothing back from Luke, opened not just her body but her heart for him. And her heart was something she hadn't intended to offer up. She raised her head to meet his gaze. "This was just for tonight. You know that, right?"

His eyes glittered in the moonlight. "Don't kid yourself, Faith."

And before she could answer, the driver was there, opening the door for her to step out of the car and begin her special evening on the town.

Her feet had just hit the sidewalk when Luke's cell buzzed. He pulled it out to turn it off and stopped short.

"What?" she asked, not liking the sudden change in his expression.

"It's from Torpedo—nobody gives a damn Dante recanted. He says get ready for the fight of our lives."

TWENTY

Sunday, August 11, 3:00 P.M.

Four more days.

Scourge's thoughts were as repetitive as the *tick tick tick* of the clock he'd purchased from Burton's Antiques that hung on his kitchen wall. He stared first at the swinging brass pendulum, then out the kitchen window, then back to the pendulum again. Ever since his reconnaissance mission to Dr. Clancy's place, he'd been ruminating about that boy Tommy and his dog. And now, through his own stupidity, because he'd sent that photo without taking his usual time to think things through, he'd pointed the police's attention to Tommy and made matters worse.

It wasn't like him to be careless. Not at all. He really wasn't himself these days.

He let out a long sigh.

The animal was an easy enough fix. Scourge had no qualms about slipping the mongrel a nice piece of beef from Hugo's butcher shop—marinated in antifreeze, of course. The mangy mutt was already sick. Anyone could see that. He'd be doing the bitch a favor, putting her out of her misery—no harm, no foul. In fact, he'd make sure Chica—yes that was what Tommy had called her—would meet her maker in style. He'd decided on filet mignon for the poisoning. How many dogs get to feast on a filet as their last meal?

But the boy was a different matter.

In many ways, Tommy reminded him of himself at that age—all curly black hair and slumped shoulders. Like Scourge, the boy seemed underdeveloped and scared of his own shadow. In other words, a puny loser. Probably got bullied more than most.

Besides, Tommy had those imploring eyes that called out, *love me love me love me,* but you just knew no one ever had. Scourge thought about sparing him. As far as he could tell, the kid hadn't told the police about their little encounter yet. But, of course, he couldn't know that for certain. He fisted his hands and clamped his jaw shut.

No witnesses.

The book was very clear on that particular point. Four years ago, in Amarillo, a kid named Jeremy Jacobs had seen Scourge with Kenny Stoddard. Scourge knew then he shouldn't have let Jeremy live. Closing his eyes, he remembered that nagging voice:

Would you forget that damn book, for once? Sometimes

*you have to think for yourself. Jeremy's become a suspect.
Killing him will eliminate him as one. No one believes him,
anyway.*

And so he'd broken the book's rule, and he'd let
Jeremy live. Now there was another witness, Tommy.
Scourge had convinced Tommy he was Faith's brother,
and he didn't think the boy would talk, but he couldn't
take that chance. If Tommy *did* give the police a description, they might put it together with what Jeremy
had told them four years ago, and this time, they'd believe it. This time, they'd come looking for the black-
haired man.

No witnesses.

Killing Tommy might not be part of the original
plan, but then again, neither was spending the rest of
his life in prison, *or worse.* His stomach knotted. He
didn't want to end up hanging from the end of a rope
like Perry, for Chrissake. They say you lose control of
your bowel and bladder when they hang you, and that
was completely unacceptable to Scourge.

Tommy had to die.

But . . . maybe he could think of a way to make
his death a positive experience. Like Chica and the filet
mignon. He'd ponder that one a while and see what he
could come up with.

Head throbbing, he went to the kitchen cabinet and
downed a handful of aspirin. He used Bayer baby aspirin because he liked to be able to swallow a handful
at a time, just like good ol' Perry used to do. Next he
made his way to the bedroom, stripped off his shirt

and slacks, hung them up neatly. As he slid the mirrored closet door closed, his reflection caught his eye.

Bending one knee, he flexed his right biceps, animating his blue tiger tattoo. Trying out various growls, he entertained himself with blue tiger sound effects until his throat started to itch. Then he dropped to the floor and did fifty push-ups. Under the bed, his guitar craved attention, so he slid it out and set the case on his bed.

He popped open the latches and removed his treasured instrument. Next he retrieved an amber bottle of guitar honey, spray cleaner, and a tin of Carnauba guitar wax from a dresser drawer.

After carefully removing its strings, he ran his hand over the smooth maple body of the instrument and trailed his fingers up the rosewood fret bar, closing his palm over the neck of the guitar. His hand slid up down up down up down. His dick warmed, and his pants grew pleasantly tight. With spray cleaner, he misted the maple and rubbed it dry, then applied a thin coat of Carnauba. The clean, crisp scents of oils and cleaners brought his senses to life and made his skin tingle with excitement. Appreciatively, he sniffed the wax tin once or twice before replacing the lid.

The guitar wax would need to dry before he could buff it out and polish the maple surface to a hard, bright shine. No problem. While he was waiting for the wax to dry, he had other, equally enjoyable things to do. Uncapping the amber bottle labeled guitar honey, he let the contents drip into his cupped hand. Next, he drew his lubricated hand over the fretboard, up down up down, until the fine rosewood must've been as ready to come as he was.

But he wouldn't come.

Not now anyway. A man should be able to control himself, and this was not the place to do his business. Gently, he laid the guitar back in its case to dry and headed for the bathroom to wash his hands. Once he'd cleaned them, he'd step in the shower and properly relieve himself in a way that wouldn't soil his sheets. There was a right way and a wrong way to go about things after all.

But a moment later, the sound of the faucet running and the tactile rush of water flowing over his hands had him ready to explode. He shut off the faucet and, gritting his teeth, dragged off his underwear and socks. He took the time to carry them back to the bedroom so they wouldn't absorb any humidity from the shower. Nothing worse than damp socks in a hamper, smelling up the place.

Another mirrored glimpse of his blue tiger tattoo acted as an aphrodisiac, and he quickened his strides.

Hurry up. You can make it. Don't soil the carpet.

His control thinning, he skidded back into the bathroom and leapt into the tub, grabbing the shower curtain and yanking it back at the same time. The plastic curtain rings made a high-pitched noise as they scraped across the shower rod.

Then came a different sound, a metallic *clank, clank, thunk.*

Too late, he remembered what he'd asked of Hugo the butcher.

His heart froze as a slackened rope tightened and jerked, sending a bucket toppling from the window ledge above the shower.

The *flooding!* It was happening now!

He covered his head with his arms as blood from the falling bucket sprayed him like bullets. His head snapped back, and more blood filled his nostrils, sickening him with its tangy smell. Warm, sticky fluid coated his eyes, drained into his mouth, dripped down his torso.

His dick responded to the tepid liquid by spurting milky jets onto his stomach. He opened his mouth, swallowed more blood and gagged on the clots. As he climbed from the tub, he stumbled, then some part of his brain went awry. His muscles seized, and he fell jerking onto the bathroom floor. His skull hit the tiles with a resounding crack, and the seizing stopped.

Half-blinded with blood, he lay still on the floor, unable to hold back an agonizing scream—a scream that made the spasms start up again. Finally, the convulsions ceased, and he hobbled to his feet. His hands were covered in toxic blood, and he smeared them on the tile wall behind the tub. Up down up down up down. His dick came to life again.

No!

Do not lose control!

He slapped his dick, sucked in a blast of air, and

waited for his member to deflate. Then he looked up
and saw his handiwork on the wall. Five bloody letters
now dripped from the tiles. He doubled over, panting,
his body spent.

The bathroom door creaked open.

A new burst of adrenaline hit him hard, and he
whirled around to find Hugo the butcher standing in
the doorway, mop in hand, mouth agape.

Don't lose control.

But it was too late. He bit his tongue hard as his
heart pumped pure rage into his veins.

"Oh, man. I thought I'd check up on you. Make
sure you hadn't changed your mind. Guess I got here
too late." Hugo's eyes rounded. "Did it work? Are you
cured?"

Digging his fingernails into his naked thighs,
Scourge crouched, waiting for the perfect moment to
strike.

He was a tiger.

A blue tiger.

He growled.

Hugo lifted his hands. "Take it easy, buddy. Just
take it easy. Good thing I came back. It's gonna be oh
k-kay."

His growl erupted into a primal scream, and he saw
clumps of hair in his fists.

"I warned you this was a wrong idea. Anyone who's
seen *Carrie* ought to know it was a crazy idea." Hugo
ventured a half step in his direction.

I am the tiger.

He pounced, knocking Hugo to the floor and straddling him, closed his paws around his throat.

The throbbing in his head and the burning bile in his throat woke Scourge a split second before he vomited a gray substance that looked and smelled like fish guts onto his lap. He had no memory of what he'd eaten that day, nor did he have any memory of falling asleep with his back against a cold wall, chin bobbing against his chest.

Fuck.

Moaning, he lifted his bowling ball of a head and used his fingers to pry his sticky eyelids fully open, which is when he saw the white toilet gleaming in the darkened room.

The bathroom.

Nighttime. He'd fallen asleep in the bathroom. This was highly improper . . . and unhygienic. Because he deserved it, he slapped himself in the face. His hand felt wet, and he stared at his black, gooey palm. His legs, stretched out in front of him, jerked and jittered. Yes, he'd mopped the bathroom with Lysol yesterday morning, but the idea of his bare hands and legs touching the floor, a place where he *walked*, sometimes in *shoes*, made his stomach heave again. This time, only a thin jet of liquid spurted out of his mouth. As his eyes flicked around the room, his vision adjusted to the dark a bit. He tried to get up but wound up on all fours, waiting for the next wave of nausea to hit.

And then he saw him.

Hugo.

Fuck.

His friend, Hugo the butcher, sprawled on his back next to the bathtub, arms flailed, neck torqued, eyeballs rolled back, skin purple as the puke dripping from Scourge's hands.

"Hugo!" he cried, his voice hoarse from retching. "Hugo, wake up!" He crawled to his friend and poked his chest with his index finger, but Hugo didn't move. "Wake up! Wake up! Wake up!" He grabbed his friend's arm. It was stiff . . . and cold like the tile.

Next, he grabbed Hugo's head, forcing it from side to side. Purplish streaks and spots marched around Hugo's neck and over his chest above his collarbone.

Dead.

Strangled.

Somebody strangled Hugo. Frantically, Scourge made the sign of the cross, squeezed his eyes closed, and began reciting his prayers.

Rosary.

He needed a rosary. Opening his eyes, he looked toward the moonlight slicing in from the bathroom window. The light shone from above, cutting through the dark like a heavenly flashlight . . . and like a flashlight held against your hand, the light shone bloodred.

Blood!

Blood. Blood. Blood.

Blood smeared the white tile walls. He looked

down. Blood soaked his hands. He crawled to the toilet and hurled another burning stream of bile. He wobbled to his feet. Looked in the mirror. More blood streaked his face and chest and stomach, even his genitals were covered in blood.

He jerked the faucets on, flooding the sink with water, dunked his head below the surface and kept it there until the lack of air threatened to explode his skull. He came up for a breath, then soaked his hair and face beneath the faucet, eyes wide open, cold water flushing them clean. A minute later, he felt his mind snap back. Then his memory came rushing at him like the water spewing from the faucet.

The flooding technique hadn't worked at all. And now Hugo was dead. Strangled. Scourge wasn't cured, and he'd lost his only remaining friend. He'd made a dirty mess in his bathroom. But he could clean it up.

He had to clean up his mess.

He yanked open the cabinet below the sink, grabbed his scrub brush, and inch by inch scoured all traces of blood from his body. During this time, he puked more than once, but eventually he got himself clean. Then he wrapped his freshly washed feet in bath towels and stumbled naked into his bedroom, turned on a light, collected what he needed: gloves, sheets, garbage bags, rope, bleach.

Rosary.

Heart thumping in his chest, he eased the bathroom door open once more. His stomach convulsed as he looked around—most of the blood was contained within the tub where the bucket had fallen. Blood was also on the back wall behind the tub and clotting in the drain. Pinching his nose with one hand, he closed his eyes and jerked the shower curtain closed. At an agonizing pace, he cleaned all the streaks of blood from the bathroom floor with bleach.

But the tub and back wall were impossible to face.

He'd have to wait until he was cured to clean them. In the meantime, he'd hide the mess behind the shower curtain, and he'd sponge bathe himself in the sink the way mothers bathed their babies. The thought gave him comfort. Besides, it was all he could do.

Unlike the tub, however, Hugo would have to be dealt with now. He couldn't leave a dead body on his bathroom floor. Then, suddenly, something akin to pride welled in his chest. He could kill again. He *had* killed again, and all on his own. True, it was a bloodless kill, but it was a kill nonetheless. He rolled his friend over and went to work binding his hands and feet with the ropes.

This wasn't Hugo's fault. The poor man had only done as he'd asked him to do. This wasn't Scourge's fault either. Dr. Clancy should've cured him faster. He was getting better in spite of her, though, and it would soon be time for her to pay.

TWENTY-ONE

Wednesday, August 14, 9:00 A.M.

As Luke ambled across the diner, each step carefully measured, his expression tightly controlled, he matched Detective Johnson's stare. Even as Luke relaxed into the booth tucked into a far corner of the kitschy café, he didn't drop his gaze.

Nor did Johnson.

Out of his peripheral vision, Luke noticed a waitress approach. Eyes still locked on Johnson, he turned up the empty cup in front of him, and the waitress filled it with a brew so acidic he could smell the bite. Just the kind of java he liked, man-up black.

"I'll give you fellows some more time," she said, wisely backing away from the booth. When she spun and bolted for the counter, Luke caught the flip of her pink-skirted uniform out of the corner of his eye.

"We do this now or wait for Torpedo?" Johnson finally dropped his gaze, breaking the face-off, picked up his knife and fork, and moved them from the napkin onto the tabletop.

"Is it true?"

Johnson's mouth pulled to the side. "What?"

He kept his voice low and steady. "They found another body."

"Can't confirm or deny." Johnson dumped a load of cream into his coffee, stirred and took a sip. He tapped a menu on the table. "You know what you want already?"

Luke grabbed the menu. Opened it. Closed it. Nodded. "I got a connection at the *Gazette*."

"I just bet you do. Jerichos got connections everywhere." The detective's voice sounded like he'd just swallowed a mouthful of Tabasco.

Ignoring the jab, Luke continued, "I got a connection at the *Gazette* who says they're holding the story until the DA gives them the go-ahead. Says a male body was found near Camel Rock Monument in mint condition."

"How do you figure a corpse to be in mint condition?"

"No decomposition. My connection says it's a fresh kill—couple of days old at most."

"Can't confirm or deny."

"My connection says the victim had a rosary clasped in his fist, same as the others."

"Others? Oh, you mean like the Saint's victims.

Hey, maybe you should get your ears washed. Like I said twice already, I can't confirm or deny."

"Like hell you can't." Luke leaned forward, slammed down the menu. Coffee sloshed from his cup into the saucer. "There's a press conference scheduled for this afternoon."

"And you can get your details then along with the common folk."

Luke was debating whether or not to knock that fat chip off Johnson's shoulder when the door to the café swung open, and Teddy Torpedo Haynes stalked inside and made a beeline for their booth. Crowding Johnson over, the attorney sat down too close and spit into the man's coffee.

The detective's face turned rage red. "How 'bout I book you for assault, counselor?"

Torpedo shrugged. "Assault with a deadly loogie? Knock yourself out."

Johnson sputtered, extended a fist, then drew it back.

Yeah, Torpedo was going to be a big help in winning Johnson over to their side. Luke rubbed the knot out of his forehead. He didn't know which man was the more unpleasant breakfast companion. No. He did, and it wasn't Johnson. Compared to Torpedo, Johnson was a regular Miss Congeniality. "Look, I'd love to sit here and watch you gentleman measure your dicks all day, but this is a serious matter."

Torpedo hocked another gem into the detective's coffee.

"Give it a rest, will you?" Luke pointed a finger at the phlegmatic attorney. "Save your antics for the courtroom." Then he jerked his chin at Johnson. "Torpedo's sorry, and it won't happen again."

Torpedo made an aw-shucks face.

Luke arched a brow. "For real, Haynes. This is no game. My brother's life is at stake here, and I'm sure the good detective is doing the best he can to get to the truth. Aren't you, Johnson?"

Johnson crossed his arms high on his chest and looked from Luke to Haynes and back to Luke again. "You can't *good cop bad cop* a cop. Let's cut the crap, shall we?"

"Absolutely. But the fact is, my brother's been charged with a string of murders whose only common denominator is a rosary left on the victims' bodies."

Johnson pushed his ruined coffee aside. "And Dante Jericho's confession. That ties the victims together, wouldn't ya say?"

Luke decided to concede the point because you can't say you're after the truth and then ignore whatever parts don't suit you. "Okay, the rosaries *and* the confession of a man who's clearly guilt-ridden and mentally fragile."

"Big of you to admit that." Johnson's tone might've been sarcastic, but he stopped fiddling with his silverware and sat forward attentively, allowing Luke to finish.

"Apart from the rosaries and a questionable confession no one can say what ties these victims together.

And perhaps more importantly, there's no physical evidence whatsoever to link my brother to the crimes. A victim found with a rosary—killed while Dante remains in custody—would obviously be important to my brother's defense, if such a victim in fact exists. So yes, we are entitled to the information according to the law, which I believe you are sworn to uphold. Now, I can go through channels and get the information, or you can stop fucking around and just tell us what's going on." He turned his palms up. "Because quite frankly, Detective, Torpedo's manners suck. I'd hate it if he spouted off unfairly to the press. I'd hate it even more if the good people of Santa Fe garnered the false impression that the police in general, and you in particular, are uncooperative and endangering the welfare of the community by refusing to follow up new leads on a serial killer."

"Nobody's being uncooperative." Johnson slapped the table with his palm, and his lower body jerked.

"Now that's assault." Torpedo interjected. "You kicked me on purpose."

Johnson kept his eyes on Luke. "I'll tell you what I know, but it's nothing gonna do your brother any good."

Luke forced himself to breathe and refrained from saying he and Torpedo would be the judge of that. He didn't want to give Johnson a reason not to trust him. He wanted to know what was going on, and he wanted to know now.

Johnson moved his silverware, piece by piece back onto the napkin and off again. Scratched his day-old whiskers. "You say you're after truth. Well, so am I. So in a way, you and I got something in common, though it pains me to say I'm anything like an overprivileged dick like you."

"And it pains me to think I'm anything like an arrogant prick like you, so I guess we do have stuff in common." Luke showed him his teeth.

Johnson hunched his shoulders. "We got a fresh body. We got a rosary. But it's not the Saint."

"You think it's a copycat?" Luke asked.

Torpedo smirked. "Here comes the old copycat excuse. These coppers never want to admit when they screw up and arrest an innocent man for murder."

Johnson bolted to his feet. "You fellows think you know what I'm about. You think I'd railroad Dante Jericho just to make a name for myself, get my fifteen minutes of fame."

"I'd say that's a fair assessment." Torpedo shrugged.

Then, apparently realizing Torpedo had him trapped in the booth, Johnson sat back down. "Well, you can both go to hell. Ever heard of the words protect and serve? Maybe those words sound corny to a slimeball lawyer like you. Or a rich asshole like you who never had to work a day in his life." He favored Luke with a poisonous look.

"I may be an asshole, but I do work," Luke didn't let his voice rise. He wasn't being defensive, just stating the facts.

"Fine, you work. But you never *had* to work. Not the same thing at all."

"Hey. Over here. Remember me?" Torpedo stuck his thumbs on his temples and wiggled his fingers. "I'm the slimeball lawyer who's never lost a murder case."

"Which proves my point." Johnson said through gritted teeth. "No way each and every one of your clients was innocent. Statistically speaking, that's impossible, and that means you've put *killers* back on the streets—the streets I'm trying to make safe for law-abiding citizens. So question anything you want, but don't question my motives. Ain't a goddamn thing wrong with my motives, and they got nothing to do with fifteen fucking minutes of fame."

The temperature of Luke's blood was rising in direct proportion to the amount of bickering between Torpedo and Johnson. Time to take things down a notch. "Okay. Nobody's saying you're a bad cop."

"Your mouthpiece just said exactly that."

Again, Torpedo nodded.

Johnson straightened his spine and drew his shoulders back. "And then you practically ordered him to mouth off to the press with that bad-manners comment."

"I'll make sure Torpedo doesn't impugn your reputation. You have my word on it." Luke narrowed his eyes at his brother's attorney and looked back at the detective. "Now, if you'd care to explain why you think this new victim is the work of a copycat, I'm all ears."

"I wouldn't even go so far as to call it a copycat. The MOs are too different. Sure, the rosary and hog-tying is an obvious homage to the Saint, but nothing else fits."

"Hog-tied, too?" Luke shuddered at the image that brought to mind.

"Yeah. Sick, like the Saint. But each and every one of the prior victims had his or her skull blown apart with a shotgun. And the bodies were found still covered in blood. But not this poor fellow."

"You made an ID?"

"We're waiting for dental records. The unsub . . . who is definitely *not* the Saint, strangled his victim, then he scrubbed the body clean. If there was so much as a drop of blood on the man's body, it's gone now, along with his fingernails—they were trimmed down to the nubs. The good news is we found trace this time."

"Trace?"

"Yeah, nylon fibers. Guys at the crime lab think they're from a toilet scrubber. No DNA, but its better than nothing."

"Just to be clear . . . there *was* a rosary."

Johnson raked a hand through his hair. "Yes."

"Then how can you discount that so early on? How can you be sure this isn't another one of the Saint's victims?"

"Because the Saint is in custody. I'm sorry for you, Luke, and that's not horseshit." Johnson's expression softened by a hair. "I know the family of a perpetrator hurts almost as much as the family of a victim. I want you to understand, I don't lump you into the same category as your murdering brother. But I cannot make this new vic as one of the Saint's. The Saint's kills were too precise."

"You call a shotgun blast to the head precise?"

"I call a murder precise when it happens the same way every time. The Saint is a cold-blooded methodical monster who's killing his victims in the bloodiest way possible. I *will* catch the son of a bitch who strangled this new guy, but no way in hell is he turning out to be the Santa Fe Saint. No way in hell this new corpse gets your brother off the hook."

Luke pressed his palms to the sides of his head. "I can't dismiss the rosary connection so easily. It's too powerful a message. I think it's the Saint's way of taking back credit for the murders. He's letting the world know the glory belongs to him. Same thing with the media texts he sent to Faith Clancy. Those pictures—"

"Those pictures could've been sent to her by anyone with an ax to grind."

"Who'd have an ax to grind with Faith?"

"Anyone who thinks she's coming down on the wrong side of the fence where your brother's concerned. Her face has been plastered all over the local news as the doctor who was treating a heinous serial killer. It's not easy to get crime-scene photos, but it can be done." He shook his head. "Off the record, the DA thinks *you* sent the photos to make it look like the

Saint is still out there. Thinks you're trying to draw heat away from your brother."

Luke rose on his haunches. "You son of a bitch. You believe I'd threaten a kid and a dog and terrify an innocent woman?"

"So now Dr. Clancy's innocent? A few weeks ago you thought she was a bitch for turning your brother in." Johnson let out a breath. "But for what it's worth, no. I think the DA's wrong about you, Luke. I'm a pretty good judge of character, and while I may not like you, I don't see you as the type to resort to terrorist tactics. My guess is the individual who sent those photos to Dr. Clancy is some pissed-off vigilante. The same type as the guy who tossed a rock at your limo." Johnson looked past Luke. "And by the way, the extra detail patrolling Clancy's block is history. With no direct threat to her safety or to the little boy's, the captain decided to reallocate those resources."

Luke came to his feet, gestured at Haynes. "I want twenty-four/seven surveillance on Dr. Clancy and Tommy."

"I got it. I got it," Torpedo sputtered at Luke, then put his hand on Johnson's shoulder. "Now then, Detective, I've been meaning to ask you. What about that other matter?"

Johnson brushed Torpedo's hand aside. "What other matter?"

"Maybe you thought we wouldn't find the report buried in all that crap the DA's Office sent over." Torpedo brought out a *gotcha* smile. "I'm talking about a goddamn eyewitness."

Wednesday, August 14, 3:30 P.M.

Here Luke was again, proverbial hat in hand, when a phone call would've sufficed. But how could he regret his decision to come to Faith's office when seeing her in the flesh made his blood pound and his heart soar? Pounding blood might be common enough, but a soaring heart was hardly a small thing, and especially under circumstances like these, shouldn't be taken for granted.

"Luke?"

"Sorry, I guess I should've made an appointment."

Faith waved a come-in. "No need. You're not interrupting anything. I'm hardly in high demand. I've visited every primary-care doctor in town, handing out my brochures. I've offered free consultations. Same-day appointments." A frustrated sigh stopped her words.

Closing the door behind him, he entered, then circled her office. First time he'd been here. First time he'd seen this part of her life. His eyes closed as he drank in the scent—her scent—filling the small space. "It takes time to grow a new business, Faith, I'm sure psychiatry is no different."

"I'm sure being the doctor who treated the Santa Fe Saint isn't attracting droves of patients to my door."

Her hand flew to her mouth.

"No worries. I'm not offended." What she said was true, and he had no problem with her telling the truth. Faith had acted exactly as she should've in regards to Dante. It was his brother's own words that had created this mess—not Faith's actions.

By now, he was the furthest thing from angry at her. Despite everything terrible that had happened, because of Faith, these past weeks had been a glorious jumble of color. There was the vibrant red of first attraction, followed by the deep black resentment over Dante, next came the cool blue of understanding, and now—some mystifying color he couldn't name. Couldn't begin to replicate even if he had a full palette of paint and a brush in hand. Of course, his brother was the true artist. He was merely a gallery owner who appreciated but could not create beauty.

"Luke?"

He raked his fingers through his hair. He'd come here for a reason hadn't he? "There may be a witness in the Saint case."

Faith's expression tightened as she waited for him to continue.

"Four years ago, a kid in Amarillo, a friend of the Saint's first victim, gave the police a description of a man he saw with his friend, Kenny Stoddard. The file's gone to shit. There's virtually nothing left of the witness's statement, but Torpedo's got his address."

"When do we leave?" If she'd given any thought to their encounter in the limo, you'd never know it by her demeanor now. But maybe that was only because this was her office, and she wanted to stay professional. He hadn't expected her to fly into his arms or anything, but a little eyelash batting, maybe a coy smile would've been nice.

"I need to take care of a few loose business ends, but I should be able to leave sometime tomorrow. I don't mean to impose, but as a psychiatrist, you have certain, interpersonal skills that might be of use in interviewing a witness."

Seemingly pleased, she smiled. "Well, I hope I can be of help."

And besides, he wanted to be near her . . . all the time. He wasn't sure how, but she'd snuck into his heart. Whenever he had a free thought, she appeared from nowhere. Her guileless face, her lush voice—her fists, raised and ready to put up the fight of her life. He wanted this woman like he hadn't wanted a woman in a long time . . . maybe ever.

"Luke?" This time he heard exasperation in her voice. She checked her watch. I'm happy you stopped by, but really, if you're just going to stand there, I should prep my patient. I have an appointment in half an hour."

"Sure. Like I said, I should've called. Maybe I'll do that."

"Pardon?"

"Call." He cleared his throat. "All right if I call you tonight? To firm up the details and discuss strategy."

"Of course." She opened and closed a drawer, twisted her wristwatch. "This trip . . . we'll keep things strictly professional, right?"

He could see her now in the backseat of his limo, dress hiked around her waist, thighs open, waiting for him. He groaned. Maybe aloud. "Yes, let's keep things strictly professional. My thoughts exactly."

TWENTY-TWO

Wednesday, August 14, 4:00 P.M.

The way Scourge's shoulders hunched when he entered her office, the way his limbs seemed to drip at his sides, made Faith think he might simply melt into a puddle on her new, stain-resistant carpeting. He walked as if his bones had been extracted, leaving nothing to pin his muscles and skin into the shape of a man. Both his whitened complexion and the guarded look in his hyperemic eyes warned that one wrong word from her might vaporize him altogether.

Her shoulders tensed up around her ears. Blowing out a slow breath, she lowered them. Today, she must be especially gentle with Scourge, choose her path with the utmost caution ,or else she might send him off to Never-Never Land. He'd hadn't ever seemed quite this fragile before.

"Shouldn't there be a couch in here or something?" he muttered, eyeing the leather chair pulled near her desk.

"This place isn't for napping." She got up, motioned for him to sit, then dragged an ottoman around for his feet.

"But what about for dreaming?" he asked, his voice near a whisper.

"Dreaming is allowed. In fact, it's encouraged." Faith squeezed his arm, then seated herself in her usual place behind her desk. Up close, the circles under his eyes seemed even darker than before—so dark she could almost believe he'd painted them on. She tried to make eye contact but couldn't. "Scourge, has something happened since our last therapy session?"

His eyes darted frantically about her office. "I'd rather not say."

"Your call, of course, but since you're here to get better, you might want to reconsider."

"I'd like to talk about it. I *need* to talk about it, but . . . I'm afraid you'll be angry with me, Dr. Clancy."

"That seems highly unlikely, but suppose I did become angry. Wouldn't be the end of the world, now, would it?" She scooted closer to the edge of her chair.

Confusion flitted across his face. "What do you mean?"

"I'm just saying it's no big deal if I get angry with you. That's just life. We'll both get over it."

He blocked his gaze with his hand to keep her from reading his expression, leaving her wondering what generally happened in his world when someone got angry.

Tugging a loose thread on his shirt, he shifted in his seat. He was dressed in long sleeves again, and again, she wondered what he was hiding underneath. Today, however, was not the day to inquire. She forced her gaze to the bookcase, hoping Scourge would find her less intimidating if she didn't look directly at him. He needed breathing room, or more accurately, talking room.

"You're a very good doctor, and I should've listened to your advice. I'm truly sorry for disobeying you."

Disobeying her? She hadn't a clue what he meant by that, and she wished he'd stop apologizing and get to the point. "Hmm."

"You remember we talked about that flooding therapy. I thought if I immersed myself in blood, I'd see there was nothing to fear, my adrenaline would eventually wear out, and I'd be cured of my hemophobia fast."

Her body canted forward, not liking where this was going. "We also talked about the fact that flooding would be too stressful to undertake at this point, that it might do more harm than good."

"I suppose you'll think me hebetudinous then when I tell you what I've done."

She waved him off. "You don't need to impress me with big words. I know you're smart, even without the vocabulary lesson. I wish you didn't feel you had to work so hard to get people to like you."

"Certain people do like me," he said. "I used to have friends . . . but they've all gone away now."

She was two steps behind him, still trying to recall what hebetudinous meant. Stupid? Foolish? Oh, dear. The light finally dawned. *She* was the hebetudinous one for not putting out a stronger don't-try-this-at-home disclaimer. "Scourge, please tell me you didn't—"

"Yes. I did." He clapped his hands together in a theatrical gesture. "I flooded myself."

"And are you feeling any better?" The answer was obviously not, but she thought she'd let him tell it his way.

For the first time since he'd entered the room, his eyes sought hers. "I'm sorry. Sorry. Sorry. Sorry."

She got up and went around the desk, rested her hip against it. "It's okay. I'm not mad at you."

"You're really not mad?" The quiver in his voice made her heart constrict.

"Not even a little. You were desperate to get relief, and so you tried something you thought might help you get well. You made a mistake, yes. But you survived, and now you've learned something."

"I barely slept last night, and when I did, I had terrible dreams." He covered a yawn and rearranged his legs on the ottoman, crossing and uncrossing them at the ankles. "Maybe I shouldn't have used real blood."

"You—you used real blood." Alarm bells blared in her head. Her hand went to her throat.

A satisfied smile lifted the corners of his mouth.

"Ha! You should see your face." His smile faded as quickly as it had appeared. "It wasn't *human* blood."

She shuddered.

"It was pig's blood. I got a friend, a butcher, and he's got buddies at the slaughterhouse. That's how he got the blood. I asked him to surprise me, so he rigged a bucket of blood to dump on my head when I pulled the shower curtain open. Now I'm thinking that if only I'd used movie blood instead, if I hadn't made my friend get the pig blood, nothing bad would've happened."

All she could think of was that scene from *Carrie*. Luckily, Scourge didn't have telekinetic powers . . . as far as she knew. "What bad thing? What happened when the bucket fell?"

"I went berserk. Completely and totally berserk, and then I blacked out. When I woke up I didn't remember what I'd done—still don't—but I had a quite a situation on my hands."

"I can imagine."

He smiled an oddly superior smile. "I'm sure you can't."

Seconds ticked by. She didn't want to press too hard, but knowing how he'd handled the trauma would help her gauge his progress. "I assume the situation you're referring to was a very messy bathroom."

"Oh, it was a mess all right."

"Were you able to clean up the blood?"

His eyes flashed. "I'm not dirty."

"Of course not. But given your hemophobia, I'm wondering how you managed to handle all the blood."

"It wasn't easy, but I took care of most everything. I cleaned the floor, the sink, the mirror . . . I did leave the shower, though. I wanted to clean it, but it was too hard, I was afraid I might black out again, so I just pulled the curtain closed instead. Anyway, I don't have to look at the blood anymore."

This was a disaster, and the least she could do was help him take care of the bathroom. "I can help you find someone to go out and clean it up for you. Then you won't have to worry about it anymore."

"No!" The urgency in his tone surprised her. "I always clean up my own messes. I'm not lazy. I'm not dirty. You want to help me? Then cure me. Once I'm cured, I won't need you anymore, and I can get rid of . . . my problem."

"I don't think it's wise to allow that blood to stay in the tub. It might stain the porcelain. Who knows what kind of bacteria will form, and imagine if someone stumbled on a tub full of blood. They'd think there'd been a murder or something."

Again, an inexplicable a smile lifted his lips, then disappeared so quickly she thought it might have been nothing more than a nervous tic. "Then you better cure me fast because I won't have someone poking around my bathroom, cleaning up my messes."

"Your call." She waited, but apparently he didn't wish to discuss this further.

He closed his eyes, and his jittery legs stilled. His head lolled back in the chair. "I had a dream last night."

He'd brought up dreams earlier, when he'd first

come in, then again later. This made the third time. This dream was important.

"Shall I tell you about it?"

"If you'd like," she said, keeping her voice neutral, not wanting to show him her curiosity.

"I dreamt I was back at school. Remember I told you I lived at St. Catherine's School for Boys until ten years ago."

She occupied her hands with a pencil though she had no plans to spook him by taking notes. "I remember. You didn't like it there. One of the nuns in particular."

"Sister Bernadette. She was in my dream." His back slid down into the chair, pushing his feet near the end of the ottoman. Apparently, he really needed that couch.

Faith recalled Sister Bernadette clearly. According to Scourge, she'd beaten him with a flashlight on more than one occasion after he'd wet the bed. She wasn't certain she believed the whole story, but she was certain he did, and that was all that mattered.

"It was Sister who gave me my name, you know—Scourge."

She hadn't known, and the fact that he'd finally revealed the source of his awful nickname signaled increased trust, maybe even an impending breakthrough. "Tell me more."

"I dreamt I was deep in the woods, miles from the boys' dormitory. It's like I'm right there again, now. My thighs are burning because I walked all the way with

Sister Bernadette on my back. Then I laid her out on the soggy ground beneath a hulking ponderosa pine."

Such detail. Could this be it? Maybe this dream would bring his fears to the surface and allow him to conquer them once and for all. "Mmm hmm."

"A bright rim of moonlight encircles her face. Black robes flow around her, engulf her small body and blend with the night. Her face, floating on top of all that darkness, reminds me of a ghost head in a haunted house."

His voice rose, and his words rushed faster and faster. "I draw back, and I pull out my pocketknife and press the silver blade against her throat. I am not a shadow. I twist the knife so that the tip bites into the sweet hollow of her throat. I'm not afraid of going to hell."

His eyes squeezed tight, and his back arched.

"It's okay, Scourge, it's only a dream. I'm right here."

Writhing in the chair, he covered his ears with his hands. "I don't want to remember the rest. I don't want her to say those words." He made a choking noise. "But I need to remember. I can't go on like this. I can't let Sister Bernadette win. She's trying to keep me from doing my work. But I won't let her stop me now. Not when I've come so far. Not when I'm so close to the grand finale."

His agitation increased with each passing second. Faith watched his body, alert for any sign he might injure himself but allowing him his space. At last, his mouth opened and a hoarse cry came out. "Yes. I remember it all, now. Sister Bernadette gurgles, and her eyes roll back in her head. She screams at me while she's dying. Over and over she screams those words: *The blood of the lamb will wash away your sins.* And then blood flows from her neck onto my hands. I run and run and run until I find a stream."

She pressed her eyelids with her fingertips, trying to gather her thoughts. "Say again, please."

"The blood of the lamb. I have to get it off my hands." He rubbed his hands together frantically, pantomiming his story.

"Slow down a minute." She reached out, touched his hands, and felt his arms relax slightly, then tense again. "You said that in your dream, you killed Sister Bernadette."

"Yes."

"Her blood is on your hands, and that frightens you."

"Yes. I have to get it off. I have to get the blood off or else . . ."

"Or else what?" At last, she was about to learn the answer to the mystery. What was it about blood that made Scourge's heart race and his head spin to the point he could no longer function?

His eyes rolled back in his head, and his whole body jerked. "I don't want the blood of the lamb on me. I don't *want* to be cleansed of my sins. I have to get the blood of the lamb off my hands before it washes me clean. I want to go hell. I *need* to go to hell." His arms and legs flailed. "Now Wilhelmina's blood is on me. Like the holy lamb's blood, like Bernadette's. Get it off me!"

Wilhelmina? Oh yes, the woman at the lab. Realization jolted through her. Wilhelmina must've called up his memories of Bernadette, the nun who'd terrorized him at school. In his mind, her blood had become Bernadette's blood. Faith squeezed his shoulder. "It's only a dream. You're okay. All you have to do is wake up."

His eyes flew open, and he bolted upright in the chair. She placed her fingers on his wrist, monitoring his pulse. "Breathe, Scourge. You can do this. Use the deep breathing to help you through this."

He nodded. His chest heaved, then filled with breath, released the breath, then filled again. His pulse normalized.

"It's only a dream. I'm here for you, Scourge. Sister Bernadette will never hurt you again." She retrieved a bottle of water from her small fridge, unscrewed the lid, and handed it to him. "Now you say it."

"I'm safe now. Sister Bernadette can never hurt me again." His hand twitched, and the water fell to the ground, spilling on the carpet. "She can't hurt me. Is it really true?"

"It's really true." Faith heard the catch in her voice as she answered.

Scourge climbed out of the chair. "I'm feeling better now. I think I'll clean up my mess."

"Don't bother." She waved her hand at the water

beading on the stain-resistant carpet. "I'll take care of it."

"No." His strange laugh echoed around the room. "I mean the blood in the tub. I think I can clean the blood up now. It's like you said, Sister Bernadette is dead. She can't hurt me ever again." He looked at her with widening eyes. "Is it possible I'm cured?"

"Freud theorized that phobias result from past traumas. I suspect your dream symbolizes your rage toward Sister Bernadette because of the horrible way she treated you in school."

He moved closer, listening intently.

"Once you uncover those feelings, bring them to the surface and face them, the fear dissipates, and the phobia goes away. I must say I don't subscribe to Freudian theory in its entirety, but in this instance, it's ringing true."

"You think I'm cured."

"I think we've uncovered the root of your hemophobia. Your fear of blood is tied to your religious upbringing, to your beliefs about heaven and hell, and even more importantly to this woman who tortured you as a boy."

"*Tortured* seems a harsh word." He ducked his head so she couldn't see his eyes again.

Classic ambivalence. He hated the Sister, but he depended on her, too, because he'd had no one else to care for him. Time to let her go. "She beat you with a flashlight and shamed you in front of all the other boys."

"She made me feel small." He laughed until his shoulders shook.

Faith felt a sense of relief. He was releasing tension through laughter, a safe enough means of coping with the harsh truths of his life.

"I mean even smaller than I am in real life." As his laughter subsided, he gave one last snort. "Sister and her talk of the blood of the lamb unmanned me so to speak. Who's afraid of a bloody lamb, for Chrissake?"

He seemed to have recovered his composure enough to wind things up for the day—and they'd gone overtime. Faith's muscles ached from the tight control she'd maintained for the past hour, so she could only imagine how Scourge felt. She looked at her watch. "Time's about up."

"Yes." He looked directly at her, and his eyes sparked. "*Time's up.*"

"I'll see you next week then, or we can schedule something sooner if you feel like you need to talk more about what happened here today."

"No." His expression was almost giddy. "You've been a big help, but I can take it from here."

His phobia had been the tip of a much larger problem. He still needed therapy. "We've had a breakthrough regarding your fear of blood, yes. But there's still a lot of work to do to on other issues."

"Other issues? Oh, you think I want to become a stable, well-adjusted individual. But you see, Dr. Clancy, that isn't what I want at all. I just want to be me. I have no desire for personal growth. I only needed to get rid of that awful hemophobia so I could get back to my old life. I have a lot of work left to do, and now, thanks to you, I can finish what I started." He stroked the leather back of the chair, then turned and walked out her door.

TWENTY-THREE

After hurrying outside, Faith saw that Luke had already arrived. They were headed to Amarillo today, in the hopes of locating and interviewing Jeremy Jacobs, a potential witness in the Saint case. When Luke shot her a cocky grin, she dropped her briefcase. The tripod that'd been tucked under her arm followed, and as she bent to gather the consent forms that had flown out of the case, her purse slipped off her shoulder, landing in her sprinkler-dampened front lawn.

Luke raised one amused eyebrow, crossed his arms, and leaned back against the hood of the coolest car Faith had ever seen, his pecs rippling beneath a white cotton T-shirt that barely contained his biceps. His Wranglers were cowboy tight and buckled with an ornate silver medallion that read PRCA NATIONAL FINALS 2010 SADDLE BRONC RIDING.

Not that she'd been staring.

He hooked his thumbs in his pockets and crossed his tan ostrich skin boots at the ankles. "What?" He drawled the word into two syllables.

Her mouth snapped shut. Like he didn't know he could give a girl a heart attack showing up looking like he'd just climbed off a bucking bronco ready to claim the award for bluest-eyed cowboy.

"Nothing." She chased down the rest of her forms, locked everything up neat and tidy in her leather briefcase, and stuck her hands on her hips. "Just didn't know you were a rodeo champion is all." She cleared her throat. "Or that you'd be picking me up in that old thing."

"Now I know you're teasing, darlin', because no woman in her right mind can resist a sweet little ride like this." He winked. "My 1977 Delft blue Triumph Spitfire and I are at your service. I'm dressed in my everyday ranch gear because Amarillo's cowboy country, and I figure I'll get more cooperation from the witness like this than I would suited up."

That's how he dressed every day on the ranch. She swallowed hard and tried not to imagine what his butt looked like mounting a quarter horse. "Makes sense. I-I just assumed we'd be taking the limo."

"Nice stammer." He grabbed her hand and pressed a kiss into her palm. "Sorry to disappoint you, but you made it clear this trip would be strictly business, and

I'm afraid I just can't trust myself with you in a limo."
He swept his arm across the tiny two-seater convertible. "This'll be safer . . . for you."

Truthfully, she'd been expecting a campaign to
mix pleasure with business, but now she saw he wasn't
going to put up any argument. She heaved a sigh, and
her chest deflated.

"If you've changed your mind, I can always call my
driver. We can take the limo and fool around on the
way." His it'd-be-my-pleasure-ma'am grin set her heart
palpitating.

For heaven's sake.

"No thank you." She stuck her chin up. "I'm just
wondering how we're going to fit the two of us and my
camera equipment in that car."

He popped the tiny trunk and scratched his head.
"Don't you have a smaller tripod?"

Half an hour later, they were on their way with a
smaller tripod, the bare minimum of camera equipment, and one consolidated overnight bag. Top down,
headed for Amarillo, with Hank Williams on the
stereo. The buzz of the engine and the flapping of the
wind made chatter difficult, so she just gathered her
hair into a ponytail, leaned back, and soaked up the
day.

They might not spend the night in Amarillo—that
depended on the witness. But they'd agreed to stay
over if necessary. Luke kept his hand on hers whenever
he wasn't shifting. The wind and sun felt so good, so
pleasantly invigorating, and the hand-holding seemed

so innocent, she magnanimously decided not to protest. An hour later, they were still holding hands when it started to drizzle.

Luke pulled over at the first gas station to put up the top and take a comfort break. When he climbed back in the car and gunned the engine, she could tell his mood had shifted. They headed back to the highway, but this time he kept both hands on the wheel. With the top up and the noise down, there was plenty of room for conversation, but none seemed forthcoming.

She let it go about ten minutes, then asked, "Is something wrong?"

He shrugged one shoulder. "You picked up on that, huh?"

"I am a psychiatrist." She kept her tone playful.

"So I hear."

More silence. She pulled the band out of her hair and let it fall freely to her shoulders. If he thought she was going to pick up a crowbar and pry whatever the hell was on his mind out of him, he was mistaken. No room in this car for a crowbar. Looking out her window, she hummed tunelessly.

"What the hell?" he said at last. "Are you tone-deaf?"

"Just passing the time."

"If I tell you what's on my mind, do you promise not to hum anymore?"

"Depends."

"On what?"

"On whether I think you're being honest or not."

"I told you already, Clancy. I don't play games."

"Seems like you're playing one right now. You haven't said a word since we left the gas station."

"That's only because I'm not sure you're ready to hear what I have to say." He turned his eyes on her, and the intensity of his gaze made her throat tighten.

She might be in over her head, but it was too late to unask the question. "Fire away." She tried to infuse her voice with confidence.

"Like I said before, I'm not nearly as noble as you make me out. You give me too much credit. I can see it in the way you look at me."

"Let me get this straight. You've been holding my hand for the past hour, but now you're not talking to me because you think I like you too much." She turned her eyes back to the road so he wouldn't see the sting of his words burning up her cheeks. "I've already told you I'm not interested in taking whatever this is into relationship territory, so just relax and enjoy the ride."

"You're missing the point. I've been thinking a lot about you lately . . . about us . . . and holding your hand like that, it hit me. I'm feeling something . . . *big*. It's important to me that once you fall in love with me, it's with the real me. Not some trumped-up dreamboat you've got floating around in your fantasy life. That's all I'm going to say."

"I don't fantasize about you."

"Yes, you do." His voice came out low and gravelly.

"You've obviously got me confused with some buckle bunny, but I'm afraid that cowboy stuff just doesn't work for me." Her voice carried a little too much bravado. She knew she was trying too hard to pretend his declaration from a moment ago hadn't affected her.

He'd said he wanted her to fall in love with him—the real him.

And she was sharp enough to read the subtext. The only time a man wanted a woman to fall in love with him was when he was falling in love with her. But that was impossible. They barely knew one another. She clutched the door handle.

"What, now you wanna jump out of the car? I said you might not be ready for this."

"Luke, I'm *never* going to be ready for this. I think *you've* got the wrong idea about *me*. Maybe I'm the ignoble one, and you're the one who needs to take off his rose-colored glasses. Ever think of that?"

"Nope. But if you want to air your dirty laundry, fine by me. I like the dirty laundry, those little everyday flaws that make you who you are. To me, that's the good stuff."

"You already had your PI check me out, so what's there to air?"

"My guess it has to do with your sister, Grace."

He might as well have punched her in the stomach as brought her sister up. But if there was even a slight chance Luke Jericho was actually falling in love with her, he deserved to know the truth. Blinking away the pressure behind her eyes she turned to him. "I'm sure you know from your background check that my sister took her own life. Postpartum depression. She needed me, and I wasn't there for her."

"You're too smart for that Faith. You can't take the blame for another person's choices."

"But I can take the blame for my own choices, and I made some doozies." She sucked in a big breath and let it out slowly. Folded her hands in her lap and looked down at them. The words she wanted to say stuck in her throat—maybe because she'd never said them aloud. Ever. "I was in love with my sister's husband. Or at least I thought I was at the time."

"The detective, Danny Benson? Didn't see that one coming."

"Of course you didn't. He was my sister's husband. So there you go, now you see I have a legitimate reason to feel guilty, not to mention heartbroken."

"You still into the guy?"

She shook her head. "No. What I mean is, I'm heartbroken about Grace. I missed out on so much time with her. All the while I was mooning over her husband, wishing I had her life, her family, I was losing the last little bit of time I could've had with her. *She* was my family. She practically raised me, and somehow I let myself get resentful and jealous. I lost sight of how special she was. Now she's gone, and I can never get that time back. I didn't lose it. I tossed it away for nothing. Grace needed me, and I wasn't there, but the truth is I needed her, too."

"Say that last part again."

This time she couldn't keep her voice from cracking. "I needed her, too."

"Think about that. Your sister had a new baby, a new husband, and she was depressed on top of everything. It seems natural you might've felt she'd abandoned you. Maybe you were looking to your brother-in-law for the attention you weren't getting from your sister."

"God, no. I mean, yes. But you make it sound like that makes it okay, when it's not. Grace took care of me after our parents died. She was there for me, then, even though she was little more than a young girl herself. After she married Danny, I was so jealous of Grace I never even noticed that *she needed me*. I never saw *her* pain because I was too busy being a selfish brat."

"You were just a teenager, though. Right?"

"I was as old as my sister was when our parents died. I was old enough to know better. Old enough to *do* something."

"Like what?"

She didn't need Luke to make excuses for her. She'd been blind to Grace's pain, period. "Like get my sister professional help."

"Seems like that'd be her husband's job."

"Yes, but he didn't realize . . ." She ran out of steam halfway through that thought. Didn't want to finish it. "Grace's death wasn't Danny's fault. And now you're the one missing the point."

"Okay. So you're a bad girl. You coveted your sister's husband. How does that translate into your pushing me away?"

She didn't have the answer. She only knew she couldn't let herself get sucked into that situation again. She never wanted to be in that head-over-heels place again. That place where nothing else matters but the man you *think* you love, because it's not real . . . and the price is far too high. "I'm fine with sex, Luke. But that's it for us."

He pumped the brake and swerved onto the shoulder of the highway, killed the engine, and grabbed her by the shoulders. "That's just not enough for me, Clancy." His eyes searched her face. "You and your brother-in-law ever actually fool around?"

"Oh God, no. He's my sister's husband, and it was all on my part. Anyway, two years ago, he finally remarried. He's a newlywed now, and trust me—he doesn't have a clue how I felt back then—and he never will."

"I wouldn't be too sure about that last part, the not knowing, I mean."

Luke sounded angry, and she wasn't sure why. "Sorry you don't understand. I never should've told you to begin with, it's just that I didn't want you to think I don't care for you, or that you'd done something wrong. This is all on me. I simply don't want to be in a relationship . . . with anyone."

His voice rose, and his grip on her shoulders tightened. "You wanted Danny, though, so why didn't you go after him when you had the chance?"

"Are you listening at all? My. Sister's. Husband."

"Which brings us full circle." The edge in his voice smoothed out. "You did nothing wrong. You were a kid who'd lost her parents. You saw your sister moving on with her life, with a new family, and you wanted that for yourself. You never acted on any of your feelings because you would never do anything to hurt your sister. Not intentionally." Releasing her shoulders, he pushed a lock of hair off her forehead. "Listen to me, Clancy. Lusting in your heart doesn't make you a bad person. Remember Jimmy Carter?"

"President Jimmy Carter? Of course, but I don't see—"

"Jimmy Carter admitted in an interview with *Playboy* magazine that he lusted in his heart after women who were not his wife. He still got elected president, and he even won a Nobel Peace Prize."

She opened her mouth, but no words came out. There really were no words to express how convoluted she found Luke's reasoning.

His face was less serious now, his lips rising at the edges. A full-blown grin soon followed, and her own mouth started to twitch. When he cocked his brow and spread his hands in an I-rest-my-case, something inside her altered. From deep within, a rumble of laughter germinated, gathered speed, and eventually erupted from her mouth.

Deep, gut-busting waves of hilarity followed, and she grabbed her knees, gasping for air. "A Nobel Peace Prize. I'm next in line for the good ol' Nobel Peace Prize."

She slapped her knees and sat up, throwing her

arms in the air. "Shove over, Jimmy Carter, because here comes Faith Clancy."

She turned to Luke. He pulled her against him, and she pressed her cheek to his chest, loving the feel of his heart beating against her ear. He stroked her hair, and soon the shaking waves of hilarity turned to sobs, dampening his white T-shirt. "I've lost her forever, Luke. She's never coming back."

"The rest of us are still here, baby. Maybe you could stop beating yourself up long enough not to miss out on that. Please don't let history repeat itself. I'd hate to see you wake up one day and realize you'd turned away the people who genuinely care about you." He kissed one eyelid, then the other, then the tip of her nose. His voice was low and rough in her ear, "I need you, Clancy. So please, don't push me away."

They'd made it to Amarillo. Luke estimated the odds of getting any useful information out of a witness after four years was close to zero, but that didn't mean he was going to pass up the opportunity to question one. After all, if you knew exactly where your big break was going to come from, you'd just dial in the location on your GPS and sit back on your haunches and wait. Absent those magic coordinates, the only thing to do was hit the pavement. So here they were in Amarillo, Texas, on Jeremy Jacobs's front stoop. Projecting confidence, he smiled at Faith and rang the bell.

"I'll make the introductions," Faith offered. "A female may seem less intimidating."

"Nothing wrong with a little intimidation. In my book, it's okay if this kid knows we mean business."

Faith gave him a look, "Knock yourself out. I'm only an expert in human behavior, which, as I recall, is why you brought me along. But hey, that's no reason to let me take the lead in interviewing the witness."

"I brought you along 'cause you've got great legs—that and you've got a few other skills."

"Like my ability to enhance memory via hypnosis?"

"Exactly. But I never said anything about your taking the lead. I fully intend to impress upon this witness . . ."

At the sound of footsteps inside the home, he shut his mouth and straightened his shoulders, used the tail of his T-shirt to buff his championship buckle. He'd dressed to impress. These people ought to know who they were dealing with. A slender woman, midforties answered the door. Brittle blond hair tinged with orange framed her round face. She raised her eyebrows expectantly. "Hullo."

"Mrs. Jacobs, I presume?"

Her eyes darted appreciatively to Luke's waist, and her mouth tipped into a welcoming smile. "How can I help y'all?"

He'd been right to wear the buckle. Like his mother always said, no use hiding your light under a bushel.

He stuck out his hand. "Luke Jericho. And that's Dr.

Faith Clancy. I was wondering if we might have a word with your son if he's home."

Her smile faded as quickly as it had appeared, but at least she didn't shut the door in their faces. "What about?"

"I understand your son Jeremy was a friend of Kenny Stoddard."

Closing the door halfway, she stepped back. "Sorry. Jeremy's not home."

"Sure I am. What's up?" A lanky young man appeared behind her just before she slammed the door.

Beside him, Faith started to hum. He gave her the stink eye, then knocked on the door, first gently, then harder.

No dice.

"Jeremy." He stopped knocking and cupped his hands around his mouth to make a megaphone. "I need to talk to you about your friend Kenny."

The muffled sound of raised voices came through the door. Luke checked his watch. Four minutes later, Faith was still humming, and the voices still argued behind the door. Luke raised his hand to knock again.

Grabbing his wrist, Faith shook her head at him. "Take it easy. He obviously wants to talk to us. We just need to give him time. Let *him* convince his mother."

Luke dragged a palm over his face, put his hands on his hip. Made a couple of 360s. Three minutes later, the door cracked open. Mrs. Jacobs tried to body block her son, who, at nineteen, was a half foot taller than her.

His head wagged over her shoulder, revealing intelligent brown eyes and a guarded expression. He poked his mother's arm.

"What exactly is this about, please?" Mrs. Jacobs voice held a faint tremor. "Jeremy talked to the police four years ago. Told the detectives everything he knows. I shouldn't have let it happen, but I didn't know better at the time. After what they put him through, you can bet I won't make that mistake again. Kept my poor son holed up in that little room twenty-three hours with four cops taking turns on him. You want to talk to my boy, Mister, you gotta charge him or subpoena him first. Jeremy's not saying a word without an attorney."

Jeremy gently shoved her arm aside and stepped forward. "Mom, I'm not a suspect anymore. They got the guy who did it already. I read it in the papers."

Her face paled. "Not one more word, Jeremy. I mean it."

"Mrs. Jacobs, I'm Faith Clancy." Faith's voice was softer than cotton candy and just about as sticky-sweet, making Luke wonder if she had some buckle bunny in her after all. "Mr. Jericho and I are not detectives—we're not any kind of law enforcement—and we know that your son played absolutely no role in Kenny Stoddard's death."

"Then why do you need to talk with him?"

"Because we believe he may have information that can lead us to the man who killed his friend, information that's been overlooked but may be important in solving the cold case. For all the interrogating the police put Jeremy through, no one ever listened to him. Mr. Jericho and I *want* to hear what your son has to say. I promise, if Jeremy talks to us, we'll listen."

Mrs. Jacobs brushed her hands together and shook her head. "No. You got the guy already."

"He confessed," Jeremy interjected.

"You don't need my boy to testify against a man who's already confessed." She pushed the door, but Jeremy caught it with his foot before it shut, then swung it wide open.

"I never saw the man who confessed. I wish I *could* testify against him. I wish I could see him fry. But I didn't see him, so I can't say I did."

Luke's fists tightened at his sides. He clamped his jaw shut and nodded at Faith. Let her keep the reins. She'd gotten a helluva lot further than he had to this point.

"Jeremy"—Faith held up one finger to signal this wouldn't take long— "do you mind if I record this?"

"Yes. We mind." The mother came up on her tiptoes.

Faith put her recorder back in her pocket. "Jeremy, have you seen pictures of the man in police custody, the man claiming to be the Saint?"

"Everyone's seen his picture. His face is all over the news in Amarillo." He looked away. "Don't forget, we lost one of our own."

"I haven't forgotten, Jeremy. I don't want to forget. That's why we're here. We want to be sure the *real*

Santa Fe Saint gets what's coming to him. We want justice for Kenny as much as you do. I just need to ask you a few questions."

Jeremy nodded.

"So let me make sure I understand what you're saying: You do not recognize the man the police have in custody. The man who claims to be the Santa Fe Saint?"

"Never saw the bastard before in my life."

Luke couldn't stay silent any longer. "You're absolutely certain the man on the news is *not* the man you saw with Kenny on the day he disappeared."

"Positive. I told the police then, and I'm telling you now. The guy I saw was a freaky little dude, a shrimp. I even met him once at Kenny's place. If I saw that creep again, I'd know him in a heartbeat."

"You actually met him?" Luke rushed forward, and Faith put her arm out, body blocking him in much the same way Mrs. Jacobs had curtailed her son.

"That's enough." Mrs. Jacobs clasped her hands in front of her. "My boy doesn't know this Saint person, he's said so, and that's the end of it."

"That's because the man in custody is not the Saint." Luke strained to keep his voice level. "He's innocent!" So much for level.

"I don't understand. He confessed, didn't he?" Jeremy stepped out onto the stoop, but his mother yanked him back inside by the collar.

"My brother, Dante Jericho, is the man the police

have in custody. The *real* Saint, who is *not* in police custody, is the man who killed your friend."

Mrs. Jacobs's eyes bulged. She shook her fist at him. "You're his *brother*! If you don't get off this property right now, I'm going to call 911."

He ignored the pressure of Faith's hand tugging at his shirtsleeve. "And tell them what? That a man and a woman are standing on your porch asking you polite questions? We're not breaking any laws here, ma'am. All we're doing is trying to get to the truth. Something I'd think you and your son would be interested in."

"You're trespassing on private property." She fumbled in her pocket and came up with a cell. "Get off my porch!"

The boy put his arm around his mother. "Look. I'd like to help you. But my mom's upset. And I can't talk about this anymore." He patted his mother's hand. "I'm asking you nicely, Mr. Jericho, Dr. Clancy. Please leave. My mom and I have been through enough. Someone killed my best friend, then the police accused me. They said I murdered the best friend I ever had. My mom lost her job at the bank. Not one girl in town will go out with me. Even after all this time."

"Look." Luke modulated his voice and bit back his anger. "I admit I don't know what it's like to be accused of a crime I didn't commit. But I *do* know what it's like to have family falsely accused." He looked pointedly at Mrs. Jacobs. "And it stinks. You wake up with a knot in your gut in the mornings, and you fall asleep with that same knot in your gut at night. Half the time you can't eat, and when you do, your food tastes like sawdust in your mouth. When you finally fall asleep at night, you dream of falling off a cliff or drowning in the ocean. Then you wake up in a cold sweat . . . and there's the knot again."

Her eyes glistened, but she made no reply.

"Mrs. Jacobs, my brother is innocent. There's talk of extradition to Texas. I know you don't want an innocent man to die."

"G-go away, and don't come back here again. We want nothing more to do with this matter."

He squeezed his eyes and gritted his teeth, knowing what he was about to do would likely get him reincarnated as a sidewinder. "Mrs. Jacobs, your son says he never saw my brother, but he did see some *other* man with Kenny."

Her eyes widened, and her hands began to tremble.

He told himself the end justified the means in a situation like this, and why shouldn't he warn the woman? "Think about what that means, Mrs. Jacobs. If Dr. Clancy and I . . ." Hesitating, he looked at Faith, who refused to meet his eyes. "If Dr. Clancy and I, who are just regular people, not detectives or anyone special like that, if *we* found out your son has seen the real Saint up close and personal, don't you think *the Saint* knows about Jeremy, too? Mark my words, someday the real killer is going to come looking for your son. Only question is why he hasn't come for him already."

She drew back her shoulders and spit in his face.

He wiped his cheek and said nothing.

"You're trying to scare me, but it won't work. It's been four years, and we haven't had any trouble. They have the real Saint in custody. He *confessed*."

"But what if they don't?" Faith asked softly.

Luke spun toward her and put his hand on his heart. He knew what that must've cost her—to join with him in frightening this poor woman, a mother who only wanted to protect her son.

"What if they don't have the real Saint behind bars? What if he's still on the loose?" Faith held out her hand. "Here's my card. You can call me on my cell if you and your son change your minds. We're staying at the Starlight Motel, room six. Mr. Jericho and I will be in town until tomorrow afternoon." Then she shrugged. "After that, I'm afraid we can't help you."

TWENTY-FOUR

Thursday, August 15, 1:00 P.M.

Luke and Faith had just checked into the Starlight Motel, and after what they'd done to Jeremy Jacobs and his mom, Faith wanted to jump in the shower and scrub herself clean. Too bad dirty tactics didn't wash off with soap and water.

Luke clicked the dead bolt on the motel-room door and gave her a look that made her regret agreeing to rent only one room. Hopefully, they wouldn't need to stay overnight, but that all depended on Jeremy Jacobs.

Luke moved slowly toward her, circling her like a wrangler aiming to coax a skittish mare. "Thanks for that, by the way."

"For joining in the scare tactics? No problem." She touched her nose like she always did when she told a lie. The knowledge that she'd added to Jeremy's pain—and to his mother's fears—was currently burning through her stomach lining like a hot coal. Maybe she could pick up some Tums in the motel gift shop.

Still, she'd do it again. The truth might be hard and

cold and scary as hell, but running from it never gets you anywhere. She thought of that corny refrigerator magnet Grace had proudly displayed.

EMBRACE THE TRUTH.

Not always an easy thing to do. The Saint was out there; she was certain of it. The menacing photos sent to her cell, a fresh body found with a rosary—those things had to be the work of the Saint, and the Saint had to know Jeremy Jacobs could identify him. The boy's life was absolutely in danger. Her fingers clenched the hem of her blouse. She and Luke had been right to use whatever tactics necessary to get Jeremy to talk. With Dante in custody, the police had simply stopped investigating other leads. Dante's life was not the only one at stake. The Saint could have another victim in his crosshairs right this minute.

Luke pulled a foil packet from his pocket and popped something into his mouth.

"Tums?" she asked hopefully.

"Breath mint." He waggled his brows, and she backed up until her knees bumped the edge of the bed.

He closed the distance between them and swept his hand down the side of her cheek. Her body leaned forward as if he'd yanked a string that connected them at the heart. Like every time he touched her, she wanted more. More fingers, more lips, more skin.

More Luke.

It was not only getting harder to keep the man at arm's length, it was getting harder to remember why she should. He slid his mouth up against her ear, and while he nibbled, she caught the faintest whiff of his minty breath. Her mouth already open and hungry, she tried to turn in for a kiss, but he relocated, nipping his way down her neck, across her collarbone, and over the hollow of her throat. He dragged his palms down her sides, molding them to the shape of her body. Her skin burned beneath her blouse, and, longing to shed it, she unbuttoned her top button. His hand came over hers. His lips retraced their path, and finally, *finally*, thank the Lord in heaven, landed on top of hers.

This particular kiss was born of more than physical need though there was certainly that—every scrap of skin she owned clamored for Luke's attention. But this kiss was hard and rough, fueled by adrenaline and fear and at the very bottom of it . . . trust. A kiss this deep demanded complete faith in the other person. She didn't know why or how, but she'd come to trust Luke to tell the truth even when it suited his purpose better to lie.

Integrity.

Yes, that's what Luke had—and she'd never been this wet in her life.

Her hands found his hips and pulled him against her body, savoring the feel of his erection pressing into her stomach.

He broke the kiss. "Don't push me away, Faith."

She trailed her fingers over the hard muscles of his arms. "Did that feel like pushing you away? My bad. Because all I want right now is to get as physically close to you as possible, and if some parts of your body happen to get tangled up with some parts of mine, then, hey, that's just the way it goes."

He put his hand on the small of her back and jerked her even closer, grinding into her through her clothes. "I'm not talking about sex, and you know it."

Panic welled in her throat as she fought for control of the situation. She lifted her right knee and draped it over his hip. "But I *am* talking about sex. And whether you like it or not, you can't hide the fact that you want that, too. You see, I'm a licensed physician, and I recognize a hard-on when I feel one." She rubbed her pelvis against his as tightly as she could and rolled her head to the side, exposing her neck to him.

He bent backward, lifting her off the ground, and she wound her legs around him. One hand came up to her nape, and he laced his fingers through her hair. His other hand was under her bottom, supporting her, and crushing her into him at the same time. His mouth slammed down on hers, and she let out a soft cry, both unable and unwilling to conceal her desire for him. She was aching and scared and desperate to feel him inside her—that quickly.

He dropped her on the bed, straddled her, still fully clothed. Grabbing her wrists, he pushed her arms up over her head. Her breath was coming in soft gasps. "Yes," she moaned.

"No way." His voice was low and raspy. She blinked hard, confused, tying to read the expression on his face, but her body kept overriding her brain. Finally, her eyes focused. The fast twitch of the muscle in his jaw, the thin hard line of his lips told her he was serious.

"Luke." He'd reduced her to begging, but she didn't care, couldn't care about her pride in this moment. "Please."

"No way," he repeated. "I can't think of any other way to tell you, so I'll say again, I don't play games."

"I'm not playing games." Not games. This was war. A battle with herself, and every instinct she had was screaming at her to surrender. Surrender not just to his touch but to his need. He'd said he *needed* her.

"Like hell you're not." Pressing her into the mattress with the weight of his body, he used his knee to separate her legs, and she writhed harder beneath him. "You're a grown woman, with all kinds of skills—a fucking Yale-educated psychiatrist no less, and you're so afraid of your own feelings, you won't let anyone get close to you. Sorry you lost your sister, and good for you for channeling that pain into helping others, but just because your sister's dead, and you're an orphan doesn't mean you get a free pass to skip the rest of your life."

His cold words were a stark contrast to the heat that poured from his body to hers and back again. This was not the moment to examine her past. Her past was what she was trying to escape, right here, right now with him. She wanted the amnesic bliss his body could provide, and if he wasn't going to cooperate, then to hell with it. She tried to roll out from under him, but his weight completely trapped her. Lifting her head off the bed, she said, "Then just let me go."

"No way."

"Would you please stop saying that?"

"Sure. Just as soon as you own up to how you really feel about me—about us." He narrowed his eyes at her. His erection, like hot steel between her legs, taunted her. "I can stay here all day, sweetheart. So if I were you, I'd start talking."

Her heart hammered in her chest so fast she couldn't catch her breath. She should just surrender. "C'mon, Luke." She controlled her voice to hide the wave of doubt washing over her. "Don't try to tell me that what we have is any different than what you have with other women, or what I have with other men. You'll get tired of me soon enough, just like I'll get tired of you."

The sound that came out of his mouth this time was feral, aggressive, and underneath it all, wounded.

She wanted to cradle his head in her arms, and if he hadn't had her wrists pinned mercilessly over her head, she might've.

"You're goddamn right what we have is different. And the only thing I'm tired of is your bullshit."

Something in her chest turned over and squeezed. Pain and hope simultaneously jetted through her veins, and for one crazy second, she thought she could love this man. Her neck strained as she lifted her head, her pulse pounding in her throat. "I'm sorry. I'm so sorry, but I just can't."

His eyes were cold blue agate.

"I've lost everyone I've ever loved. So maybe you could cut me some slack if I don't feel like getting overly attached to you." She forced herself to hold his gaze, willed herself not to let him see her cry.

"I'm not cutting you an inch of slack. Not one single inch." Keeping her pinned between his thighs, he released her hands. "But hell if I'm walking away without a fight."

Her body started to shake, and despite her will, moisture slicked her cheeks. His heart was beating against her heart, the rhythm hard and fast and demanding. Something inside her tore open, and need swamped her. She *needed* him. She *trusted* him. "Don't. Please don't," she begged.

He froze, but didn't take his eyes from her face. His rasping breath told her how difficult it was for him to stay so silent, so still. Even now, he was protecting her.

Lifting her hand to touch his cheek, she whispered, "Please don't walk away without a fight."

Faith gave her hair one last stroke of the brush and frowned at her reflection in the mirror. No more stalling. She'd showered and changed and even blown out her hair, and she couldn't stay in here forever. Sooner or later, she had to face Luke, or face herself, or face whatever this thing was between them. Little shivers of excitement rushed over her at the thought of seeing Luke again even though they'd just spent the past hour making love.

Making love.

Yes, that was the correct term for what she'd done with Luke. To steady herself, she hauled in a deep breath and stepped out of the bathroom, flashing Luke a shaky smile.

He came to her, turned her palm up, and stroked the underside of her wrist. "You okay? I'm afraid I might've been a little rough."

"Oh no. It was wonderful." Her face heated. "I mean *you* were wonderful. And you're right, it's time I stopped feeling sorry for myself—"

"That's not what I meant, sweetheart. I meant . . ."

There was a fast rap on the door. Luke stopped mid-sentence. They exchanged a glance.

Jeremy.

"We'll finish this later." Luke's voice was low and gravelly and full of a sexy promise that made her insides melt.

"Damn right, we will." She'd been acting a fool, and she knew it, but she wasn't sure where to go from there. "I'll get it."

She tugged her blouse to be sure it was in place, slipped back into her shoes, and opened the door, and just as she'd hoped, there stood Jeremy Jacobs.

Hands fidgeting at his sides, he said, "Is this a good time? I guess I should've called."

"Your timing is perfect." He didn't know *how* perfect.

She ushered Jeremy inside. "Look who's here," she said lamely to Luke, then shrugged one shoulder.

Luke had swept her clean off her feet, and she needed a minute to regain her professional demeanor.

"I came here to talk about Kenny." Jeremy got straight to the point.

"This okay with your mom?" she asked.

He clenched his teeth. "I'm nineteen. I don't need her permission, and anyway, I got a right to protect myself *and* my mom—whether she likes it or not. That man I saw with Kenny, I know he's the one who killed him. Way too creepy. You can't tell me this weirdo's showing up in Kenny's life, then Kenny's winding up dead is all a big coincidence."

"It might be. Coincidence can be very convincing sometimes." Luke crossed to Jeremy and laid a hand on his shoulder. "Just so we're clear, we're not here to get you to say what you think we want to hear."

"You mean that your brother's innocent."

"Right. How would you even know a thing like that? We're here to find out from you only things you actually saw, only things you actually know. We want the truth, Jeremy. Nothing more and nothing less."

"I want the truth, too. I *need* to know who murdered my best friend . . . and I don't want anyone else to die. What he did to Kenny . . ." Jeremy cast his eyes nervously around the room, started to cough.

Faith pressed a bottle of water into his hands and led him to a chair. A few minutes later, his coughing subsided, and the color came back to his lips.

Good. For a second she'd thought their witness was going to faint. "We've got snacks, too." Faith opened the minifridge and swept her hand across the contents. "Peanut M&Ms and Chips Ahoy . . ."

"Pringles." He straightened in his seat. "I like Pringles."

"Pringles it is."

The tension in the air had just begun to dissipate when Jeremy fixed his eyes on the video equipment in the corner of the room.

Luke tracked his gaze, and offered, "We hoped you'd agree to talk on camera."

"Fine by me." Jeremy shoved a handful of Pringles in his mouth and chased it with bottled water. "Only I don't remember too much anymore. It's been four years, and I told the cops everything I knew at the time. Don't they have what you need? They interviewed me for hours."

"Unfortunately, those tapes are nowhere to be found. All that's left of your interview is a pad of paper with mostly illegibly scribbled notes."

"I guess I can see that. The cops weren't too interested in my description of the guy I saw with Jeremy. They thought I was making him up because I did it." His voice rose an octave. "They thought I killed my best friend."

"We know you didn't do it, Jeremy. No need to worry about that anymore, not now, not after three other murders the police tried and failed to tie you to." Faith sat beside Jeremy and made her voice reassuring. "I guess what I'm trying to get across is this: You have nothing to fear anymore from the police and nothing to gain by lying. If there was no other man, just say so, and we'll be on our way."

His eyes glittered, and he wiped his nose with his sleeve. "It's the truth. Why won't anyone believe me? If I could have made the police believe me back then, maybe they would have found the Saint and stopped him before all those other people died. If you look at it that way, those deaths are on my head."

"Whoa. Don't even think of taking the blame for what the police did or didn't do. You volunteered all the information you had. You could've lawyered up, but you didn't. And you can still help catch the Saint." Faith passed Jeremy an informed consent form. "This just says it's okay with you if we record the interview on camera."

"Sure." He scribbled his name. "But how can I help if I don't remember? The guy was shrimpy, with wavy black hair. He got into a truck with Kenny on Bell Street, and I never saw either one of them again. That's it, that's all I remember. I'm sorry." He wiped his nose with his sleeve again.

Faith went to the bathroom and returned with a box of Kleenex.

"Thanks." Jeremy blew into the tissue, then landed a nice shot into the trash.

"What if there was a way I could help you remember more? Would you be willing to let me try to enhance your memory of that day?"

"How?" He sounded more curious than frightened.

"Hypnosis." It had only a small chance of working to begin with, and unless Jeremy felt comfortable, there would be no way she could even get him under.

"You can hypnotize me?" He grinned like a kid who'd just been given permission to play in the dirt. "Cool."

On the other hand, a motivated subject was a hypnotherapist's dream. "Yeah. I guess it is kinda cool."

While Luke set up the recording equipment, Faith gave Jeremy more information on the small risks associated with hypnosis and reassured herself he was still comfortable proceeding.

"Ready when you are." Luke focused the camera, then motioned for Faith to sit facing Jeremy, her back to the camera.

"I'm ready," Jeremy said, looking Faith hard in the eyes as if he couldn't wait and was trying to hypnotize himself already. "Are you going to swing a watch in front of me and say *you're getting sleepy, very very sleepy?*"

That made her smile in spite of her determination to stay neutral, professional. The technique was really quite simple, and hardly as glamorous as it was made out to be. "I'm afraid not. Clinical hypnosis isn't the same as what you see in the movies or even in a Las Vegas show. It's really not much more than a state of deep relaxation and heightened awareness. There's nothing to be frightened of." Fortunately, Jeremy didn't seem a bit worried, at least about the idea of being put in a trance. "Let's begin by having you close your eyes and imagine someplace safe and warm. Take your time and let me know when you've found that place."

The room wasn't noise-free, but with a little luck, the sound of cars buzzing by on the street could be used to some advantage. A constant hum like that might serve to cover up more distracting noises, like chatter in the hallway.

A smile played across Jeremy's face, suggesting he'd followed her instructions.

"Where are you, Jeremy? Can you describe your safe place?"

"I'm camping. I'm camping out in the woods with Kenny, and there's this mountain stream."

"That's good." Very good. The fact that he'd brought Kenny into his safe place meant he was trying hard to help, and she could work with that mountain stream. "Do you hear the stream rushing by? Smell the must of the woods?"

He nodded, still smiling. The buzzing of the cars had likely just turned to rushing water in Jeremy's mind. She could almost hear that babbling stream herself. "Good. Now then, imagine your body is getting heavy, very heavy."

His body sank deeper into the chair.

"Now your left arm is getting lighter. Imagine a balloon tied to your left hand."

Slowly his left arm started to lift off the armrest.

Jeremy was proving an excellent subject. Less than five minutes later, she had him in a deep trance. "Good, Jeremy, you're doing so well. Are you comfortable?"

He nodded.

"Is your friend Kenny still there with you?"

Again, he nodded yes.

"Ask Kenny if he'd like for you to remember the last time you saw him."

Jeremy's chin tilted up. A few seconds passed, and then, "Yes. He wants me to remember. *I* want to remember."

"Good. Tell me about the last time, before today, that you saw Kenny. What are you doing?"

"We're at the mall. My mom dropped us off to get haircuts, but we don't want haircuts." He shook one hand like it was hot. "We just ran into two babes at Yo Yo Yum's, that frozen-yogurt place. Carmen and Jennifer. We even got their numbers." A look of disappointment crossed his face. "They're probably fake. Carmen and Jennifer just ditched us for two jocks."

"Their loss. What are you going to do now?"

"Go to Chili's."

"What do you order?" If he could remember a safe detail, that would be a good lead-in to more troublesome memories.

"Nachos. Loaded with jalapeños." He swiped at his mouth and sipped his water. "Damn, those are hot."

"I bet. Do you need more water?"

His brow drew down, and he crossed his arms over his chest. His chin jerked sharply to the right, and she thought he was about to come out of the trance, when suddenly he started talking, his head turning and nodding like he was speaking to another person. "I don't like him, Kenny. He gives me the creeps. How'd he even know you play the guitar?"

Jeremy fell silent again. Faith cast a glance back at Luke. His eyes were wide, his face rapt with attention.

Jeremy leaned forward, resting one hand on his knee. "But how did he know, Kenny? You didn't put an ad out or anything."

"Are you and Kenny still at Chili's, Jeremy?"

"No. Kenny just left. I told him that guy was bad news. I told him not to give that guy guitar lessons. You don't let someone in your house who just shows up from nowhere with a guitar and offers you money for lessons."

Sensing motion behind her, Faith looked back at Luke. He scribbled something on a piece of paper and held it up.

Good question.

"You met this creepy guy at Ken's house? On a different day? Before Chili's? Before Carmen and Jennifer?"

"Yeah. I was at Kenny's place after school. His mom wasn't home, and we were about to smoke some weed when this freak and his guitar show up. Says he heard Kenny knew how to stroke a guitar—that's exactly how he put it—gave me the willies."

"What else do you remember?"

"His guitar was maple, and all oiled up. Had a fancy rosewood fretboard. Had a sweet sound to it. Kenny took it off the guy and strummed it. Then he told the guy he'd do it—give him lessons. But to come back a different day." He shuddered. "Creepola."

"Besides the way the man talked about the guitar,

do you remember anything else that bothered you about him? You seem to have a strong dislike for some-one you'd never met before."

"His tattoos. One said *Cookie*, which is just plain stupid. The other was a green, no, a blue tiger. And the guy kept flexing his biceps and growling—like he was the tiger. The way he kept eyeing Kenny, I knew he was a pervert. Perry the Pervert."

"Perry the Pervert?" Her fingers twitched, and her palms tingled. "Did he say his name was Perry, or did you just think that fit?"

"Yeah. He said his name was Perry, but I added the pervert." He smirked.

"And you saw him again, at Chili's?"

"Yeah. I told Kenny not to go with him, but he didn't listen. He left with Perry the Pervert. I looked through the window and saw them get into a truck. It was one of those landscaper's truck with a tarp in the back." His lip shivered. "Kenny got in the truck with Perry the Pervert and left me holding the check."

A tear rolled down the side of his cheek. "I don't want to remember anymore."

"It's okay, Jeremy. You've been a big help to Kenny, and to us. You can wake up anytime you're ready."

Tears were streaming down Jeremy's face now. "Kenny left me holding the check, and I went back home and cursed him. That night, I sent him a text that said: *Asshole. I hope I never see you again.*" His voice broke. "And I never did."

"Wake up, Jeremy." She squeezed his knee firmly.

Jeremy opened his eyes and looked at her, pure anguish written on his face.

"I have to say, that was impressive." Having finished packing up the camera equipment, Luke turned to Faith.

"Thanks." She twirled a long piece of her flame-colored hair, then pulled it between her teeth. Chewing her hair might be childish and innocent, but her body was anything but, and it was calling to him right now.

He raked a hand through his hair and took a turn around the room. His brother's life was on the line, and all he could think about was throwing Faith down on the bed for one more round before they hit the road. *What a guy.* "No, seriously. That was amazing the way you had Jeremy under so fast." He'd been skeptical about the whole mumbo-jumbo hypnosis deal, but it'd worked in a big way. Recorded on video, and also in his handwritten notes was a wealth of detail about the person of interest last seen with Kenny Stoddard—right down to the color, location, and shape of the man's highly unusual tattoos.

Faith leaned forward, intent on her laptop screen. "What did Torpedo think?"

He shrugged. "He says he'll pass the information to the DA, but he's not hopeful they'll follow up on this Perry guy. They had a lot of the same information when they first interviewed Jeremy, before they *lost* it, but nothing ever turned up."

"Because they didn't take Jeremy seriously. They were focused on him as their prime suspect and didn't even look for Perry the Pervert." She shot him a frustrated look and kicked the leg of the desk in a very uncharacteristic display.

"Preaching to the choir here. I'm just the messenger. And it gets worse. Torpedo says he can't alibi Dante out for any of the murders, and the cops can place him at an Amarillo Walmart buying a case of beer a week before Jeremy's body was found in Lubbock. They're convinced Dante's the Saint. So if we want to find Perry, it's on us. Unless we can connect Perry to some or all of the other murders, nobody is interested."

"What was Dante doing in Amarillo?"

"Four years ago? Beats the hell out of me—rodeo maybe, lot's of folks come out for that, but one thing I do know: He didn't kill Jeremy Jacobs while he was here . . . so let's get going and connect Perry to another case."

"How are we going to connect the other murders to Perry the Pervert if we can't even connect the murders to each other?"

"You mean apart from the rosaries, the hog-tying, and the shotgun blasts to the head." He leaned against the wall and stuck his hands in his pockets.

"Yes, there's that." She sighed. "But what you've

just described is merely the killer's MO. I'm talking about the victims themselves. What do Nancy, Kenny, William, and Linda have in common that made them targets? Maybe if we knew that, we'd know what connects them to Perry."

Faith had a way of seeing things he didn't. He went to her and massaged her shoulders. "I like the way you think. I say we do what any PI worth his salt would do and sign on to Google."

She patted his hand in a disappointingly platonic way. "I'm in. Let's start with Perry and those odd tattoos. Jeremy said Perry the Perv had a blue tiger tattooed on his . . . left biceps?"

Luke checked his notes and nodded. "Right. I mean, yes, left—left biceps."

He paced the room some more while Faith googled.

"Oh, boy. Well this is very interesting."

"You got a hit for *Perry* and *tattoos*?"

"Yep. But this may not be quite what we had in mind."

He waited.

"Says here Russell Brand and Katy Perry have matching tattoos, and he's having his removed—had, I mean. This an old story."

"Google's a wealth of information. Try again, would you please?" He cracked an imaginary whip in the air.

"I already tried Perry, Nancy, William, Ken, Linda."

"And?"

"Pulls up a *Matlock* episode."

He dropped onto the bed on his back and groaned.

"C'mon. Don't give up so fast. Why don't you see if you've got the magic touch?"

He rolled off the bed and came and leaned over her shoulder. Why did she smell so damn good all the time? They hadn't been around flowers all day. He dropped a kiss on her neck, reached around her, and typed in *Perry, short guy, black hair, blue tiger tattoo*.

The screen refreshed.

She reached for his hand and squeezed.

Then her head dropped. "I'm so sorry."

"I guess the police were right, Jeremy was fabricating the whole thing." According to Google, the man Jeremy described was Perry Smith, one of two men who murdered a Kansas family called the Clutters back in 1959. The murders were the subject of a famous book by Truman Capote: *In Cold Blood*. A book most kids read for high-school English.

He pushed his hands in his pockets and blazed another path around the room. "We don't know for sure that Jeremy borrowed his description from Capote's book. Is there any way possible this could be the same Perry who killed the Clutter family?" He was reaching, he knew, but he didn't want to let go of the only lead they had so easily.

"Not possible."

His fist came down on the desk where Faith was set up. "I suppose that guy would be pretty old by now. Probably still in prison."

Faith nodded and typed something else into the computer. "Perry Smith would be in his eighties today. But that's irrelevant." She slammed the laptop closed. "Because he was executed by the state of Kansas in 1965."

TWENTY-FIVE

Thursday, August 15, 4:00 P.M.

They'd be back home in Santa Fe by dark. Luke gunned the engine of his Spitfire and cast a sideways glance at Faith, riding shotgun. He wished Jeremy had waited until morning to come by the Starlight Motel. Luke had been picturing waking up with Faith in his arms since the first moment he saw her at his family's gallery. But now that they'd concluded their business in Amarillo, there was little excuse to stay the night.

A heaviness in his gut set in. Not only was he not going to wake up next to the woman of his dreams, but what had looked like a promising lead on the Santa Fe Saint had turned out to be a work of fiction. Quite literally. It seemed Jeremy Jacobs had lifted his entire description of the mysterious man last seen with Kenneth Stoddard from his high-school English assignment. Perry the Pervert was quite obviously Perry Smith from the nonfiction novel, *In Cold Blood*. And Perry Smith couldn't be the Santa Fe Saint unless he was setting upon his victims from beyond the grave.

Jeremy had been so believable. Luke's hopes had soared higher than they'd been since his brother's arrest, then, with the click of a mouse, they'd been dashed to an all-time low.

Thanks, Google.

At least he had Faith all to himself for the ride home. Nothing enhanced intimacy like being trapped together in a small vehicle for hours on end. There's a reason chicks dig road trips.

Faith was currently working her smart phone hard, but at least she wasn't humming. One of the many little things he loved about Faith was that she rarely used her phone. It hardly beeped, buzzed, or played a tune to indicate an incoming call, and she kept her focus on the people in the room, not on her electronics. A path he tried to follow himself. As Chica's due date grew near, however, things began to change. The texts between Faith and Tommy had become much more frequent. "Checking on Tommy and Chica?"

"I tried, but no response. Now I'm downloading a book."

He gripped the steering wheel tighter. Faith would rather read on the trip home than talk to him, and he'd really been looking forward to all that small talk. *What's your favorite color? How old were you the first*

time you did it? Beer or champagne? "Anything special?" A nice romance wouldn't be so bad. She could
read it aloud, might put her in the mood.

"*In Cold Blood*." Then, reading the what's-the-use
look on his face perfectly, she added, "I've got sort of
a hunch that Jeremy's not entirely full of hot air. It's
been a long time, but I read this book in school, and my
gut is telling me we're missing something. I just wish I
could remember the story clearly."

"Maybe I could hypnotize you."

"Maybe I could read the book."

"My way's more fun."

But she was already scrolling down the page. He
didn't understand people who read on their phones. He
preferred the feel of a leather-bound volume in his
hand, the crisp smell of ink on paper. But what the hell,
maybe he'd try it someday.

A few miles of silence went by. He cleared his
throat. He was tempted to hum. "Wanna read that
book aloud? Maybe I might get a hunch, too."

Her response was a sharp intake of air, as if something was very wrong. He waited, but she said nothing, and time beat on making his own breathing
accelerate—maybe, just maybe something was *right*.

Clutching her heart, she said at last. "I need a fast
connection . . . fast."

He tried not to let his excitement show in his voice.
His hopes had been dashed too recently. "What's up?"

"Just get me somewhere with wireless . . . and coffee

would be good. I think I found something important."
She reached over and squeezed his thigh. "I think I figured out how the Saint has been choosing his victims."

Fifteen minutes later, Luke and Faith were crammed
side by side into a half booth at Starbucks, laptop
blazing. Hard to believe the connection between the
victims was so simple, and yet so hard to recognize.
Perry the Pervert was the key. If only the police had
taken Jeremy Jacobs at his word all those years ago,
maybe Kenneth Stoddard would've been the Saint's
last victim.

"Here." Faith's low voice rang with urgency. I've
created a document with the names and ages of the
members of the Clutter family—Perry Smith's victims.
Herb Clutter, age forty-five, Bonnie Clutter, age forty-
four, Nancy Clutter, age sixteen, and Kenyon Clutter,
age fifteen."

Luke scribbled down the info on a napkin to keep
it within easy reach while she navigated to the *Santa
Fe Gazette*. "And here are the names and ages of the
Saint's known victims: William Carmichael, age forty-
five; Linda Peabody, age forty-four; Kenneth Stoddard,
age fifteen, and Nancy Aberdeen, age sixteen."

"Not a perfect match," he said, playing devil's advo-
cate. She was onto something all right, but they were
going to need a lot more than the coincidence of a few
first names to convince the police.

She drummed her fingers on the tabletop. "A man

calling himself Perry asks Kenny Stoddard for guitar lessons."

"According to Jeremy."

She held up her hand. "Let's assume Jeremy's telling the truth. He's got no reason at all to lie anymore. This Perry fellow has a tattoo of a blue tiger on his right biceps and the word *Cookie* tattooed on the left. The guy's short, a muscle-head with wavy black hair. Either the guy *is* Perry Smith, which is impossible, or the guy's *trying to be* Perry Smith, which most certainly is not . . . impossible I mean."

"I have to admit the tattoos seal the deal for me. A blue tiger, a short guy named Perry who plays the guitar, could maybe be coincidence, but *Cookie*? Who the hell gets *Cookie* tattooed on his arm?"

Faith hadn't touched her croissant. He eyed it sideways, and she dumped it on his plate.

"*Gracias.*"

"*De nada.* We've only got a 50 percent hit on the victim's first names. We need this airtight, or the cops are gonna think we're spouting bullshit to get your brother off the hook." She covered her hand with his. "But the thing is we're not spouting bullshit. So all we have to do is put our heads together and solve the puzzle."

He liked the idea of putting their heads together. He liked the idea of putting their other parts together, too. But he decided to keep that tidbit to himself for now. "Google Nancy Aberdeen. The girl's a real good stand-in for Nancy Clutter, so let's start with her. What else do we know about her?"

Faith's fingers jumped over the keyboard. A smiling image of poor Nancy Aberdeen popped up—the same one that'd made national news—the one of sixteen-year-old Nancy wearing a blue ribbon on her chest and displaying her prizewinning cherry pie. Your all-American girl personified. "That cherry pie is like the cookie tattoo. It cinches the deal almost as well as a DNA match. According to Capote's book, Nancy Clutter was *the* all-American girl, and get this, on the day she died, she taught a friend how to bake a cherry pie."

"You're kidding," he said.

"Don't know for sure that she actually helped a friend bake a cherry pie that day, but that's what Truman Capote wrote in his book. So as far as our Perry wannabe's concerned, that's the model he needs to follow—assuming he's getting his information about the Clutter murders from *In Cold Blood,* of course."

"I think that's a safe bet. Okay, so we've got one perfect victim fit. Let's move on."

"How about Kenny? The Clutter boy was named Kenyon, but I'm calling this a match. Unlikely the Saint could find another Kenyon. Kenny's close enough, and both boys were fifteen, from a rural area. Good students, maybe a little shy."

He let out a deep breath. It all seemed so perfect until you factored in the others. "But aside from age and the rural connection, the adults don't match. Herb Clutter versus William Carmichael? All the cops need to discount this complicated theory, and it is complicated, darlin', is one logical flaw."

"Hang on, I want to try pulling up the men's obituaries side by side." Seconds ticked by, then Faith's eyes widened. "Bingo!"

He nearly choked on a bite of croissant. She passed him her water, and he gulped what was left in the glass. "You can say that again. Full name: Herbert William Clutter. Occupation: farmer. Deacon in the Methodist church. And here's the Saint's victim: William Herbert Carmichael, also a farmer. Also a Methodist. The two men even look alike."

An electrified look passed between them. He knew it. She knew it.

Dante was not the Saint.

Perry the Pervert was real, and he was deadly. Luke didn't know yet how Linda Peabody matched up well enough to stand in for Bonnie Clutter, but Faith already had the women's obituaries up in side-by-side windows. Both were mothers of four children—three girls and a boy. Both married to farmers. Both Methodists. It was a good fit, but . . .

"This bothers me." Faith's words echoed his thoughts. "All the other names match in one form or another, but not Bonnie's and Linda's. Why would the Saint veer off course?"

"An evolving MO? A dearth of suitable victims named Bonnie? Bonnie's an old-fashioned name, and maybe the Saint decided it was more important to match the victims on other characteristics rather than the names."

"But he made it work with the others, even though

he had to resort to *Herb* as a middle name. The Saint seems so organized, and yet this feels sloppy to me."

"Google Bonnie." Luke jabbed his napkin.

"I already did."

"No. Just the name Bonnie. Doesn't Bonnie mean pretty?"

"I don't have to google that. A bonnie lass is a cute girl."

The words sizzled in the air, charging the space around them with excitement. In unison they said, "*Una chica linda!*"

The Saint couldn't find a forty-four-year-old *Bonnie* with four kids, so he chose a forty-four-year-old *Linda* with four kids. This was New Mexico after all. People were facile with Spanish. Linda and Bonnie both meant cute or pretty.

"I don't see how the authorities can fail to act on this. The Saint is targeting individuals who mirror the victims in Capote's book. And he's using a shotgun— just like Perry Smith and Dick Hickock did. Jeremy Jacobs saw a man calling himself Perry with Kenny Stoddard shortly before he disappeared. This is compelling stuff."

"The Saint has already killed a stand-in for every member of the Clutter family who was murdered in cold blood. Does that mean he's finished?"

Faith looked so hopeful, he hated to remind her. "The Saint's not done. If he were, we wouldn't have the butcher."

"The butcher? Is that a moniker for a famous serial killer or something?"

"No. The latest victim, the one they found with a rosary last week, was just IDed today. Torpedo texted me. The guy owned a butcher shop downtown called Three Little Pigs."

Faith's face went ashen. Her coffee cup spun onto the floor, and he grabbed the laptop, jumping out of the path of hot liquid.

She stared at the coffee dripping from the table onto the floor. "I didn't know the new victim was a butcher . . ." she whispered. "I-I can't believe this." She dropped her face in her hands.

A young girl—a barista—stood behind Luke, her mouth agape and a rag in her hand. Luke grabbed the rag and sopped up the coffee mess. The girl just stood there staring. He found a wad of bills in his pocket and closed the barista's palm around it. "Thanks very much," he looked at her name tag. "*Linda.*" Who knew how much she'd overheard.

"We need a change of scenery." He tugged Faith to her feet and shoved her out the door.

The minute they were out of Starbucks, she sagged against the brick building. Leaning in, he put his arm against the wall protectively, and also to encourage passersby to keep their distance from the two love-birds. "What's going on? Why did you react like that when I told you the new victim was a butcher?"

She shook her head. "I-I don't know. It just reminded

me of something a patient told me. I'm not even sure myself what it means. Let me figure this out first. I don't want to violate patient privacy."

He felt his face heating. He could barely contain the urge to shake her by the shoulders. He'd trust Faith with his life, yet she couldn't trust him with whatever was on her mind, and it clearly had to do with the Saint and a connection to the butcher. Dante was facing extradition to Texas, a state that made full use of the death penalty, and suddenly her lips were sealed? For the first time in weeks, he felt the need to remind her. "You turned my brother in to the police."

"I can't talk about a patient."

"*Now* you get your panties in a wad about doctor-patient privilege? I want to know what's going on." He pressed his body against hers. The feel of her heart beating against him made him want to protect her, keep her safe from harm, and here he was pushing her. But he couldn't let up, not with his brother's life on the line. He brushed his lips over her ear and growled again. "Tell. Me."

A man stopped, then took a step toward them. Faith shooed him away with a hand signal. "We're newly-weds," she said in a shaky voice.

Luke backed away from her.

Once her would-be rescuer had moved on, she said, "Dante is in jail for crimes he didn't commit precisely because I ignored doctor-patient confidentiality. I did it for the public good. I'm not saying I made the wrong decision, but I simply cannot go down the path my mind is taking me without more information. Your brother confessed. The man I'm thinking of now did not, and he's very, very fragile."

His mouth gaped, and he sucked in a blast of dry air. "It sounds like you're saying you think this patient of yours might be the Saint. If that's the case, you owe it to me to tell me why. If you won't give me his name, at least tell me what's driving your hunch."

"I-I suppose you're entitled to that much." As she spoke, her lips quivered. She brushed a long, silky lock of hair off her face. "For one thing, this person has a friend who's a butcher."

His anger cooled, he dropped his hands to his side. There had to be more to it than that. "And that's it? That's all you have to go on?"

"He also fits the physical description of Perry to a T." Her lips had stopped quivering, and she seemed to be in thinking mode again.

"Even the tattoos?"

"I wish I could say, but he always wears long sleeves. I thought he might be hiding scars under them. But yeah, he might be covering up unusual tattoos."

Luke rolled his head back, closed his eyes, then jerked them open and squared his gaze with hers. "That's not exactly an open-and-shut case you're making."

"I agree, it's hardly proof. Anyway, I have his address in my laptop contacts. As soon as we get back to Santa Fe, I'll pay him a visit." She must've read the look on his face because she added, "I've been meeting with him alone for weeks. He doesn't scare me. And like I said, I may be completely wrong."

"No way in hell I'm letting you go to this man's home alone."

"You can't go with me. That wouldn't be ethical." She planted her hands on her hips.

"The second you told me there was a chance this guy might be the Saint, we passed the point where I gave a damn about ethics. So either I'm coming with you to talk to him, or I'm hauling your ass straight to the Santa Fe PD. Choose your poison, Clancy."

As she drew her shoulders back and set her jaw, he prepared himself to make a stronger case.

"You're right," she said.

His chin jerked back in surprise. "I am? Since when?"

A flinty look of determination darkened her eyes. "Since just now. Since I figured out I'm tired of following rules that don't work. I don't want you to take me to the police, and I don't want to talk to my patient alone again. In fact, until we know more, I don't want to talk to him at all."

He loved the sound of that *we*. A million questions were racing in his mind, but he held off, not wanting to interrupt and risk her changing her mind.

"I'm sick of playing by the rules only to have innocent people end up hurt. Suppose, heaven forbid, he really is the Saint. Confronting him would be dangerous, and going to the police would be foolish. Look how Detective Johnson reacted to those text messages.

He practically accused us of engineering the whole thing. Even if he takes us seriously, he'll need more information to get a search warrant. We, on the other hand, don't need a warrant. I trust you, Luke. And I don't trust Johnson."

"What are you suggesting?" His admiration for this woman was growing by the minute.

"My patient is a creature of habit. He dines every evening from 7:00 P.M. to 8:00 P.M. at The Blue Moon Café. He's told me so many times. So I'm suggesting we pay him a visit at 7:00 P.M. And if his door just happens to be unlocked . . ."

He held up his hand. "I'm sure I can jimmy the door, and I have no problem going to his place while he's not home to take a look around. But what if we find evidence? Maybe it'll get thrown out in court because we broke into the house. Then we'll have done more harm than good."

She shook her head. "That's the beauty of it. If we find nothing, no one knows but us, and that means no one gets hurt. But if we do find something, it's all admissible—just as long as the police know nothing about our plans."

TWENTY-SIX

Thursday, August 15, 6:00 P.M.

*F*ive hours.

In five short hours, I will fulfill my destiny.

A quiver of excitement traveled through Scourge as he opened Dr. Clancy's back door with his bump key, but not because the key worked—he'd established that the last time he was here. He turned his arms palms up, opened and closed his fists, pumping hard until his beautiful purple veins congested with blood and popped to the surface. The blood coursing through those veins electrified his skin—just as it had earlier today when he'd finally cleaned up the mess in his bathtub.

I'm cured.

I am not a shadow.

It's time.

Tonight, his timeline was of the utmost importance. Eleven o'clock would mark the ten-year anniversary of Sister Bernadette's death. So he needed to hurry. First, he'd abduct Faith and take her with him to The Big Kill, the grand finale, the pièce de résistance. Then, at precisely 11:00 P.M., he'd send the Donovans to heaven one by one and buy himself a first-class ticket, *nonstop*, to Satan's playground—with Faith as witness to his sin. Finally, he'd come back around and take care of the boy and the dog before Faith's body was discovered, and the cops questioned the neighbors again.

After, he'd retire to the beaches of Mexico, just like Perry had wanted to do. And Scourge would be at peace—confident in the knowledge he'd secured himself the kind of afterlife he so richly deserved. Sister Bernadette would probably ridicule him for his worry over this point. According to her, he'd secured his place in hell as a boy at school, just by wetting the goddamn bed. But Sister Cecily had said no, no matter how black the heart, light always remains. According to Sister Cecily, it was impossible to extinguish every bit of light in a man, and thus the possibility of forgiveness would always be there.

That assertion had troubled Scourge for a long while, until he'd found the book. Once he read about Perry Smith and the Clutter murders, Scourge had devised a plan for getting into hell that he considered foolproof. He liked to think of his soul as the night sky, and taking an individual life was like cutting a single star from that sky. The light diminished . . . though not enough. But if Scourge took an entire family at once, it would be like cutting out the moon. His soul would become so dark, it could never be redeemed.

And Dr. Clancy was such a lovely bonus. His other targets had never excited him the way she did. If his justification for taking her had been weak before, now it was completely sound. In therapy, he'd had to confide too much in order to obtain his cure. She was clever enough that sooner or later, she'd realize the dream he'd shared about Sister Bernadette was not a dream at all but a memory.

No witnesses.

That had been Perry and Dick's cardinal rule. Now that Dr. Clancy had become a potential witness, taking her life would be by the book, and that would make his pleasure that much greater.

He closed the door behind him. Dr. Clancy's home smelled good.

He liked the way she kept fresh flowers from the yard set out on every surface that would accommodate a vase. He liked the way she smelled, too. When he sat across from her in her office, he could always detect the faintest trace of flowers perfuming her body. The scent she carried with her was more intoxicating than the finest draft of whiskey. Her scent reminded him of a funeral.

Ironic.

Laughing aloud, he wished Faith would come home, so he could share the joke with her. He checked his watch—6:15. It wouldn't be long now. He'd left his shotgun in the truck. He cared too much for Dr. Clancy to make a mess of her lovely home; besides, he wanted her to see him in all his glory. He'd take her with him to the farm, lay her next to the Donovan girl, and explain all to her. He'd keep her alive until the very end, show her how he'd sent the others off to heaven. He'd be sure she knew how and why he was going to send her there, too. He'd give her plenty of time to cleanse her soul before joining her parents and her sister. He'd give her his favorite rosary.

He sighed. He doubted she'd thank him, though. No one ever did.

In the kitchen, he opened the fridge and found some Tejava pure Java tea. He poured himself a tall glass, sat at the table, and drank it. Then he rinsed his glass and put it in the dishwasher. He dried his hands on a dish-towel, but water had seeped inside his gloves, and his fingers began to itch. He checked his watch again— 6:30. Time to hide in the bedroom. No fireplace poker or knives there to stab him. He slipped behind the bed-room door and waited.

Time ticked by, and his fingers stung inside his wet plastic gloves. He shifted positions, stretching his stiff legs. He decided to take a quick stroll through the house to ease his soreness, then come back and crouch behind the bedroom door again. He'd only just wan-dered into the living room when he heard the sound of a key in the front door. No time to get back to the bed-room. He hid behind the sectional, removed his chlo-roformed rag from a Ziploc baggie in his pocket, and made himself ready. Blood zinged through his body. The door flew open, and a slight figure jolted inside, dragged by a tight leash.

That damn kid.

That damn dog.

In his surprise, he hesitated, and in that moment the boy spotted him, crouched and ready to pounce.

"Get back!" The boy yelled bravely, but then he made the same mistake they all make, he turned his back to Scourge in order to run, and that was just the opening Scourge needed to leap on him. He knocked Tommy to the ground. Tommy screamed and tried to crawl away. Scourge grabbed him by the leg and twisted.

Crack!

Tommy's head fell back, and he stopped struggling. Scourge dragged him close and pressed a chloroformed rag over the boy's mouth and nose. The little fellow never had a chance. His body went limp in Scourge's arms.

As he got to his feet, his arms stiffened beneath the boy's weight. His palms itched. Where was the dog? Looking carefully to his left and right, he saw no sign of the mangy mutt. Probably hiding under the bed with her tail between her legs by now. He hoisted the kid over his shoulder like a bag of flour. He'd stash him in the truck and come back for Faith.

Scourge's overalls made a perfectly good disguise. The boy would fit easily into his wheelbarrow, and no one would question the sight of a landscaper wheeling out a pile of trash, dumping it in the back of his truck, and covering it with a tarp. Landscapers were invisible.

But he had to hurry if he was going to stow the boy and make it back inside before Faith got home. He slipped out the back door, not bothering to close it behind him, dropped the kid in the wheelbarrow, tossed a tarp over him. No time to tie the kid up now. He lifted the wheelbarrow by the handles and heard a long growl behind him.

Damn dog.

He stuck his arm under the tarp for a pair of gardening shears. A sharp pain cut into his flesh. Not the shears.

The kid.

He should've used more chloroform, held the rag in place longer. The kid clawed his arm, sunk his teeth into his wrist. Pain bellowed up the nerves in his arm.

I am not a shadow.

As he yanked his hand back, he bit down on his tongue to stop himself from laughing. He was cured all right.

He looked up just in time to see the dog flying through the air like a missile locked on target. The dog landed on his chest and chomped down on his arm. Penetrating pain seared through to the bone. The kid was out of the wheelbarrow, limping for the gate. Scourge shook his arm, but the dog clamped its jaws tighter, holding on for the ride. Scourge reached down and, summoning all his strength, all his will, pried the dog's jaws open and hurled her into the bushes. Then he bolted out the gate before the dog could give chase.

He wouldn't be able to take Dr. Clancy with him tonight after all.

Damn kid.

Damn dog.

Then he grinned. He'd be back for *all* of them later.

TWENTY-SEVEN

Thursday, August 15, 7:00 P.M.

After the third knock, it seemed certain Scourge was not at home. Faith didn't know how she felt about that. Yes, this had been her idea. No, she didn't want to turn back, but that didn't stop her stomach from clenching tight as a fist.

"You sure this is the place?" Luke asked.

"I'm sure it's the address my patient listed on his face sheet, yeah. It's possible he gave me a false one, of course." She hurried after Luke, who was headed to the backyard.

"I sure hope not." Luke picked up a mammoth rock. "Stand back, Clancy. Waay back."

Before she could put two and two together, he'd shoved her aside and hurled the muddy missile through the back window. The sharp sound of breaking glass was followed by the dull thud of the rock hitting the floor.

"Luke!"

He wrapped his arm with his windbreaker and cleared out the glass, then scrambled through the window. Over his shoulder, he called out, "I lied about knowing how to pick a lock."

Somehow, breaking a window seemed much worse than picking a lock, but she supposed it was all the same in the end. Besides, the damage had been done. She clambered through the window after Luke. With lives at stake, this wasn't the time to hesitate. This was the time to act. She placed her hand on her protesting stomach. They'd know soon enough if Scourge was the mystery man, Perry the Pervert. They'd know soon enough if Scourge was the Santa Fe Saint.

"You might've waited for me to open the back door, Clancy. I can be a gentlemen when I want to be." Luke shot her a cocky grin. He signaled her to wait there and strode ahead of her, straight-arming a pistol he'd pulled from the Spitfire's glove box. He cleared every room, then came back for her, bearing rubber gloves from the kitchen. No point leaving their fingerprints all over the place.

A quick perusal of the rooms convinced her they had indeed come to the right address. Not a speck of dust marred the furniture in the living room. The floors in the kitchen gleamed bright as mirrors. She opened a cabinet and found it loaded with cleaning products, all facing the same direction and ordered alphabetically.

This was definitely Scourge's place—she hesitated to call it a home. It was more like a hospital ward.

Luke kicked open the hall closet. Empty. They made their way to the bedroom, where she noted a military-style bed, made with all white bedding, pulled smooth and tight.

As she thought of how Scourge would react if he could see the way Luke ripped off the covers and dumped them on the floor, she cringed. A thread of hope still remained that her suspicions were unfounded, that there was a perfectly good explanation for everything. The idea that Scourge might be the Saint made her stomach twist and her limbs shiver like an army of ants was marching up her arms.

Luke lifted the mattress and tossed it aside as if it were featherlight. Then the pillow went flying, and something went with it, landing with a thunk on the hardwood floor. Their eyes met.

A book!

Together, they dove for it. Faith grabbed the volume first, and her throat constricted.

In Cold Blood.

There it was. The smoking gun.

Squeezing her eyes closed, she fought for air, then managed to rise from the floor. She clutched her heart and with a sharp inhale, resumed breathing.

Scourge Teodori was the Santa Fe Saint.

Maybe this wasn't all the proof a jury would need, but it was proof enough for her. Her hands balled into fists, and her heart drained of sympathy. A revolting taste flooded her mouth as her eyes fell on Scourge's clean bedding. She spit onto his sheets.

When he'd first come to her office, he'd been terrified of blood, and she'd cured him of that fear. If he killed again, it was on her.

But had she really cured him?

Her heartbeat amped up.

Hope rocketed inside her. "Bathroom. Now."

"Okay." Luke's eyebrows rose. "Any special reason you're so anxious to get to the bathroom?"

She'd already filled Luke in on Scourge's hemophobia on the way over. And now there was no need to withhold his name any longer. She had all the proof she needed. "Because Scourge—"

"You're fucking kidding."

"No, his name is Scourge. Anyway, Scourge had his friend the butcher rig a bucket of pig's blood to fall on him in the shower." She pulled in a breath. "Never mind why, I'll explain it all later. But the point is the blood made a huge mess in the tub. Scourge managed to clean outside the tub, but he left all that pig's blood congealing in the bath. He just closed the curtain and worked around it. He was so overcome by the idea of cleaning up the tub, he's been bathing in the sink ever since."

"Okay. Freaky. But what are we looking for in the bathroom? We already know there'll be blood in the tub."

"I *hope* the blood is still in the bathtub." Now her heart was in her throat. "If he's cleaned it up, it means he really is cured. It means *I* cured him to kill again."

Luke led way to the bathroom and jerked the shower curtain aside. Clean as a whistle. Her throat spasmed as she struggled to bite back a scream. The floors were white, the tub pristine, the wall behind the tub scrubbed clean . . . except for five letters, all caps, scrawled in blood:

FAITH.

Luke pushed Faith out of the bathroom, slammed the door behind them, then turned and punched his fist into the wall. The bastard was primed and ready to kill again. He rubbed his knuckles, then rested his hands on Faith's shoulders. His blood chilling at the thought of Faith shut away in her office with Scourge, listening to his stories, soothing his anxieties.

Luke had wanted to save his brother all along, but now he had an even more compelling reason to nail this Scourge bastard. Luke had spent the past few hours learning about the lives of the Saint's victims. These were real people—not just photos on the news—and not only had their lives been cut short, the lives of their friends and family had been devastated. Kids like Jeremy were collateral damage, even though they still lived—and Faith.

If he didn't stop Scourge, would Faith be next?

He couldn't pull his gaze away from her.

"I'm fine." She read the unspoken question in his eyes and jerked away from him. "Let's not waste time talking about my feelings." And then she was off, moving quickly through the bedroom, searching for more evidence, more answers.

"Look at this." Faith motioned him over to the dresser, where she was busy going through the drawers. "Bottom drawer is locked."

A minute later, he returned with a butter knife and a mallet for pounding meat. He turned it over in his gloved hand and hoped like hell it had only pounded meat. *Crack!* The latch on the drawer split and flying shards of wood stung his arms. He yanked the drawer open with such force it careened off track, landing sideways on the floor.

Faith gasped though she couldn't have been surprised. There, spilled on the carpet were rosaries, maybe fifty, maybe more. He used his cell to snap a photo.

With Faith on his heels, he headed into the kitchen, where they'd placed the book on the kitchen table. Still gloved, he lifted the book. The pages gaped in the middle, and the novel fell open to reveal a folded paper. Faith unfolded the sheet while he snapped away with his camera. Turned out to be not one but two sheets of waxy paper, stapled together. On the top sheet, someone had sketched the floor plan of a three-level home. A satellite photo was taped to the bottom sheet . . . along with GPS coordinates.

He began taking close-ups of each section of the sketch and photos. Faith went back to the bedroom and returned with an ebony box. "I found these in the box. I jimmied the lock myself," she added although there was no pride in her voice, only sadness. "Looks like a journal, and look at these pictures."

He thumbed through the photos and with each successive one his pulse pounded harder in his ears. The first shot captured a stately farmhouse, then came four years' worth of Donovan family Christmas cards. Scourge had been stalking this family for years, and he'd clearly been inside their home on a number of occasions.

"They're next—the Donovans are next." Faith shook her head and touched the corner of one of the Christmas cards. Blinking hard, she looked away.

He rested one hand on her forearm, unable to forget that just a few yards away, her name was scrawled in blood on the bathroom wall. "Probably. But, I'm not entirely following this. Our theory, and it's a hell of a good one, is that Scourge is emulating Perry Smith and re-creating the *In Cold Blood* murders."

"Yes. Scourge has a very meager sense of self. Several times, over the course of therapy, he's talked about feeling like a shadow, like he's not even a real person. The parallels between Scourge's life and Perry Smith's are uncanny. I think Scourge only feels real when he's acting as Perry. In a nutshell, he's stolen the man's identity because he doesn't have one of his own."

"But why would he choose to re-create a crime that was originally carried out by two men? And the Clutters were murdered en masse, inside their home. Scourges' victims were taken elsewhere and slaughtered one by one, spread out over the course of time. He's already killed a stand-in for each member of the Clutter family."

Another piece of the puzzle clicked into place. "Practicing. Of course, he's practicing! Scourge is compulsive, a perfectionist, and exasperatingly plodding. He doesn't want to be caught. Perry Smith was executed for the Clutter murders. I think Scourge is practicing on surrogate victims, as a way of building his nerve and honing his technique. It's far easier to take on one person at a time, and it's also a way of testing potential pitfalls."

Luke nodded. "Scourge isn't replicating the Clutter murders so much as perfecting them. He's trying to commit the perfect crime."

"**G**oddamnit, Johnson, I'm handing you the Saint on a silver platter, and you say you're not hungry." Mouthing the word *asshole*, Luke turned to Faith, who sat beside him in the Spitfire. The trunk was full of evidence, and they were parked a few blocks east of Scourge's place.

"I said"—Detective Johnson's tone on the other end of the line was patronizing—"I'll get an officer out there as soon as one's available. This is about the most cock-'n-bull story I've heard in all my years on the force, but I promise I'll check into it. I'm perfectly capable of handling things from here."

"I hope you do handle it and soon, because if I get

the chance to take this guy out, I just might do it."

"Hold up, Luke." Johnson struck a more concilia-tory tone. "Don't even joke about going vigilante on me. Surest way to get yourself killed."

"Then send someone out to the Donovan farm before it's too damn late already."

"According to you, this guy's been planning this for years. He's not going to act hastily. If he's got the nerve to act at all, that is—why hasn't he done it already?"

"Because he *didn't* have the nerve to act. We've been all through this. He lost his edge. An incident at the blood lab where he worked traumatized him, and he developed a fear of blood."

"Right. Good old convenient hemophobia. The serial killer was afraid of blood, but now he's cured. Dr. Clancy, bless her heart, cured him. Now he's off to murder the Clutter family all over again, only this time he's gonna do it up right. Commit the perfect crime. Does that about sum it up?"

"Look, I know it sounds crazy. But once you see the evidence . . ."

"Evidence that you might have planted."

Luke's knuckles were white. He loosened his grip on the phone. "Listen to me, Johnson. I'd do almost anything to get my brother cleared of a crime he didn't commit, but I would *not* frame an innocent man."

"How about a guilty one? Would you frame a man you believed to be guilty in order to get your brother out of jail."

He silently counted to ten . . . then twenty. He

rubbed the back of his neck. "You think I'm even capable of concocting a scenario like this—that I'd come up with something this wild to cast suspicion on another man? You're not making sense. The Saint's victims are all stand-ins for members of the Clutter family—and you can't deny that. Or at least you won't be able to when you see the evidence. You've got a witness who says one of the victims was last seen with a guy who called himself Perry. And that man fits the description of Dr. Clancy's patient, Scourge Teodori. I can't *plant* those facts."

Johnson waited a beat, as if mulling things over. "You say the victims are stand-ins for the Clutters. But I have to look into that, I can't just take your word. Besides which, you could've found that book—what's it called again?"

"*In Cold Blood*, by Truman Capote."

"First off, you could've found a copy of *In Cold Blood* among your brother's things, and you could've planted that same book and those Christmas photos of the Donovans in Scourge's house. Or maybe you're just saying you found them there. And who has a name like Scourge, anyway? *Second, third, and fourth,* you expect me to believe that Dr. Clancy had the extremely bad luck of having two patients in her practice, one of whom *confessed* to being the Saint and the other who *actually is the Saint*. The odds of that's happening are astronomical. A coincidence like that isn't just hard to swallow, it'll choke you dead. So I gotta believe there's something else going on here. Maybe the good doctor is helping you frame this poor Scourge schmuck."

He pulled the phone from his ear, then replaced it. "Faith wouldn't do something like that."

"Tell me the truth: You fucking her or what?"

And that was absolutely none of the detective's business.

"That's what I thought."

Luke controlled his voice by speaking very slowly. "Accuse me later all you like, but in the meantime, you've got to get someone out to the Donovan place. Scourge could be there right now while you're standing around speculating about my sex life."

"Even if I wanted to, I can't send someone out there just like that. Not my jurisdiction. I gotta call Rio Arriba County, and I'll make a case as good as I can, but I can't promise how fast they'll move on it. Depends on their manpower."

"That's just not good enough."

"You think I want to see more innocent lives lost, you're dead wrong. I'll make sure we get someone out in the next twenty-four hours to do a wellness check on the Donovan family. Meanwhile, you ever think you could give them a call?"

He had a point. Luke hung up and dialed Torpedo. After a brief conversation, during which Torpedo provided him a landline number for the Donovans—no cell service in that corner of Rio Arriba—he turned to Faith. "Torpedo's on it. He's applying all the pressure he can to get the authorities moving on this. He'll try to get the police out to the Donovan place tonight, but it might take longer."

"I can't sit around and wait for the wheels of justice when I know a family may be in grave danger."

That made two of them. "We'll give them a call, but if they don't pick up, or if they don't believe me." He paused, and they exchanged a glance. Who in their right mind would believe a crazy story like that coming from complete strangers? "If they don't believe me, I'll drop you at your place and head out to warn them in person."

"You're not dropping me off." Faith glanced at her nails, like she'd just said she didn't care for more tea, thank you.

"You're not going with me." He pushed up from the table, leaning toward her.

"Scourge is my patient. I agree with Johnson. He's a planner and not likely to be there at this particular moment. But if by some chance he is, I'd have a far better chance of reasoning with him than you."

"No offense to your shrink skills, but if the bastard's at the Donovan place, reasoning with him is the last thing I'm going to do. You won't be trying that either because you're not coming with me."

Still looking at her nails with that same casual demeanor, she said, "Let me put it another way. My name's written on the bathroom wall in blood. So who do you think is next on Scourge's list, the Donovans or me? Where do you think I'd be safer, at my place all alone, or riding out to Rio Arriba with you?"

He couldn't argue with that. Truth was, he wasn't keen on letting Faith out of his sight. He heaved a sigh. There was something else bothering him. "How did Scourge find you, Faith? You're new in town, your practice isn't even a practice, and yet . . ."

"I found a brochure advertising my practice inside the box with the family's photographs. I didn't show it to you because I didn't want to worry you. I've handed those pamphlets out to just about every primary-care doctor in town, trying to drum up referrals. I guess Scourge's physician thought he could use some mental-health services. He probably found me from my brochure."

Luke shook his head. "That doesn't explain the coincidence. You have two patients. One confesses to the murders, the other is the actual killer. How does that happen?"

"Not by coincidence, I'm sure. Let's dismiss the brochure, then. He could've picked it up later I suppose."

Luke dragged a hand through his hair. To him, everything fell apart unless they could explain how both men happened to turn to Faith.

"Try this on. Scourge was enraged when he heard Dante had confessed to being the Saint. When Dante took credit for Scourge's crimes, Scourge felt impotent, powerless, terrified. Think about it. His traumatic incident in the lab happened right around the time Dante's confession hit the papers. Scourge is both drawn to blood and repelled by it at the same time. Just as he's drawn to religion and repelled by it at the same time. He was undone by Dante's confession, and that impotence manifested itself in his fear of blood. He could no longer carry out his crimes so . . ."

"He needed a shrink."

"My name was all over the local news as the woman who turned Dante Jericho in to the police. *That's* why Scourge picked me. In a way, I'm complicit with Dante in trying to steal his glory, don't you see? Since I'm the one who turned in the *false Saint*, I'm as much to blame for his problems as anyone."

He raised an admiring eyebrow. "And that's why they call you *Doctor*." Grabbing his windbreaker, he added, "Road trip?"

TWENTY-EIGHT

Thursday, August 15, 10:00 P.M.

Faith clamped a hand over her mouth to stifle her gasp. Luke had been right to insist they proceed with caution. They hadn't been able to reach the Donovans on their landline, and with no cell coverage, they couldn't call Torpedo to find out if help had been sent. Once they'd sighted the Donovan family's farmhouse, Luke had pulled his Spitfire off the road, and they'd walked the remainder of the way just in case Scourge had already set his plan in motion. Just in case he'd arrived at the farmhouse before them, ready to do his worst. Just in case, while peering through a downstairs window, they spotted Scourge brandishing a shotgun.

Just in case had just turned into her worst nightmare.

She caught a glimpse of Scourge, shotgun slung

over his shoulder, in the hallway. Then he disappeared into a room and closed the door.

He's inside the house.

Luke's arms came around her from behind, shoring her up even before her knees could think about wobbling. He spun her toward him, noiselessly pressed his finger to his lips. Like she needed a reminder to keep quiet. Her body shook from the effort of holding back a powerful scream—a scream that pounded the inside of her chest like a fist demanding to be let out.

And it wasn't just her body she was fighting but her mind as well.

We're too late. Too late. Too late.

From inside the house, a male voice cried out, but she couldn't make out the words.

At least one member of the family was still alive.

Whatever Scourge had planned, she was certain he'd be sticking to a strict schedule, and that might buy the family time.

Closing her eyes, she willed away the thoughts of helplessness, replacing them with a single empowering one.

Stop him.

Yes. That was much better. If her heart hammered any harder, she'd need a defibrillator, but that was fine by her.

Fuck fear.

She'd used all the extra oxygen her panicked heart provided to fuel her muscles and her brain. "We have to stop him before it's too late." She mouthed the words to Luke, not wanting to chance so much as a whisper this close to the downstairs windows.

Nodding, he took her by the hand, and together, they backed away from the house and into a copse of trees where they could quietly strategize.

Lucky for them, Faith had read the pertinent parts of *In Cold Blood* aloud to Luke on the trip, and that just might give them the edge over Scourge, who had no idea his master plan was about to be disrupted. Considering they were armed only with one Glock and the can of pink pepper spray clipped to Faith's belt, they were going to need all the edge they could get. "If Scourge is carrying out the scenario described in the Clutter murders, the daughter will be bound with cord in her upstairs bedroom, and the mother will also be upstairs, bound in her own bedroom."

"Bonnie Clutter slept separately from her husband, but no reason to think Mrs. Donovan does. I say the mother is most likely in the master bedroom."

"We'll find out soon enough." Her gaze traced the upper story, looking for an open window. She'd studied the blueprint they'd found at Scourge's place and knew the master bedroom was on the east side of the house. Which of the several smaller bedrooms on the west side would turn out to be the daughter's room, they'd learn once they got inside the home.

"I'd like to proceed on your assumption—that Scourge is following the book. Since the book is what led us here in the first place, I say we dance with the one who brought us." Luke offered her a weak smile, but his expression was drawn.

"How are we going to get past Scourge to get to the women? He's downstairs with a shotgun, and we'll never be able to climb the stairs without his spotting us." Her blood was rushing in her ears.

Fuck Fear.

Then it came to her. "I say we start at the top and work our way down."

Luke cast a glance toward the farmhouse.

She followed his gaze to an object glinting against the side of the house—a ladder. A ladder, a Glock, pepper spray, and each other. That was what they had, and they had better make the most of it.

"We'll get the women out first." Suddenly, he dropped his eyes, and she knew they were both wondering the same thing. Were all the family members inside? How many were still alive? "Let's take this one step at a time and be ready to improvise," he said, meeting her eyes again.

And just like that, she knew they'd made a silent pact to trust that the family was alive and to *act* to keep them that way. "Agreed. But improvisation starts now. No way that ladder will reach the upstairs windows."

"Upstairs window second from the left is open. We'll find a way to get to it." Luke outlined the split-level roof with his pointer finger. "We can get to the lower section of the roof with the ladder. From there, we'll have to scramble to the next level. And then . . ."

Faith was already pulling him toward the ladder. They were on the same page. Whispering instructions, they positioned the ladder under the lowest section of the split-level roof. Luke put a foot on the ladder's bottom rung, testing its stability.

Scrape.

The noise amplified in Faith's ears, and her heart jumped to her throat, but around them, all remained still. No door swung open, no shot rang out, and that's when she realized the farm's natural sounds would cover their small infractions. Unless they sent the ladder crashing to the ground, the night's noises would absorb the sound track to their rescue mission. She let out the breath she'd been holding.

Luke's arms wrapped around her and pulled her body against his. "Luke," she whispered, her hands trailing down his arms, his back, his buttocks, trying to feel and hold as much of him as she could.

"Just in case," he murmured in her ear, his breath hot and sweet. Then his mouth came down hard on hers. She opened for him, and in that brief moment, they shielded each other from the evil they were about to face, taking only strength, only good from one another.

They broke apart.

As noiselessly as possible, they stabilized the ladder and began the climb. Faith scampered up ahead of Luke. When she reached the top rung, the roof was just within her reach. Grateful for the upper-body strength her workouts had provided and that extra jolt from adrenaline, she pressed her forearms on the slick tiles above and heaved her body onto the roof with a soft grunt.

Luke's eyes came into view at the edge of the roof. "Nice ass, Clancy." And then he hoisted himself up beside her without so much as a quickening of his breath. "Get on your belly."

"What?"

He eased into a prone position and motioned ahead. Oh. They were going to crawl over the roof. Less noise. Less chance of falling. They combat crawled a ways, then Luke clambered onto the second level of the roof and pulled her up behind him. More combat crawling.

They reached the window to the master bedroom.

Luke grabbed her hand. "Its not too late for you to climb back down, get in the car, and drive like hell to the police."

She shook her head. It was an hour to the nearest town, and the first forty minutes were in a no-cell-service zone. She'd never make it back with help in time. "I'm not leaving these people here with *him*. I'm not leaving *you* here with him."

He squeezed her hand. Opened his mouth, but then shut it again. Took a breath. An eternity later, he said, "Okay. So here's the plan. I lower you by your arms through the window. You get the mom back to the window, and I'll get her onto the roof and down to safety. Repeat with the girl. You strong enough?"

"Hell yes." She sat up and flexed a biceps. "You see me flip up onto the roof?"

He winked, but his face was pulled tight. "On three."

She pressed a kiss to his forehead and extended her arms.

"Wait." He pulled something shiny out of his jeans and tucked it between her breasts. It felt cold against her skin. "Pocketknife. I've got another."

"You could've just handed it to me."

"My way's more fun."

The look he gave her was so full of tenderness, she thought her heart might burst in her chest. "Thanks," she said.

"You'll need the knife to cut their ropes."

"I meant thanks for being here. I couldn't do this alone."

"Tell you what, Clancy, neither could I," he said, his voice hitching. Then he took her by the wrists. Her arms jerked in their sockets as he lowered her from the roof. Her feet scrambled for purchase and found the bottom sill. The window was open halfway, but she had no way to open it more. After exhaling all her breath to make her body smaller, she squeezed feetfirst through the window and into the master bedroom.

"Easy darlin', you okay?"

She heard Luke's low voice but didn't take time to answer. She'd found the mother. The full moon varnished the room in light, revealing a feminine form on the bed—Mrs. Donovan. Midforties. Brown curls, eyes fixed on Faith, telegraphing the kind of desperate plea a mother sends when she knows her husband and children are about to die.

Not:

Help me.

But rather:

Help them.

The woman's hands were bound together in front, as if in prayer, and more ropes connected her body to the footboard of the bed. Her mouth was covered in duct tape.

Just like Bonnie Clutter.

Now Faith was glad they'd not been able to give the family details by phone. Scourge was no doubt already here, and better Mrs. Donovan didn't know what Scourge had planned for her loved ones. Faith lifted a rope, inspecting the elaborate knots. She'd definitely have to cut through, no way to quickly untie these. She pulled Luke's knife from her bra, and the mother struggled, violently jerking her head toward the door.

Faith got the message loud and clear.

Help them.

But she couldn't give in to the mother's silent pleas. There was no time to rearrange the plan. Faith had no intention of leaving the mother bound in this room while she went off searching for others. She steeled her jaw. She couldn't let her heart overrule her head, or else none of them would make it out alive.

No pity.

She shook the woman by the shoulders, and mouthed, "Don't say a word."

The woman struggled harder, talking incoherently beneath the duct tape.

"Shut up!" Faith gritted her teeth and slapped Mrs. Donovan's face.

The woman whimpered again but then nodded.

Faith whispered in her ear, "If I take this gag off, you have to promise not to scream. If you make a sound, your whole family will pay the price. Do you understand?"

The woman nodded again, and Faith ripped the tape from the woman's mouth. Blood from Mrs. Donovan's raw lips dripped onto her chin.

No pity.

Faith sawed the ropes that bound the mother's hands. The sawing rubbed Faith's own hands raw, and the hemp she held turned pink.

Move on to the feet.

"Why?" The softest whimper from Mrs. Donovan. "Why us?"

Faith kept sawing rope. She couldn't stop to think about what kind of a monster would inflict such terror on another human being because *she* had been helping that very monster every day. Supporting him, calming him, making him strong again so he could do . . . *this*.

She spit bile from her mouth.

"There. The ropes are gone. Get up slowly. I don't want you to faint."

The woman made it to her feet, and Faith stuck her

hands beneath her armpits and walked her toward the window.

"No! Please, I can't leave my children."

Faith closed her heart to the woman's desperate pleas.

"You're going first. I'm not making any bargains with you. I won't leave them. I'm going for your daughter next."

"No. Please." The woman was edging away from the window.

Faith threw both arms around her and dragged her back. "I won't leave your family. I promise, but you have to go now. You're wasting my time when I could be helping the others."

Mrs. Donovan's body went limp. "Okay."

"Good. Now, I'm going to hand you up to a man on the roof. His name is Luke. He's going to get you to safety. I don't care if you're scared. Your children need you alive, so you will do exactly what he tells you."

Another nod. And then Mrs. Donovan leaned backward out the window. Luke's muscular arms gripped on to her, and while Faith held her by the feet, Luke eased the mother onto the roof.

Three doors down, Faith found the daughter. Also hog-tied, also terrified. But a certain resilience on the girl's face told Faith she had a thinking partner on her hands, one who'd make the process a lot easier than her mother had. Sure enough, the girl sat quietly, positioning her hands and feet as best she could to make it easier for Faith to saw through the ropes.

Minutes later, they were back in the master bedroom. "Your mother's already outside. Don't worry about finding her, just run as far as you can and hide," Faith said as she helped the teenager through the window.

The girl looked at her with misty eyes. "Thank you."

"Go. Go. Go." Faith ordered. And handed her off to Luke.

They'd been arguing in whispers ever since Luke had returned to lift Faith through the window to safety—like he'd done with the Donovan mother and daughter. But Faith flat-out refused to leave the house until the father and son were out safely. With no one to lower him, Luke couldn't get down and in through the window himself, or else he'd drag her out of there by force. As matters stood, she'd left him with no choice. He clamped his jaw hard enough to crack a tooth and dangled his right arm over the edge of the roof, lowering his Glock down for her. "Take the gun."

A beat passed in silence. Then, "I don't know how to use a gun. You keep it."

"Point center mass and pull the trigger."

"Isn't there a safety or something? You should keep it."

A muscle spasm shot up his arm, and he nearly dropped his Glock. He'd felt something snap in his shoulder earlier, and now his hand tingled, his fingers had long since gone numb. "Either take the gun or get the hell out of the house. My vote is get out now."

"I won't leave them."

"But you expect me to leave you," his words hissed out.

"You're not leaving me. You're just attacking the problem from another angle. If for some reason, you can't get to the men from below, I'll still have a chance to sneak downstairs and free them. This is a team effort."

As much as he hated to leave her, time was running out. The longer he stayed here arguing, the greater the chance he'd be too late to save the father and son, and the greater the chance Scourge would head upstairs for the women and find Faith instead. She wasn't going to budge. She was too goddamn stubborn. "One condition—take the gun and hide. Do not come downstairs. Leave the men to me. Then I'll come back for you. Are we clear?"

"Crystal." First her voice floated up, then her arm.

What the hell was that?

Pepper spray!

She was trading him her pink pepper spray for his Glock. He took it, and for a split second, smiled. As he handed the gun off to Faith, the world turned grim again. "Pull the trigger hard. That's how you disengage the safety." Then he was on his belly. Combat crawling back to the ladder, forcing his mind to focus only one step ahead.

Make it to the ladder.

He reached the bottom rung, stepped nice and easy, nice and quiet onto the ground. He secured the ladder against the side of the house, just in case Faith came to her senses. Meanwhile, the best he could do was get to the men, who, according to the book, would be in the basement. The only way to stop Faith from confronting Scourge would be to get the father and son out before she changed her mind and tried to free them herself.

Find the son.

From the roof, he'd had the advantage of distance to distort and cover his noise. But on the ground, he needed to be even more stealthy in his approach. Scourge might be anywhere—doing God knew what to anyone. His stomach clenched. He wiped his palms on his thighs.

Find the boy.

Back pressed against the wall, he sidestepped to the nearest window, closed his eyes, and prayed to whoever was up there for a little help. *Please let the book be wrong. Please let the boy be on the first floor and not in the basement.* He darted his head in front of the window. The room was lit up inside, and it only took a split second to process what he'd seen—the boy.

And the boy had seen him.

Thanks. I owe you one.

He stuck his head in front of the window again, this time pausing long enough to search the room for signs of Scourge. The kid shook his head violently. His eyes pleaded for help, and in that moment, Luke understood Faith completely.

Impossible to leave this family at the mercy of a sadistic maniac.

The son's hands and feet were hog-tied. His body stretched on the couch, head elevated by a pillow.

Kenyon Clutter's head had also been elevated by a pillow. The Kansas Bureau of Investigation had speculated Perry Smith had propped the boy's head to make it an easier target for his shotgun.

Luke's whole body tensed. His hands fisted so hard, his knuckles popped. A wave of sheer hatred for the man who'd done this threatened to swamp him. He rolled with that hate one second, then pushed it aside before it could disable him.

Focus.

The chances of the window being locked—he couldn't guess. Under normal circumstances, people keep their downstairs windows secured. But out here in the middle of just-good-folks country, families often neglected to lock their homes. He leaned his weight against the bottom ledge of the window and felt it give, heard a creak. Another break. The window was unlocked.

Opening it fast, like ripping off a Band-Aid, would make the least noise, or at least make noise for the shortest amount of time. Either way . . . he shoved hard, the window screeched open. In a heartbeat, he was inside the den, sawing at ropes, watching with rising alarm as the boy's chest heaved in an unnatural rhythm. Luke heard wheezing seep out from under the duct tape that covered the kid's mouth.

Fuck.

The kid had asthma.

"Don't scream. I've got you," he whispered in the boy's ear, still sawing at ropes with one hand as he ripped the gag from the boy's mouth with the other.

A gasp, a violent coughing attack, and finally a wheezy cry. "Help!"

The ropes were almost off.

"Quiet!" Luke grabbed him by the shoulders, shook him hard. "Your father's still inside. What's your name, son?" he asked, keeping his voice as low as possible.

"Carl."

"You're going to be okay, Carl. But you gotta run, fast as you can, find someplace to hide."

"My dad. He can't—"

"Your mom and sister are already out of the house. I won't leave anyone behind. I promise, Carl. So when I say run, you run and do not look back. My job is to get your dad out. Your job is to run and hide. What's your job, Carl?"

"Run." Carl wheezed out the word.

"That's right." Luke cut the last bit of rope. The boy had been tied like an animal waiting for the slaughter. Luke climbed out the window, took a fast look around to make sure the area was clear, and helped Carl out behind him. "Now, Carl! Run!"

Carl took off, coughing and gasping. He made it

under fifty yards before tripping and landing flat on his face.

Get up. Get up.

Luke had one foot back in the window already. He hesitated.

Carl bolted to his feet, but he didn't run. Instead, he looked back at the house, searching the high windows, trying to glimpse his family.

Boom!

A gunshot split the air. Carl turned and ran. The shadow of a male figure emerged from behind a tree, short, and stocky, a long gun in his hand.

Scourge.

Scourge loped after the boy.

Goddamnit!

Luke's foot caught on the windowsill as he scrambled back out. He yanked it free and took off after Scourge and Carl. Faster and faster his legs pumped, but the boy and Scourge had a head start. He lost sight of them for a few seconds, then rounded a corner and saw a barn door swinging open.

Boom!

Luke crashed through the barn door in time to see a dark shadow disappear atop a ladder and into the hayloft.

Quiet. All was quiet now . . . and dark.

The scents of hay and manure and sweat mingled with something more disturbing. Luke wouldn't have believed it if someone else had told him, but evil has a smell—dank and putrid and saturated with hate. The sickly-sweet odor in the barn made his eyes water. He covered his mouth with his sleeve. And then a scraping sound made him forget all about the smell.

He pressed his back against the wall and waited for his eyes to adjust to the dark. Long moments passed. Seconds seemed like hours. Time stretched and strained, helping him milk every nanosecond out of the time he had left on this earth. Like the barn, his brain had quieted, allowing instinct to take over. He was all muscle and nerve now. No emotion. No doubt. Just a crystalline understanding that this was the moment that would determine everything. What he chose, right now, would make him into either the man he wished he could be or the man he feared he might become. His father's face flashed before his eyes. His chin came up, and he swiped moisture from his cheeks.

I won't let you die, Carl. Not by this monster's hand.

He edged forward, the ambient light illuminating shapes and forms but not defining them.

Not tonight, Carl. You're not going to die tonight.

Luke's muscles coiled into tight ropes of energy. His eyes searched the barn.

There, in the corner, he spotted a long shape with spiked shadows sticking up like a crown.

Pitchfork.

Keeping to the walls, he crept to the corner, all the while willing the night to creak its natural sounds alongside his footsteps. Let a coyote howl, a mouse scamper, branches scrape. He was almost there.

His senses sharpened to the point he could practically feel his pupils widening in the dark, and he focused all his energy on his eyes. It crossed his mind that if he survived, he should try to remember how to do this, how to control his body so completely.

He blinked. Imagined himself with night-vision goggles and damn if he couldn't see clearly now. The pitchfork. His hand darted out and clamped on. The splintered wooden handle scraped his skin. He gripped his weapon tighter, until it became an extension of his arm.

More noises from the loft.

How long had he been in this barn? A minute, an hour? He had no idea. He crept forward, making his way to the bottom of the ladder, not knowing for certain if Carl was in the hayloft, too. The figure he'd seen on the ladder he believed to be Scourge.

"Come out come out wherever you are, little buddy. Come out with your hands up, or I'll make Mommy and Daddy pay."

And there was his confirmation. Scourge had chased Carl into the barn.

Don't do it, kid. Don't look back.

"Don't make me angry, Carl. I'm going back to the house with or without you, and you really don't want me to be angry when I get back there. Come out now, and I promise not to hurt you or your family."

Silence.

The kid was too smart to be fooled.

One hand clutching the pitchfork, Luke placed a

foot on the bottom rung of the ladder. It groaned beneath his weight.

Boom!

His body jumped in response to the blast, and the ladder jerked up and back down with a *crack*. He covered his ears. Hay and bits of wood rained down from above. The barn filled with smell of gunpowder. He swung his body behind the ladder and climbed the rungs, gripping the wood with one hand, the weight of his pitchfork, a comfort in the other.

Boom! Hard to localize the gunshot in the dark. Scourge could be shooting at Carl, or at him. Either way, it didn't change the plan. He kept climbing the backside of the ladder until he felt the floor of the loft bump the top of his head. In a nonstop series of movements, he pushed his body to the front of the ladder and leapt into the hayloft, pitchfork sweeping out in front of him. "Stay down, Carl!"

Boom!

He heard mostly ringing now. But the flash of light had come from behind him.

He whirled, and there, standing a yard in front of him was the devil himself. Shotgun in hand, aimed just to the side of him. He jumped the opposite direction just as the shotgun swung and fired. Heat from the blast singed the air. Rage rose inside him fueling his muscles, overriding his fear.

He charged.

Straight for the shotgun, straight for the devil himself. Pitchfork to the leg, and the devil howled, yet with nearly superhuman strength, wrenched it from his leg and tossed it aside.

It was like fighting a machine. This devil was made of steel and hate. Luke kicked him in shin and grabbed for the long barrel of his gun. The gun pulled back, blasted into the air, and hay and bits of barn battered his body.

Whoosh.

The gun fell from the loft and landed on the floor below with a thud.

Luke grabbed Scourge by the throat, and a fist slammed into his face. His nose cracked. Pain shot all the way to his eye sockets. Scourge slipped from his grip, and Luke's hand brushed against his side, closed around a cool canister.

Pepper spray.

Scourge leapt on him, and as they rolled through the damp hay, Scourge yanked the canister from Luke's hand. Then a strobe flashed, blinding him. An alarm rang out, and he covered his burning eyes. For a split second, Luke's lungs seized, and he couldn't move, only watch as Scourge raced down the ladder.

Recovering his breath, he bolted to his feet, but the devil just laughed and tossed the ladder across the barn like a toy. Now Luke had no way down from the loft. Through blurry eyes, Luke saw Scourge hobble across the barn, dragging one leg behind him. Luke had gotten him good with the pitchfork.

Without looking behind him, Scourge found his gun and limped outside. The door to the barn slammed shut, then Luke heard the screech of metal against metal as the latch engaged. Scourge had locked them inside.

Suddenly, the room was filled with the sound of coughing and gasping. "Help me. Please help me."

"It's okay, Carl. He's gone."

"I-I can't breathe."

Fuck.

The fallout from the pepper spray had triggered Carl's asthma again. The boy rose out of the hay, then fell back flat.

Luke raced to Carl and lifted him in his arms.

"Can't." He wheezed and wheezed. "Breathe."

And then the wheezing stopped altogether. The kid was barely moving air. Luke dropped to his knees and ripped open Carl's shirt. His chest heaved and retracted, the outline of his ribs exaggerating with every shallow breath. Luke cleared the hay from the boy's mouth and nose and felt for a pulse.

Strong.

Carl's chest stopped moving. He was no longer struggling to breathe—he wasn't breathing at all. Pinching Carl's nose, Luke blew air into his lungs and watched for the rise and fall of the chest. He gave another breath, then another.

Carl's head jerked, and he coughed, spewing warm liquid down his shirt . . . and the wheezing started again.

Good!

At least he was breathing. Luke lifted Carl in his

arms and looked for a way out of the loft. He couldn't risk jumping with the boy in this condition. There, to the left, he saw a way—crates stacked clear to the loft. "Stay with me, kid. I need you to put your arms around my waist. Can you hold on?"

Carl couldn't speak, but he nodded.

Luke's vision was starting to clear after the pepper spray. His skin stung, and his lungs ached, but that was of little interest to him at the moment. He had to get Carl out of this barn.

With the boy clinging to him, he hopped onto the highest crate. It wobbled slightly beneath his feet, but luck was with him. Whatever was in that crate must've been heavy, because it held the weight of both men. The crates were staggered just enough to allow Luke to find purchase with his feet and use them like a staircase.

At the bottom, Luke propped Carl against the barn wall. "Keep breathing, Carl. I'm going to get us out of here."

Behind the crates, he found a sledgehammer and used it to bust up the door's planks. Then he dragged Carl out into the fresh night air. "Stay quiet." He almost laughed, then. There was no need to tell Carl not to talk. He couldn't cry out if he wanted to. Not to mention they'd sledgehammered the barn door. "You did your job, Carl. You ran. Now you've got a new job, and that's to keep breathing. Let me worry about everything else."

Carl's hand reached up, and Luke squeezed it. Then Carl's arm went limp.

Don't you dare die, Carl. Don't you dare die.

And then Luke was carrying the boy again. By now, his right shoulder had gone completely numb, and about a hundred yards from the barn, his left arm started to cramp, but he had to get Carl out of sight. At last, he found a good hiding place, a metal toolshed.

He kicked open the door and choked back a grateful cry.

Inside the shed, on her knees, with her hands clasped in prayer, was Mrs. Donovan. Wordlessly, Luke lay Carl on the ground and checked his pulse—still strong. The boy's chest heaved, but no breath came out. He looked to Carl's mother. "Asthma?"

She didn't answer. Instead, she fished something shiny out of her pocket and stuck it in Carl's mouth. Two soft *whooshes* sounded.

Nothing.

She squeezed the inhaler again and waited. A loud cough followed a wheeze, and Carl's chest started to lift higher. He was breathing—not exactly with ease, but nice and steady. It seemed Mrs. Donovan had been thinking of her children throughout her ordeal. And despite the risk, she'd managed to find Carl's inhaler and stuff it into her pocket sometime between the moment Scourge entered her home and the time Luke and Faith had dragged her out of that window.

Luke let out a soft, admiring whistle.

Mothers.

TWENTY-NINE

Thursday, August 15, 11:00 P.M.

Faith opened the final closet door in the last upstairs bedroom in the Donovan home, and a pungent, chemical odor hit her in the face. Other than a conglomeration of old coats and worn boots and a spilled container of mothballs, the closet was empty. If either Mr. Donovan or his son was upstairs, they were well hidden. Well hidden was exactly what she planned to be when the police and Luke arrived. She'd given Luke her word she'd wouldn't go downstairs, and she didn't plan to break her promise—not unless she had to.

Boom!

She'd given Luke her word—he'd given her his gun. That wasn't Luke firing off shots. She rushed to a window and ducked below the sill.

Boom!

The second shot sounded faint, farther away than the first. Edging her face above the windowsill, she peered into the night and spotted a stocky figure darting across the yard. She heard a softer boom and saw a flash of light. Another figure darted after the first.

Her breath released all at once. Luke was alive. But then her heart skipped and stuttered—Luke was alive, and he was chasing Scourge, armed only with her pepper spray. The weight of Luke's Glock felt heavy and cold in her hand. She turned it over in her palm, wondering if she'd find the inner strength to pull the trigger if it came down to it. All she'd ever wanted was to help others live their best lives. She'd never envisioned *taking* one of those lives. She shook her shoulders out.

Don't second-guess yourself.

Don't second-guess Luke.

Scourge was running away from the house. How or why didn't matter. What mattered was this was a chance, and it might be the only one she had to get downstairs and free whoever remained alive.

If anyone remained alive.

A sour thought fermented in her belly like a cake of yeast. Had Scourge done his worst to the men while she and Luke worked to free the women?

She flew to the staircase. With Scourge out of the house, there was no need for quiet. She raced down the stairs and, taking them too fast, tumbled. Her back cracked against the wooden steps, and the gun fell from her hands. She wrapped her arms around herself and craned her neck to protect her head as best she could, but she didn't try to stop the fall. Every sharp blow to her arms and legs and torso brought her one second closer to the bottom. Once the fall happened, she welcomed it.

Fastest way down.

An instant later, she saw the floor coming toward her. She stuck out her hands to break the fall and catapulted to her feet. Her body was a collection of throbbing muscles and aching bones, but that was nothing compared to the urgent voice in her head.

Hurry.

Scourge might be back any minute.

Gun!

There, at the bottom of the steps. The Glock had tumbled down, too. Thank heavens it hadn't discharged. She stuck it in the back of her pants.

She saw a door to the right and ducked inside. Too dark to see. She decided against searching for a light. "Is anyone in here? Can you hear me?"

No response.

Hurry.

She moved on. In the next room, the light was on. Curtains flapped. A breeze cooled her burning cheeks. A couch, magazines, and cups littered the floor, and rope—lots of it—cut into pieces was scattered everywhere. Two things were notably absent: blood and bodies. Her chest felt as though a constricting band had burst open, allowing her heart to beat freely again.

Luke must have rescued at least one of the men.

Next she flung open the door to a downstairs office and was greeted by muffled cries. To her right, a man in a wheelchair was bound and gagged with duct tape. "Mr. Donovan, I have to get you out of here now," she said, and rushed to his side, ripped off the duct tape. "Can you walk?"

He shook his head. "Back injury," he rasped the words and drew a deep breath of air.

His hands and legs had been tied, and his injury was a blessing in at least one way—she could wheel him out now and work on the ropes later. From the corner of her eye, she noticed an open door on the other side of the room, and that jogged her memory of the home's blueprint and what had happened to the Clutters.

The basement.

"Is anyone down there? Anyone home beside you and your wife and children."

He sputtered, then started to cry. "My children. My wife."

"They're safe." They *had* to be. "Is anyone else in the house?"

His chin trembled. "No." His eyes flicked to basement door. "He-he was going to take me down there, but he changed his mind."

The injury must've been recent. Scourge wouldn't be expecting to have to carry or wheel the man down to the basement, so he'd taken the easy way out and bound him in this room instead. Clearly, Scourge followed whichever parts of the book were convenient and tossed the others aside, which was good for her and good for Mr. Donovan. It would've been far more difficult to get him up those basement stairs. "Let's get you out of here."

She released the hand brake and heaved. The chair rolled forward, and she worked her quads to gain speed and momentum. Out of the office, down the hall, around the corner. They were almost to the front door.

Crack!

Her muscles jumped. She looked up to see Scourge lounging in the front doorway, his body leaning against the frame, his shotgun pointed straight up.

"Hello, Dr. Clancy. I'm glad you could make it. I wanted you with me, and now here you are."

Her heart boomed in her ears like a stereo with too much bass, muffling his words. His oily smile made her gag. Steeling her legs, she gripped the chair to stop her hands from trembling. For one crazy second, she thought about charging Scourge with the wheelchair, or drawing the Glock from the back of her pants and facing off with him, gun to gun. She bent at the knees, gritted her teeth, but then a strange calm overtook her.

His advantage was a shotgun and the will to use it. Her advantage was her wits.

She should try those first.

"I've scared you speechless it seems." Scourge tilted his head sympathetically.

Mr. Donovan was crying softly.

Before speaking, Faith let out a long breath to steady her voice. Focusing on the distorted face in front of her, she told herself to see Scourge as a man in pain, a man in need of help and not some monster with a gun.

Then an image of Nancy Aberdeen and her prize-winning cherry pie came back to her, and she knew she couldn't do it. All she could see here was a villain of the worst sort. Devoid of empathy, she was going to have to fake it.

"Run, Scourge. Run now." *Sounds wooden. Next time do better.*

"No need for that, Dr. Clancy. We have plenty of time. Your friend is locked in the barn. He can't get out, or if does manage, it's going to take a while, and we'll be . . . finished by then."

"Run while you still can, Scourge. The police know everything. They'll be here any minute." She released her grip on the chair and extended her hand. "I care about you, Scourge; I don't want to see you hurt. Please run, run now," she said, suppressing the need to retch.

He leveled his shotgun at Mr. Donovan. "If you'd been able to convince the police, you'd never have come on your own." He shrugged. "You and your boyfriend. I mean."

She jerked her head up. "Leave now."

"Absolutely not. You're starting to irritate me, Dr. Clancy. Maybe we should stop chatting and just get started."

Summoning every ounce of cunning in her body, she said, "We can put a stop to this right now. I can help you."

"You already have helped me. You cured me to kill again." He wagged the gun at Mr. Donovan.

"And I'll help you again. Put the gun down right now, and I promise you I'll convince a jury you're insane. *Not guilty by reason of insanity*." She stepped to the side of the chair, then in front of it, blocking Mr. Donovan with her body. "You'll walk away a free man. I can sell that to a jury, Scourge, but only if you put the gun down now." Her arm snuck around her back, and she gripped the handle of the Glock, slowly inching it from her waistband.

"What a lovely offer, Dr. Clancy, but I won't be needing it because I'm not going to get caught." In one long stride, he came to her, and before she could stop him, he'd grabbed her right arm and wrenched. She tried to hang on to the gun, but the crushing pain of his fingers gouging her wrist caused her muscles to go slack. Her hand opened, and the gun slid to the floor.

He smiled. "The good news is I've saved my best rosary for you, and I just happen to have it on me."

She'd dropped the gun.

Luke had trusted her with his own weapon, given her his one advantage, and she'd wasted it. Her mouth went dry. She couldn't swallow, couldn't breathe.

"Today's your lucky day, Dr. Clancy." Scourge kicked the Glock across the room, dropped her wrist, and pulled a rosary from his pocket. "Sister Cecily gave this to me, and now I'm giving it to you." He twisted his arm and let the rosary wind around it like a bracelet.

A flash of headlights, the sound of wheels screeching up the drive made both of them jump.

The police.

"They're here, Scourge. Time to take my advice. You listened to me before, and I didn't steer you wrong."

"I'm not going to surrender, and I'm not going to trial, so take your offer and—"

"Then let *him* go." She slid her gaze to Mr. Donovan. "You have nothing to gain by keeping this man."

"Nothing to gain except my freedom. Sorry, Dr. Clancy, but the two of you are my ticket out. I need living hostages, and, you see, I lied before when I said I'd locked your friend in the barn." A sadistic smile cut across his cheeks. "Luke's already dead."

Her breath caught in her throat. He was lying. He'd lost control of the situation, and now he was trying to hurt her any way he could. In her mind, she pictured punching him with her fists, kicking him in the groin, gouging his eyes, but she held perfectly still, didn't move a muscle while she waited for her hatred to die down enough for her to fake a civil tone. "*I'm* your ticket to freedom. You don't need two."

For the first time, his eyes flickered with something akin to reason. His chin thrust forward. He was listening.

"In fact, you'll never get away if you try to take both of us. You can't hold me at gunpoint and wheel him out at the same time."

She'd expected the police to do something—

anything by now. What the hell was going on out there? Did they know the Saint was here and holding hostages, or were they still under the impression this was a simple wellness check?

"You can wheel him for me," Scourge said.

"All the way to Mexico? That's where you're headed isn't it—like Perry? Do you have a treasure map like Perry, too?" Oh God. She'd let sarcasm slip into her tone.

His eyes snapped. "You're right. A man who can't walk is a liability. I'll shoot him now."

"No!" She spread her arms and widened her stance. If Scourge wanted Mr. Donovan, he'd have to shoot her first.

"Get out of my way! You're making me lose my temper, and you're not going to like it if I lose my temper."

"You want a living hostage? Do as I say." Through gritted teeth, she bit out the words. She didn't know what the cops were doing out there, but she wasn't leaving her fate, or this innocent man's, to someone else.

"You're not the one in charge here. I've got the gun."

"But *I'm* your ticket out. And if you so much as look at this man again, if you so much as say one more cruel word to him, I won't cooperate. I'll force you to shoot me. You can't manage a man in a wheelchair, and you'll have no more ticket. Tickets aren't free." The last thing she wanted to do was look at Scourge. She squared her eyes with his. "The price of your ticket is Mr. Donovan's life."

Another set of headlights flashed.

Backup!

Scourge gaped at her a split second. Then jerked his shotgun. "Over here. Hands in the air. Slow. No sudden moves."

"Or what? You'll shoot me? I believe we've covered the fact you need me alive." She sucked in a breath. "I'm taking Mr. Donovan back to his office, so he can lock the door from the inside. He stays here. Once he's locked safely in his office, you and I walk out this door together. You'll be holding me at gunpoint, naturally. That's the deal. Take it or leave it."

Luke hurled himself down the hill, aiming straight for the farmhouse. Not so much as a pitchfork would stand between him and the devil when he got there, but he had to get to Faith, and he had to get to her *now*. His muscles still coiled and humming, his vision as sharp as it had ever been in his life, he plowed an easy path through the brush and cut out into the open.

He could see the Donovan place up ahead. A lone patrol vehicle in the driveway.

The wellness check.

His arms and legs worked furiously until he'd reached shouting distance of the cop car. An officer crouched beside the vehicle, radio in hand, pistol drawn. He must've called for backup because from somewhere behind Luke, headlights suddenly lit the road.

"Gun! He's got a gun!" Luke prayed the officer wouldn't turn and fire on *him* in confusion. "Up at the house!" He panted and held both hands high in the air to show he was unarmed. Then, like a punch to the gut, a realization hit him—the officer would detain him. The police would need time to sort out the good guys from the bad guys, and Luke with his six-foot-four build would be viewed as a serious threat. Making a sharp change in direction, he zipped past the patrol car.

"Police! Freeze!"

The words carried plainly in the wind, but Luke didn't stop, couldn't stop. He waved his hands high over his head, fingers stretched wide and called as loudly as he could. "Don't shoot! I'm unarmed. Civilians in the house!"

"Police! Freeze!" The command repeated close behind him. The officer was giving chase, but whether because of instinct or information from Johnson, he wasn't firing on Luke.

He kept running.

About a yard from the house, he saw the porch light flicker on, then off, then on again. He pulled up short and from his peripheral vision, he saw two patrol officers do the same. Faith appeared in the doorway, hands high in the air, just as his had been. Relief so intense it hurt washed over him. He grabbed his knees and kept breathing.

Faith was alive.

Then his heart and his breath stopped at the same moment. The barrel of a shotgun was stuck in her back. As Faith took another step forward, Scourge appeared behind her.

Both officers had pistols trained on Scourge and Faith. "Police! Drop your weapon!"

With his shotgun, Scourge pushed Faith down the steps. "Dr. Clancy and I are going for a ride. I'm afraid I'm going to need to borrow someone's car. My truck's a ways down the road and not too fast."

"Drop it now, asshole," the police officer barked back.

A painful spasm shot through Luke's legs, but he stayed crouched and at the ready. Sucking in deep lungfuls of air, he fueled his body with oxygen.

With flat eyes, Scourge stared past the officer.

Something was wrong. The expression on Scourge's face was so . . . indifferent.

Luke's hands squeezed at his sides. He had to get Faith out of the line of fire, and soon. A laugh from Scourge . . . and Luke knew.

Suicide by cop!

One. . .

Scourge's shotgun swung toward the officer.

Luke had meant to go on three, but that was shot to hell now.

Two!

He charged in from the side, knocking Faith to the ground just as the *pop, pop, pop* of gunfire rang out. A minute later, his ears were ringing, and he felt Faith's back heave beneath his chest.

"Luke, Luke are you okay?" she cried out, and he rolled off her, looking up to find an officer staring down at him.

"Helluva nerve, buddy. What'd ya say your name was again?"

"Luke Jericho!" Faith grabbed his neck and clung on tight, just about choking the life out of him—and all he could think was he hoped to hell she never let him go again.

THIRTY

Sunday, August 18, 3:00 P.M.

Scourge Teodori, the Santa Fe Saint, was dead. But Faith's pulse still rushed at every unexpected noise, her gaze still darted around every room she entered. Just now, she'd checked the corners of her kitchen and the space beneath the breakfast table. The sensation of danger lurking in the shadows hung in the air like the damp musk of an approaching storm, raising chill bumps on her arms and keeping her nerves on high alert.

Scourge is dead.

Faith shaded her eyes against the glare coming in through her kitchen window and reminded herself that the Donovan family was safe, and so was she. It was time to resume a normal life—one that included wonderful Luke and did not include sitting across the desk from a serial killer. And, with all the publicity surrounding the rescue of the Donovan family, Faith expected she'd finally be able to scare up some patients and pay back her loan to the bank.

As it turned out, Scourge had no family or friends. At least none the authorities could track down. Closing her eyes, she dropped her chin to her chest. She'd heard from Detective Johnson that a Sister Cecily from St. Catherine's school had offered to provide a mass and burial in the event no family came forward. Johnson was checking into the legalities of turning Scourge's body over to someone other than a relative but said he thought that in the end, the state would welcome the chance to spare the taxpayers any further expense on the Saint's account.

Ironic.

Isn't that what Scourge would say? Faith felt quite certain he would hate the idea of a mass and nuns praying for his soul. Her head jerked up, and her eyes flew open. She hadn't the slightest interest in intervening on his behalf. Scourge would have a proper Catholic burial, and she would think of him no more. Wiping clammy hands on the sides of her jeans, she took a deep breath. *Eventually,* she would think of him no more. For now, she would have to settle for getting on with her life as if she'd already forgotten.

All day yesterday and today, she'd been busying herself doing exactly that—by cooking. Humming off-key, she applied the last label: GREEN BEAN CAS-SEROLE, AUGUST 18, to the final Tupperware container and packed it in with the others. No thanks to Torpedo, who'd failed to keep a protective detail in place for Tommy while Luke and Faith traveled to Amarillo, Tommy had come through his encounter with Scourge with only a broken leg and an assortment of scrapes and bruises. Faith's security system had been installed this morning, and she'd happily paid extra for Sunday hours.

Faith's care package for the Bledsoes was overflowing with zucchini bread, beef Wellington, and homemade cinnamon rolls. Anything and everything that might make life a little easier on Angie Bledsoe while Tommy recovered from his surgery. Her heart squeezed as she lifted the box and headed for Tommy's house, Chica at her side.

"Wait here, girl," she whispered to Chica, then climbed the front steps. Before she could knock, Angie threw open the door and ushered her inside.

"More? But where am I going to put all this food?"

Faith shrugged. "If you can't fit it in your freezer, I can bring it over in smaller batches. I just thought this way you'd have more variety at your fingertips."

Angie sorted through the box. "Oh, good. You brought more mac and cheese. That's my—Tommy's—favorite. What's that yummy sauce you put on it?"

"Gruyère. I'll show you how to make it sometime if you like."

Angie stopped unloading the box. "I'd like that, Faith. Maybe you could join us for one of these awesome dinners sometime."

She'd like that, too, very much. "Sure," she said, and pulled her lower lip between her teeth, careful how she broached the next topic. "Chica's home from the hospital, too. I'm very grateful you took the time to make sure she got to the vet once Tommy was safe."

"It was Ann from three doors down who took her, all I did was ask. That dog saved Tommy's life—if it hadn't been for Chica, I wouldn't have my little boy."

Her heart lifted, and at the same time, a sense of loss weighted down her shoulders. Angie Bledsoe appeared to be very receptive to what Faith was about to propose, which meant her furry friend would be residing with Tommy for a while. "Speaking of Chica, I know Tommy can't come to her, so I wondered if it would be all right for Chica to drop by here, for a quick visit . . . or maybe even until Tommy's recuperated. I thought she might cheer him up. I don't want him to be lonely."

"Absolutely not."

Faith couldn't hide her surprise. Chica was no longer full of ticks and fleas, and as Angie had just pointed out, the dog had saved Tommy's life. "Oh, okay, well whenever Tommy's able to come by—"

Angie threw her arm over her chest. "Oh, no. I'm afraid you misunderstood. When I said I didn't want Chica to come by for a quick visit or a little longer, I meant I was hoping you'd let her stay here . . . permanently. Tommy loves that dog." Angie hesitated and looked at Faith beneath her lashes. "I know you love her, too, but it would mean the world to Tommy."

Faith waved her hand. "Of course. I'll be right next door if you need me, and I've always said Chica is Tommy's dog. I was just minding her until you two were ready. And now you're ready, so that's that. I'll bring you a list of her medications, and just between you and me, you may want to prepare Tommy for some news."

"This is about the puppies, isn't it? I've been wondering if they survived her injuries."

Faith filled her voice with optimism. "The puppies survived, but Chica had a through-and-through fracture of her right front leg. She needed pins, and they had to gas her down with Isoflurane to do the surgery. So the pups may or may not make it. The vet's hopeful, but she says we should be prepared for the worst."

"They couldn't take them early?"

"I asked, but that wasn't a good option. Dr. Culpepper said they had a better chance if we left them alone." Faith aimed her thumb over her shoulder. "I've got Chica waiting outside. Is it okay if I bring her in to Tommy now?"

Faith matched Chica's hobbling pace through the back door, which was the door closest to Tommy's room. Chica managed remarkably well with her front leg casted, and she looked rather adorable with a leopard-skin vet wrap covering her cast and not quite matching her natural Catahoula Leopard fur. The sound of children's voices carried down the hall, making Chica's ears prick.

Faith scratched her underneath her chin. "Tommy's got a visitor. That's good." She hated to think of

Tommy convalescing in isolation. Even children with lots of friends had a hard time being confined to their rooms, and Tommy . . .

"Chica." She knelt and put her face in the dog's fur, felt it grow damp. "I'm *not* going to cry." She lifted her head and swiped her eyes. "You'll be right next door, with Tommy. Right where you belong. After all, you found him first. You've always been his dog." Sniffling, she got to her feet. "I'll bring your white chocolate bones over later. Don't worry about a thing."

When Tommy's voice floated out to them again, Chica's tail wagged furiously, and Faith smiled in spite of the hole in her heart. "Let's go see Tommy."

The door to Tommy's room was half-open, and his voice was louder now. "And that's when I bit him."

"But weren't you scared?" a young girl asked.

"Nah. I had my dog with me."

Faith had never heard that bravado in Tommy's tone before.

The little girl continued, "My mom says the Saint had a shotgun. My mom says if you hadn't stopped him, he might've murdered the whole entire neighborhood."

"Yeah, Tommy. You're a hero," said a third voice, this one belonging to another boy.

"Like I said, I had my dog with me. But yeah, I suppose I was brave."

"Tell us again about the—"

"Tommy, you have another visitor." Mrs. Bledsoe swung the door wide. There reigned Tommy, propped up on pillows, his casted leg occupying a large portion of his narrow racecar bed. Around him, most every child in the neighborhood huddled in folding chairs.

Mrs. Bledsoe caught Faith's eye. "He's had so many visitors, I had to borrow chairs from my bridge club."

A hush fell over the room. And then one of the boys asked, "Is that Chica? Is that the hero dog?"

"Doy. Do you see the cast on her leg? She got a broken leg saving my life. Saving *your* lives." Tommy glanced meaningfully around his circle of friends. "Take it easy." Tommy instructed, as the children jumped to their feet. "Don't crowd her, but you can line up and pet her one at a time if you like."

The children fell into line, waiting their turn to pet Chica, the hero dog. A newfound confidence shining from his eyes, Tommy threw a glance at Faith, then his mother, "How long can Chica stay, Mom?"

"Oh, I don't know Tommy." Angie Bledsoe dabbed her eye with the corner of her apron. "How 'bout forever?"

Tommy let out a whoop. Faith gave him a hug, and clearly being too old for this crowd, left with a promise to return tomorrow. As she made her way back across the lawn toward her house, her cell phone beeped. She looked at the message, blew out a long breath, then typed her response to her brother-in-law.

Can't wait to see you, too.

THIRTY-ONE

Sunday, August 18, 4:00 P.M.

Faith smoothed her shaky hands over her hair and opened her screen door to admit her brother-in-law, Danny Benson. "I wasn't expecting you until tomorrow." Regretting the aloofness in her voice, she took a step forward.

Danny ducked his head and strode through the front door. Even when she was in heels, the man dwarfed her. He stretched out an arm and pulled her in for an easy side hug. Her body stiffened, a defense against crumpling against his chest and telling him how desperately she'd missed Katie and him.

His hands still on her shoulders, he backed up to arm's length, surveying her. The worry in his brown eyes made her want to crawl into a far corner of the room. She'd hurt him, and worse, she'd hurt Katie. They didn't understand why she'd been keeping her distance, and Danny certainly didn't understand why she hadn't told him about what had been going on with the Saint until now.

"We've been out of our minds, all of us, until we could get here. Why the hell didn't you tell me what was going on?" He pulled her back, this time for a bear hug.

"I'm perfectly fine. At least I will be once I can breathe," she sputtered.

Danny loosened his grip, then tightened it for one more hug before releasing her. He raised a brow, "You look surprisingly good, kid, considering you just tangled with a serial killer."

"And won." She raised her chin and self-consciously touched her cheek near a bruise she'd worked hard to camouflage.

Danny gave her the eyebrow lift again. "You're not fooling me with that pancake makeup over those bruises. I see them all right, but that's not what I meant. I meant you look happy."

"What're you? Ninety? I'm not a kid, and I'm not wearing *pancake* makeup. I'm wearing Chanel concealer. But thanks for noticing—I am happy." Even now. Even banged up and bruised and standing toe-to-toe with the man she'd been avoiding for the past two years. And thank heavens for that bear hug. It had taken her nerves away. "Can I get you some tea?"

Danny dragged a hand through his hair. "Nah. Let's wait for the girls."

Her heart did three flips in her chest. *The girls.* He meant Sky and Katie. Faith was about to see her niece, Katie, for the first time in forever. The worst part about avoiding her brother-in-law was that meant avoiding

Katie, too. And she simply could no longer bear to keep that up. "There's something about almost dying that really makes you want to live," she murmured to herself.

"I hear you." Danny looked at her with a comprehension that went beyond those simple words. He'd come close to death more than once himself, and he must know how that sort of thing makes you want to put your life in order, screw up your courage, and be honest about your feelings.

"I've missed you." She reached out to him.

He took her hand. "I missed you, too, kid. And I think I deserve some answers."

She didn't pretend not to understand him, just waited for him to finish.

"Sky and Katie will be here any minute, so maybe now would be a good time to fill me in on why you suddenly put Katie and me on the blacklist." He held up his hand to stop her protest. "Don't say you haven't blackballed us. You barely take our calls, and we haven't seen that pretty mug of yours for over two years. Sky says I need to give you your space, and I sure as hell tried, but I gotta say, I'm done with that. This has gone way too far, and if Grace were alive . . ."

"You don't have to bring Grace into this. I admit it." Her hand went to her stomach. *Suck it up, Faith.* "I've been avoiding you. Not because I don't love you guys, but because I do—so much. But you've got Sky now, and you don't need your former sister-in-law interfering. I only wanted to give you and Sky and Katie a chance to be a real family."

"Interfering? *Former* sister-in-law? What the hell are you talking about, Faith?"

She didn't look away. She was tired of keeping secrets, and even more tired of missing the people she cared for most. "I didn't want to horn in on your new family or your happiness—the way I did with you and Grace."

His grip tightened around her hand, and she tried to pull it free, but she was no match for Danny. "Never say that again, Faith. You never horned in on our happiness—Grace's and mine. That's a flat-out lie, and it kills me to hear you say such a thing." He paused, his eyes misting over, his voice lowering an octave. "You have no idea how much your sister loved you. You were Grace's whole world, at least until I came along. I'm the one who horned in on your territory, not the other way around. But I don't regret it. I'm selfish that way, and I wouldn't take back a minute of the life I shared with your sister."

She shook her head. "I wasn't a good sister, Danny. I didn't deserve Grace, and that's the truth. I'm sorry if it hurts you to hear me say these things, but it's time you understand."

"I already understand. Grace loved you with all her heart, and you loved her, too."

"That doesn't make me a good sister."

"In my book, it sure as hell does. Nobody's saying

you were *perfect*. None of us are, Faith. There's no such thing as the perfect wife, the perfect daughter, the perfect sister. We love each other in spite of our flaws, and that's all the perfection we need."

He didn't get it. He just didn't. "Listen to me, Danny. When Grace married you, I resented it. At first, it was like you said, I thought you'd horned in on my private world with my big sister. But when Grace got sick and started to pull away from us both, it was you who was there for me. Then things changed. I started to wish *I* was your wife." She held her breath and waited, and waited some more, but nothing happened. Danny's expression didn't alter, he didn't look away from her or drop her hand. The earth didn't rise up and swallow her whole. Eventually, she had to inhale.

Danny brought his fingers under her chin and tilted her face up. "I know that, too, kiddo."

She stumbled back, collapsing onto the couch. Danny sat beside her and put his hand on her shoulder. "That's right, I knew. It doesn't take a degree in psychiatry from Yale University to figure that one out. You were a lonely teenager. Your parents were gone, taken from you without warning. You looked up to Grace, wanted to be just like her." He winked. "And let's not discount the fact that I'm one helluva good-looking guy. Women swoon on the street when I walk by." He tweaked her chin, "C'mon, Faith. Please stop looking at me like that."

"Like what?" She held her back stiffly and tried to

keep the swirl of emotions off her face, at least until she could sort through them.

"Like you're embarrassed. This is *me*, Faith. I've known you since you were a kid, and I love you just like Grace did, and that's a fact."

"Even though I made a fool of myself over you? Even though I let Grace down when she needed me most of all, you still love me?"

"I do. Show me a person who never made a fool of themselves, and I'll show you a robot. You and me, Faith. We're not robots. You want me to say we didn't let Grace down, and I wish I could, but I can't. Neither of us recognized how deep her depression ran. Neither of us knew what to do to help her. Just remember, I was the adult. I was the one who missed the warning signs. But I know you and I both feel that weight on our shoulders every day."

She let the tears stream down her face, didn't try to blink them away.

"We feel that weight because we love Grace, and we always will. Our love for her isn't perfect, but it's real. Faith, you have to go on living even though you've lost such a beautiful part of your life. I think it was easier for me to move on because I had Katie, and I had no choice."

"I should never have stayed away from Katie this long. I just didn't want to interfere with her bonding with her new mom, and I didn't want Sky to resent me."

"No chance of that. Sky thinks you're the cat's meow."

Faith sniffled, and then smiled. "I think she's the cat's meow, too."

"So let's not do this again, okay? Grace would've wanted me to look out for you. Katie misses you like crazy. And I *miss* you. Our family's not complete without you. It's like trying to have Thanksgiving without the turkey."

"Umm. Did you just call me a turkey?"

He gave her a soft knuckle to the top of her head. "Yes, I did. Because you're acting like one."

"Gobble. Gobble." She flapped her elbows, then they were both laughing. It was the kind of laugh that bubbles out when you feel free to be just exactly who you are instead of who you think you ought to be. "Funny. All this time I've been carrying around my deep dark secret, and it wasn't a secret at all. You knew the whole time."

He shrugged. "And speaking of funny, that secret of yours wasn't nearly as deep and dark as you thought. It's human nature to want to be loved, Faith. Grace and I both knew that as you matured, your feelings would change, that someday you'd grow up and fall in love—real love, with another man, and then I'd have to run his prints through IAFIS, and let him know he better treat you right, or he'd have to answer to me."

That made her smile. "Hey, you never said why you flew in early. I really wanted to pick you up at the airport."

"Sorry, but right after I booked our flight, I got a call from some guy named Luke." Danny's grin was high-wattage. "Man, is that guy pushy. He wanted to send a private jet for us, which I thought was completely unnecessary and a waste of money, but he was insistent. Then Katie got wind of it . . . and as you know, I'm not good at saying no to my daughter. So Luke got his way. We flew out on his private jet, and now Katie thinks that's the only way to travel."

"Why didn't you tell me?"

"It was supposed to be a surprise. And when Luke suggested I meet with you alone, I knew it was a good idea." He lowered his brow. "I don't ever want to hear another word about your being an outsider or horning in or any other *bullshit* like that."

"I promise." She crossed her heart, then took a deep breath. This might be the only chance she had to talk to Danny alone, and now that they'd cleared the air, there was something else on her mind.

He cocked his head, studying her, as if he knew by the look on her face she had something important to say.

She prowled the room, debating whether or not to bring it up. It would be so much easier to let everything go, to ignore the niggling voice in her head that was telling her something still wasn't quite right. If anyone would understand, though, it would be an experienced cop like Danny. She stopped pacing and came to stand in front of him. "You ever get hunches. About a case I mean?"

"All the time."

"And . . . do those hunches usually turn out to be true, or do they just lead down a wrong path and waste your time."

His brows rose with interest. "Depends. The thing about hunches is there's usually something behind them. A forgotten fact that's nagging at us, but buried so deep we don't recognize it, a detail so small we've forgotten it. So we say, *I got a hunch*. Listen to me, I sound like a shrink."

Picturing Danny as a *shrink* made her smile. He never let anyone get away with bullshit. He didn't have the temperament to do her job.

"You got a hunch about the Saint?"

She made her voice casual, like it was all a big nothing. "I do. I tried to talk to Detective Johnson about it, but he practically threw me out. He said the case is closed, and it's time to let it go. Get back to my normal life. He didn't want to listen."

"I'm listening, Faith. What was it that Johnson didn't want to hear?"

"I told him Scourge had a dream about murdering a nun, back when he was a teen. I told him I thought it wasn't a dream at all. That it really happened. The murder would've been about ten years ago." She started wandering around, picking up cushions and putting them down again.

"He ought to look into that."

"He says he will, but a ten-year-old murder committed by someone who's already dead isn't a priority.

Then I told him something wasn't adding up for me. Scourge is such a follower. So susceptible to suggestion—he sees flooding on *Dr. Phil,* and next thing you know he's off flooding himself—but he didn't come up with the idea on his own. And the plan for killing the Donovans came from a book. He copied the idea from *In Cold Blood.*"

Danny tipped his head. "Let me guess. That's when Johnson tossed you out."

"No. He was very patient right up until I said that something feels unfinished—like it's not over yet. Then his face turned purple, and he showed me the door."

"What does Luke think?" Danny asked evenly.

"Luke thinks I'm having some sort of posttraumatic stress reaction. He thinks I'm experiencing natural anxiety, and I'm looking for an explanation as to why I still feel fearful even though Scourge is dead."

A low laugh, then Danny said, "Now *everyone's* a shrink. But, that sounds right to me." He scratched his chin. "Still, I wouldn't dismiss the feeling altogether. If your hunch is based on some detail you've forgotten, you'll remember it eventually. That detail is like a word on the tip of your tongue. Relax. Stop trying so hard, and eventually, it will come to you. Once it does, go back to Johnson and make him listen."

There was a knock on the door.

Faith answered, and Katie barreled in, nearly knocking her to the ground with her hug. "Aunt Faith. Aunt Faith. I love you!"

"Katie. Katie. I love you more!"

A long time passed before Faith and Katie stopped hugging. When they finally broke apart, Danny's new wife, Sky, took a quick turn. "Good to see you, Faith. I know Katie and Danny will try to hog you while we're here, but I hope you and I can steal some time for shopping and girl talk." Sky beamed at Faith. "I'm dying to hear about your new man."

Faith's cheeks grew warm. "You mean . . ."

Another knock sounded, then Luke, carrying three bouquets of gardenias, let himself inside. The sweetest fragrance filled the room as he handed a bouquet to Sky and Katie, then tried to hand the last one off to Danny. Laughing, Faith intercepted the final bouquet for herself. "New man? You must mean Luke Jericho." Then her heart cracked open. "Luke," she said, "I'd like you to meet my *family*."

THIRTY-TWO

Saturday, August 24, 5:00 P.M.

Luke drew Faith's eye like the last morsel of chocolate on a dessert platter. Amidst the buzzing throng at the art gallery, she could tell which ladies were Santa Fe royalty by their Dolce and Gabbana frocks belted with turquoise. Their male counterparts she knew by their Armani shirts adorned with bolo ties. Luke boasted the same garb, but one glance was all she needed to pick him out from across the crowded room.

The way he held one shoulder slightly higher than the other; the way he bent one leg at the knee when he was concentrating had become as recognizable, as essential to her, as her own heartbeat. His back was to her, so she took her time, raking her gaze across his broad shoulders and down his arms, where the hard contours of his muscles strained against the sleeves of his best silk shirt.

Luke.

Luke had been planning this art gala to benefit the Big Brothers and Big Sisters of Santa Fe for the better part of a year. Proceeds from all works sold would go to the charity, and a large and very generous crowd was in attendance. When the event coincided with Dante's release from jail, Luke came up with the brilliant plan of including Dante's works in the exhibit. What better way to reintroduce his brother to society than as a gifted artist rather than a demented serial killer. Town gossips had been flaming about Dante since his arrest, and Luke knew it was a risk to show Dante's work here tonight, but that was exactly why he'd insisted on doing so. Luke wanted his brother to know he wasn't ashamed of him. He wanted to celebrate Dante's talents in a big way.

Faith glided to Luke's side and slipped her hand in his, studied the painting he was studying. For a long time, they stood together in silence, letting the intensity of the piece in front of them suck them inside its strange, foreboding world. Of all Dante's works, this mixed-media was the best she'd seen, the one that evoked the most emotion. Tilting her head, she cocked her front foot back on its stiletto and focused all her attention on the dark forest depicted in the painting. The greens and browns and watery textures seemed so familiar, so real she could practically smell the musk-soaked night. Suddenly, a restless beat began drumming in her ears, slowly at first, but then picking up speed, beating fast and hard, like rain falling on a canopy of trees. Dropping Luke's hand, she shook her head slightly, then cupped her ears, but the beat only played louder.

There was something troubling about this particular painting, something sinister about its inky woods with rivulets of water cutting through layers of moss and dead fronds on the ground. With a hypnotic rhythm still drumming in her ears, her gaze honed in on a patch of moonlight illuminating flat eyes. The eyes belonged to an old woman—a faint, nearly translucent image on the canvas—which must be why she hadn't discerned her form until this moment. Black robes flowed around the woman, blending seamlessly into the night. Her face seemed eerily disconnected from her body, floating in a starless sky.

A ghost head.

A shiver hummed down her spine.

In her mind, she heard Scourge's grotesque whisper:

In my dream, we're deep in the woods, miles from the boys' dormitory, and my thighs are burning because I walked all this way with Sister Bernadette on my back. Now I've got her laid out on the soggy ground underneath a hulking ponderosa pine. A bright rim of moonlight encircles her face. Black robes flow around her, engulf her small body and blend with the night. Her face, floating on top of all that darkness, reminds me of a ghost head in a haunted house.

A ghost head.

As she let herself be drawn deeper into the wooded

scene, her stomach clenched, flushing acid up the back of her throat. This reminded her of Scourge's dream—a dream so detailed, so powerful, she believed it *had* to be real. She swallowed down the bitter taste in her mouth. This painting held that same power. It was almost as if the artist—as if *Dante*—had been with Scourge in the woods that night, as if Dante had recorded the murder of Sister Bernadette in his mind and later reproduced it in this painting.

But that was impossible.

She passed a hand in front of her face, waving away the horrible thought.

"Your fascination fascinates me." Luke said, making her jump back. One high heel collapsed. Her ankle twisted. She barely managed to keep her balance.

She'd been so lost in the painting that she'd forgotten where she was. Now the pain in her ankle pulled her back to reality. This painting was a work of art, the source of which was Dante's undeniably brooding imagination. There was nothing more to it than that. Her breathing slowed, and she raised her hand, touching the notch of her throat where her pulse throbbed hotly against her skin.

In therapy, she'd ventured so deep inside Scourge's head, it was understandable that at times she'd see the world through his eyes. He'd described what she now believed to be the *very real* murder of Sister Bernadette to her in such sickening detail, she worried she'd never be able to see the world the same way again. She doubted she'd ever be able to free herself entirely from the vile images that had been burned into her brain, courtesy of Scourge Teodori. A hard sigh escaped her lips. According to Dr. Caitlin Cassidy, the weight of Scourge's diseased thoughts would grow lighter and more bearable with time.

Please let that time come soon.

This was not how Faith wanted to view the world or the people around her—with suspicion and dread. One person, though, she knew she could trust. Seeking the comfort she'd come to find in Luke, she turned to him. "Sorry. I'm afraid my mind was somewhere else. What'd you say, again?"

He reached out, his fingers brushing her cheek, sending a frisson of electricity across her skin. "I've been trying to tell you for the longest time, Clancy. You're the most fascinating woman I've ever known." He tucked a lock of hair behind her ear. "Seeing your mind far away like that makes me want to crawl inside your head and eavesdrop on your thoughts. I want to go to that faraway place *with you.* I have since the first moment I laid eyes on you."

"Be careful what you wish for," she said, a little more sharply than she'd intended. Being inside another person's head wasn't a picnic in the best of cases, and in the worst of cases . . .

Her mind was wandering again. She jerked her attention back to Luke. She could never forget that evil existed, but Luke reminded her of all that was good. He gave her the strength to move forward.

"The first time I saw you," he said, "you were

standing in front of this very piece, wearing that same white-hot blue dress with that same intense look on your face, your mouth pulled sideways, just the way it is now. You couldn't take your eyes off Dante's *Dark Woods*, and I couldn't take my eyes off you. And now here we are again, only now I can touch you, and you won't disappear." He lifted her chin with his thumb. "Promise me you won't disappear, Faith."

Her breath released in a rush. "I promise."

A moment ago, she'd been staring at this painting, feeling as though she stood witness to a murder in progress. And a trace of a tremor still ran through her arms, but just knowing Luke wanted to stand by her side made her shoulders feel lighter, the world less heavy. Luke was here with her, and he'd provided her a perfectly good explanation for that sick feeling of déjà vu she'd had—a perfectly good explanation that had nothing to do with the Santa Fe Saint or Sister Bernadette's murder. The tightness in her chest all but vanished. "So that's why this scene seems so familiar. I've actually *seen* this painting before—the first time I came to your gallery."

"The day we first met." He nodded, then continued, "Believe it or not, as evocative as this painting is, it's one of Dante's earliest pieces." He rested his cheek in his palm. "I think he actually started on this one while he was still at St. Catherine's. Can you imagine? I really think it's his best work."

The sensation that her entire world was about to irrevocably change replaced her momentary sense of relief. When she turned back to *Dark Woods,* she could feel its bleakness chill her skin, taste its poison on her tongue, *see* its evil wafting from the canvas in greasy black waves. Unable to look away, she leaned closer. Now she saw that the old woman lying prone on forest floor clasped a string of beads. Faith briskly rubbed her hands against her sides, trying to brush away the tingling in her palms. She closed her eyes, reopened them one at a time, wishing the image away. But the beads remained.

The *rosary* remained.

"Clancy, are you listening to me? Have you heard a word I've said?" Luke's tone seemed more amused than angry.

"Of course," she murmured, and stumbled back, her ankle throbbing in protest. She looked up at Luke, tried to focus on the warmth in his eyes, tried with all her might not to let her gaze return to *Dark Woods.* But it was no use. The woman in the painting called out to her, a desperate soul begging for help. As she gazed in horror, the black-and-white brushstrokes swirling across the canvas no longer seemed abstract, open to the viewer's interpretation. The subject of this painting was perfectly clear to her now, and she couldn't unsee it—a nun sprawled lifeless beneath a hulking ponderosa pine.

Yet . . . it was possible she'd misheard . . . wasn't it? Her tongue felt thick in her mouth. "W-where did you say Dante painted this?"

"At St. Catherine's School for Boys. Our father

claimed he sent Dante away to that awful place to straighten him out, to socialize him and teach him right from wrong. Dad said that if Dante kept heading down the path he was on, he'd wind up in jail or worse. But I know the truth. My father banished Dante from our lives because his presence at the ranch was a constant reminder to my mother and me that, for years, Dad had been living a secret life. Once Dante's mother died, there was no one to stop my father from turning his back on Dante. Dad tried to persuade mother and me that Dante had no moral compass, but we both knew it was really my father who didn't know right from wrong."

His words floated around in the air, and it took her extra time to hear and process them. She braced her hand on Luke's strong shoulder.

Dante was sent to St. Catherine's School for Boys.

Depending on the years he attended, he might have known Scourge. And that meant it was possible he'd been in the woods with Scourge that night. It was possible Dante had witnessed Sister Bernadette's murder.

It was even possible Dante had been more than a witness.

But . . . Scourge never mentioned a partner.

She shuddered.

The voice.

More than once, Scourge had referenced a voice—a voice that issued commands and had opinions all its own. She'd assumed the voice had been an auditory hallucination . . . but what if it hadn't been? After all, Scourge's dream probably wasn't a dream at all, but rather *a true memory*. Maybe the voice wasn't in Scourge's head at all. Maybe the voice belonged to *a real person*. The same way she remembered Scourge's voice in her head, Scourge might remember his partner's.

His partner.

Feverishly, she scanned the painting.

And then her breath stopped.

There!

She gripped Luke's shoulder tighter. In the corner of the canvas, she could make out two boyish figures escaping into the trees.

Two boyish figures.

Her knees threatened to buckle, but she couldn't allow herself to give in to fear. Locking her legs, she imagined a steel rod running through her spine, forced herself to breathe, slowed her racing thoughts.

Luke unclasped her hand from his shoulder. "You learn that grip in Krav Maga, darlin'? Maybe we can try some of those moves out later night, but right now, I have to go. The mayor just came in. I'm going to go politic a little, then hit the guy up for a massive contribution to Big Brothers and Big Sisters."

"Luke, I have to tell you something." Shock steadied her voice, numbed her fear.

But Luke had spotted Dante across the hall and was gesturing him over. "Can it wait till after the mayor?"

Dante was all smiles as he headed toward them.

"Yes." She tiptoed up and kissed Luke's cheek, let her fingers trail across the nape of his neck. If she was right about Dante, the news would crush this beautiful man. This man who'd brought her heart to life again. "It can wait."

When Dante was close enough for Faith to catch a whiff of his camouflaged whiskey breath, Luke said, "I think you've got a fan in Faith, she can't take her eyes off this painting of yours. Keep her company for me for a minute, will you?"

"Of course, brother. Anything for you." Dante gave Faith an extravagant bow, then grazed her cheek with his fingertips. "I'm at your service, madam."

His touch left her wanting to scrape slime from her skin.

As Luke strode away, Dante said, "You do seem uncommonly interested in my painting. Why is that, Dr. Clancy?" His lips curled up to reveal his teeth in something closer to a snarl than a smile.

Her eyes jerked involuntarily to the spot on the canvas depicting a rosary in a dead nun's grip, then her hand went to her own necklace.

Stupid.

Too late to escape Dante's notice, she stuffed her hands in her pockets.

Dante's gaze went to *Dark Woods*, then flicked to her face. She didn't want to look up at him, but she couldn't let him intimidate her. Raising her chin high, she matched his stare.

An eternity passed. He watched her with such intensity his pupils threatened to black out his eyes. "Are you afraid of me, Dr. Clancy?"

She didn't drop her gaze. "Should I be?"

"Always the psychiatrist. Answering one question with another question. Never revealing your true feelings. I find that rather tiresome, really. I can't imagine what my brother sees in you." Dante turned his back and stalked away.

Frantically, Faith scanned the room for Luke. But the crowd was too thick and the air oppressively hot, almost suffocating. She put her hand on her chest, forcing herself to breathe, and hurried to the door, still searching for but not finding Luke. Checking back over her shoulder to be sure Dante hadn't followed, she ducked out of the gallery.

Faith's feet flew over the sidewalk, carrying her away from the gallery and toward her office. She needed time to think. Maybe she was reading too much into things. Maybe she was projecting her own memory of Scourge's dream onto the painting. After all, no one else around her seemed to see a dead nun in *Dark Woods*. Yes. She was projecting. That's all it was.

But a sick feeling still sat like a piece of rotting fruit in the pit of her stomach.

Dante started this painting at St. Catherine's School for Boys.

That was not her projecting. *That* was a fact.

Dante attended St. Catherine's.

Scourge killed Sister Bernadette at St. Catherine's.

She was sure of it.

Are you afraid of me, Dr. Clancy?

As much as she wished it weren't true, she knew—and Dante *knew she knew*. He'd been present in the woods that terrible night. Had he been a witness, or an active participant in the Sister's murder?

Had Dante been *the voice* that commanded Scourge: *Do it! You want to make it into hell, don't you?*

Then slowly, understanding dawned—not like the rising of the sun, but like its eclipse. A black curtain fell across her heart. Scourge never mentioned a partner because he wanted to protect that partner. Just like Perry Smith wanted to protect his partner, Dick Hickock. Before his execution, Perry Smith took the blame for all the murders, claiming Dick never pulled the trigger on any of the members of the Clutter family. Perry said he didn't want Dick's family to suffer, so he changed his story to accept full responsibility. She drew up short and spewed undigested hors d'oeuvres onto the sidewalk.

Scourge planned to re-create the Clutter family murders in order to guarantee himself a place in hell, but there was a reason he'd chosen that particular path. Like Perry Smith, Scourge had spent time in a Catholic school. Like Perry, Scourge was small and ridiculed for wetting the bed. If Scourge was to be taken at his word, and she didn't know if she could or not, he'd been beaten with a flashlight, just like Perry. Scourge had taken on the role of a cold-blooded killer, in part, because he'd become overidentified with Perry Smith,

even to the point of combing his hair the same way and
branding his body with the same tattoos.

And Perry was nothing without Dick.

Of course Scourge had a partner.

Scourge was nothing without Dante.

When Dante confessed to being the Saint, he left
Scourge to carry out his master plan on his own. No
wonder Scourge came unglued and developed a crip-
pling fear of blood.

He'd never killed on his own before.

Bolting down the sidewalk, she crashed into a man
carrying a bag of groceries. Oranges, apples, and pota-
toes flipped out of the bag and rolled down the sharp
incline of the street. A kid let out a whoop at the splat-
ter of eggs exploding onto the sidewalk, then gave
chase to the fruit.

"Sorry! Sorry!" Faith yelled, barely glancing back at
the man who'd lost his groceries and now stood shaking a fist at her.

Her heel caught a crack in the sidewalk, wrenching
her already pained ankle. She threw out her hands to
break her fall, and her palms scraped the ground. As
she catapulted upright again, she cast another glance
over her shoulder. No one was following her—not
Dante, not even the man with the spoiled groceries.

*Get it together. Breaking your neck won't accomplish
anything.*

Deliberately, she slowed her steps, threw back her
shoulders, tried to blend in with the tourists on the

busy street. She stopped and feigned interest in a bouquet of gardenias from a street vendor. The pungent fragrance of her favorite flowers somehow distracted the panicked part of her brain, and reason seeped in, albeit a little at a time.

A block from her office, she ducked behind the corner of a building. Keeping an eagle eye out for Dante, she slipped her cell out of her clutch and speed-dialed Luke.

Straight to voice mail.

Not a huge surprise. Luke didn't usually carry his cell at gallery functions. He liked to lavish his undivided attention on patrons of the art. "Call me. It's urgent," was all the message she left Luke. Dante might intercept her voice mail, and there was always a chance he didn't realize she'd put the pieces of the puzzle together.

Are you afraid of me, Dr. Clancy?

Yeah. Right. Dante had no idea she was onto him.

Despite her slowed pace, her breath came in hard pants. Her heart ticked in her ears like a metronome set too fast by a sadistic piano teacher. She had to call the police—now. But she still remembered Detective Johnson's scorn when she'd told him she thought Sister Bernadette had been murdered, and that things were still unfinished.

If she called Johnson now with yet another turnaround—and that based on her personal interpretation of an abstract painting and a single menacing comment from Dante—Johnson would be slow to act. And she couldn't blame him. Not really.

But there was someone she could call.

Special Agent Atticus Spenser had given her his card and told her he had the power to make things happen, and she still carried his card inside the back of her cellphone case, so she could be sure to find it quickly. She snapped her phone out of its case, plied Spense's card out, and entered his number.

"Spense here," a deep voice answered on the first ring.

"Special Agent Spenser?"

"Dr. Faith Clancy. Talk to me."

Her number was blocked, but she didn't bother asking how he knew it was her. He was FBI. "Dante Jericho. Dante Jericho is the Santa Fe Saint." She had no intention of burying the lead in small talk.

"Nope. We got DNA says that's Scourge Teodori. But while you've got my attention, please explain yourself."

She threw a hand over her racing heart. "Right. Scourge Teodori is the Saint. But he's only one-half. Dante and Scourge are, that is they were, a team. There's this painting . . . look, I know it sounds crazy, but Dante painted a picture depicting the murder of a nun. Scourge described the same murder to me in therapy in the guise of a dream. Turns out Dante attended St. Catherine's just like Scourge. Can you check to see if both men were at the school at the same time?

I believe Scourge and Dante cooked up the idea *together* to replicate the Clutter murders."

"Say no more, Dr. Clancy. I got it."

"You do?" She'd been too excited to explain things clearly.

"Scourge Teodori and Dante Jericho are Perry Smith and Dick Hickock wannabes."

Thank the lord for Special Agent Atticus Spenser.

"Think hard. Does Dante know you suspect him?"

She squeezed her eyes shut. "Probably."

"Where are you? Can you get someplace safe until I can get someone to you?"

"I'm near my office on—"

"I know your office. Go now. Lock your doors. Keep your cell on. I'm still in Phoenix, but I'll call back to let you know who's bringing you in. Do not call anyone. Do not open the door for anyone until I give you the go-ahead."

"But I have to warn Luke."

"The only thing you have to do is stay out of sight. I'll warn Luke. You're to go straight to your office and lock the door. Don't tie up your phone."

She nodded.

"Stop nodding and hustle."

Pulse pounding in her throat, she rounded the corner and raced up the stairs of her office building. When she reached her office door, her shaky hands made it hard to fit the key in the lock, but she finally managed. Once inside, she slammed the door behind her and flipped the dead bolt in place. Whirling around, she searched the dimly lit room. With the window shade drawn, only a scant amount of light edged inside. She debated whether or not to open the shade. It would let more light in, but she'd be visible through the window if Dante had followed her somehow. If she kept the shade drawn and turned on the lights, Dante would know she was here, too.

At least she'd locked *both* entrances to her office before going home last night. She'd made that a habit ever since the first time Dante followed her here from the gallery.

The thought of that day, the day he'd confessed, set not only her pulse but her head pounding.

Why did Dante confess?

He clearly didn't intend to go down for the Saint's crimes. Despite his early protestations, he'd instructed Torpedo to enter a not-guilty plea, and in the end, he'd proven more than anxious to be set free. It simply made no sense.

Unless . . .

Dante's confession was his get-out-of-jail-free card.

Her hands clenched. That son of a bitch had used her.

By now her eyes had adjusted from the outside brightness. She could see perfectly. Cell in hand, she moved forward.

Creak.

Her shoulders jumped.

What was that?

Silence. And then . . .

Thud.

A small gasp escaped her lips, and her heart slammed into fifth. Dante leapt out from his hiding place behind her desk. Then she screamed, long and loud.

"Oh dear, now I've gone and frightened you again. You're a jumpy one aren't you, Dr. Clancy?" He leveled a pistol at her. "If I were you, I'd stop screaming." The pistol jerked. *"Now."*

She heard a soft *pop.* A muzzle flashed, and a burnt odor filled the room. The glass covering her framed diploma shattered. The cylinder on the tip of Dante's gun was a silencer, suggesting cold-hearted premeditation on his part. He must've known she'd put things together eventually, and he'd been prepared.

Forcing herself to look directly at him, she stuffed down her screams. Tried to slow her breathing. Dante had every advantage but one. He didn't know help was on the way. All she had to do was stall him until that help arrived. "How did you get into my office?" Not like she didn't want to know.

He clucked his tongue. "Really, dear, is that the most pressing question you have for me? Not: *Are you going to kill me here or do it elsewhere?*"

She shrugged.

"All right then. I'll tell you anyway. I'm going to kill you elsewhere and dump your body where it will never be found. Along with the other whores. Of course, if you give me any grief, I'll have to improvise—do you here and move your body later. So don't give me any grief."

Other whores. He's killed others, not just the Saint's victims.

Her tongue felt swollen, and her throat closed. She gulped air, and her throat opened again.

Stay calm. Help is on the way.

All she had to do was stay alive one more minute. Then stay alive another. She could manage that. Wishing she still had her pink pepper spray, she patted her beltless waist.

No pepper spray, but letter opener in the desk drawer, globe on the bookshelf, Taser hidden in the plant stand.

Stay alive one more minute.

Dante had always enjoyed talking. Perhaps he'd like to unburden himself a little before traveling. He was egotistical enough he'd surely want her to know how clever he'd been. He'd want her to see all the brilliant ways he'd outsmarted her. Well, she'd give him an open invitation to explain his superiority to a mere mortal like her.

"How'd you get in, Dante?" Her tone held real fear, and she dusted in a bit of deference. He wanted to watch her squirm, and she knew it. Careful not to overplay it, she let her voice quiver a bit more. "I'm absolutely certain I locked both doors."

"So you did, my dear. But you see I've had a set of keys to your office since the day you moved in. I lifted a set from your landlord, had a copy made for myself, and replaced the originals."

She drew in a sharp, shocked breath. He'd been

stalking her since before she moved into her office. "But why?"

"Because I had my eye on you. My friend Scourge showed me your brochure. I believe you know my good friend, Scourge Teodori." One side of his face squashed up. "Make that *knew* my friend Scourge Teodori. He was quite fascinated by you, and I thought, why not? She might be just the ticket I've been looking for. And as it turned out, you fit the bill perfectly—greener than grass with no patients, no real experience to draw upon. You made a perfect foil for my plan. And what a bonus to learn you were all alone in the world with no one to miss you or protect you."

She'd known it was no coincidence that both men had wound up in her office. Only she'd assumed Scourge had found her from the publicity she'd garnered when she turned Dante in. But it was the other way around. *Scourge found her first, through her brochure, then Dante latched on to her as a means to an end.* "I suppose I ought to be flattered you chose me, but I'm afraid you only picked me because you thought you could play me."

"I *did* play you, dear. Scourge had it in mind to make you the Saint's next victim—I guess he was tired of watching me have all the fun with the ladies. He wanted a little of his own before he retired to the beaches of Mexico. But I had other uses for you, so I made him wait. Scourge also wanted to take Jeremy out, but I convinced him the kid was more useful as a living suspect. So you see, I saved two lives—yours and Jeremy's—you'd both be dead right now if I hadn't needed you. Aren't you going to say thank you?"

"Thank you." She cast her eyes to the floor in a show of submission, much like a housecat who rolls over and plays dead for the family dog. On the way to her toes, her gaze fell on her watch.

Ninety seconds.

He hadn't pulled the trigger yet. Why settle for a minute? She was going for another ninety seconds. Amazing how when your time is so short, every second expands into a lifetime. She wouldn't waste it or take it for granted. She'd use her time to remember her loved ones, Luke, her niece—Katie, and Danny and always, always Grace. She'd also use her time to scheme—a multitasker to the end. "You mentioned you had your own plan? I assume you don't mean killing the Donovans."

"No. Though I wouldn't have minded sticking around for that. The idea of killing the perfect family always appealed. I'd rather have killed my own, but I liked Scourge's idea, too."

"I see." She was back in therapy mode, and strangely enough, Dante had fallen easily into the role of patient—a patient with a pistol.

"The problem with Scourge was he was simply too slow. He wanted to plan *for years,* then practice and practice, with *more years* between kills, mind you, before taking on what he called The Big Kill. He wanted to wait for the ten-year anniversary of Bernadette's death. Can you imagine? I simply didn't have that kind of patience. Besides, he wouldn't shut up about hell and purgatory and fucking Truman Capote. Scourge was not all there. But you already know that."

"Hmm. So the whole *In Cold Blood* thing, the Perry and Dick thing, that was only Scourge's obsession?"

"I went along with it for years. Scourge was a handy guy to have around; he handled most of the mundane details of our trade, and I rather enjoyed the way he looked up to me. I did my own thing in between our Saint kills, of course."

"The whores, you mean?"

"Scourge just kept getting crazier and crazier on me. The way he insisted we had to leave the rosaries on the bodies to save their souls. Bodies don't have souls—dead or alive. There's no saving something that doesn't exist. He'd spend a good thirty minutes saying a rosary over a corpse. Those goddamn rosaries were going to get us caught sooner or later. When I couldn't persuade Scourge to stop with the religious crap, I decided to ditch him."

"And that's where I came in."

"You're brighter than I thought you'd be, Faith. Too bad that's not going to save you."

She waited.

He sighed and glanced around, as if growing impatient with the conversation.

She needed to keep him talking. "Tell me about your plan."

"You're so smart, why don't you tell me?"

She gestured toward her desk. "I'm tired, do you mind if I sit down while we talk?"

Waving his pistol, he shook his head. "So you can stab me in the back with that letter opener? I found it and got rid of it. If you look around, you'll notice that big glass globe is gone, too."

Tears stung the back of her eyes, and she blinked them away. He hadn't mentioned the Taser. Maybe he hadn't found it. She continued on, as if two-thirds of her arsenal hadn't just been obliterated. "Your plan—let's see if I can guess. You wanted to get rid of Scourge and escape blame for the Saint's murders all at the same time. So you decided to confess—to me. You knew that, by law, I had a duty to warn. You knew I'd have to turn you in whether I believed you guilty or not."

"Very good. And don't forget the green-as-grass part."

She tilted her head. This, she wasn't so sure about. "You studied up on personality disorders, then . . . you role-played a depressed man with a schizotypal personality disorder." That's why she hadn't been able to diagnose him. He was *playing* at being at one thing, but his true psychopathic traits occasionally broke through and knocked her off course. "You figured an inexperienced psychiatrist like me wouldn't know the difference. You figured I'd think you were too ineffective to pull off an organized-murder scheme. You figured I'd figure your confession resulted from paranoid delusions. Well played."

His eyes glittered as he spoke. "Exactly. And then you'd begin the fight to set me free. Meanwhile, the Saint would kill the Donovans while I remained in custody. I'd be turned loose, free and in the clear. Afterward, I'd find Scourge and get rid of him, put his body with my whores. The trail for the Saint would grow cold, and with no more rosary killings, eventually the authorities would stop caring about catching the Saint."

"Why not just kill Scourge to begin with and go on about . . . your business?"

"Too boring. I like danger—I *crave* danger. And I wanted to be cleared as a suspect. That way, if evidence of the Saint's crimes ever led back to me, no one would pay attention. The only thing that nearly went wrong is that Scourge developed that absurd blood phobia. I guess he was just too damn scared and weak to keep going without me—until you cured him, of course. I really don't know what I'd have done without your help, dear."

His words chilled her bones all the way to the marrow. Dante was right. She'd cured one serial killer of a blood phobia and been an unwitting accomplice to another killer's master plan. Well, guess what? She wasn't going to let Dante get away with another murder. Not hers. Not anyone else's.

She looked down at her watch again.

Four minutes.

She faked a backward stumble, put her hands out like she'd grown faint, and nearly lost her balance. She wound up one step closer to the front entrance, and to the plant stand, which might or might not still contain a Taser.

"Take off your shoes."

"What?" Was this a foot fetish or some other sick game?

"You had your shoes off the last time."

"When? What do you mean?" But she remembered. This was Dante's way of showing he was in control. Apparently, holding her at gunpoint wasn't enough. Next he'd want her cell.

"Toss me your cell."

She did as he commanded.

"You had your shoes off the day I confessed. So take them off now. We're going to play another little game. Only this time, the end is going to be different. This time I'm going to confess to you, and then I'm going show you just exactly how bad a man I am. Dying's not going to be the worst thing that happens to you today. Are you afraid of me, now, Dr. Clancy?"

She could see the bulge in his trousers. He was getting off on her fear.

Fuck fear.

Now *she* was going to play *him*.

"Y-yes." She scurried backward like a frightened mouse, all the way to the door, before he could protest. "P-please, I'll do anything you say." Head down, she kicked off her shoes.

"Good girl. Now, take off your dress."

She swallowed hard. This time, when she felt tears

prick the back of her eyes, she let them fall. Not tears of fear—tears of rage. Dante wanted a show? She'd give him one. Reaching behind her back, she fumbled with her zipper and finally managed to slide it down. It made a little whirring noise in the process, and Dante licked his lips in anticipation.

Slowly, she slipped one arm out of her dress.

"Take it off."

She got down on one knee.

"What are you doing?"

"I-I can't stand up, I'm too afraid. Just put the gun down, then I'll come to you. I'll do anything you say, only please don't kill me."

He hesitated, then slowly lowered the gun. "Why not? A little thing like you has no chance against me with or without a pistol in my hand." He laid the gun on her desk and grabbed his erection. "Come to Papa, dear."

She elbowed the panel on the plant stand, and it opened with a soft *pop*.

Taser!

Thank God. She pointed it at Dante and heard him growl as he lunged for her. Without hesitation she fired. A thousand tiny *clicks* . . . and then, like confetti, the tags that branded the Taser fell through the air. Dante's body jerked once. Then again. Back on her feet, she released the dead bolt on the front door, unlocking it, but Dante was on her now. She pressed the stump of the Taser to his chest. His body convulsed only a second before he grabbed her by the neck and cut off her air, strangling her cries and sending crushing pressure to her head. The room went fuzzy and started to spin, sending the Taser falling from her hand as her body slumped against the door. She knew her weakened legs would soon give way completely. Above the din of her heartbeat, she heard footsteps in the hallway.

The police?

Stay alive one more minute.

She opened her eyes. Dante's face was red. Saliva was dripping from his mouth like a rabid dog's. His hands squeezed her throat too tightly for her to cry out. Suddenly, the door flung open, knocking both her and Dante to the floor. His hands released her throat, giving her back her breath. Giving her back her hope. She kicked him in the groin just as a man she'd know anywhere blasted into the room.

The hope that flickered in her heart ignited to a full blaze. *Luke*.

Dante leapt to his feet and bolted across the room, found his pistol on her desk.

Oh, God.

"Gun!" Through her raw throat, she screamed to Luke, then saw his Glock. Both men faced each other, pistols aimed.

"Oh brother, brother, brother. You'd do this to me?" Dante's voice held only hatred for Luke.

The sight of Dante's pistol pointed at Luke had Faith's heart dumping adrenaline into her veins by the barrel. As her muscles sprang back to life, she managed to get to her feet again.

His gaze on Dante, Luke said, "Don't make me shoot you. Drop your gun. The police are on their way."

"What happened to all your promises to right our father's wrongs? You vowed you'd never be like him, and yet look at you. You *are* our father. You're ready to sacrifice me, just to protect *her*."

"Shut the fuck up and drop your weapon." Luke's voice shook, but his hand held steady.

Dante twisted slightly, aiming his pistol at Faith now. "Sorry, brother, but I believe it's you who needs to drop his gun."

Eyes trained only on Faith, Dante crossed to her and pressed his pistol into her temple. Her body stiffened. The eerie feel of the muzzle pushing against her skin made her dizzy, and she had to will her knees not to give way.

Lowering his arm, as Dante had clearly anticipated he would, Luke's face went ghostly pale. Dante whirled, jerking his pistol.

A muzzle flash.

The stench of burnt powder.

With a harsh grunt, Luke clutched his arm, and Faith saw his gun tumble to the floor.

"No!" she cried.

Never turn your back on your enemy.

But that's exactly what Dante had done, leaving Faith an opening. From a crouching stance, she leapt onto his back. Just as quickly he reared up and bucked her off. After hitting the floor with a resounding crack, she lay stunned and stilled beneath an oppressive cloud, heavy with the smell of blood and smoke. She heard Luke cry out and saw Dante turn toward the sound. Then her mind, too, went gray, and the room faded altogether.

Stay alive one more minute.

Forcing her eyes open, she spotted the gun on the floor nearby. A long stretch of her arm, and she had Luke's pistol in her grasp.

Do not waste this chance.

Luke had fallen to the floor. His back to her once more, Dante straddled Luke, pistol aimed. "Beg me for your life, brother."

While images of Grace flashed through her mind, Faith flipped onto her stomach, stuck out her arms, and braced the gun with both hands.

No more wasted chances.

She squeezed the trigger hard and emptied the magazine.

EPILOGUE

The sun had been up for hours by the time they gathered around the big mosaic breakfast table at the Jericho ranch, but even without the sunrise, the view of the Sangre de Cristo Range still stole Faith's breath.

"Luke"—Faith gently rubbed his arm, all healed at last—"this was a wonderful idea to bring Tommy for a day at the ranch—thank you." With her free hand, she reached over and petted the wiggly puppy in Tommy's arms. Luke had selected a beautiful spotted girl as a gift for his mother—the one Tommy called *Chicita*, meaning little Chica.

Each and every one of Chica's seven puppies had been born healthy. Practically a miracle, according to Dr. Culpepper. Faith smiled and dotted the corner of her mouth with a fine linen napkin. They were all due for something good, and the puppies were a wonderful portent of a bright future. Her eyes slid once more to Chicita, whose small body was currently stretched to the max as she stood on her hind legs in Tommy's lap, madly licking his face.

Fleetingly, she thought of the empty spot beside her bed where Chica had slept such a short time ago. She cast her gaze to her lap. Ridiculous. She was hardly the type of person to begrudge another the joy of a pet. Chicita had been the only puppy not spoken for, and Luke had been right to claim her for his mother.

The rich aroma of baked apples preceded Rose Jericho as she entered the breakfast room, carrying yet another silver platter piled high with warm pastries. She took a place on the other side of Tommy, broke off a corner of an apple Danish, and held it out in her open palm for Chicita.

"Don't spoil her, Mother," Luke said.

"I'll do as I please. She's my puppy." Rose winked at Tommy, who looked positively hypnotized by the pastries. She forked a Danish onto Tommy's empty plate. If Faith wasn't mistaken, this would make his fourth pastry, and he'd just finished a whopping portion of bacon and eggs.

"My son thinks this puppy is going to keep me too busy to look for another husband." Rose broke off another bit of Danish for Chicita. "But what he doesn't realize is that the dog park is a great place to meet single men. Maybe we could walk our dogs together sometime, Tommy, find you a nice young lady."

Tommy's cheeks, puffed with pastries, flushed. His throat worked in a swallow, then he sputtered. "I don't need a nice young lady. I've got Chica." Chicita yapped happily at the sound of her mother's name.

Taking the puppy in her arms, Rose said, "When you finish your Danish, Tommy, we can check out the horses, maybe go for a ride."

"You mean ride a horse?" He threw down his napkin and raised his hands in the air in an all-done gesture.

"I certainly do. The lovebirds can mind Chicita for me." She passed the puppy to Luke. "Careful, she might need to piddle soon."

Ten minutes later, Tommy and Rose had wandered off to find the horses, and Luke and Faith were wandering in the opposite direction, taking Chicita to piddle.

The puppy bounded through the tall green grasses, an occasional yap letting them know she was nearby. With the sky the same clear blue as those famed Jericho eyes, the fresh smell of hay and wildflowers permeating the air, and Luke by her side, Faith couldn't imagine wanting more than what she had right here, right now. The day was perfect, and she understood why Gran Cielo meant so much to Luke. She stopped and dropped his hand. "Luke, I've been meaning to tell you something."

"What a coincidence, I've been meaning to tell you something, too. All right if I go first?" He pulled her against him and ran his hands down her back. "See that puppy over there?"

As usual Luke hadn't waited for permission to go

first. She didn't know why he'd bothered to ask. "Chicita? Of course I see her. Your point? Because I have something important to say."

"Me, too. Chicita is yours." He threw his arms around her, crushed her to his chest, and lifted her off the ground.

Her heart raced, not just because Chicita was hers, but because Luke had seen the way she'd looked at those puppies and taken matters into his own hands. "You've been paying attention again." She laughed, and he set her feet on the ground, but she didn't let go of his neck. "I love you, Luke Jericho."

And then his lips were gliding over hers. The sun warmed her back as they kissed, and his hand slipped down to her bottom. She molded herself against him. Being in love with Luke didn't frighten her. Yes, he made her heart beat too fast, but for all the right reasons. She took her time, tasting him with her tongue, caressing his muscular arms, then his buttocks with her hands, enjoying the moment, enjoying the man with every fiber of her being. Finally, she broke the kiss.

"I love you, too, Clancy." He smoothed his hand over her hair. "I wanted to be the first to say it, but I guess you beat me to it."

"I guess I did." She didn't hide the boastful tone in her voice.

By now, Chicita was yapping at something up ahead. Hand in hand, they made their way toward her as she chased an imaginary object up a hill. "What about your mom?" Faith asked. "She seemed really keen on getting a puppy."

"Oh, she's still getting a puppy. She's actually the 'neighbor kid' who claimed Chico. As you might've guessed, she prefers boys."

Faith smiled and touched his lips. "Thank you, Luke . . . for everything."

"I'm glad you finally came to your senses and figured out how lucky you are to have me."

She shoved his shoulder, and he shoved her back. Then they crested the hill.

In the meadow below stood a small house. Faith stopped short, her body stiffening. She shaded her eyes for a better look. "Is that the casita where Dante and Sylvia lived?"

He nodded. "What's left of it anyway. The police took an ax to the floor and walls, looking for evidence."

Faith grabbed Luke's hand and turned to him. "I'm so sorry about Dante. I mean I can't be sorry that he's gone. But I know how much you wanted to put your family back together."

He shook his head. "That's just it. I had the wrong idea about family the whole time. Dante wasn't really a brother to me. I was chasing an abstract ideal that doesn't exist—the perfect family."

She didn't understand, but she knew he'd explain.

"Family isn't defined strictly by blood, Clancy. Look at you and Danny. And Faith, you're more family to me than Dante ever was—I never even knew him."

He looked out over the horizon and up at the sky, then back at her. "In a way I *have* put my family together again. I feel like I've gotten my father back. After so many years of hating him for what he did to Dante, I found out he was actually protecting my mother and me."

Faith knew the police had found Dante's journal in the casita. She shivered, as she thought of what it contained—the location of Sister Bernadette's body, and of a dozen others—prostitutes Dante had killed on his own while Scourge was obsessing over the Donovans. Had there been something more, something she didn't know about?

Luke ran his hands briskly over her arms. "I waited to tell you the last piece because I didn't want to spoil our happiness, but there was something else in Dante's journal. Even as a child, he loved to draw and paint. Anyway, he sketched page after page, depicting me, my mother, and my father." He paused. "Even his own mother. In those drawings, Dante had mutilated us in just about every manner possible. One day, Sylvia found the pictures. She found other things, too. Dante had tortured animals and buried them in her garden. According to Dante's journal, the night Sylvia died, she'd drunk herself into near oblivion and showed the whole thing to my father—the drawings, the animal graves. Later that night, she got in her car and drove off a cliff. In his journal, Dante talks about how excited he felt thinking about her car going over that cliff."

Her hand went to her throat. "So your father really did send Dante away to try and straighten him out. That's why he sent him to Catholic school, hoping the nuns could turn him around."

"And to protect our family." Luke put his arm around her. "The thing is, Dad knew both my mother and I hated him for his cruelty to Dante. But he never told us about the drawings. Dad was more concerned with whether or not we felt safe than with whether or not we were angry with him. My father was far from perfect, Faith, but he loved me the only way he knew how. I can't find it in myself to hate him any longer. But I do hate that damn casita." He put his hand on the small of her back and steered her toward the ranch. "I've got a special team coming out here later today. I love Gran Cielo, and I won't allow that casita to scar this beautiful land. I'm tired of trying to fix my father's mistakes."

He'd been dealing with his father's legacy his whole life. She held her breath, waiting for his confirmation of what she'd been hoping he'd do.

"I'm burning the casita to the ground. I don't intend to let the past define me, not anymore."

Then he bent, feathered his lips softly over her forehead, and her chest opened, making room for his affection, welcoming his touch. While he'd been trying to rewrite his past to bring his family together, she'd been running from hers. As she contemplated his words, her fingers went to her necklace.

His gaze traveled to her throat and lingered a moment before lifting. "I've been meaning to ask about that. I'm not the jealous sort or anything, but it is a heart, and you do wear it all the time . . ."

She let go of the necklace and took his hand. "Half a heart, and it's not what you're thinking. Grace gave it to me—just before she married Danny. She said it was to help me remember that no matter where our futures led, we would always be part of the same family, part of the same heart."

"And you still wear it."

"Yes, I always have, even during the bad times." Her chest tightened, but she didn't care, she welcomed the ache the same way she welcomed Luke's comfort. "Grace always wore hers, too."

"How wonderful, to have a sister like that." His voice had grown low and hushed.

Looking up, she watched as a bank of clouds drifted away, and the sun brightened the hilltops to a breathtaking green. "It is," she said, entwining her fingers with his. "It really is."

His gaze traveled to her throat and lingered a moment before lifting. "I've been my turn to ask about that. I'm not the jealous sort or anything, but it isn't hers, and you do wear it all the time."

She let go of the necklace and took his hand. "It it wasn't, and it's not what you're thinking. Grace gave it to me. Just before she married Diany. She said it was to help me remember that no matter who came, fea- tures led, we would always be part of the same family, part of the same heart."

"And you still wear it."

Yes, I always have, even during the bad times." Her chest tightened, but she didn't care, she welcomed the ache the same way she welcomed Luke's comfort.

"Grace always wore hers, too."

"How wonderful, to have a sister like that." His voice had grown low and husked.

Looking up, she watched as a bird of cloud drifted away, and the sun brightened the hilltops to a breath- taking green. "It is," she said, entwining her fingers with his. "It really is."

ACKNOWLEDGMENTS

Leigh LaValle, Tessa Dare, Courtney Milan—you will always be my favorite geniuses, my staunchest allies, and my greatest inspiration in this endeavor we call writing. Much love to my husband, Bill, and my children, Shannon, Erik, and Sarah. I'm sorry for shushing you when I'm writing . . . kind of. Lena Diaz—what would I have done without you? Much love and many thanks to my Kiss and Thrill crew: Lena Diaz, Sarah Andre, Diana Belchase, Manda Collins, Rachel Grant, Krista Hall, Gwen Hernandez, and Sharon Wray. Lindsey Faber, thank you so much for all your wonderful support. Thank you to my awesome agent, Nalini Akolekar, and finally thank you to my incredible editor, Chelsey Emmelhainz, for all your insights.

The suspense doesn't end here.
Be on the lookout for Carey Baldwin's
next thrilling novel

LABYRINTH

Coming from Witness Impulse in Fall 2014

ABOUT THE AUTHOR

CAREY BALDWIN is a mild-mannered doctor by day and an award-winning author of edgy suspense by night. She holds two doctoral degrees, one in medicine and one in psychology. She loves reading and writing stories that keep you off-balance and on the edge of your seat. Carey lives in the Southwestern United States with her amazing family. In her spare time she enjoys hiking and chasing wildflowers. Carey loves to hear from readers, so please visit her at www.CareyBaldwin.com, on Facebook https://www.facebook.com/CareyBaldwin Author, or Twitter https://twitter.com/CareyBaldwin.